HER FATHER'S DAUGHTER

Eroica von Heyditch had grown up despising her immensely powerful, utterly ruthless industrialist father.

She had watched him drive her brother to suicide. She had seen him destroy her mother's sanity. She had vowed never to let him mold her to his iron will. She would kill him—or herself—before he forced his desires upon her.

Now, as she looked into his smiling face, saw the triumph in his eyes, and surveyed the terrible choices open to her, she knew she had failed . . . he had won . . . and her life was to become a hell with no escape . . .

EROICA

a novel that plunges to new depths of horror—and reaches a new high in breathtaking suspense

"Fascinating, impossible to put down . . . I loved it"
—Mary Higgins Clark
author of *Where Are the Children?*

A NOVEL BY MARA ROSTOV

A JOVE/HBJ BOOK

Published by arrangement with G. P. Putnam's Sons

First Jove/HBJ edition published May 1978

Library of Congress Catalog Card Number: 76-30824

Printed in Canada

Jove/HBJ books are published by Jove Publications, Inc. (Harcourt Brace Jovanovich) 757 Third Avenue, New York, N.Y. 10017

To Michael, Erin, and Christopher

And I know even more, more I can tell.
Once, by his violent hand, a dragon fell.
He bathed in blood, grew hard, and can't be slain.
And many have seen this again—and yet again.

—*Das Nibelungenlied*

Part I

1

In our house no one spoke of the war, although I knew my father had received an award of some kind. It had all been over for seventeen years, almost three years before I was even born, and Cologne had long since been rebuilt, with Father back in full control of his factories and assembly plants. Our family lived comfortably in a large, balconied house which my father's grandfather had built in another century and which suffered only slight damage from the bombing. Our extensive gardens were surrounded by spacious parks where I played at being an Apache Indian girl with a few casual friends who attended the same private school I did.

Except for my dance class, school was rather dull, with only an occasional interesting bit of information floating down to me from my teachers: the Nile, like the Rhine, flows north. Mathematics: if one added zeros to the ends of numbers, the numbers became larger—tens, hundreds, thousands, millions. Languages: English and French—"English is a Germanic language, therefore, more interesting," said a teacher one day. Science: oxygen is a colorless, odorless, tasteless, gaseous element which makes up about ninety percent of water, two thirds of the human body. Without oxygen a candle's light will go out (charmed by teacher's experiment). History: World War II was fought for economic reasons. Thirty-five million people lost their lives. Six million of these were Germans. As retribution for losing the war, Germany was divided.

It was all rather remote and unimportant.

Then, one day while I was at school, my seventeen-year-old brother hanged himself. He and my father had had a row the night before, and Gerd ran out of the house, screaming. I saw him from the window on the second landing of the stairs. Outside, he threw himself at a tree; I mean he actually raced toward the tree and hit it with the full force of his body. I ran down the stairs and out into the garden, where I found him dazed and weeping on the ground under the wide branches of the pine tree he had seemed to try to knock down. I dropped to my knees beside him. When I touched his shoulder, he shuddered; but when he saw who it was, he raised himself into a kneeling position, put his arms around me and wept for a long time. Asking him what was wrong did no good. I was crying, too, by then because he felt so badly about something and because the look on his face was too terrible to bear. "But what has happened, Gerd? What has happened?" For a long time he merely wept, shaking his head and apparently unable to speak. My father had come out of the house during this time, and after looking down at us from the terrace, he muttered something I could not hear clearly and went back inside. I knew that my mother was lying down in the dark in her room with one of her terrible headaches. For a fraction of a second I saw her as I had so often—one arm bent above her forehead, which was covered with a wet multifolded cloth, her other hand more or less over her heart.

When Gerd finally spoke, his voice was very steady and determined. "Eroica, as soon as you can, leave home, leave Germany, leave Europe." He had stopped crying. "It does not matter where you go, but leave this country."

"Gerd, I don't understand. Leave home? Leave Mother and Father? Why, Gerd?"

"Don't ask why, just leave as soon as you can." He

placed his hands on my shoulders, his arms stretched straight out in front of him. "Leave. You must leave. Go to England, America. Anywhere."

"But . . . but why?"

"That does not matter. Go as soon as you can." The light from the entrance terrace shone on his face and his eyes looked black, although they were actually a beautiful blue, like the new variety of iris Mother had brought back from Holland the year before. "Go, just go," he said again. "As soon as you can."

"But what about you?"

"I shall go very soon," he whispered.

"What about Mother? She is always sick."

"Let her die. No one can help her."

"Oh, Gerd, what a dreadful thing to say."

"It is not dreadful at all," he said in a perfunctory voice. "Mother does not have real headaches. She lies in the dark for other reasons." He stopped.

"Why?" He shook his head. "What about Father?"

Gerd laughed in a horrible way. "Father has Germany—and his monuments. Leave Father to his monuments."

"What monuments?"

He began to weep again, his whole body shivering. I believed he was ill, and I tried to get him to come inside. "You will catch pneumonia if you stay here. The ground is cold." I held him in my arms. "Oh, Gerd, you must tell me what it is. You must." He shook terribly, but he would tell me nothing. When we finally went inside, I had to help him up the stairs to his room. He did not want the light on; he lay on his bed shivering, even after I covered him with the eiderdown, and he still had all his clothes on.

The next morning, before I went to school, I stopped by his room to see him. He was sleeping. I thought about him all day. My dance teacher made a stupid joke about my mind's being elsewhere: "And when can we expect a return visit from Fräulein von Heyditch, who seems to have forgotten that a *grand jeté* takes both physical *and* mental concentration." The other girls laughed. It made no difference to me. All I knew was that my brother felt terrible about something and that I should be with him. I was desperate while school dragged on forever, keeping me away from some unknown important thing that I should have been doing. When the limousine finally came for me, I told Wilhelm, our driver, to drive as fast as he could, but he was his usual cautious self and ignored me completely.

At home, I raced to Gerd's room. He was not there; nor was he in my room, where he sometimes came to talk. I considered this a great honor and adored him for it. Frankly, I adored him for everything. He was strong and beautiful and talented; he played the piano without having to use musical sheets; he collected rocks (he wanted to be a geologist), writing away for specimens from all over the world. But best of all, I knew he loved me, and this love was the best thing in my life. Our parents were rather distant people with whom we had very little in common. On our vacations—Spain, Greece, Yugoslavia—we always managed to get away from them for whole days at a time. In Greece we got to the Acropolis before it opened and we were the very last to leave it. He explained everything to me in a very clear and dramatic way. "Here stood Athena, the protective goddess who gave man both justice and mercy when she acquitted Orestes of his crime. Blood begets blood. Vengeance begets vengeance. Let us end that. Let justice be objective, but let us temper it with a compassionate heart." We were standing in the Parthenon and Gerd spoke with intense emotion. "Her gifts were many, from the invention of the potter's wheel to the feminine guardianship of peaceful life. Also, she was an intellectual." "Intellectual" was one of Gerd's favorite words. Lately, he had begun to talk of the "obligations of the intellectual." It was beyond me, but I began to throw his phrases around with considerable aplomb. "It is the obligation of the intellectual to question what most people take for granted." At the time I had no idea what this meant, but it sounded fine.

I thought of all this while I searched the house for him. Neither the cook nor the maid had seen him since morning. Both my mother and father were out. I assumed my father was at one of his factories or his office, and I suddenly remembered it was Friday and my mother was getting her hair washed and arranged.

The only place I did not look was my father's study; we were forbidden to go there, so I wandered about the garden and under the trees. After a time I went in and sat on the stairs. The house was still and cold. Fog had begun to roll in from the north, dripping heavily over the Rhine and I watched it for a while rather abstractly, feeling a vague uneasiness. Then, for no reason I could remember later, I went through the foyer, the drawing room and on to my father's study. The door was locked. I went outside to the terrace and walked around to the tall Gothic windows that faced the rose garden, where I cupped my hands against the glass and peered inside. My brother was hanging from one of the ship's beams that held the ceiling.

The rest of the day and night had the clarity of a repeating nightmare—always the same except for a few minor differences. I broke the window with my fists, cutting my hands badly. When I reached his body, I discovered it was very cold; he was barefoot. I put my face against his feet and knew at once that he had been dead for some time. His face looked black and his tongue protruded in an almost comical way. In my real nightmares, in the years to come, his face would be green or blue or red, even beautifully tanned, but his tongue's sticking out would always have the same grotesque humor about it that would cause me to wake up screaming.

I tried to get him down, but I couldn't reach the rope. He was hanging over the middle of my father's great mahogany desk. There were some books on the floor that he must have pushed away with his toes. (This was reasoned out later by someone else.) His right hand was in his sweater pocket, which caused his arm to protrude from his body at an awkward angle. It was only when I tried to release his hand from the narrow pocket that I realized he held something in his curled fingers. For a few seconds I even tried to open his hand, but his bones triumphed and they held in place for him the one thing he wanted Father to find on his dead body—and not merely impassively on his body, but actually clutched in his hand. However, more than a year was to pass before I discovered Gerd's and Father's shared secret.

Vaguely I remembered seeing all the drawers of my father's desk and cabinets open and papers strewn about the room. There was a claw hammer on the desk. In later years, in my very special dream, it would turn into an ax, a gun, and once, when I was very ill, a human penis.

My screams brought all the servants who were banging on the study door. I could never remember opening it for them, though they all said I did. They cut his body down and covered it with a sheet. Someone tried to pull me away from that white stiff form on the sofa, but I struck at them with my bleeding hands. I cursed them and shrieked at them to leave us alone—my brother and me.

After the funeral my mother rarely left her room. She no longer went shopping or visiting, and she stopped going to the beauty parlor. After a time she took all her meals in her rooms, while my father and I sat opposite each other at the formal table in the dining room and ate in silence. One night I asked him the question that had been waiting in my mind since my brother's death. "What did Gerd have in his hand?"

"Nothing." My father spoke calmly and kept on eating.

"He had something in his hand."

My father looked at me without anger. "If I say he had nothing in his hand, then he had nothing in his hand. Your brother was a fool, a sentimental cowardly fool."

A dark hatred toward my father began to ferment in me. "Why does Mother not eat with us anymore?"

"Because she is behaving stupidly."

I watched his hooded eyes glance briefly at me, then back at his plate. "Your brother had everything to live for. He threw his life away for nothing, for less than nothing."

"What did you fight about the night before he died?"

"Nothing."

"He was crying."

"He was weak and cowardly and stupid. He betrayed his responsibilities to his country, to our name, to me. He had no right to do what he did. It is a black mark on our name. He was a perfect Aryan and he betrayed his potential over some silly sentimentality." My father gazed at me fiercely then and with great anger. Time to keep quiet.

Later I looked up the word "Aryan" and discovered that it applied to a hypothetical parent language of the Indo-European family of languages. I decided that my father must have used the wrong word.

When I visited my mother each day after school, as she sat propped up in bed with her many pillows, she would stare at me with her dry, dead eyes. She always asked the same question: "How are you doing in school?" I always told her what we were studying, although I knew she was not listening. One day she frowned at the scars on my hands (the stitches had been removed, but their marks left red welts and depressions). "You hurt your hands?"

"Yes. But they are fine now."

"That's a good girl." She would close her eyes and seem to sleep, but I knew that she did not sleep very much. At times I could hear her walking around her room for hours. It was about this time that my own insomnia began.

One night, some months after my brother's death, I

heard someone weeping. It was long after midnight and I left my room without turning on any lights. There was a three-quarter moon, one of those odd-shaped moons that seems to have an uncertain, blurry edge on one side. The glow from it shone on the stair landings where the arched windows delineated oval frames of light. In one of these oblong shapes I found my mother lying face down on the carpet, wrenching hideous sounds out of her throat. I knelt down beside her. "Mother, Mother, please! Mother!" I pulled at her shoulder to turn her over. For a terrifying moment I felt as though I were touching Gerd's body as I had that night under the tree. But she was much thinner than Gerd had been, and I was able to move her easily. Faceup in the moonlight and curiously indifferent to my motions, she continued her wretched sobbing. When I touched her face, I thought for a moment or two that I must have screamed, for my father's door at the far end of the mezzanine suddenly swung open and a slanting triangle of bright light caught us at its perimeter. My father moved rapidly, his dressing gown slapping around his bare muscular calves in a way that I remembered for years afterward. I had never seen my father dressed in anything but his gray vested suits. He pulled my mother up to a standing position and dragged her up the remaining stairs, her bare feet thumping lifelessly against each step, her blond hair, which she once wore in a graceful figure eight on the back of her head, hanging over her face. At the top of the stairs my father, with his gasping burden slumped in one arm, turned to me and said without emotion, "Go to sleep."

What had caused me to scream—if I did scream, and I am still not sure of this—was that my mother was weeping without tears.

After that night I spent more time with her. When I was much younger, she had taught me to embroider and knit, but I had given it up for the Indian cause. I took it up again as I sat beside her bed and waited for her to get well. The Apaches would have to raid the plains of the Cologne parks without me.

My mother and I did not become any closer in these long, dead afternoons. The doctor came several times a week and listened to her heart, left some medicine for her to take, and made irrelevant comments to me. "So you are looking after your little mother, are you? That's a good girl." I disliked him; he was a pudgy little man with a cheerful round face and fat thighs. He smelled of cough drops and rubber.

One afternoon as he was snapping closed his black case on a table in the upper hall, I asked him if my mother was really ill. His dwarf face lost its cheer and he said with a grim voice, "That is an unkind thing to ask about a brave lady, especially since she is your mother."

"Gerd told me before he killed himself that Mother wasn't really sick."

He looked at me sternly and told me that Gerd had lost his senses. "What he did to your parents was selfish and cruel."

I followed him down the stairs and out the great oak door to the terrace. "But he cannot be blamed if he lost his senses, can he?" At this question, the doctor's face took on one of my father's expressions; his mouth tightened and flattened out, but he did not answer me. I started a new tack. "What does the word 'Aryan' mean?" We were standing in the open sunlight.

"Where did you hear that?"

"Father said Gerd was a perfect Aryan."

The doctor looked away toward his expensive black car parked in the circular drive in front of our house. I saw that the man's nose had a whole network of purple veins all over it. This was the first time I had seen him under the bright truth of the sun. "Your father was right; that is enough for you to know." He was sweating.

"What did my brother have in his hand?"

He glanced at me with another of Father's hostile expressions. "You are too young to be concerned with that. I hope you are not upsetting your mother with such questions." He left hurriedly without looking back at me.

So! It was more than just an uncertain language. My Indo-European brother had died with something shameful in his death-clutched hand. It was inconceivable to me that I should question my mother about anything. I sat beside her and embroidered pillow slips while her desire to live slowly died before my eyes. There were times when I knew that she was not aware of my presence. Sometimes she moaned as she lifted her tombstone eyes up toward the ceiling. Even raising her eyelids seemed to require a monumental effort of will. By late fall she weighed under ninety pounds. She was starving to death. I do not know what she held on to for so long. On the day the first snow fell, in November, my mother died.

The item in the newspaper said that Frau von Heyditch died of natural causes. The servants said she died of a broken heart. My father never commented on the matter at all. She was buried in the huge ornate von Heyditch crypt, next to my brother. She was thirty-nine years old.

For some weeks I spent every afternoon in the tomb, sitting on the marble floor, rereading the names of the many von Heyditch dead or just remembering things about my brother: his beautiful blue eyes, his gentle concern for me, his last advice—"leave Germany." More and more, the secret in his closed hand haunted me. Sometimes I talked aloud to him: "Gerd, give me a sign. Let something happen so I will know. They will not tell me." I had already asked the servants, who gave each other quick secretive glances and then said that they did not know. I knew they were lying.

Father and I still sat across the table from each other at dinner and ate in silence. He looked like Rembrandt's painting of the man with a gilt helmet. Gerd had pointed that out to me once in an art book that he kept hidden in his room. Since Father's study was closed to us, we had access only to our schoolbooks and a collection of classical-literature volumes that were kept in a glass-door cabinet in a small alcove off the drawing room. I knew that Gerd had been secretly buying books. We were not allowed to have any money, but about a year or more before my brother's death, Mother had secretly been giving him money. He shared these small sums with me from time to time, and I would buy Swiss chocolates or an occasional sticky éclair and once a marvelous black and white crane feather (from a hat shop) which I casually passed off as having belonged to an American eagle. The other Indians were fierce with envy. I made a headband for it, and for the remaining months of the Indian troubles I was Bright Eagle, beloved true warrior-daughter of Chief Great Eagle of the Apaches. Somehow during my education I had unconsciously brought Odin's warrior maidens, the Valkyries, who could ride through the air on horseback, and the American braves (and bravesses), who could move as soundlessly as shadows, into complete harmony with one another. Gerd, who had first told me about the greatness of the American wilderness people, failed to include any information about the U. S. cavalry. It was those stupid, clumsy, treacherous, depraved and generally evil cowboys, who tried to enslave and kill the noble Red Man, who were the real enemy.

One night at dinner, my father suddenly spoke to me, as usual without looking up from his plate. "Wilhelm tells me that you spend much time in the cemetery. Stop that. There is no point in crying for the dead." Also as usual, he spoke in that calm, rational voice that was oddly flat yet totally sincere.

"Other people weep for the dead." It was a brave statement in face of the two-word edict which had just been issued. A girl at school had recently lost her grandmother, who had raised her and whom she had loved, and sometimes she would begin to cry suddenly and talk haltingly about the dead woman. After crying, she always seemed less sad.

"It does them no good."

"Who?"

"What?"

"Whom does it do no good—the dead, or those who have been left behind?"

"You are a stupid girl. It is obvious that it does the dead no good. It should also be obvious to you that it does the living no good."

I watched him eat. The man in the gilt helmet ate methodically. The only sound in the room was of his knife and fork, clinking on the china plate occasionally. In the foyer the tall floor clock chimed eight-fifteen. I loved the clock, not because it was beautiful, or antique, or expensive, but because of the little man with the long white beard who lived in it. When I was five and Gerd eight, he had told me about the little man who inhabited the clock and made it chime. I had wanted to bring the little man food, but Gerd assured me that he lived on the music of the chimes, and for extra-special feasts he ate the music which he, Gerd, played on the piano in the music room. Sometimes when I passed the piano I would toss him a few melodious chords which Gerd had taught me. I was not very good at music, but these chords were long and sonorous and full of roast meat, especially when I stepped on the pedals at the same time as my hands pressed down the keys.

As I heard the clock, I knew I would never abandon the crypt in the cemetery. What would it mean to disobey my father? He had never touched me. In my entire life he had never touched me, neither kissed me nor hit me. But I was afraid of him. For reasons I never understood when I was a child, I knew that violence did not necessarily mean hitting. There was another unexplained absolute that I held: my father was a violent man. Yet, to my knowledge, memory, and experience, I had never heard him fight with my mother. I had never seen him hit anyone; I had never even heard him raise his voice above his normal speech. During that one fight with my brother, it was Gerd who had been doing all the shouting and screaming.

The next day after school, I told Wilhelm that I was going to the crypt and that he could tell my father anything he wanted to. The man laughed a dirty little laugh as he sucked on a cigarette. There was always a cigarette hanging out of his mouth. He rarely held it in his hand; he simply puffed on it until it almost disappeared, and then he would take it between his thumb and forefinger and flick it away. Sometimes, before he reached the end of it, a long limp ash, the ghost of its former self, hung on in defiance of all the physical laws I knew about. Wilhelm wore a dark-green uniform and a visored black cap, and under it his face had the bright, inquisitive expression of a hairless rat.

That night my father said nothing to me during dinner. Perhaps Wilhelm wasn't such a bad rat after all. My cue to leave the table was in the form of the maid, bringing my father his coffee. I hesitated a few moments, waiting to make sure he did not want to say anything. After the maid was gone, he picked up his coffee cup and looked at me silently over the rim of it. He had eyes the color of wet clay. Time to go to my room, but I felt that I had won something indefinable.

When I reached the cemetery the next day, I almost walked past the crypt; the wrought-iron gate was gone and a huge metal door was in its place. I knew even before I tried it that it would be locked. I tried it anyway. The door had no handle or knob; it was a huge rectangle of metal with a short panel on one side with a keyhole in its center. I sat on the grass and considered the door for a long time: the rivets that held the key panel in place looked like gray flat bugs, marching. Left, right, left, right. Turn ninety degrees. Left, right, left, right. . . .

After a time I walked away from the door and out of the cemetery. Our home was about two kilometers away. At any other time I would have enjoyed the walk between the rows of tall poplar trees, through a lovely fountained park, past the manor houses of the rich (one of which was ours); but on that day I saw nothing except the metal door and the orderly marching bugs. Somehow I had to live with the man who was my father, the man I hated above all things. In my small life I had disliked this or that or something else. None of that mattered any longer; all my dislikes vanished in the presence of that enormous hatred.

At dinner that night we did not speak to each other, and when the maid brought the coffee, I left at once for my room. On the floor of my armoire, under a folded blanket, were my brother's secretly purchased books. I had not yet found the interest (or perhaps the heart) to look at them. As I sat on my bed, thinking of Gerd, a longing to go to his room came over me. I went there often to lie on his bed and conjure up bright moments of the past when we had both been happy. But on that night, when I got to his room, the door was locked. I kept thinking it was only stuck as I pushed my shoulder against it. Then I began to beat at it with my fists. How dare anyone lock my brother's door! I shouted and screamed and wept convulsively, but no one came to my repeated loud demands that the door be opened. I ran down the stairs to the dining room, but my father was not there. I pounded on his study door, but there was no answer, although I knew he was in there. I ran to the kitchen, where the maid and cook were cleaning. The two women, both thickly built and in their fifties, did not answer my question: "Who has locked my brother's room?" They did not look at me at all. With their closed faces and averted eyes they did not have to answer: I already knew.

I stomped out of the house and ran around to the back where the windows of Gerd's room faced a terrace garden; my mother's primulas and winter roses continued to bloom after she died with what I considered to be treacherous indifference. I picked up a rock and threw it up against the window, vindictively anticipating the sound of shattering glass. There was a wooden thud. I had missed. I threw another rock, and still another. Something was wrong. I raced back into the kitchen and snatched a flashlight out of a drawer. The two women continued mopping and polishing as though nothing were going on. Outside I flashed the light along the ivy to the spot where Gerd's room began. The windows were gone. Wide panels of wood covered the area where the windows had been. The last shrine had been nailed shut.

The knowledge of defeat came upon me quickly, but I was beyond weeping, beyond feeling pain. The only thing alive within me was a white, hot hatred. Bright Eagle of the Great Apaches stood alone in the middle of a hostile continent and contemplated murder.

However, there was nothing I could do. My father and I continued to live together in open estrangement. I did not mind the silence; I preferred it. There were no words I wanted to hear from him, and I did not trust myself to speak first. I often thought that if I ever began to talk to him, I would end up screaming and shouting, as Gerd had done, and he would only sit back and watch me with his unblinking mud eyes.

Some weeks after Gerd's room was lost to me, I awoke one morning feeling vague mild pain in my chest and that same night I began to menstruate. When I saw the blood on my underclothes, I was surprised, not frightened. Gerd had told me this would happen, but he was off by a year. He had told me to expect it when I became fifteen, but here I was still in my fourteenth year. Much time passed before I realized the great kindness my brother had done for me by telling me about this monthly cycle of blood, and other information he thought I might need someday.

I tore a towel into strips, folded the pieces into little pads and pinned one to my underpants with a safety pin. When the pad was soaked, I replaced it with a fresh one and washed the used one, drying it on the window-sill in my room at night. Briefly I wondered what American Apache girls did about catching the blood. Gerd had said that once I began to menstruate I would be able to have babies. What he had not told me about were the headaches, the terrible, excruciating headaches, that seemed to begin behind one of my eyes. At first there was a horrible stab of pain that lasted only a few seconds; then, about a half hour later, one side of my face felt as though it were going to explode. Bright lights or loud, strident noises increased the pain. Also, strange noises were going on inside my head: the sound of crinkling cellophane, the hum of bees and a ticking that continued for hours. The first attack lasted three days. On the fourth morning I awakened to silence; all the static and buzzing and clockworks had moved out. My head was mine again, and for that I was grateful. But I had entered the state of womanhood in secrecy, alone, alienated, and isolated with a dark enemy that went in and out of my head without my wishes and against my will.

The hatred for my father never left me; I awakened with it and carried it around with me all day like some heavy weight that had replaced my empty heart. In the last moments before sleep, before the insomnia abandoned me for a few hours, the loathing loomed out of me like a living thing, some monstrous, nameless creature that laughed a most inhuman laugh. While the ugly sound shrieked at me, the corners of the ceiling became inverted, and kaleidoscopically fell into patterns that reached down heavily to hover only a millionth of an inch over my face, my body. I was being crushed with hatred. I fought the claustrophobia with all my will, for to relinquish myself to it was to go mad. And I had to stay sane if for no other reason than to keep Gerd alive in my memory. Also, I knew I had to kill my father.

My plans for this murder were opiates for my suffering. I would poison him, pour liquid cyanide into his wineglass when he wasn't looking. Was there liquid cyanide, and, if so, how did one get it? I would run him through with one of the crossed swords over the fireplace in his study. The swords were riveted to a plaque. And anyway, would he stand still long enough for me to dissect his liver? I would make a bow and an arrow with a long metal tip; then one night before I got up from the dinner table I would casually reach under my chair, raise the weapon as he sat with his cup of coffee and shoot the arrow into his heart. He would jerk back sharply, without a sound, twitch briefly and be still. Afterward I would move around the table and stand over him (he had fallen out of the chair). "That is for Gerd and for my mother and for me." His hateful eyes would glaze over, and after making sure he was dead I would take the keys he kept in his coat pocket and open Gerd's room. But there was a problem: how does one make a lethal, metal-tipped arrow? And how could I be sure my father had a heart?

The notion struck me that my father would thrive on poison, that he could be stabbed and shot without any impairment to his health. The man in the gilt helmet, the protected, invulnerable, enduring horror of my life who sat across the table from me, chewing methodically, could not be killed.

One night I sat on the floor in front of the armoire and carefully examined Gerd's books and a few other possessions of his that I had moved out of his room in the months before it was sealed. Besides the books there was very little: a few seashells (three, to be exact, from his rather large collection), a tiny jade Buddha which my mother had given him, and a small piece of gnarled olive wood we had found in Greece on our last vacation. The shells consisted of a fine sample of the chambered nautilus, a green turbo with part of the outer husk removed, and a bonnet shell with exceptional cameo markings and a deep clear roar. Gerd had frequently been amused at my absolute belief that the ocean's roar could be heard in the shell. "But you have to know the truth, Eroica: it's only an echo of things around you."

"It's the ocean roaring," I announced with monumental conviction.

One night he had held the shell lovingly in his hands. "My dear little sister, it's perfectly all right if you wish to think that there is a little man in the clock who sounds the chimes, but you must know that the clock is a mechanical device invented by man in the thirteenth century. It has wheels and weights and springs and little pointers, humorously called 'hands' in English, that move over a dial, and all these parts cause it to make the sounds you hear. If you wish to think that the roar of the ocean reverberates through this exquisite shell, you are, of course, free to do so, but the truth is"—he had stopped, his blue eyes wonderfully laughing and capricious—"the truth is, you are right: it is the ocean roaring." We had rolled on the floor in his room and laughed hilariously, both of us knowing it was not true. After a while he told me to hold the shell and stroke it and listen to it.

Something very curious happened to me that night as I took the books from the armoire: I stayed up all night, reading. It was the first of hundreds of such nights in my life. The first book I read was Franz Kafka's *The Trial*. I might never have read Gerd's books if he had not underlined passages and made notes in the margins and on the end sheets. When I flipped through one of the books and saw the first notation, I thought my heart had stopped. I had the fascinating conviction that he was talking to me. My wounded mind and barren heart let me believe that he was in the room with me. This necrophilia, in a sick and paradoxical way, kept me alive for some years. Unless I saw him, I did not think of my father at all. Gerd's shade was more alive to me than all that was living. He spoke to me from the pages of every book. His questions became mine. *"Aber Herr Kafka, wer ist Joseph K.?"* Indeed, who *is* Joseph K.? *"Und das Verbrechen?"* And the crime, Kafka? What was the crime? My brother and I want to know about the crime. Even after I read the book carefully, I still did not know Joseph K.'s crime.

At the end of the book, on one of the blank pages,

Gerd had written the following: "Why the trial? What is the crime? Who are the executioners?" After that Gerd had written "Franz Kafka (1883–1924) b. Prague, Czechoslovakia." And added later, at least I assumed it was added later because the ink was a different color, "He was a Jew."

2

What did I inherit from my father? Certainly not the color of his eyes; mine are green. I silently thanked my good luck. Years later when I came to understand something about genetics I wondered what green-eyed ancestor-monster I should have thanked. However, in the fifteenth year of my life I came suddenly to discover that my father had contributed something to the nature and essence of whatever I was becoming: I found out late one evening that the violence I sensed in him was also in me. Regardless of the books I read later, I was convinced that this was an unfortunate inheritance, even though the intellectual side of me said, "You were taught to be violent; you were taught by a master of violence." But back in that lonely time, I only saw my meanness as part of the natural von Heyditch cruelty. I did not feel that the wish to kill my father was violent; this curious paradox existed in my mind without confusion or tension, because in my thinking killing him was a matter of execution—a right and justifiable and necessary execution.

The violence which I managed to effect with impunity began in small, seemingly insignificant incidents. There was the matter of the keys. One day after school I returned to the limousine for a notebook which I had forgotten, and while I was in the car, I saw that Wilhelm had left the key. On an impulse I pulled it out of the ignition and returned to the house. Off of the kitchen there was a small storeroom and in it hung a keyboard with dozens of keys in orderly rows all clearly identified with little labels above the hooks from which they hung. The room had two openings; it had once been a passageway from the kitchen to a smaller dining room which my mother had turned into a conservatory since it had a solid wall of glass panels that faced the garden. I passed through Mother's old plant room to the passage storeroom, where I took the other key to the Mercedes as well. There was no particular plan in my mind, but I knew that with my father's penchant for order, the loss of the keys would at least cause someone some discomfort. I walked to the street beyond our driveway and dropped the keys through the grates of a storm drain.

Sometime after dinner that night I heard my father tell Wilhelm to bring the car around. I was sitting at the piano, trying to find the chords Gerd had taught me.

A few minutes after Wilhelm returned to the house, I heard angry voices from the kitchen. The cook was shouting at Wilhelm, "What would we want with your stupid key? What would anybody want with it? You are the only one who drives the car."

"You don't understand! Two keys lost on the same day, and you were in charge of the keyboard. You must have misplaced it."

"Misplaced it? You idiot, I don't even know how to drive, and neither does Lena. You took it yourself and forgot that you did and now you've lost both of them. Well, *you* tell the master. It's nothing to do with us."

Wilhelm stalked out of the kitchen in a black fury.

"Have you seen the key to the car?" he asked me, his voice cramped with rage and frustration.

I was all innocence. "What does it look like?" I looked up at him with concern and interest.

"Look like? It's just an ordinary car key, you stupid girl."

"I've never seen an ordinary car key."

"Well, you've seen keys, haven't you?"

"Of course. I have a key to the front door."

"It's like that, only smaller," he snapped.

"I'm sorry, but the only key I have seen is the door key." I brought my fingers down and by chance found one of the chords.

A moment later I heard Wilhelm knock on my father's study door. There was a brief exchange of words, low and not distinct enough for me to understand; and a few minutes after that Wilhelm strode, white-faced, through the dining room and back into the kitchen, where a bitter argument began almost at once. I listened to it with enormous satisfaction. In my mind I saw the keys lying in the sewer, under the street, where no one would ever find them. I left the piano and went to the reading alcove, where I sat in a big wing chair that faced another part of the garden. It had begun to rain and as I watched it I became aware of my father's voice. In his pique at Wilhelm he had left his study door open—something I had never known him to do.

"Nonsense. Of course I can't take a taxi, you fool. Either send a car for me or hold the meeting without me." He hesitated. "You are reckless and therefore dangerous. I recommend you cancel the meeting. We shall meet next Saturday." He was talking on the phone, and after the word "Saturday" I heard him bring the phone down with a loud crash. The rain fell steadily and I watched it with vicious pleasure. At the time my father's conversation meant nothing to me. All I knew was that I had spoiled his evening.

On Monday morning there was a taxi waiting to take me to school, but that afternoon Wilhelm picked me up with the limousine. "Oh, you found the key," I said.

He looked at me with bitter eyes and said nothing. For several days there was periodic bickering among the help. Wilhelm was sure that one of the women had removed the key from the keyboard, and they were equally sure that he had done so at some earlier time and had forgotten about taking it.

It was obvious to me that all I had to do was wait and watch for opportunities that would enable me to disrupt the household. After the key business, the incident of the rats occurred. My father had a particular hatred of rats, and it was this unreasonable aversion to them that excited my curiosity. Father was not an unreasonable man: in all that he did he remained cool and dispassionate, yet the very thought of rats paralyzed him with a frenzied rage.

The incident which set the whole rat business into motion occurred when the cook, Vera, said rather casually, early one Saturday afternoon, to the gardener, "Another thing, Karl: while you're straightening up down there"—she was referring to the wine cellar—"see what you can do about the rats."

My father, who was just coming home for lunch, stopped stone-still in midstep on the front terrace. "What rats?" I was sprawled in a lounge chair, reading. Again he said, "What rats?" His voice had not risen; it had lowered. I looked at him as he gazed first at Vera, on the terrace near the French windows, and then at the gardener, in the driveway.

The cook was very offhanded and casual about the matter. "We have rats in the cellar. They will eat the corks from the wine bottles and spoil the wine. We should do something about them." As with Karl, the look on my father's face must have stopped her. "Are you ill, sir?"

Apparently my father was unable to answer this solicitous question immediately. His face seemed to turn gray, and then green. I watched him carefully. He recovered quickly. "Don't be ridiculous. Of course I'm not ill." He hesitated; he was breathing deeply, heavily. "If we have rats, we must get rid of them at once. Use poison, traps, anything. But get rid of them. And I want a report. They are a danger to health, the filthy, disease-ridden beasts! In twenty-four hours there is not to be a single rat on this property. Get Wilhelm to help. There will be no rats!"

Neither Vera nor Karl moved and my father too stood motionless, his usually controlled face twisted with agony, the mouth pulled down, showing only his lower teeth, the eyes sunken in slate-gray pools. For a dreadful moment I saw the three people gripped in a tableau of frozen forms rendered blind and mute, turned stone-cold under the midday sun. Vera, her dough-heavy face with its thick jaw and half-open mouth jutting forward toward my father, had stopped drying her hands. Karl too leaned toward Father, his body in an attitude of beginning a turn which all the earth's dead weight defied him to complete. For a few moments I was unreasonably terrified. They appeared to be listening to something I could not hear, something horrible—as though the distant voices of the dead were calling to them. I held my breath while this scene entered my memory down to the minutest detail: Vera's square hands holding up the edge of her apron to dry them; Karl's loose, too-long tweed trousers stained with dark spots which looked like grease or gas or blood; my father's black fedora crouching on his head like a squat, angry bird.

Then the universe moved again. Vera dried her hands and opened the door for Father; Karl completed his turn and walked away toward the side of the house; and my father's face moved back into its familiar, controlled expression of invincibility.

I leaned back in the chair and thought about my father and rats. A short time later Wilhelm and Karl came from the garage. "The Old Man still has the thing about the rats," said Karl.

"Yeah? Well, if he keeps thinking on that, he will drive himself crazy—like the kid."

"No, the kid didn't know about the rats."

"I didn't mean that; I mean he will go crazy like the kid, but for a different reason. The kid didn't know what to make of it. He got it all wrong. The Old Man should have talked to him years ago, trained him better, and he would be alive today and working with us. But today's kids aren't worth anything, full of stupid ideas—unworkable. We have to rely on the Old Guard."

They walked past me without looking toward the terrace, their shoes crunching on the gravel. I had long sensed that there were things going on around me of which I was ignorant, and more and more I began to remember remnants and echoes of old conversations and bits of scenes that were like flashes of lightning in a dark sky. In another country, in a half-remembered house in an uncertain year, Gerd and I, exploring a long corridor flanked with dusty rooms of squat ugly furniture, opened yet another door and heard Father's voice low and thick through the cigar smoke. "Gentlemen, let the rats eat each other. We prevail as always. We—" At that moment a large man motioned toward the door with his brandy glass, and Father turned his head sharply, catching us in the full force of his distracted gaze. "Go to your mother." His voice was without anger, but in it—in the last word—I felt his rancor as surely as if he had struck us.

The rat annihilation began with Wilhelm's drive into the city. He brought back several large cartons which I watched him unload at the side of the house. There was a small stone balcony off my bedroom and from it I could see him quite clearly; his lips were pulled back in a grimace, and the eternal cigarette was clamped between his teeth. I knelt on the stone floor and put my face between the balusters and listened to him grumble into his own puffs of smoke. He was in a burning rage, throwing the boxes out of the car in a careless and indifferent manner.

Karl joined him after a few minutes and the two began a curious conversation that made no sense to me at all. "If the people at the top go to pieces, the whole thing will go to hell again," said Wilhelm, banging down the trunk lid. "I say they police each other. That other one had no one to keep him in check, so he went crazy. Sure, he was a genius, but he went nuts. Geniuses go nuts quicker than other people. It's too big a job for one man; a committee is best."

"There *is* a committee. What do you want—a committee inside the committee?" Karl took some packages from the back seat of the car and dropped them on the grass.

"I know there is a committee," sneered Wilhelm, "but there is no one to watch each of the members. Any one of them could go off the deep end at any time. With von Heyditch it's rats. With Müller it's kids; he can't stand to be around little kids. With Vogal it's the smell of you-know-what. With all of them it's something. Even Hauser has something; that tick under his eye is a sign of it. That twitching of his has something behind it, all right. It will all go to hell again."

"No it won't. This time we will succeed. The Old Man knows what he is doing. He isn't scared by all that saber-rattling." Karl had pale eyes and blackened decaying teeth that he sucked constantly with his tongue. "I tell you there is fine music for Germany in that clash of armor," he laughed. "When they have eaten each other up, who do you think will be there to collect the goods?"

"Look out. I hear the Old Man." Both men began to move cartons around to the kitchen entrance.

My father appeared from the front of the house just as they were returning from the back. "What is taking all this time? Do you mock my orders?"

Karl and Wilhelm quickly picked up the remaining packages. "No, sir, the rats will be gone, as you ordered."

"See to it. If not, it will go badly for you."

I could see his face contorted and twisted almost as though he were in pain. It gave me a strange satisfaction to see him suffer. Perhaps he finally felt some remorse for the death of Gerd and Mother. In my ignorance, I pictured their bodies as my sanity and spirit demanded: they were simply lying in their satin-cushioned beds, rather cozy and comfortable, never feeling cold or pain, and never being sad or lonely. They slept peacefully and serenely forever. My life was an unsolvable paradox: I wanted to be dead with my brother and my mother, and I wanted to be alive so I could kill my father. At that frightful time in my life, I could not see that killing my father would put him where I wanted to be. There were a good many unconsidered conclusions floating around. There was also another feeling that I did not look at too long or too hard: I wanted to live for other reasons than ridding the world of my father, but the reasons were unclear to me, although I knew I would have been sorry never to dance again, never to hear music again, never to feel the sun on my skin again. Lately, too, I liked the feel of my own skin. My breasts were growing and that interested me. Gerd and I had seen each other naked when we went swimming in a cove on the Adriatic, and he had said then, as we lay on the white sand, that I would "probably fill out very nicely—like Mother." My mother had been full-bosomed and round-hipped before she stopped eating and became a skeleton.

The rat raid upset the whole routine of our well-ordered household. Wilhelm and Karl came in and out of the kitchen all Saturday afternoon in order to get to the cellar. This irritated the cook, who disliked having anyone around while she prepared the meals. She complained loudly and often. "Use the old door underneath the stairs," she shouted at the two men when they tramped through the kitchen to check their snares and traps.

"We can't," Karl hissed at her. "We have locked it so no one will leave it open by accident. If the rats escape, they will only return when it rains again. And then we'll be in for it."

I had gone to the kitchen to watch the parade by then and the bitterness between the chauffeur and the cook was of interest to me. Apparently the key incident still rankled both of them, each convinced of the other's guilt. They berated each other colorfully.

A short time later, when both Wilhelm and Karl were outside again and the cook had gone into the pantry, I raced across the kitchen and slipped into the cellar, closing the door behind me quietly. It was cold and silent in the rank darkness and the smell of sour wine and mold pervaded the dead air. Although I knew the layout of the cellar well, I was angry at myself for stupidly not having taken the flashlight when I had the opportunity. The stairs, which had no rail or hold on one side, were steep and narrow and ran down along the wall. I risked turning on the light for a few seconds in order to imprint the room in my mind: it would not do to stumble over any of the traps and cages that Wilhelm and Karl had set up.

The cellar was a large square room with wine racks placed not only against the walls but also in three double rows that nearly filled the center of the room and reached almost to the ceiling. Between these central shelves were narrow aisles; with care I could remain hidden if the men returned before I could get back out again. I turned out the light and descended the stairs and carefully inched my way along one of the wall racks. My brother had told me that although Köln had been heavily bombed during the war, our house had sustained relatively minor damage: most of the windows had had to be replaced and part of the roof had needed repair. There was also settling of the house that had damaged the plumbing and left some kind of cracks. But all that was taken care of before I was born.

Gerd and I had explored the wine cellar whenever the opportunity arose, looking for ghosts that might have invaded the house during its long history. We spent much time in our early years tapping on walls and searching for secret chambers and passageways with fearful expectation of tongueless spirits moaning to us in the heavy darkness. It all came to nothing.

I had barely followed two of the walls when I heard a new fight break out in the kitchen. There was some kind of crash: something made of glass must have been knocked to the floor. The fight lasted a few minutes and then the door to the cellar opened and the light went on almost at once. "Those bitches, those damned bitches! I'd happily like to strangle them. I tell you: deal with women and you deal with idiots."

"Forget them; we have work to do."

Both men were coming down the stairs. I slid between the farthest row of wine racks and held my breath, my heart pounding.

"Not one of the beasts! And you know he will want evidence that we got them." It was Karl who spoke. Peeking around the edge of the shelf, I could see his blunt face with its mean eyes. "What if there are no rats? All we have is the cook's word on it anyway. We could go to the dumps or the riverfront and get some there. There's plenty of them around the wharves and on the barges. If the old man wants to see some dead ones this badly, we are going to have to find some. If the war were still on, I'd know where to find plenty." He laughed a thin, high laugh that made me shiver.

"Don't be an ass. Of course there are rats here. There is ratshit all along the baseboard here and over there." He motioned vaguely toward the opposite wall. "The rats must be coming in from the old cellar. There are probably openings by now to the outside. The thing to do is give them plenty of arsenic and forget about the traps."

"Yeah, well, then they crawl in their holes and die and we got dead-rat smell in the house. You think the old man will give us a medal for that?" They were silent, looking at the empty traps and cages with various bits of food in them. "We have to bait them better. We have to get them to come out and eat." He paused. "Now, if we could get some Jew meat . . ." They both began to laugh—an absolute roar of laughter. I wondered what meat that was and decided that I would try to find out what kind of meat Jews preferred and why it should so amuse anyone.

Wilhelm picked up one of the traps. "This is stupid.

I'm going to get some more bait, plenty of it. Then we mix it with larger amounts of poison. They die quicker and that's all there is. If a few crawl back in their holes and stink up the place, von Heyditch can rest easier for the smell. He's had a worse smell stuffed up his nose. He shouldn't mind a dead rat or two." He spat into the corner and picked up one of the traps. "Hell, half the bait on this one is already gone. Those damn rats are smart. Come on, let's get on with it."

The men left the cellar without turning out the light. I waited for the battle to start upstairs again, but nothing happened. The traps had cheese, bread and pieces of radish in them. In the cages there were various grains and more bread. The only thing I knew about rats was that they would eat anything. I decided that it was time for me to find out more about them.

I opened the other entrance under the stairs, reasoning that the men would feel no need to check the bolts again. Still I was terrified and held on to the handle of the door on the other side, imagining all kinds of horrors. For one thing, I was in the dark, standing on the lowest level of a flight of stone steps that led to a trapdoor opening to the garden. Gerd and I had used this entrance in our ghost-hunting days, but he had always had the foresight to bring a flashlight. The darkness and the damp stones pressed heavily on my fear and I felt a disgusting nausea in my throat. Then something walked over my foot and I lurched up the steps, struggling for the bolt to the trapdoor, gasping for breath, for light. The fresh air hit my face, and it was only then that I became aware of the bad smell. Down below, on the lowest step, which was three times as wide as the others, small frightened eyes glittered back at me. There were piles of bits of paper and cloth and other material I could not identify heaped liberally in the corners. It occurred to me somewhat slowly that I had my own private community of rats.

Once outside, I tossed some leaves and twigs on the closed doors and hurried around the far side of the house. It was late in the afternoon by then and no one was in sight. When I was safely in my own room, I thought about the rats—my rats, which Wilhelm and Karl knew nothing about. I remembered the conversation between the two men. *"The Old Man still has the thing about the rats. . . . If he keeps thinking on that, he will drive himself crazy. . . . The kid didn't know about the rats."*

It became increasingly obvious to me that my father must have had a particular experience with rats that had nothing to do with sanitation problems. What would happen if my father came face to face with a big ugly rat?

I looked up rats in my science book and found out that they could eat a third of their own weight in food in one day and that they gnawed on things constantly to grind down their teeth, which never stopped growing throughout their whole lives. But there was information even more astonishing than that: under ideal conditions—enough food and good weather and no one killing them—a pair of rats could have twenty million new relatives within three years. In the fourteenth century rats carried bubonic plague to Europe and twenty-five million people died from the disease. Thus, rat control was one of man's oldest problems, particularly since rats were smart and caught on to traps quickly and soon learned to shun them. Apparently poisons worked best.

However, if Father was going to face a rat, it would have to be a healthy, lively one, not one that would crawl under the furniture and die. No, one of Wilhelm and Karl's poisoned rats wouldn't do. I needed a well rat and access to my father's study. What I had to do was feed my private rats to keep them from being poisoned.

For a week all the servants lived in hysteria, with seething rages and frenzied dispositions. My father cursed them and raged at them about their "inefficiency." A single rat had been caught. Meanwhile I gave banquets for the sanitation problems belowstairs. I dug up some of my mother's flower bulbs and the rats enjoyed them hugely, especially the tulip bulbs. I pocketed much of my own food and at night crept to the back of the house and fed my rats. There was little difficulty in getting things from the kitchen. One day after school, when Wilhelm had gone to pick up my father and Karl was out in the garden (I could see him from my room), I heard the cook go into the water closet off the main upper hall. She apparently suffered from constipation and usually took a magazine with her. The maid, Lena, was sorting linen in the upstairs linen room. I could hear her slamming cabinets. Everyone had begun to slam doors in their state of constant agitation and the house echoed with slams all day. I hurried to the pantry with a pillowcase; I took potatoes, radishes, carrots, stale bread and some candle ends (there was a whole drawer full of them).

I took the flashlight and my pillowcase of food down into the cellar, using the inside entrance. I fed the rats. They seemed to be waiting for me and were not at all as skittery as they had been during my first few visits.

I had made some remarkable discoveries that week: the more chaotic life became in the house, the more freedom I had; the people who moved around me with such nervous and turbulent actions seemed to have forgotten me completely.

The second discovery I made that week was that under violent stress, it was "each man for himself." The servants fought among themselves viciously: they cursed each other and accused each other of being troublemakers. However, it was my father who interested me most. At dinner, sitting silently across the candlelit table from him, I began to take surreptitious looks at him. One night I saw that his hands were trembling. On another night he dropped his fork into his plate; it made a loud clang, and he got up awkwardly and hurried to his study, his empty chair teetering crazily for a few seconds. One night he rang for the cook and asked her about the food. "What is this you expect me to eat?" He glared at her suspiciously.

"Oh, it's a very fine ragout, sir, the very best ingredients."

"What is the meat in it?"

"Why it's . . . a lamb ragout, sir."

"It stinks; throw it out; bring me some bread and cheese." He got up and stormed out of the room.

Late Saturday morning I saw my father's study door open. The maid was cleaning the ashes from the hearth. I slid in silently and hid behind the draperies, where I could watch her as she grumbled petulantly, her plain face troubled and anxious. When she left the room to take the ashes to the garden, I unlocked one of the windows and climbed out, closing the window as tightly as I could. I returned to the front of the house, let myself in with my key and went to my room, making sure that the maid heard me slam the front door.

Back in my room, I took out a box of rock specimens which had arrived by mail some weeks after Gerd was already dead. I had met the delivery man, and after leaving the letters on the usual table, I had quietly taken Gerd's package to my room. I carefully took out the rocks and put them away, seeing in that moment Gerd's bright excited face as he explained a vein in a rock to me. I wondered how many other packages had come for him without my knowledge of them.

On Saturday night after dinner Wilhelm drove my father to his usual meeting, leaving me to myself. The cook went to bed early, as always, and the maid listened to the radio in her room. At ten I watched Karl climb the outside stairs to his rooms over the carriage house.

I took Gerd's rock container and the flashlight, and, dressed in my black leotard, black sweater and black stockings, with my hair parted in back and tied in a knot under my chin, I went to visit my rats. They came to me quickly and I took some food and gave them a little. Then I placed the open box on the cement and put a tulip bulb inside of it. One rat sniffed the box and jumped into it; a second rat followed. I had not considered two rats. But why not two? If one rat enraged my father, two would certainly get him twice as furious. I placed the lid over the box and wrapped my sweater around it, twisting the arms back and forth knotting them. I gave the rest of the bulbs to the remaining rats and quickly made my way to my father's study. The rats seemed glad to get out of their cramped quarters and rapidly began to run about sniffing everything. I was careful that none of the remains of the bulb fell from the box. I left the room, checking the low window ledge for any odd marks, and reentered the house through Mother's garden-room door. I decided to keep the flashlight. It was a remote risk, but it might come in handy some day.

Once back in my room, I cleaned the box, returned the specimens to it, and flushed the remains of the tulip bulb down the toilet. Then, dressed in my long cotton nightdress, I lay in the dark and waited. Bizarre imaginings filled my mind: the rats would attack my father; they might even give him the plague and he would be horribly sick with blisters all over him filled with black pus.

Then my father drifted out of my mind, and Gerd and I were lying on the warm sand in a cove off the Adriatic, and he touched me the way I had discovered to touch myself that gave me pleasure. He murmured some indistinct words, yet his face was close to mine, his warm sweet breath mingled with sea air and the taste of green grapes.

Then, not in a dream, I heard a horrible howl followed seconds later by a series of gunshots. I ran to the hall. Below me lights began to go on in the rooms. I descended to the second landing on the stairs. From there I saw my father's study door open and his tall form—crouched down—come backward into the drawing room, carrying a pistol, which he continued to shoot into his study. I heard the women running. "Get Wilhelm! Run!" It was the cook's voice. My father continued to howl, clicking his gun furiously (empty by then, apparently). The cook stood in the doorway to the drawing room crying, "Sir. Oh, sir. Calm yourself!"

He turned on her, still clicking the gun; if it had had any bullets left, he would have shot her. She shrank away as he raced to the cabinet and grabbed a new box of shells. He filled the gun and ran back to his open study door and began firing almost at once. Suddenly Wilhelm and Karl were in the drawing room. They gave each other a quick look and went up behind my father, each one grabbing one of his arms. He screamed curses at them, but Wilhelm managed to get the gun away from him. They dragged him to a chair. "Brandy!" Wilhelm whispered harshly. Lena, who had come in with the men, went out of my range of vision. She returned with a bottle and a glass. Wilhelm filled the glass and put it in front of my father's mouth. "Drink!"

It was odd watching my father become docile. He was making snuffling noises; then he began to retch. In the next minute, as the others moved back from him, he vomited in a long arching stream which splattered over a wide area of the carpet and some of the furniture. The cook ran out of the room, returning moments later with towels. Wilhelm and Karl stood my father up and began to lead him out of the room. It was obvious that they intended to bring him upstairs. I retreated to my room with haste, leaving my door, which was in the shadows anyway, open enough to hear anything they might say.

"Rats," whimpered my father, "there are rats in there, hundreds of rats crawling all over everything." His voice was shaking, and he kept repeating the word "rats."

When my father's bedroom door closed, I returned to the stairs and quietly crept along the wall to the foyer, where I hid beside the clock and listened to the two women cleaning up the mess.

Lena was on the edge of tears. "But what was it?"

she cried. "I don't understand. He seemed well at dinner."

"He thinks he saw some rats. Who knows how much those men drink when they get together. It's all a bad business. He had a very bad experience near the end of the war. He never got over it."

The clock chimed four and scared me for a moment. Then I picked up Vera's voice again.

"You might as well know about it, in case we have any more scenes like this one. When the war ended, the Americans or the British gathered together some people in Bergen and forced them to carry the dead in the camp to grave sites. Von Heyditch was somehow rounded up with the others and forced into this monstrous thing. It was horrible for him. In any case, when he and another man lifted a dead body, a rat came out of it and ran up von Heyditch's arm and into the collar of his shirt. The beast ran around on his bare back, looking for a way out. It couldn't have lasted more than a few seconds, but it drove the master almost out of his mind. The rat had something hanging from its mouth. I suppose it was flesh."

Lena spoke then. "Oh, the poor, poor man. Will we ever be through with those dreadful Jews?"

They began to talk mundanely about the need to get more soap and some antiseptics. I crept back up to my room, from which I could hear my father making odd gutteral sounds pierced occasionally with high, thin cries. I heard Wilhelm say he was going to phone for the doctor. A door closed, quietly for a change, and I heard fast-moving footsteps on the stairs. I peered out. Karl was running down to the foyer; then Wilhelm opened my father's bedroom door and called out, "And close the door to the study while you're there." Karl shouted back something. It was not clear. My father's bedroom door closed again, but the cries still came from it muffled and, therefore, all the more terrible.

I left my door partially opened and sat on my bed in the dark. There was that word again: "Jews." Before, the word had only identified people of a given religion, but now it was suddenly bigger. One thing, though, was becoming clear to me: I was certainly my father's daughter. How else could I have done such a terrible thing?

3

In the following weeks I took to brooding in my room as my headaches came more often and I sank into hours of depression. I began to have small accidents, causing myself physical injuries which left me in pain and rage.

One afternoon coming home from school I slammed the car door on my hand. Wilhelm, who had turned around at the exact moment that I cried out, said, "What the hell? Are you trying to cut off your fingers?" He looked at me anxiously. "You dummy! Go to the kitchen. Tell Vera to call the doctor." Surprised at this attention, I went into the house and up to my room. Lying on my bed, I held the hand in front of me and watched it become huge. I let the blood run down my fingers and drip on my chest. A few minutes later the cook came in.

"What's this about your hand?" She stopped, and loomed over me, her face as large as a full moon. "Heavens! Get up." She was tugging at my shoulders. "This must be seen to."

I pulled away from her. "Get out and leave me alone. I hate you."

She took a step backward and looked at me coldly. "That is of no importance. Your hand must be tended to. The doctor will be here soon to see your father, I shall have him take care of your hand at the same time."

"He is a pig. I don't want him to touch me."

"You will do as I tell you. We are not going to upset your father; he is not a well man, and while he is ill I shall run this house as it has always been run. Now be quiet. There will be no nonsense. You may have broken some bones." She left the room.

My hand hurt terribly and it was about twice the size of the other. I lay back on the bed and suffered in satisfaction.

When the doctor arrived, he washed my hand with some smelly solution that burned. "How did you ever slam the door on your own hand? Don't you watch what you are doing? Fortunately there are no bones broken from what I can tell, but it should be x-rayed anyway. Wilhelm can bring you by in the morning; I'll make the arrangements with him myself. No need to upset your father." He blathered on about how I should pay more attention to what I was doing, that I should stop daydreaming and being difficult, that I should be particularly good just now because my father was ill. It seemed that everyone made a great point of telling me that my father was "not a well man." They apparently all thought that I had slept through the entire rat incident, and many afternoons when Vera and Lena were having their coffee in the kitchen, making no attempt to lower their voices, they spoke about me, thinking I was in my room, safely sleeping. I had taken to lying in a deeply pillowed wicker settee in Mother's plant room, eavesdropping. One rainy day their conversation included Mother and Gerd.

"Does the girl know about the master's terrible experience at Bergen?" Lena spoke with food in her mouth.

"No. She knows nothing. And it's just as well. Von Heyditch made a bad mistake with the boy. He wasn't ready." There was a moment of silence. "To tell you the truth, that boy would never have been ready. He had his mother's softness, playing the piano, collecting rocks like a child. It was a bad mistake from the beginning: the master should have married a strong woman who could have given him many fine sons. Financially, of course, it was a good match; she brought a tremendous dowry with her and, of course, a nationally known name. But she was weak from the beginning, and the flaw passed on into the children."

"But she was so much younger than he. Do you suppose that caused the weakness?"

"No, no. That has nothing to do with it. Her young blood was going to be good for the von Heyditches; he is the last and was desperate for a son. But she was soft. She was one of those idealistic little convent girls who know nothing about the world; and when it came time to show strength and courage, she went all to pieces. She never understood his work. She tried to get him to go to church. Can you see von Heyditch in church?" Both women laughed. "Well, it was doomed from the beginning. She had three miscarriages before the boy was born. It would not surprise me if she was responsible for them herself, but of course, you must never breathe a word. Anyway, it is not a certainty, and she *was* Catholic. No one would believe a Catholic girl would do such a thing.

"She hated Cologne and I think she hated von Heyditch. Without a word to anyone she would leave for Bavaria. Yet, I believe he was fond of her. Each time she ran away, he went himself to Regensburg to bring her back. When the war was over and the boy was born, she must have reconciled herself. She never left again. She adored that baby and then she began to pray for a daughter." The cook paused. I was afraid she would stop talking. I wanted to shout to her, "Don't stop now, don't stop now."

Vera continued slowly. "The only time I ever heard her scream at him was when he gave the girl that name. She was inconsolable."

"That's not her real name?"

"Of course it is. The master never gave in. Eroica is

her recorded name. But the mistress wanted the girl to be called Theodosia."

"Whatever for?"

"Oh, some silly romantically religious meaning the name has. It's not even German; it's Greek."

"And the boy's name?"

"Oh, I don't know if she objected to his name or not. The master named him after the field marshal, of course. Another mistake—not the name, but telling the boy whom he was named after. So many mistakes. Everything has gone wrong. What a family! Cursed they are; and him, such an important man.

"And now the girl, injuring herself, mangling her hand in the car door, and then falling on the stairs and hurting her head. It's unnatural to have such bad luck. And what a disposition; he should send her away to school."

I breathed silently so that I could hear everything; they were deciding my life with their careless opinions.

"Perhaps relatives could take her. The mother's people. There is that uncle of hers."

"No. There is bad blood between the families. Those wretched people in Regensburg wanted his wife's body to be placed in their vault. He would not hear of it. So now there is a break with them. If I know the master, it will never be mended. A school would be best for her, but he refuses to do this."

"Why?"

"I don't know."

"Perhaps he wants her near him. He has no one else."

The cook gave an ugly laugh. "Don't be stupid. He can't stand her. He wanted sons. What good is she to him? The best thing is to send her away where he isn't constantly reminded that all he has is a useless girl who is nothing but a bother and a nuisance to him. It is obvious that her very presence is vexing and bitter for him."

"But she will be an heiress someday."

"Yes, he's stuck with that, and how it must gall him."

When the two women turned their attention to preparing the evening meal, I slipped back to my room and thought over what Vera had said. That my father hated me was not news, but that he had picked my name and that my mother had loathed it made me despair. Gerd had thought "Eroica" was beautiful, and he had researched the whole story of how Beethoven had named his Third Symphony, but apparently he never realized that it had been Father's choice.

"Originally Beethoven called it *Bonaparte*, until that huge dwarf proclaimed himself emperor; then the composer scratched out the '*intitolata Bonaparte*' on the title page with such fury that he tore a hole in the sheet. He finally settled on *Eroica* with the idea that it was meant to commemorate the life of any great man. At least that is the opinion of the historians. But more interesting than all that title business is what other musicians and critics thought of it." He smiled at me and said drolly, "You will be glad to hear that no one said it was altogether rotten. Berlioz said that the *Eroica* Symphony is so powerful in ideas, so spirited and at the same time noble in style, and so poetic in its form that it is equal in stature to the most exalted of its creator's inspirations.

"You might also be interested in knowing what Richard Wagner wrote in 1851, that's twenty-four years after Beethoven died. '. . . . this work is filled by all the manifold, interwoven feelings of a strong, complete, individuality, to which nothing human is unfamiliar, but which contains everything truly human within itself, and expresses it in such a way that, after most sincerely presenting all human passions, it attains the fulfillment of its nature with a combination of most deeply felt gentleness and most energetic power. The progress towards fulfillment is the heroic element in this work.' Rather a lot to live up to if that's why they named you 'Eroica.' Odd for Mother to give you such a name," he added.

"But it suits your black hair and your passionate nature."

"Do I have a passionate nature?"

"Did you ever hear of an Apache who didn't?"

In retrospect, it is not odd that neither Gerd nor I asked my mother about my name. My mother always seemed distant, and we tended not to disturb her, because she suffered hideously from her headaches. Later, when I had my own headaches, I understood her physical suffering and was glad that my brother had taught me consideration for her. "You must know that she is in pain and that bright lights and loud noises make her pain worse. We must not ever disturb her; it is best if she can sleep." I was about six or perhaps seven when Gerd told me this. By that time he and I had become the closest of friends.

We had a series of nurses until I was about seven. New ones came and went with such rapidity that all I remember about them is the uniform—a dark-blue dress with a white cape and white stockings and shoes, and they all smelled of starch.

After the last of the nurses left, Gerd and I were alone together more often and we began to share our secret feelings with each other. Uncle Teddy, Mother's older brother, was of great interest to us: he had a dueling scar. It was shaped like a perfect crescent high on his left cheek, and Gerd speculated over the "affair of honor" for which he had earned it. "Someone must have insulted the family name," he concluded one day. Father's frequent references to the importance of our two families' names was one of my earliest recollections, although we only visited Mother's estate in Regensburg twice in my memory and each time we stayed but a few weeks. Father was not with us, but I always remembered those holidays with immense joy: Mother was not as sick. Gerd and I explored the deep silence of the forest on the estate in the late afternoons and often saw deer drink from a silvery stream. When we told Mother later, she laughed with delight and hugged us, and one day she even walked with us a short distance under the quivering aspen, her face serene and loving.

But she was never like that when we were on holiday anywhere else. Father knew people everywhere, and as soon as we arrived at someone's estate in another country, he would make arrangements for guides for Gerd and me, and then he would be off to "conferences." Mother stayed in bed most of the time. Sometimes Gerd and I managed to get up before sunrise and go off on our own and a few times we managed to lose our assigned guides. Mother gave us money for souvenirs and sweets on these adventures, and although we had wonderful times, I knew that toward the end of each day, Gerd would start worrying about Mother and want to get back. She was almost always sleeping.

After Gerd killed himself, the doctors would not give her large amounts of sleeping medicine. One day after school, as I came near my mother's room, I heard the doctor tell her that she must not be foolish. My mother was pleading with him in a sad and hopeless way. "But I must have more. I've built up a tolerance to it, and I need to sleep. I do not sleep at all. If I could only get one good night's sleep, I should be all right. Please, please, please."

"My dear madam, it's too dangerous. The risk is too great. You must build up your strength with good, healthy food. And I recommend a glass of sherry before bedtime. And get some exercise during the day; some nice long walks would do you a world of good."

But my mother did not take any long walks, and when I offered to bring her the sherry later in the day, she only shook her head and patted my hand.

After my mother's death, I tried to think out what Gerd had meant about letting Mother die. I could not understand how he could have thought something so contrary to his kind and gentle nature. I worried over that perhaps more than I worried over anything else.

Ultimately it was this unacceptable paradox that made me realize I had to reenter my father's study. There was nothing else to do except return to that terrible room and search it until I found the thing that had made living unendurable for Gerd.

Lena alone among the servants had a key to the study, and she carried it on a large ring with other keys attached by a leather thong inside the pocket of her heavy apron. I would have to steal it.

My plan was to become friendly with her, distract her attention in some way when she had the apron off, steal the whole ring, unlock the door and return the keys without her ever knowing that they had been missing.

Pretending to be friends with any of the servants made me wild with anger, since this was a betrayal of Gerd and Mother and myself, but it couldn't be helped. One morning I rose early, made up my bed and took the towels from my bathroom and brought them to Lena in the linen room. She looked at me with astonishment. "Whatever are you doing?"

"They need to be washed."

"Well, I would have picked them up in due time," she said crabbily.

I shrugged and looked sullen.

She looked at me with curiosity. "You shouldn't be up this early until you are completely well. You had a bad fall."

"I am well," I mumbled.

"The doctors will decide that. A relapse would be very bad right now. I'll be up in a little while to make up your bed."

"I've made it up."

"Whatever for?" Again she looked astonished.

I shrugged again and looked away. "I had nothing else to do."

"Well, this calls for a little inspection. We'll see how well you did." She smiled at me warmly. I decided it was too early to smile back at her, but I went along with the inspection. Apparently I knew how to make a bed.

It occurred to me that it might take a long time before I could steal the keys and I was bitterly impatient. Everywhere the crocuses were pushing up, and in the rock garden under Gerd's sealed room the golden-green shoots of the remaining tulip bulbs and daffodils were just breaking through the wet earth. The sky was partially cleared and I could hear the calls of migrating birds filter down over the land. I looked up. An airplane was passing high over the city, but I could see no birds.

I longed for Gerd, remembering the year the cranes had flown in magnificent formation over the Rhine far to the west of their usual migrating pattern. "They are going back to Russia—all the way from Africa," said Gerd with wonder. To Gerd everything was wondrous. Once he had held a sprouting onion in front of me. "Do you see: it looks dry and dead, but life is secretly waiting inside of it. It has to bring forth its life, its claim. Even if it dies now, it will at least have made its demand to live. All things have a demand to live."

I looked up at the boards that covered his windows. They were dead eyes. Everything hungered for life and growth and becoming. Everything around me was making its demand, everything except my dead brother, and I raged at his death.

I increased my efforts with Lena. I helped her water the plants in Mother's indoor garden, folded linen, sheathed the silver. She soon began to expect me to be in certain parts of the house when certain duties were to be done and she took to calling me endearing names: "That's a dear child" and "What a thoughtful girl." But the keys never left her apron.

By the third week I was helping her dust the knickknacks. But she was subtle about the study. "Now you can put a shine to the music room if you like while I straighten up your father's office." My heart sank each time I heard the jingling keys while she locked the crucial door. Silently I pleaded with her to forget to lock it, but she never did.

Vera's view of my helpfulness was predictably caustic. "So, a little pain did her some good."

Lena's defense of me led to a curious exchange between the women. "It's not that. She is really a considerate and thoughtful girl. In some ways she is much like her mother. Poor dear child."

"Nonsense, the girl is the worst of both her parents: she has her mother's weakness and her father's vile temper."

"No, no. She is in her way a good girl. You forget the shocks she has been through."

"We have all had our share of shocks," retorted Vera. "Your sentimentality over the girl will get you into trouble. You know that he does not want any show of weakness toward her."

"He is unfair to her. There is no love. It's cruel."

"It's what he wants. Do you intend to disobey direct orders from him? He wants no sentiment shown her."

"That's unkind. He could make an effort to like her. She can't help her coloring." Lena's voice was whining and defensive.

They talked of other things, and I went to my room, where I held the chambered nautilus in my hand. *"The echoes of things around you,"* said my brother's voice, but the reference to my coloring made no sense. My skin was not as light as Gerd's or Mother's had been, but it was pale in a different way: whereas they had rosy cheeks, I never did, not even in the snow. Once, when we spent a month wandering around the Aegean Islands on a boat that belonged to a friend of Father's, one of the Greek crewmen asked me if I were Greek, and Gerd told me that the sailor's question was a compliment. "It's your black hair and your golden skin," he said.

My plans to distract Lena were going nowhere; I had to get her to invite me into her room. One day, when I heard her come up the stairs, I quickly went to my brother's locked door and leaned my face and arms against it. I heard her stop suddenly a small distance away.

"Here, here, you mustn't grieve like that. Your brother wouldn't want you to be unhappy." She came to me and touched my shoulders in a soft and loving way. "This won't do at all." She turned me gently to face her, but I looked down at the floor. When she lifted my chin with her fingertips, I saw that her eyes were glistening with tears. "You must be brave," she said with a trembling voice; and then she hugged me and called me her poor little girl. I remembered Gerd's statement about Lena's having a good heart as I felt one of her tears fall on my forehead.

In the next few days it took some effort for me to keep things straight in my mind. I was uncomfortable in the presence of Lena's kindness to me: on the one hand I did not want it; yet on the other I found that it was not altogether unpleasant. This was disturbing and something I had not counted on. If I was to get into my father's study, I had to steal from Lena. I could not be concerned about who got into trouble, and yet Gerd would not hurt a person with a good heart. Then, quite suddenly, the opportunity to steal the keys arose. Lena had removed her apron and had fallen asleep in a chair in the linen room. I had only to take the whole apron, since the keys were in the pocket and would not jingle about, find the right key, open the door to Father's study and return the apron before she awakened. Yet when I looked at her sad sleeping face, at the closed blue-veined eyes that had wept for me, I could not do it. Twice I picked up the garment and held it tightly in my hand. Finally, with rage and disgust, I put it back and went to my room.

My head began to hurt as I cursed my weakness and stupidity. I wished Gerd had not told me she had a good heart. I wished she had not wept for me. On Saturday I did not go to help Lena; I raged in my room, cursing my lost opportunity. I skulked around the house and told Vera I was not hungry. Back in my room, I read, fell asleep, awakened angry and hating the world. By late afternoon Lena came to ask me if I were "feeling badly." I did not answer her. She looked at me sadly and left. Ten minutes later she returned with a tray with hot chocolate on it and a sweet roll, some cheese and an apple. She took off her long black sweater and put it over my shoulders as I sat on the window seat looking out at the gray twilight; it was a time of day I particularly hated. Lena left without saying anything. I wanted to tear off the sweater and throw the tray at her, but instead I pulled the sweater on tighter and ate the food and drank the chocolate. Everything had failed.

That night I could not sleep. Long after my father returned from his evening out and I heard him go to his bedroom, I lay awake listening to the night sounds. A wind was rising and some branches scraped against the house. On the river the foghorns answered one another like owls in the dark. I got up and turned on my lamp. The room was cold. Lena's sweater hung over the back of the chair at my desk. I put it on and pushed my hands into the deep pockets. For a few seconds my mind reeled; then, almost mechanically, I withdrew my right hand slowly: I was holding a key.

I knew at once the door it would open. Quickly I changed into my black clothes. I folded Lena's sweater and hid it under Gerd's books, and with the flashlight I left my room without a sound. Gerd's room was closest to Mother's old room. She had changed rooms some years before. At one time she and my father had adjacent rooms with a connecting sitting room between them, but Mother had moved down the hall when I was about ten. The room next to mine was a guest room, although we never had any guests.

I carefully fitted the key into Gerd's lock; the door opened easily without any creaking sounds. If Father was awake and also listening to night sounds, he would hear everything. I flashed the light around the room: nothing had been moved. I did not sit on the bed or any of the chairs for fear of making a noise. Instead I sat on the floor, and after a few minutes I realized I was weeping. I clutched the key in my hand and thought of Gerd's closed dead fingers. Then, as I felt the ridge of the small bit of metal, something clicked in my mind. There was no key to Gerd's room on the board in the storage room, just as there was no key there to Father's study. I thought of the way my father always organized things so that two different purposes served a single action. Our holidays always seemed to coincide with his business trips.

I got up and went stealthily down the stairs in the dark. At the study door I slowly put the key into the lock. Like Gerd's lock it took an almost full-circle twist, and like Gerd's door it opened without a sound.

Inside I could use the flashlight safely, since the drapes were closed and the backs covered with some metal-painted cloth that looked like tarnished silver. I was drawn to my father's desk, although the room contained many cases with glass doors and tall five-drawer filing cabinets. The top of the desk was orderly, with stacks of papers and workbooks of some kind on it.

I sat in his chair and slowly pulled open the wide, shallow center drawer. It contained only a flat, black velvet box perhaps five inches long and three wide. I looked at it for a few moments and tried to think where I had seen it before. I placed it on top of the desk and carefully opened it. Inside there was a single object: a gold-framed medallion. On a red background gleamed a golden eagle, its claws holding a ridged wheel. In the center of the wheel was a black hooked cross called a swastika, which Gerd had once said meant "good luck" in Sanskrit and which had been on all the flags during the war.

I took the medallion out of the box and held it in my hand: my fingers closed over it, easily concealing it. Then I recognized the thing that I had pushed away, beyond memory, as I had touched my brother's cold feet that day. It came rushing back to me, starkly clear:

there on the desk lay the box, empty—just as it had been that other time.

I turned the medallion over and over in my hand, realizing with increasing despair that it meant nothing to me. Yet, in the final terrible seconds of his life, Gerd had gripped it in his hand; and in my sorrow I imagined that his last thought was on this enigmatic bit of metal. My despair turned to rage, and for a wild moment I felt the impulse to start a fire in Father's study. I saw flames reach up through the ceiling and curl into Father's bedroom, on the next floor. He would be trapped, burned to ashes. My breath came fast and violently for a time while I fought the dreadful urge with all my will. At last my rage subsided and I was able to think calmly again.

I traced the outline of the medallion on a piece of blank paper, drawing in the eagle and the wheel with its hooked cross. After returning the medallion to the drawer, I examined some of the files in the cabinets and cases. They appeared to involve business matters with people and companies in many parts of the world: North Africa, South America, the Near East—all over Europe. I knew that my father exported machinery to many countries. It seemed odd that he should keep business records at home when he had a skyscraper full of offices with hundreds of people working in them.

Before I left the study I had the curious need to take something from my father, actually to steal something that was dear to him. But this was not possible, because I was convinced that my father loved nothing: at Gerd's and Mother's funerals he had not even wept.

Back in my own room, I stared into the darkness. I should have taken something of Gerd's from his room: a jacket or a sweater, something that still had his scent on it. All I had was the drawing of the medallion and my bad feelings toward it because I knew that in some horrible way it had caused Gerd to die. The servants probably knew what it meant, but I was certain that they would tell me nothing. Anyway, no one must know that I had been in the study. I would return Lena's sweater and pretend that I had never found the key. If Father had told everyone not to have anything to do with me, Lena had risked herself. I could no longer use her as I had. Gerd would not do that. I would have to wait for an opportunity to get a book on such things, but I despaired at the idea: it could take months, a year, longer.

I thought about the medallion. It was an odd thing for my father to keep in his desk. The house was filled with collections of fine porcelain, old engravings, antique clocks, all openly displayed. If he had received it as a prize, why hadn't he put it with his shooting trophies, in the glass case in the music room? I shook away the thought. How absurd I was being: Gerd would not kill himself over some trophy Father had received.

In deep despondency and wretchedness I finally slept, and dreamed of eagles.

4

The first eagle hung suspended for a long moment in the red sky and then shot toward me like a diving airplane. It screamed like an airplane but still looked like a bird, and when the earth stopped shaking, a man stood near me where the eagle would have landed. He was an Indian with a full-feathered headdress, like those I had seen in pictures. He held his hand out to me and smiled. "Here, take this." It was Gerd's voice, but there was nothing in his hand. As I looked at him and tried to get closer to him, he turned into Father. I backed away, and it was then, in that moment, that I heard the second eagle. I looked up: there were hundreds of them wheeling and turning in a bloody sky. I began to run, but I fell almost at once. Unable to rise, I pushed agonizingly against the earth, crying, pleading. Then I heard the gentle waters of the Adriatic lap against the white flat stones where I was lying with Gerd. Sea gulls circled overhead. Cloud images drifted above us, changed, vanished, returned.

I came out of sleep slowly, lying absolutely still. On the wall the pendulum of the clock swung back and forth with hypnotic repetition, the vanishing seconds making me feel terrifyingly alone. It was a few minutes after ten and no sound came from the rest of the house. Pain beat behind my right eye, and I knew that in another hour I would be staggering with agony, looking for a dark room where there was no sound, knowing that even that would do no good. I remembered the dream, the shrieking airplane, and in that remembering the pain increased: a sudden violent streak of it ran from my forehead through my eye and down into my jaw. I knew this particular variety: it could last for hours or for days. There was no way to prepare for it, no way to escape from it, and no way to endure it.

There were things to do before it got to the stage where I no longer cared about anything that happened. After dressing slowly, I wrapped Lena's sweater (with the key in the pocket) into a towel and took it to the linen room, where I hung the garment over the back of a chair. There was no one in the kitchen. I remembered that it was Sunday, generally a relaxed day: Father went to his office, as usual, since his factories never shut down; Vera and Lena went to some kind of church; and Wilhelm and Karl usually disappeared until dinnertime. On other Sundays I read for a while and then walked to the park. But on that day I knew that nothing was possible. I drifted back to the drawing room and looked at my father's study door, thinking how strange it was that I had been in that room during the night, had found what Gerd had held in his hand, and yet had not discovered why he had chosen to die. My headache deepened and I returned to the kitchen with the idea of making some hot chocolate. The sugar canister was empty, and as I opened various cabinets and storage bins, I absently opened a tea tin with oriental paintings on it. There was money in it—over fifty marks.

Ignoring my headache, I took ten marks, put everything back in its place, and raced to my room feeling vaguely dizzy. I put on raincoat and boots, stuffed the drawing of the medallion and the ten marks into my pocket, and left through the back terrace. Beyond the outer gardens, I walked for a few blocks and then took a bus to the inner city.

For a time I walked around, until I came to the museum where there is an art library, and I asked the woman behind the information desk if they had a book on medallions.

"Do you mean architectural medallions, such as are used for decorative purposes on buildings?"

"No, something small that one might wear on a chain around the neck."

"Then you mean a pendant."

"Perhaps."

"Well, we have books on antique jewelry: necklaces, bracelets, earrings, brooches, and such things. Some of them dating back to Roman times."

"No, these are oval with pictures or perhaps carvings on them. They are made of metal."

"Are you looking for something like that to buy?"

"No, I only want to see a book that has such things in it." The pain in my head was sharper.

"You'll have to be more specific. Why don't you try some of the shop windows and get some ideas."

Nausea rose with anger and I lowered my voice to keep from screaming at her. "I already have the idea; I know what I want. I mean, I'm not looking for a pendant, just a book about pendants."

"We have no books on only pendants. You're holding up other people. Now, be a good girl and be off."

I looked behind me: there were several people waiting to talk to the woman at the desk.

"Perhaps the young lady means a badge of some kind." The man who spoke behind me gave me a rather paternal smile. I was too suspicious to smile back. Gerd had never said not to talk to strangers, but he did say that it was a good idea to listen to them first, before committing oneself in any deep way.

"I'm sure I have no idea what she means." The woman behind the counter who wanted me to be a good girl and be off was no longer looking at me. She spoke directly to the man. "Can I be of help to you, sir?"

"Yes," he said smiling. "You can help me locate a book on medallions, pendants, badges, crests, emblems, medals, charms, tokens, cameos . . . shields, yes, possibly even shields." He did not look at me at all, but moved directly to the desk. He had light-brown hair and a little red-blond beard. He was older than Gerd and much younger than Father.

"We have no such book, as far as I know." The woman's face tightened as though he had insulted her.

"And how far is that?" At this she really did knot up her face. The man looked at me with a little grin. "Time to look elsewhere." We moved away from the desk and stood next to a display case hanging on the wall. "Now, then, describe to me what you are looking for and perhaps we can find it in another library." I did not answer at once, and he smiled at me again. "Did you really come to look at a book, or were you to meet a young man here who is waiting this very minute with his heart in his mouth, anxiously wondering if you will keep your promise?"

I had an impulse to run, but decided against it: too rude, for one thing (after his help); and also, he might know something of the medallion, and if he did, I would not need to find a book at all. Time to play "dumb": "What young man?"

"Oh-ho, that's a good one. Next you'll say that you have no young man."

"I have no young man." In those days I found that most adults fit into one of three categories: they were cold and cruel, they were cold and indifferent, or they were disgustingly condescending (Lena was not too disgusting). "Thank you for your help." I quickly walked away. Even with my head coming apart I knew this silly business was only wasting my time.

"Wait a moment." He followed me as I left the building. "You seem to have something serious on your mind. I'm sorry. I see that I spoke foolishly to you. Come, I'll buy you a coffee, and we can talk about your medallion."

I stopped on the sidewalk when he put his hand on my shoulder. It was quite a decent apology; perhaps I could commit myself just a little more. We walked to a café nearby and sat at a small table where he ordered two coffees. "All right, now, you want to find a medallion. Tell me about it. No, first tell me your name."

I followed a recently sharpened instinct. "Theadora."

"Theadora? Just Theadora?" I did not answer him. "All right, just Theadora, I am just Jans. Do you live in Cologne?" He had a kind face. Gerd had said one could tell a good deal about a person by his face. The man had very good eyes that did not look away when he talked.

"Nearby," I answered, tasting the coffee the waiter brought. "I have to leave soon."

"Where do you have to leave for?"

"Home."

"But we haven't found what you are looking for yet."

Adults are forever stating the obvious as though it were some sort of extraordinary revelation: "Oh, it's you, is it"; or "Here it is, Sunday again"; or "I see you've put on the blue dress." It drove me crazy.

The man was looking at me appraisingly. "How old are you? Sixteen or seventeen?"

I looked him straight in the eyes. "Twenty."

"That old? Then it will be all right if I call on you. We could go to the films, or perhaps you'll have supper with me one night this week. We could go dancing or take a boat ride." He stopped talking for a moment; then he said slowly and seriously, "Tell me about the medallion; then I'll drive you home, and tomorrow I'll find the book you want and I'll bring it to you."

I knew, of course, that as agreeable as all that sounded, it was impossible. "That's too much trouble." I took the piece of folded paper out of my pocket. "If you can tell me where I can get such a book, I can get it myself." I unfolded the sheet and flattened it out on the table between us. "I want to find out about this." I was looking down at the drawing, but the sound he made, a strange wordless noise in his throat, caused me to look up quickly. Something terrible had happened to his face.

"Put that away at once." His angry whisper frightened me and I crunched the paper into a ball and thrust it back into my pocket. He stood up, an expression of absolute horror on his face. He started to leave, but after a few steps stopped abruptly and returned to his place. Pulling the chair close to the table, he leaned toward me. "Who are you? What is your name? How old are you? Where do you live?" His face, though still appearing shocked, had lost its look of loathing. He lit a cigarette and offered me one. I shook my head. "How old are you?"

"Seventeen. What does the medallion mean?"

He motioned to the waiter for more coffee. As we waited, he said, "I will tell you nothing unless you answer my questions." I gave him a false family name and the street of the cemetery as my home address. I stuck to seventeen as my age. He appeared to believe everything. "How did you come to see this medal?"

"Is that what it is?"

"Yes."

"What kind of medal?"

"It is a wartime medal."

"It is a soldier's medal, then?"

"No. It is not a soldier's medal. It was given to civilians for . . . a variety of reasons."

"What kind of reasons?"

He was looking at me closely; then for a moment he looked away toward the street. "Certain . . . services to the state." Again he faced me. "Do you have it?" I shook my head. The waiter brought the coffee and left. "Do you go to school?"

"Yes."

"Where?"

"It is a private school."

"What is the name of it?"

I gave him the name of a convent school outside the city. (Thank you, Vera.)

"Are you Catholic?"

"No."

"Why do you go to a Catholic school?"

"People say it is good for discipline."

He looked at me as though he were memorizing my face. "Why did you not ask your parents about the medal?"

"I have no parents."

"With whom do you live?"

"Some relatives." I knew that I had better remember all this since he might reword the same question.

"Please tell me how you managed to see the medal." His eyes were troubled and anxious.

"Someone who lived with my family had it."

"Why are you so interested in it?"

I did not know what to tell him. "It's a very interesting medal. I like eagles, and I thought perhaps I could find a medallion . . . medal . . . like it." My head was hurting horribly.

He suddenly grasped my wrist—not so that it hurt, but firmly. At first I felt fear, but his face was still kind, even though he was frowning. "Theadora, ever since I saw you at the desk back there, you have only wanted to know about the medal. You even said that you did not want one of the medals. You only wanted a book on medals. I interceded because I didn't like to see you being pushed around, and your urgency and caution intrigued me. Then, when you showed me the drawing . . . well, it was more of a shock than you can possibly know. The war . . . you see, it was from something in the war. Now, you may tell me all the lies you wish, but I want the truth to this one question: Why does the medal interest you?"

"It killed my brother," I whispered. Tears I did not want filled my eyes. He let go of my wrist and breathed in sharply. His face had lost all of its fury. He took out a handkerchief and blotted the tears on my cheeks. I felt terrible; yet all I could do was dig my fists deeper into my coat pockets and try not to make a sound as the tears streamed down my cheeks. Jans moved his chair closer to mine; he was still trying to dry my face.

"Are you a Jew?" he whispered.

I shook my head. "No, we never had a religion."

This seemed to amuse him. "The irony of it," he said with an odd little smile on his mouth. Then he brushed my hair away from my face. "Come on. This is not a good place to talk." We left the café, his hand holding my arm. I concentrated on not crying, but it was hard to stop. My head hurt and I had found out what the medallion was for and it meant nothing to me. It was only a war medal and no one talked about the war; it was over years ago. What did I care if my father had done something which had earned him a medal? I was no closer to the reason for Gerd's killing himself than I had been a year ago. Again, everything had failed.

We walked for a short distance in silence, until he stopped at a car, which he unlocked. "Get in." I did as he said, but I could feel myself coming back from the dark hopelessness. A clear voice in my head said not to do that again.

The man sat behind the wheel, looking at me. "When did your brother die?"

"A year ago."

"How did the medal kill him?"

"He had it in his hand when he died."

This apparently sounded nonsensical to him. "He held the medal in his hand and it killed him? I don't understand."

"It's too hard to explain. I'm sorry, but I cannot talk about my brother's death."

"How old was he?"

"He"—I paused to think about this—"he would be eighteen now."

"Was he in the university?"

I turned to look out the window. The university. I had not even thought of that. Gerd killed himself soon after he began his studies at the university. Was there a connection? "Yes, my brother died not long after he entered the university. Why did you ask that?"

He looked at me with that same memorizing look he had had on his face earlier. His eyes were gray, a very deep dark gray. "Only because you seem to have led a very sheltered life. Have you always lived in Cologne?"

"Yes, but we used to travel to many places." I was irritated that he thought I had been so protected.

"Where did you go?"

"Spain, Greece, Yugoslavia, Switzerland, Italy."

"Where did you stay in those countries? I mean, did you stay at hotels? And did you go sightseeing, like ordinary tourists?"

"Yes, we visited the Acropolis and Delphi, and Delos and many museums and scientific displays. My brother wanted to be a geologist. As for where we stayed, once in a while we stayed at hotels, but usually we were guests at the homes of friends of my father's."

"When did you lose your parents?"

"My mother died last winter."

"And your father?"

"I don't remember. A long time ago, when I was little." Instantly I realized that that was a contradiction of sorts; yet even if Father had died a long time ago, we might still have visited his friends. After all, they were Mother's friends, too. But that wasn't really true, either; in a way which was too subtle for me to intellectualize at the time, the people with whom we stayed were not Mother's friends. Gerd had made a comment about that once. "Father knows more strangers." He said it more in jest than in earnest, but on reflection I realized that it was true. There was always a distance between ourselves and the people we stayed with. Once, in Switzerland, our hosts kept forgetting Mother's first name. She was called Caroline, but the hostess kept calling her Christina. Gerd and I had waited for Mother to correct her, but she never did. Gerd had said after two days, "Mother's right: why bother?"

Jans had stopped asking questions. When I looked at

him, he was staring at me with a questioning expression.

"You know," he finally said, "you are a little hard to believe. I don't mean that what you say is hard to believe; I mean you—*you* are hard to believe. What do they teach you at that school?"

I thought about my school, certainly the dullest place in the world. "Oh, nothing, nothing that I can remember. I should go home now." I was content to change the subject since I had no idea what went on in a Catholic school.

"I'll drive you. Then, if you like, I'll call you tomorrow and perhaps we can visit some museums, if you still like to do that kind of thing."

What I wanted to do most was get away from him and get home. He asked me for my telephone number. I made one up. He told me that his name was Deblin and that he had grown up in Belgium. I pretended to be very interested. It is even possible that I *was* interested. As he began driving in the general direction of my home, he kept asking about things I liked to do, and in my anxiety I gave him all sorts of nonsensical answers. Yes, I liked to play chess (I had never touched a chessman). Yes, I enjoyed watching soccer games (I had never seen a soccer game). Yes, I thought Sartre was a great writer (who was Sartre?).

He drove unerringly toward the cemetery. There was a small footpath and a narrow gate at one end of the huge complex, the part called the Old Ones. Here the graves dated back hundreds of years and the monuments were huge and rather grotesque: angels with chipped faces flew about with only their toes touching a stone arch or cross. If Jans drove to the main entrance, it would be difficult to explain all those dead people living in my yard.

I told him to stop at the small gate. A few drops of rain splattered on the windshield. He said, "But there is no—" He stopped: on one side of the street was a park; on the other, the wall of the cemetery. I opened the door to the car. "Wait, please," he said. "I thought perhaps we still had some time to talk."

"No. I'm sorry. I have to go now."

He laughed incredulously. "But you can't live here. Where is your house?"

"Thank you for your help, and the ride." As I started to get out of the car, he put his hand on mine.

"If I call, will you talk to me?"

I shook my head. "No, they would not permit such a thing."

"Then will you meet me here next Sunday, at this time?"

"No, I cannot do that." I pulled away my hand. "Thank you again. Good-bye." I ran to the gate and pushed my way through. It took only seconds to lose myself among the saints.

Jans came to the cemetery and stood just inside the gate. "Theadora." The rain was getting heavy and in a few moments his hair was plastered down over his forehead. He called again. I watched him pull his coat collar up around his ears; then he began to walk up one of the avenues between the elaborate memorials, trying to find me. The rain was like a waterfall; there was no difficulty in losing Jans.

Lena and Vera were in the kitchen when I got home. I would have preferred not to see them, but having forgotten my key, it was a matter of ringing at the front door or coming in through the kitchen. Unless I made sure they were open in advance, the other entrances to the house were always locked.

"Good heavens! You look like a drowned cat. Where have you been?" Vera was preparing Sunday dinner, and the aromas of vegetables and meat reminded me that I had not eaten.

"To the cemetery." I saw the sideways glance they gave each other. Lena was wearing her black sweater, but as usual I pretended that nothing interested me. The rain had drenched my clothes completely and Lena was concerned about my catching cold.

"Now leave the coat here and the boots and go up and change your clothes. Get into bed and get warm. I'll bring you something hot to drink."

Vera grumbled something about a "stupid girl" and returned to her cooking. "Dinner will be at five. Be on time. We don't want to upset your father," she said without looking at me. I was content to go to my room and get rid of my clammy clothes. My father and I were eating together again. His illness and my accident had stopped this for a time, but we now took up our old ways, eating in silence in the dining room with only the knife-and-fork sounds breaking up the stillness. But something had changed; he looked older and he seemed always nervous and irritable. Sometimes he stared off into space as though he were listening to something far away—a summons perhaps—a distant sound only he could hear. I wondered what service he had done for the nation: perhaps he thought of those days when he was a hero. How glorious that must have been for him to receive an award from the state. Still, why did Gerd hold the medal in his hand? Slowly I came to the conclusion that Gerd had held that medal in defiance of Father. "I don't care if you did get an award, I hate you anyway, you and your cold, unloving life." But this last was really what *I* felt. Gerd had been more forgiving. "Some people are like that," he had said one day when Father had left for a trip without saying good-bye. "They don't know how to love. Mother said that they think it's a sign of weakness, so they build up barriers in their hearts. Grandfather raised him to think of love as being silly and unnecessary. Poor Father, he can't help himself. He just doesn't know how to show his feelings after keeping everything inside the barrier for so long. I think he's very unhappy. Perhaps the war made it worse, not just the constant bombing but the damage to his pride. Father cannot really endure the nation's being divided. No one talks about the war because no one wants to talk about his own failure; but I think that's wrong: the best thing to do is to learn from it." But what was there to learn from it except not to have any more of them if they were going to kill so many people and break up the country?

That night, as we had almost finished dinner, Father suddenly said, "I shall be away for a few weeks; I expect you to do as Vera tells you." He had actually stopped eating and was staring at me with a vaguely perplexed expression, as though I were some detail he had overlooked while packing. His face almost said, "Where did I leave my gloves?" or "I wonder if I should take a sweater."

The last time he had left on a business trip, he had not said anything to me at all; but then, he was only gone for about a week, and anyway, Vera told me the day before that he was leaving. That trip had taken him to Egypt, I discovered through my usual eavesdropping methods. "I can remember when we would have used other means with the Arabs," Wilhelm had said to Karl as they sat at a kitchen table, drinking beer.

Vera had disagreed. "The new methods are not only less expensive, they are more effective. Others do the work."

"What do you know about it? You think this is for women?" Wilhelm's disgust came out in an explosion of questions which he apparently did not feel needed answering.

On this longer trip Father was going to South America. He did not tell me this; Lena did, rather casually, after he had gone. But that Sunday evening, when he spoke to me, he added nothing about his own plans; the remaining statements were about me. "You will not return to school tomorrow. I have retained a tutor, who will acquaint you with subjects more relevant and practical for your future. There are specific ideas which will be explained to you and which you will accept. This should have been seen to earlier." His eyes narrowed and filled with a dark anger. "But that error can be rectified. There will be no foolishness this time. You will be ready to take instruction at eight in the morning. You will do the work that is required of you and you will do it well. You are not an overly intelligent child, therefore you will have to work harder"—I heard his voice tighten with his anger—"harder than the other, who was gifted."

This sudden disruption of the order of my own life so stunned me that I carelessly blurted out a question. "But why?" He did not answer. In his face I saw the bitter eyes of the man in the gilt helmet. "What about my dance class?"

"You will abandon such frivolities and get on with the business of learning essential matters which will prepare you for your position in life. You are a von Heyditch. Your mother came from a noble family; there are responsibilities that go with such names." He stood up and walked out of the room, leaving me staring at his vacant chair. What position? What could I learn from a tutor that I could not learn at school? I felt wretched and angry. Another door had been closed in my life. School was boring and monotonous, but I had friends there—not close friends, but still friends.

The girls there all came from rich families, but I knew that some were treated better than others. Gerd had been annoyed when I told him about one of the girls who was a constant target for ridicule. "Don't you see, Eroica, they don't want her there. Her name is not very well known, and schools like yours and mine survive because of their exclusiveness; they are supported by old families with old money. No one picks on you, do they?"

"No."

"Of course not. Pick on a von Heyditch and you pick on a national monument. If you wanted to burn the place down, they would probably tell you not to hurt yourself in the process. It's the same at my school. It's disgusting and undemocratic" (a word I had heard before, but I was somewhat unsure about the meaning).

"At the university, I intend to lead quite a different life: I shall study whatever I want and I shall choose my friends myself."

Again the idea came to me that Gerd's entering the university and his death were somehow connected.

Perhaps a tutor might not be so bad. At least it would be someone new in the house and perhaps, just perhaps, he might be able to answer some of my questions.

That night in my room, I lined up all of Gerd's rocks and shells on my desk. How alive they were for me: Gerd had held them in his hands, carefully inspected them, loved them. For a time after I went to bed I held the bonnet shell to my ear and listened to its deep roar. Then, still listening, I slept and dreamed. Gerd and I had agreed to meet at the small gate at the cemetery. It was raining and I kept hearing him call my name. I ran in all directions, crying out, but I could not find him. Then suddenly he was there, only a few feet away from me, standing quite still, his hair drenched. "Gerd, Gerd!" I rushed to him, but when I touched him, he was cold: he had turned to stone. I woke up and found the shell lying on my shoulder.

Suddenly I heard the sound of voices downstairs. Someone was laughing. I looked up at the clock: it was two in the morning. I got up and opened the door to the mezzanine. The smell of cigar smoke drifted up thickly from down below. I crept to the landing and knelt behind the ornate baluster. My father was standing in the foyer with a group of men. "Gentlemen," he was saying, "tomorrow each of us sets out on his mission. Each of us has a rendezvous with the future. This time, not a single shot will be fired. Our Barbarossa will be without guns. Our Siegfried Line will be aboveground. We have no need to strut like puppets, we have no uniforms, and we carry no regalia. We do not even need slogans, and only madmen and fools act from their horoscopes: neither our strength nor our destiny rests with the stars. Our armor lies inside our briefcases, and there will be no Bohemian-peasant carpet-eater to force any rash actions. We cannot fail, and the world will applaud our victory." The men clapped and murmured approvingly. Then they put on overcoats and one by one shook my father's hand as they left. From one of the arched windows I saw them get into cars and drive away.

After they were all gone, I heard my father move about in the music room. A few minutes later, Beethoven's Third Symphony resounded through the house. My father returned to the foyer and entered the drawing room, where he sat in a large winged chair. I could see his face quite clearly in the lamplight. For a few moments he nodded his head to the beat of the music; then he opened his mouth wide and thrust his head far back. I could hear him clearly, even above the crescendo of the drums: he was laughing wildly.

5

"It appears that we have a clean slate to start on: your record in school was not exactly inspired." My tutor said this without looking at me; he had an open file on the table in front of him. I stood opposite his spare, seated figure and was surprised that I was not surprised at his appearance. In a curious way he was what I had imagined he should be, right down to the rimless glasses that left red indentations on both sides of his nose. In the course of twenty minutes, as he sat at the table in the music room, he had already taken the glasses off twice and cleaned them with some little papers he took out of his vest pocket. He looked up at me slowly. "It is evident that you did not take your studies seriously." He had the unblinking gaze of a fish. As he began to list my academic flaws, particularly my tendency to daydream, I wanted desperately to yawn, to sleep, at least to find a dark room and put my head down. I had awakened just before eight with deep pain behind my right eye. Finally he said, still in his soft monotone, "Why do you squint like that? Is something the matter with you?"

"I am blind in one eye."

He lurched back as though I had thrown something at him. "Impossible. No one told me that."

"It just happened today."

"What?" He got up and rang for the cook. "You say you became blind today? That is not possible!"

I shrugged. There was no point in talking to someone who refused to listen to the truth. He continued to stare at me in an outraged way as though I were doing something obscene.

"She says she is blind in one eye!" he blurted out when Vera appeared.

"Nonsense." Vera's puffy face breathed onions and sour cream at me. In fact, I could smell her much more clearly than I could see her. "She is lazy and troublesome and careless. We've had such a time with her." She turned back to me. "What do you mean by telling Professor Pemsel such a lie? You are very lucky to have a great scholar here just for you, and all you can think of is to insult him with a ridiculous story."

Lena had followed Vera into the room. "She does get terrible headaches, like her poor mother." I could not see Lena's face clearly, but she leaned toward me and touched my forehead with her hand. "She's quite warm; she may have a fever."

"Children don't get headaches," said Vera emphatically.

I remembered my mother's constant suffering, and Gerd's statement that she was not really sick began to bother me again.

"Of course she could have headaches." It was the professor who spoke, silencing the two women and astonishing me with his defense. "Please leave us," he said in his tight-mouthed voice, and as soon as we were alone he continued his questioning. He was seated again by then. "How long have you been having this pain?"

"I don't remember."

"Well, think. Days? Weeks? Months? Years?"

"Months."

"How often?" He steepled his tiny pink hands in front of him. I shrugged, and shook my head. "Come now, once a month, twice, three times?"

"Every day."

"Every day?"

"Yes."

For a moment he did not speak; he seemed to be sucking air through the lipless lines that were his mouth. Finally he stood up again and began to walk back and forth.

"Do you ever take anything for them?"

"Take anything?"

"Medicine."

"No."

"How long do they last?"

"Sometimes only a few hours. Sometimes all day."

"And at night?"

"Sometimes at night."

"Do you ever wake up with them?"

"Yes."

He returned to the table and sat down again. "The headaches you get are called 'migraine.' Did you ever hear that word before?"

"No."

"Then let me say this to you: migraine headaches are painful, but you can easily overcome the pain if you want to. You need only use your will and the pain is gone."

"How do I use my will?"

He seemed irritated at this question. "What do you mean, how do you use your will?"

"I don't know what you mean by using my will."

"Haven't you learned anything? The will is a mental faculty by which one decides upon—chooses—a given course of action."

"I don't choose to have headaches."

"What I am telling you is that you can choose *not* to have them."

"How?" This was certainly good news, and I was eager to learn how to begin.

"You simply decide that you are not going to have a headache." He looked at me the way older people always do when they think they are letting you in on a great and irrefutable truth. "You need only to will it. Say to yourself, 'I do not have a headache.' "

I closed my eyes and saw the words clearly. "I do not have a headache. I do not have a headache." I repeated it a half dozen times more. My head disagreed. The pain crawled through my left eye and stretched into my cheekbone and continued down to my upper jaw, where it scratched around looking for a place to settle.

"Well?" The professor was waiting for news from my head.

"It doesn't work. What is the trick to it?"

"It's not a trick," he said angrily.

"Maybe this is not that kind of headache."

"You're being ridiculous. If you really want, you can will any kind of headache to stop."

"But I really want it to stop." How stupid of him to think I did not want to get rid of the pain.

"Then you can do it. You are German, and Germans have the strongest wills in the world."

"People who aren't German can't do this?"

"No. They cannot."

This information took a little time for me to consider. The professor had his arms folded across his chest and was leaning back in his chair. "What about Indians?" I asked.

"Indians? What Indians?"

"Apaches. When they get hurt, they do not even cry. My brother and I saw a film about Apache Indians, where a boy was hurt very badly and they had to cut a bullet out of his shoulder. He did not cry at all."

"Do not be stupid. The boy did not really have a bullet in his shoulder; that was all make-believe. Anyway, primitive peoples have no will to speak of; they are like animals and act from instinct."

"My brother Gerd believed they were gifted and strong-minded as the ancient Greeks."

"What Greeks?"

"The ancient ones in the plays. Gerd read the plays and told me the stories."

"All those dramas did not pertain to real life. You will stop reading such nonsense."

"My brother said that the dramas show the possibilities in life."

"Your brother was a fool," he said in a very offhanded way. For a few moments I did not know what to do. Then my vision cleared, and I saw that he looked even fishier than before. I stood up and knocked to the floor all the books he had stacked next to his elbow. "You lying bastard," I shouted, and ran out of the room and through the house to the garden. I did not stop running until I reached the cemetery. The morning was still fresh and everywhere the grass and flowers shone with dew. I sat down on one of the long flat tombstones.

What was I going to do? I could not study with a person who said terrible things about my brother. But neither was I ready to run away and leave Gerd's room and all the places in the garden and the house where we had shared our plans and secrets.

Suddenly I realized something extraordinary: my headache was gone. I could read the faint letters on the stone quite clearly. What had made the pain stop? Certainly it was not old Pemsel's idea of willing it out of my head, yet it was gone.

I decided to return home; with my head clear and my father gone it was a good time to face the professor and let him know that my brother was not to be insulted.

Back at the house I found Vera and the professor in a state of fierce agitation. Vera found her voice first. "You should be strapped, you little witch."

I looked at her calmly. "You touch me and I'll cut your throat when you next get into the bathtub. Better yet, I'll hack you into little pieces with an ax until the tub is full of your stinking blood."

Her face became very red and blotches appeared on her neck, but she did not speak. She rushed from the room, and the professor, finally blinking, said, "Your father will hear of this."

I looked at him. "If you ever say anything to my father, I shall hang myself and leave a note saying you did something horrible to me." I had no idea when I said this that the words would have such a devastating effect on him. His nose twitched obscenely and he gulped huge quantities of air, like a wretched fish left out of water. He sat down abruptly, obviously to keep from falling, and I took advantage of his silence. "If you ever say anything insulting about my brother again, I swear I shall kill you."

At that time of my life it never struck me as odd that I had such an easy and casual attitude about killing. Since my brother's and mother's deaths, my mind coursed relentlessly through fantasies of murder and suicide, and the words of those twin terrors flowed from me with unburdened rashness.

The professor and I finally began to work seriously at getting me informed although not necessarily educated. He never again called me stupid, even when I was. When I forgot the tonnage of iron ore imported into Germany in a given year, he would merely repeat the information without making any other comments. He stuffed my head with a thousand facts about Germany's industrial productivity, the amount of food and raw material the country needed to import, the amount of money and exchange goods involved in the country's exports, favorable world markets and unfavorable ones, economic competition with other European countries, with Japan, with England and with the United States.

Casually he began to talk about the war, sometimes referring to it as "the interruption," and showing through graphs and charts the various countries' standing in the world of raw material since that time. "Resource development is everything. We always knew that, of course, and it was with this enlightened view that Germany took the lead in the thirties in bringing the world out of economic stagnation. It led all other nations in the recovery from a world in ruin. Germany reached the highest pinnacle of civilization ever known to man. Other nations became envious of our advancements and ganged up against us in order to destroy our incredible progress. But we were not defeated."

"But Germany lost the war," I said.

"Lost. Lost. What was lost? We are stronger than ever. Our machinery is the most modern in existence. Our methods of production are far more expedient and progressive than any other nation's. The engineers of Von Heyditch Industries are the greatest geniuses of advanced technology in the world today. We are years ahead of everybody."

"But the country was divided." With this statement I used up my knowledge of the war.

"It is not divided," he said angrily. "Wherever German-speaking and German-thinking people live—there is Germany. And the world will be made to realize this again—and soon. Do you think a people like ours can be kept down for long?" He looked at me with fierce eyes.

"But the other part has a whole different government," I said, feeling an odd anxiety at his vehemence.

"Different!" he spat out the word. "Do you think we stopped our way of thinking because of a little setback? Do you think we changed from being Germans because a few fools decide that an artificial barrier can be set up among peoples of identical intentions and goals? You must begin to think clearly. Germany has lost nothing. In a way the interruption serves our advantage." He had risen and was walking back and forth in front of me. I thought of Mother's beginning to cry one day when Gerd had asked her something about the war. She had never permitted anyone to talk about it, and Gerd never asked again when he saw that his questions hurt her.

"How did the war serve our advantage?" I asked.

Pemsel stopped and stared at me in exasperation. "Haven't you learned anything from what I have been teaching you?" He hesitated only a moment. "By now you know our economic advantage over other nations.

We do not spend vast resources on self-defense. Others do that for us. This releases our energies for more enduring power. Warehousing weapons of war is a waste when everyone has the same weapons. The only political weapons today are economic—fuel, food, energy. These have real bargaining power, far greater than guns, I assure you." Again his expression was rancorous and bitter. "You have to begin considering these matters. Your father expects you to understand them."

"My father expects me—? What does all this have to do with me?"

"Your father was deeply disappointed in his greatest expectation. And it all could have been avoided if firm discipline had been effected. Your brother—"

"Don't talk about my brother." I was standing, too, by then and we glared at each other across the table. He was breathing rapidly, and his hands twitched and shook.

"You are obstinate and undisciplined. It is not your place to interrupt me."

"It is not your place to talk about my brother. He is none of your business."

At this he exploded into a rage. "Quite the contrary! Except for a weak woman's foolish whims, he would have been my sole business. And now we have to make do with whatever we can."

Vera entered at this point to announce lunch. She looked at each of us quizzically. "What is wrong here?"

"We can discuss it later," said Pemsel, straightening out some books on the table.

It did not take me long to realize that I was the "whatever" with which Pemsel had to make do. I detested him even more when his slurs against my mother dawned on me.

One morning some days after this, Pemsel got on the subject of other countries' "resource weaknesses." Saudi Arabia, for example, had oil, but almost no food and no industry to speak of. It was true that with their oil money they could buy what they needed. But still, someone with enough force could threaten to take their oil or place them in some other kind of perilous situation in which they would lose their bargaining power. Such nations were ideal markets. "Then, too, the Arab countries in particular are in need of our industrial genius since they need a large army, and armies must be fed and clothed." I listened to all this with increasing boredom, but then I noticed that Pemsel was talking faster and his fists were tightly clenched. "They cannot endure the enemy in their midst," he said furiously. Apparently I had missed some piece of information and waited for him to repeat it, which he usually did with deadly monotony. "This nation of two million is a creature of politics, criminally created, and an abhorrence to the Arab peoples. As long as it exists, with immigrants daily adding to its number, no one—not the Arabic people, however inferior, nor the Aryan peoples, however superior—can rest easy."

Something scratched across an unhealed wound. "What Aryan people?"

Pemsel seemed startled by my question. "You're not paying attention. All Aryan peoples know that Jews are a threat to their purity."

"What is the matter with them?"

"With whom?"

"With Jews. Is it a bad religion?"

The professor's eyes narrowed suspiciously. "What do you mean, 'a bad religion'? Why do you ask about the religion?"

"Aren't Jews a religion? I mean, aren't Jews people who have a certain kind of religion?"

The professor's forefinger of his spread-out left hand was tapping softly on the table. It was a little habit he had whenever he was working something over in his mind. "Yes," he said quietly.

"What is wrong with the religion?"

"No one said anything was wrong with the religion. It is not a matter of religion. They are Jews."

"What?"

"It is the kind of people that Jews happen to be."

"I don't understand."

"It is in the blood." Tap, tap, tap, went the finger.

"In what blood?"

"In Jew blood."

We sat looking at each other for a few moments of silence. "I don't know what that means," I said finally. "If it is not a religion, what is a Jew?"

The professor sucked air through his closed teeth, forming a grotesque smile that made me want to run from the house and keep running. I saw myself racing through the park, past the cemetery, beyond the city and far out into the country where I knew there were fields and mountains and forests, where I could drop in the soft moss and listen to the murmuring of trees: Regensburg: Mother's estate. Among the silver leaves, bright songbirds sliced the patterns of sun rays and rested on quivering branches and sang their golden notes. In my forest of memory Gerd and I watched the birds and held our breath at the loveliness of the secret place that was ours. "Eroica, beauty is everything," he had said, lying back on the dark moss, flicking his blond hair off his forehead with a quick casual motion of the back of his hand. "Without it, the world would be terrifying, unspeakably horrible."

Pemsel's tightly controlled voice dissolved the pattern and my heart hurt in a bad twisting way. "You pose a question no Aryan girl your age should have to ask. It all should have been clarified years ago." Again he sucked air and made his ugly smile. "The Jew is a dissembler, a destroyer. At one time the Jews controlled the best positions in the universities for the sole purpose of corrupting the young. They dominated the major newspapers, controlled the leading banks, monopolized important industry. Their foul practices threatened every area of ordered society with decay. They are subhuman, and—"

"Don't they bury their dead?"

"What?" Pemsel was frowning deeply.

"Don't they bury their dead?"

"What a question! Of course they bury their dead. What does that have to do with what I'm talking about?"

"Subhuman creatures do not bury their dead." Gerd's voice came to me across a museum display case where the dusty bones of a primitive man lay surrounded by his ancient tools. "You see, Eroica, man, like other animals, evolved into what he is. No one seems to know why his brain developed the way it did, why he can make choices and judgments—in short, think things over. But his advanced intelligence does not really answer the most important question, which is, What made him human? What gave him that special quality of humanness that makes him feel compassion and love? No one seems to know, but we do know that somewhere in his development, he began to bury his dead and bury them with things they might need in another world. This is a human act. Subhuman creatures do not bury their dead."

Again Pemsel interrupted. "You are seeing this all wrong. Jews are inferior in a different way."

"If they are so inferior, how did they get control of the banks and newspapers and universities and everything? They must be very intelligent to be able to do that."

Pemsel's nose twitched in a ludicrous way. "They are not intelligent. They get their power and wealth through criminal acts."

"Didn't the police stop them?"

"You are not thinking clearly. He who controls the money controls the police."

"But how did they start? I mean, before they had the money and the police, how did they work it? One has to come before the other. If they can only get control of the police once they have the money, and they can't get the money until they have control of the police—? I don't understand. And where did they live before they had their own country?"

Pemsel pulled his nose back so that his nostrils, with their pink hairs, were quite expanded. "They lived everywhere, all over Europe; but they originally came from the east. They invaded Europe in secrecy, like a disease—twelve millions of them. They wanted to Hebrewize the world, and especially Germany, since it is the most desirable of nations. As soon as some of them got settled in Europe, they instigated mass immigrations for their own kind. They brought horrible diseases: mental retardation, bone deformities." He was gesturing with his hands and talking fast. "They intended to Jewify every area of human life with their vile practices. In Jewish families brother and sister mate and bear morally depraved offspring. There is not a corner of the world where they are not despised."

"What happened to them?"

Pemsel stopped all gestures and drew in his breath, tightening his nostrils. He removed his glasses and took a long time cleaning them, holding them up to the light, breathing on them and then resuming the polishing. I waited patiently. He picked up some papers and moved them a few inches away and then moved them back again. "I told you, they had a nation created for them."

"You said that only two million of them lived there."

He glanced at his watch. "Perhaps we should take up this problem at another time."

"What problem?"

He looked at me in his old unblinking way, and then he said something extremely curious. "You know, don't you?" The expression on his face, the slight twist of one side of his mouth, inclined me to remain silent. I stared back at him, hoping that I looked as though I knew whatever it was that I was supposed to know. Casually we turned to English grammar.

A short time later we had lunch. Pemsel kept taking little cautious glances at me which I pretended not to notice. We may have started with a clean slate, but now there was a question on it. And that question burned in both of us: Pemsel wondered what I knew and I wondered what he thought I knew.

For the first time in weeks I thought of Jans, whom I had last seen walking in the rain in the cemetery, calling my name, which was not my name at all. How gently he had asked me if I were a Jew.

6

As my father's absence continued, Professor Pemsel slowly insinuated himself into our household. He stayed longer and longer each day, until finally he was having dinner with us as well as lunch. He was particularly ingratiating toward Vera. "What a superb chef you are," he would say to her while she smiled coyly and murmured how wonderful it was to prepare delicacies for one who had "an appreciative palate." He complimented the men on their ability to "take over the difficult responsibility of keeping order" while the master was away. One afternoon at tea he wondered whether it wouldn't be a good idea if he temporarily lived "in residence," so to speak. "It will give me further opportunity to help the girl with her languages." Vera thought this was an excellent idea, and as I listened from the terrace, she showed him a small bedroom off the reading alcove.

"It's not very large, but it's quite comfortable and there's a bath. The master has occasionally used it for business guests, so you'll find it quite convenient for reading and such."

Pemsel smiled broadly when he saw the room and said it would be fine—in fact, perfect for him to continue work on the book he was writing. "It's a plea for a return to traditional values, particularly in raising our children. They have not had the proper discipline, and I for one feel that it's time to return to measures that will assure obedience and order."

"Professor Pemsel, you cannot know how deeply I agree with you," she said, unaware I was near. "Today there is so much hooliganism, and if you knew what we have had to put up with here. The boy was more respectful, and although I do not wish to speak ill of the dead, I feel that if the master had had more of a hand in raising him, the young man would be alive today, fighting the elements that want only to keep Germany down. Do you know the boy was never whipped? Their mother was adamant about punishment. Well, you see the results: the boy is dead and the girl is vicious. You heard her murderous threats. What she needs is a good whipping."

"Quite true, but she is not exactly a child. She is quite tall and rather well developed for her age. Still—"

I could tell he was contemplating with pleasure the prospect of hitting me.

"I tell you, professor," Vera broke in, "it would be the right thing. Her father left me in complete charge. Also, you must consider that you are her teacher. If she fails von Heyditch's expectations—such as he has—it might reflect back upon you."

"Hmmm. Perhaps. She is obstinate." The professor moved into the house that night.

One night a few days later there was a light, timid knock on my door. When I opened it, Lena quickly came into my room. "What is it?" I asked her. She put her finger to her lips. "Is my father back?" She shook her head, walked to the window and pulled the draperies.

"You must not irritate them in any way," she said fearfully. "Do exactly as they say."

"Who? I don't understand."

"They are up to something. I know it." She was blinking rapidly to keep from weeping. "I cannot help you and the men won't. Your father will be away another two weeks at least. Don't do anything to give them a reason."

"Lena, you're not making sense to me. Who?"

"Vera and the professor."

"I'm not afraid of them."

"You should be. Stay out of their way; don't antagonize them. Please, don't do anything to give them a reason." She was actually weeping.

"A reason for what?"

"I can't say. It's too impossible, but please be very careful with them. Be polite." She kissed my forehead and left with the same disconcerted and dismayed attitude with which she had arrived.

I tried to ignore Lena's warnings, though Vera seemed to be watching me more and more lately. One day she bought me some new clothes. In the months after my mother's death I had outgrown everything, and I told Lena that nothing fit anymore. But it was Vera who had gone into the city and brought back some new skirts and blouses, some sweaters and a coat. She had failed, however, to buy me any underwear. When I mentioned that I needed a brassiere, she told me it wasn't necessary yet, that my breasts were firm and didn't need support.

Lena had come into my room with her warnings on Friday night. On Saturday the professor and I worked all day. I didn't mind, particularly, since we were on the subject of Greek history. The professor was quite surprised that I had already read Thucydides months before. Gerd had loved studying the ancient civilizations, and I took up his interests as though I had inherited them.

On Sunday morning Vera shook me awake. "The professor wants to see you at once." She seemed excited about something.

"What time is it?"

"Never mind that; get dressed and come down as quickly as possible."

It was half past nine. I dressed in my dark skirt and

white blouse, pulled on knee socks, shoes and a sweater.

In the music room Pemsel was sitting at our usual study table. "Since you failed to get up on time, you'll have to forget about breakfast. Sit down."

"I didn't know we were going to work today."

"Did I say we weren't going to?"

"No, but we didn't last Sunday or any other Sunday."

"This will teach you not to make irrational conclusions. Sit down." He had a disgusting smirk on his face. "Today you will take an examination on the Peloponnesian War."

"I did that yesterday." He ignored my statement and passed a dozen sheets of paper toward me. It was the identical examination I had taken the morning before, one in which I had not made any errors. "You said you were pleased with the result."

"I want you to take it again."

"Why?"

"Are you questioning my authority?" His voice was calm but his eyes glittered.

"I'm asking you why you want me to take it again when you said yesterday that I did it perfectly."

"You are being insubordinate." He stood up. "Mrs. Oper."

Vera came into the room at once and without comment grabbed my hair, pulling me out of the chair. I screamed at her to let me go. She twisted my right arm behind my back, while Pemsel, who had come around the table, took my other arm. I reached down to bite him, but Vera pulled my head back. They dragged me toward Pemsel's room, where Vera pushed me face-down across the bed. "You should have taken your belt off before," Vera snarled.

He mumbled something I did not understand. Vera pressed her knee into my back and Pemsel raised my skirt to my waist and began pulling down my underpants. I screamed curses at them. At the first stroke of his belt I bit into the bunched-up bed covering. The belt came down three more times. "You fool, give it to me,"

Vera shouted at him. I saw Pemsel, the belt still in his hands, pull violently at his own trousers, ripping at the buttons. He grabbed his penis and began to wiggle it furiously with one hand. Again the belt came down several times. I screamed. Pemsel began to make strange high squeaky noises. Vera reached for the belt, and as she stretched over me I realized she had on no underclothes. She was quite wet underneath. She brought her huge body back over mine once she had the belt, but in doing so she had to release both my arms. Pemsel shouted as she brought down the belt with much greater force than he had, and faster. Reaching behind me, I scratched at her back with my fingernails, but with no effect. She continued viciously with the belt. On the bedstand was an iron owl about nine inches high. I reached for it. She brought the belt down only once more before I hit her on the back with the statue. She gave a loud cry and raised her arm toward my head. In the same moment I twisted violently around and hit her in the face as hard as I could with the carved owl. Blood began to spurt from her mouth and nose. I hit her again, this third time on the forehead, which also began to bleed. "I am dying! I am dying!" she shrieked as she collapsed on the floor. Pemsel, his mouth open, his hand still holding his wet, limp penis, stared down at the bloody face.

I scrambled off the bed and for a moment was too frightened to run. Then I threw the statue on the floor and fled from the house. I felt ill but had nothing to vomit, although I retched dryly several times. At the outer edge of the garden, where the scent from the citrus trees sweetened the air, I tore a lemon from one of the branches and bit into it.

Some time during the struggle with Vera and Pemsel I had lost my sweater, and there were large blotches of blood on my blouse. I was cold: I had no shoes on, and as far as I knew, Pemsel still had my underpants.

By the time I reached the cemetery I was numb with horror. I had killed someone! I was a murderer! I walked to the family vault, and only then began to weep. "Oh, Gerd, Gerd, I didn't mean to do it." I leaned my forehead against the cold metal and promised that I would hang myself at the first opportunity. While I was furiously whispering these plans to the metal door, an arm suddenly covered my shoulders. I started to scream, but a hand covered my mouth. My first thought was that the police had already caught me.

"Don't cry out," a voice whispered to me gently. I turned to the face beside me. It was Jans. "Come." He put his coat over me and led me out of the cemetery to his car. Inside he looked at me, gently pushing my hair out of my face. "There is blood all over your clothes. Are you hurt?" I shook my head. "Whose blood?" he asked. I began to cry hysterically. He put his arms around me and held me close to him for a long time. "Tell me and I can help you."

I shook my head. "I killed someone." He breathed in sharply and held me more tightly.

"Who?"

"A woman who works for us."

"How?"

"I hit her with an owl."

"Is this the owl's blood or the woman's blood?"

"The woman's blood."

"How is the owl?"

"Oh, please don't joke. The owl was made of metal."

"All right, I'm sorry. How do you know the woman is really dead?"

"She said so."

"Eroica, you make it impossible for me not to joke."

I stopped crying. "How did you know my name? How did you know I would be at the cemetery today?" I studied him closely. He had a kind face. Gerd would probably say he had a good heart.

"What a suspicious girl you are. I found out your name by going over old newspapers. You said your mother died at the beginning of winter and your brother last spring. I only had to find a seventeen-year-old boy who had died and a woman with the same name who died within the same year. It took less than twenty minutes. On your mother's death notice there was the information that she is survived by her husband, Rolf von Heyditch, and a daughter, Eroica. As for being here today, I have been here every Sunday, knowing that sooner or later you would come. There was no way I could get to your home, because of the guards. It is somewhat unusual to have a house so protected." He was silent and I started to cry again. "She may not be dead, you know. People who say they are dead rarely are. Why don't you tell me about it from the beginning?" I shook my head. The horror of the scene was too terrible. "Now, listen, I'm going to take you where you can clean up. I'll find out exactly how dead the woman is and then we can decide what to do." He started the car and drove into town, where he pulled into a parking lot behind a tall apartment building. Not until I saw the name Deblin printed in front of the car slot did I remember that he had told me his family name. His apartment was on the ninth floor.

Once inside, he told me to relax and make myself at home. "What is your telephone number?" I told him. He wanted to know Vera's name. I gave it to him. When someone answered on the other side, Jans' voice changed. He became perfunctory and businesslike. "Yes, we would like to speak to a Mrs. Oper." Silence, and then, "Ill? I'm sorry to hear that. We have an important personal message for her. Some very good news. Yes, I'll wait." Jans looked at me and smiled. "Yes, hello Mrs. Oper. This is the law firm of Hermes and Son. It seems that you are the recipient of some money. We are looking for the heirs of a certain Otto Oper, a recluse who recently died leaving a fortune but almost no heirs. I'm sorry to hear that you are presently ill. May we contact you in a few days?" Silence. "That would be splendid. Friday it is, then, at two." Silence. "Indeed it is quite a large sum. Your first name is—? Vera. Of course. There is no doubt that we have finally found the rightful heir." He put down the phone. "Alive and greedily waiting to come into distant cousin Otto's wealth. You see, you are not the only accomplished liar running loose. Now then, you must tell me everything that happened." I was still standing in the middle of the room. "Come now. It's all right; you're not headed for the gallows, after all." He took my hand and stared at the raised welt around the wrist. "How did you get this?" He was suddenly serious. I shook my head. "Eroica, how did you get this?" He was looking at my wrist closely. "Now, listen to me. Do not be frightened." He drew me close and brought his hand up under my skirt. The welts burned at his touch. He quickly took his hand away. "Who dared do this?" His anger deepened. He went to a cabinet and poured something into a glass and brought it to me. "Drink it down." I did as he said, but it burned my throat and made me cough. He took his coat off me. "Now, listen to me. I want to know everything that happened and why, but first take off that bloody blouse. You can wear a shirt or something of mine. There is the bath. Is there anything I can do?"

I said, "No."

"There is a robe hanging on a wall hook. Put that on. You'll find a comb and brush in one of the cabinets. Use whatever you need." He opened the door to the bathroom; then he closed it softly behind me.

I took off my clothes and threw them in a heap in the corner. Everything had Vera's blood on it. I showered and put on the robe.

When I came out of the bathroom, Jans was sitting on a sofa, lighting a cigarette. He stood up and offered me one. I shook my head. "Eroica, I want you to lie down." He took my arm and led me to the bedroom. "Leave the robe on and lie on your stomach." I did as I was told. "Now, don't be alarmed, and you can save your modesty for another day. It's best to estimate the damage." He lifted the robe over my buttocks and then wordlessly covered me again, bringing a blanket up over me to my shoulders. "Not too bad. How did you manage to interrupt her? I'm sure she intended much greater harm."

"I hit her."

"With the owl?"

"Yes."

"Does your father allow this kind of thing?"

"He is away on a business trip."

"Does this go on often?"

I shook my head. "The first time."

He sat down on a chair beside the bed. "Eroica, will you please tell me everything from the beginning?"

The beginning? Where was the beginning: the history examination of Saturday? Pemsel's first day at our home? my brother's death? my birth? I began at Saturday's history examination. Several times Jans asked me to repeat something: was the test exactly the same? Then, how soon did Vera come into the room after the professor called her? Was I sure of what Pemsel was doing with his penis?

As I talked I could not stop crying. I tried to hide my face in the pillow, but the more I remembered, the harder I cried. Jans put his hand on my hair, which made me cry all the more. The shame of it had finally reached me, that dirty little Pemsel touching me, that flabby disgusting Vera crawling over me like a slimy garden slug.

"You must not let this linger too long in your mind," he said quietly. "You must also know, if you do not already, that their aim was to molest you sexually. Look at me." I turned my face toward him. "The whole thing was planned; they counted on your refusal to take the examination again since it would have been a meaningless thing for you to do. Don't you see that the whole filthy thing was planned in advance?" I was unable to say anything. All of it began to come clear to me as Jans spoke. He stood up and walked back and forth. "Vera is probably a lesbian. Do you know what that is?" I nodded. I had looked up the word in relation to

Sappho when I read her poetry. "The professor gets his orgasms by whipping girls' bottoms. You understand 'orgasms'?" I nodded again. That was something Gerd had explained to me—graphically.

Jans paused and sat down beside the bed again. "Tell me one more thing: how did your brother die? The paper merely said that he was killed in a freak accident involving a fall."

I did not answer. The days after my brother's death were filled with screams and nightmares. Jans suddenly touched the side of my face very gently. "You don't have to answer that. Please don't look that way. Forgive me for bringing it up." He had tears in his eyes.

"My brother hanged himself. My mother killed herself, too." I was surprised that I could say it to this man whom I didn't even know. He got up again and turned his face away from me.

In a thick voice he asked, "And the medal?"

"My brother had it clutched in his hand when I found him hanging in my father's study."

"You found him?"

"Yes."

After a long silence, he asked, "How did your mother die?"

"She just quit living: she stopped eating, she no longer got out of bed, she could not sleep. She starved to death so that she could stop living."

There was another long silence. And then he asked, "When will you be eighteen?"

I almost told the truth, but for reasons I could not explain I let the lie live. He had found out about my family, but he still did not know my age. "In three months."

"Have you other relatives?"

"In Regensburg, where my mother was born, I have an uncle Teddy. He is my mother's brother. I have not seen him since my mother died. I never hear from him."

"Were you ever close to him?"

"No. My parents' families hated each other."

"Any other relatives: cousins, aunts, grandparents?"

"No. My father had no brothers or sisters, and Uncle Teddy never married. All my grandparents are dead."

"When will your father be back?"

"I don't know. He was supposed to be back last week; then someone called to say he would be gone three more weeks."

"Where is he?"

"I don't know. He was in South America for a while, then Africa. I don't know where he is now."

"What will he do when you tell him about Vera and the professor?"

"I will not tell him."

"What?" He looked at me in astonishment.

"I will not tell him."

"You have to tell him!"

"We do not speak to each other."

"Why not?"

"I don't know." I was beginning to feel very tired and sleepy from the whiskey Jans had given me to drink. "I think I have to go now."

"Just where do you think you're going?"

"Home."

"My God! You're not going there, at least not right away. We're going to scare the hell out of them first."

"Scare them?"

"Eroica, do you know who you are?"

"Who I am?"

"Yes."

"I'm me."

"Very sane answer. But you are also more than that. What do you think those people at your 'home,' as you put it, will do when you do not return? They are mere servants and they have let one of the last von Heyditches disappear. Can you imagine the hell they will go through in a few days when you have still not returned? Do you think they will dare to call the police, since they know you could tell the authorities that you were abused? No, Eroica, they are going to be terrified when you do not return."

"I have a friend there."

"You do?"

"Lena, the maid. She tried to warn me about Pemsel and Vera. And once she helped me get into Father's study, where I found the medal."

"Then you didn't find it in your brother's hand?"

I told him that Gerd was holding something in his hand when he died but that for a long time I didn't know what it was. I told him the details about Lena and the key that fit both doors and how I had finally searched the study and then taken the money from the tea tin and ridden the bus into town. The rest he knew himself. For a long while he sat looking at me without speaking. "I put the rest of the money back; I only used enough for the bus. Someday, when I get some money, I'll return it. You must not think that I am a thief as well as a liar."

He smiled. "Is that what you are worrying about—what I would think of you?"

"You must have a bad opinion of me. I hid from you that day in the cemetery when it was raining and you got all wet. I'm sorry."

"Don't be sorry. Because of it I found out who you really were." He smiled his warm smile. "So you don't have any money. Poor girl, poverty-stricken. Not even clothes to wear."

"I could sneak back into the house and get some of my clothes and I could leave a note for Lena where only she would find it so she would not worry."

"No. I'll work something out later. Now I want you to sleep, and after you are rested we will have something to eat. Tomorrow I shall go into town and buy you some clothes. How does that sound?"

"I need a brassiere. Vera wouldn't buy me one."

He looked at me very oddly, his expression changing from confusion to some other look I didn't understand. "I'll buy you a brassiere," he said. Then he pulled the draperies to darken the room and left me alone to sleep, which I did almost at once.

It was night when I awakened and the door to the outer room was partially open. A triangle of light sliced into the room where Jans was sitting, beside the bed. "How do you feel?"

"All right."

"Eroica, we don't have to lie to each other." He took my hand and held it in his. "We can be good friends and tell each other the truth."

"What good would it do to say I hurt or that I feel terrible?"

"A great deal of good, because I want to know how you feel and what you think."

"Why?"

He remained silent, looking down at my hand. His eyebrows were much darker than his hair, like Gerd's had been. And when his hair fell over his forehead, he flicked it with the back of his hand the way Gerd used to. Finally he looked at me and smiled. "I prepared some dinner for us. We'll eat in here."

I got up and went into the bathroom deciding I would shower again: I couldn't seem to stop feeling dirty. This time I even washed my hair, although it always took all night to dry. It hung almost to my waist, so I parted it in the middle and braided it. Jans' bathrobe was warm and white with an interesting smell to it. I felt much cleaner after I had it on again.

When I returned to the bedroom, there was a tray of food on the nightstand: cheese, bread, wine, fruit, some meat and tarts. Jans was peeling an orange, but when he saw me, he had the same confused look he had had on his face earlier. The lamp was lit and the bed folded back for me to get into, but I sat on the edge of it, opposite Jans' chair, realizing how hungry I was. "You look a little different with your hair in braids," he said.

"Different in what way?"

"More German, I would say."

"Don't I look German?"

"Well, yes, only you have unusual coloring: black hair, green eyes, and an odd gold touch to your skin."

"You don't like it."

"Oh, no. I mean oh, yes. I like it very much. You are unusual-looking, beautiful."

"Am I?"

"Yes. Didn't anyone ever tell you that before?"

"My brother. But I thought he only said it because I was his sister."

"No. He said it because it is true. Come, you must eat." He buttered a piece of bread for me and put some cheese and meat on it, and I obediently ate it. Then he poured some wine into a stemmed glass and told me to drink. I did. It was delicious. He filled my glass the second time. "Now, don't drink it all at once. Don't you drink wine at home?"

"Yes, a glass at dinner, but I was very thirsty."

"How stupid of me. Can I get you some beer?"

"No."

"Well, I know you don't like coffee. Tea? Cider?"

"Hot chocolate."

"Hmmm," he said. "Haven't any. I'll get some tomorrow. You must make a list of all the things you like." He talked casually and urged me to eat.

We ate almost everything on the tray and drank all the wine. Sometimes I felt that he was staring at me and I wondered if he had guessed my age. Once, he stopped in the middle of a sentence and just stared at me, shaking his head.

"What is it?" I asked him.

"Well, it's just that you are here. I waited all those Sundays at the cemetery, hoping to get a glimpse of you. And now you are here. I am only sorry that such rotten circumstances brought us together." He smiled. "There are so many things that I want to ask you, but all that will have to wait. What I want you to do now is sleep again." He went to a bureau and took out a pair of pajamas. "I'll take my clothes out, too, so you can sleep as long as you like. I write a travel column for a magazine, but I don't spend much time in the office. I'll be back early in the afternoon." He stood in front of me. "You'll have to tell me your sizes."

"I don't know them."

"Hmmm, and I threw your old clothes into the garbage chute. Well, let's find out how tall you are. Stand next to me." I did. "Hmmm, I'm five feet eleven inches. I would say you are about five feet seven inches."

"Are you sure?"

"No, I'm only guessing, but it's a reasonable guess. Also, you are very small in the waist and quite . . . well, quite nice and round above and below. No problems."

"I know my shoe size."

"Good."

"I wear a four and a half ballet shoe and that is the same as a six and a half in other shoes."

"Fine. Now, you change into the pajamas and I'll take care of some other things." He left the room.

He seemed rather funny, hurrying around the apartment, making up the couch for him to sleep on. I put on the pajamas and got back into bed. After a while he came in and stood looking at me. "Eroica, I want you to take these two pills; they will make you sleep quickly and for a long time. Don't think about anything except going to sleep." I took the pills. He leaned over me and kissed my forehead, his warm mouth seeming to rest a long moment on my skin. It was a very pleasant sensation. Then he straightened up and quickly left the room.

Gerd used to kiss me on the back of my neck the same way. Once, while we were lying on the beach, his hand supporting his cheek, he suddenly asked, "Eroica, do you know what it means to make love?" I told him that I was not sure, that older girls in school said things that were unclear to me.

"I don't want you to learn from silly talk, and Mother will never speak to you about it; she is simply unable. You have seen me without my clothes on, so you know what a man looks like, and I know what you look like." He took off his swimming suit. "This is called a penis." He was sitting cross-legged and held it in his hand. "This is the scrotum, which has two egg-shaped glands in it that secrete a substance that comes out through the penis when a man makes love." Slowly, gently, he described the act of love.

At one point he stopped. "Is this frightening to you?"

"No, no, no."

"Do you want to know more?"

"Yes, yes, yes."

"All right." He massaged his penis up and down with his hand curled around it. In a short time some white liquid gushed out at the end of it. He was breathing heavily and his eyes were closed in the last few seconds. "That," he said, "is called an orgasm. Usually this happens when one is inside the woman, although it is perfectly all right to do this by oneself if one feels like it because it feels wonderful and does no one any harm." He pulled his suit back on again.

"Is it pleasant for the woman?"

"Yes, but the man has to make her want it. He has to touch her very gently."

"Where?"

He flicked his hair back. "Well, many places."

"Show me." I took my suit off. He put his hand very gently between my legs and explored the area with his middle finger; then he seemed to have found what he was looking for. He began to rub very gently, but then he stopped quickly and said almost harshly, "That's where." I could see that his penis had risen again under his suit.

"Why did you stop?"

He grasped my shoulders. "Eroica, you are still too young. Anyway, it's not something you do with everyone."

"I like it. I don't want anyone except you to do it to me."

"Someday you will be with someone you love very much. He will do it."

"I don't want to love anyone else. I want only to love you."

He smiled. "You are still very young. You have to give yourself some more time for this."

"But I want you to do it with me."

He looked away toward the sea; when he turned his face to me, his eyes were a wonderful deep blue. "Next year, perhaps, when you are a little older."

"Promise?"

"Promise."

Two months later he was dead.

In Jans Deblin's bed I wept for my lost brother not only because he was dead and the promise had not been fulfilled but also because the man in the next room had kissed me and I had understood the kind of kiss it was. When he had stood up to leave the room, I had seen the bulge push out of his clothes and I wished he had stayed and touched me.

7

If I had dreams during the night, I did not remember them in the morning, when Jans woke me, asking, "Are you all right?"

"Yes. What's happened?"

"You slept around the clock and then some."

"Oh, how lovely. I cannot remember when I slept so well."

"Do you know that you talk in your sleep?"

"What did I say?"

"Well, I don't eavesdrop on other people's dreams," he said laughing. "Actually I listened very hard, but I couldn't make it out. I would like to say that you kept saying my name, but you didn't."

"How do you know I didn't if you couldn't make it out?"

"I can see that you are going to be deplorably logical about everything." He smiled. "If you feel like getting up, we can start the day all over again, as though it were morning."

"Isn't it?"

"No. But we can still do anything we want to. I'm using the rest of the day for research and if you like you can help. I need an assistant who can look up trivia."

"Like what?"

"It doesn't matter. Anything that will fill up the column and that makes the reader think he has read something truly important."

I laughed and was surprised to see his face become sober. "What is it? What is wrong?"

He stood at the foot of the bed with the bathrobe in his hand. "I never heard you laugh before. I have never even seen you smile."

I did not know what to say to this, so I got up and put my hand out for the robe. He looked different and it was in that moment as we stood looking at each other that I realized he no longer had a beard. "Why did you shave it off?"

He put the robe over my shoulders. "Because I want to look young again."

"Are you very old?"

"Yes."

"How old?"

"I am twenty-seven, going on thirty-eight hundred."

"I don't understand that."

"I know you don't, but someday, when we know each other better, I shall explain it to you." He seemed troubled in a way that I could not understand. "Here's a toothbrush and a few other things from the chemist's I thought you might need. If you'll go take care of that, we can have some lunch."

I took the package and thanked him. "I like your chin." I couldn't think of any other way to say how beautiful he looked without his beard, and it dawned on me—too late—that I might have told him just that.

He smiled. "That's one way of putting it, but I don't know if that's a statement from a sophisticated twenty-year-old or a backward ten-year-old."

Alone, in the bathroom, I did some serious thinking about what he had just said. I had better figure out how to sound like a sophisticated twenty-year-old. Perhaps if I listened to him more carefully I could pick up some clues.

The package he had given me held a fine hairbrush and a comb made of tortoiseshell, some hair ribbons, hairpins, hand lotion and a toothbrush. After bathing, I undid my braids and tied my hair back with one of the ribbons. When I came out of the bathroom, he was just cutting the last string from some packages he had placed in a row on the couch. He looked at me with one of those funny expressions people get on their faces when they are expecting you to be surprised.

I thanked him for the beautiful brush and comb and the other things, but I took no notice of the parcels. This was a game I knew well; Gerd and I had always given each other wonderful things, pretending to be very blasé about it and giving each other "thank you" kisses.

I walked past the couch. "The lotion has a very pleasant jasmine scent. Thank you again." His face dropped, all thirty-eight-hundred-plus years of it. But he recovered it very quickly.

"Oh, by the way, those are for you; I would like my bathrobe back someday, if it won't inconvenience you too much."

"Not at all. What is all this?" I took the lid off one of the boxes: inside was a pleated cashmere skirt in a green-blue plaid, and a green sweater. The next box held a white coat, and the next a whole collection of lace lingerie with a brassiere placed prominently on top

"I was unsure about the style of shoes you preferred, but I did remember that you wore boots to the museum." He was maddeningly casual. The last box had a pair of white kneehigh boots in it.

"Well, I suppose I had better get dressed, then, so that you can have your robe back." I was still in control on the surface.

"Yes, why don't you do that, and I'll get lunch." We carried the packages into the bedroom.

When he had gone, I leaped at the clothes with a delight I had not known before in my life. When Mother was living and was still well, she bought me pretty dresses, but that was years ago. The lingerie was all filmy with lace edges, beautiful underpants with a matching brassiere. I put them on and did pirouettes all around the room. The skirt came slightly above the knees and fit beautifully; the sweater was a little snug. There was a pair of sheer stockings that came all the way to the upper thigh and were held there by their own elastic band at the top. The boots fit very well. I retied my ribbon so that my hair hung loose. There was also a nightgown and a lovely rose-colored bathrobe, which I hung in his closet along with the coat. Then I stacked all the empty cartons on the floor of the closet. With monumental control I walked out into the other room with his bathrobe in my hand. He was standing by the window, nervously smoking a cigarette. "Here's your bathrobe." He turned quickly and took a deep breath; then, slowly, with the most extraordinary attention to his action, he put out the cigarette. "Uh, yes, why don't you just hang it in the bathroom."

I started across the room. "Of course." I never reached the door; in two strides he was barring my way.

"Eroica." He took the robe and dropped it on the couch. "Eroica." I put my arms around his neck and we began to kiss each other, a long sweet kiss. His mouth was exquisitely warm and soft. He held me closer and kissed my eyes and ears and hair. "Eroica?"

"Yes."

"Do you know that I want to make love to you?"

"Yes."

"Do you want me to?"

"Yes."

"Now?"

"Yes."

"You're sure?"

"Yes."

He flicked his hair back, and touched my face with his fingertips so softly I could barely feel them. "Eroica, I don't mean to invade your privacy, but have you made love before?" He seemed distressed at asking this question. If I said no he might not make love to me; on the other hand a "yes" would soon prove me false.

"Would it make a difference to you if I had?"

Jans smiled. "No, of course not. It was unfair of me to ask, and unkind." He had misinterpreted my question perfectly, but he still hesitated.

"Is there something else you would like to ask?"

"No, no, of course not." He took my hand and we walked into the bedroom. He seemed surprised that the bed was made and voiced one of those obvious facts that used to irritate me. "You've made up the bed." But coming from him, it did not irritate me at all. He took off his jacket and I became acutely aware of the bulge in his pants. The more I looked at it, the more strange and restless my legs felt. He took off his tie and carefully hung it over the back of the chair. Then came his shirt, another exercise in slow-motion neatness. I had already unzipped my boots and stood them up neatly by the wall. I pulled my sweater off over my head and straightened out my hair. The skirt fell next, but before I could retrieve it from around my ankles, Jans was beside me, kissing my neck and shoulders, his hands loosening my new brassiere. He took it off and looked at my breasts, his mouth slightly open, his breath terribly controlled. Then he was kissing them, cupping them in his hands, murmuring, "Too beautiful, too beautiful." He lowered me to the bed slowly. I watched him take off his trousers and his underclothes. His penis absolutely fascinated me; it stood almost straight up against his body, with the heart-shaped end of it a deep rose color. Slowly he rolled off my stockings, kissing each one before he dropped it on the floor. Then, for a moment, he paused, his face preoccupied, as though he were listening to something. I reached out my hand and brought it around his penis. If he stopped now, I knew I wouldn't be able to stand it. I had waited more than a year and a half for this and I was through with waiting. Jans caught my hand. "Not too soon. Not too soon," he whispered. He took my last garment off very tenderly and lay down beside me, his fingers between my legs, exploring. I remembered a distant day on the Adriatic.

Everything seemed far away: the sound of the water lapping against the white stones spread outward in a long unrelieved sigh; the blue sky became wider and deeper; sea gulls drifted in slow motion past us. My whole body seemed to rise toward the sky; in a moment, in another moment, yes, yes, in one more moment, I would be spread against the sky. "Yes, yes, yes," in one more, one more moment, in this, this moment, I became the sky, floating over the earth, over the stars, over the universe.

Then, first distantly and then closer, I heard Jans' voice murmuring my name. Then he moaned and sank his face into my hair on the pillow.

The room was still. I waited for him to say something. One of his hands was resting against the side of my cheek; I turned my face and kissed it. We were both perspiring slightly and his moist body had a wonderful spicy odor to it. I touched his shoulder with my tongue; he tasted delicious, but he did not say anything. He was shivering, but it took me a few minutes to realize that something was wrong. "Jans, are you all right?"

"No." His voice was muffled and hoarse.

"What's wrong?"

He did not raise his head, but spoke into my hair. "In my heart I knew it; even in my goddamned stupid head I knew it. You were a virgin!" He raised his head then, his face filled with anger. "Of course, my cock didn't know it; so I suppose that part of me is innocent. How's that for irony?" He started to roll off me, but I held him as tightly as I could.

"Would you rather I remained a virgin the rest of my life? I wanted you to do it. You asked me and I said yes."

"But you said that you had made love before."

"I did not."

"At least you implied it."

"I did not. I asked you—"

"I know what you asked me." His face softened. "All right, you're not a backward ten-year-old. You outwitted me. No man will ever understand women; you're all too complex. You can lie magnificently without lying at all." A clear voice inside my head told me that I had better keep lying about my age. When we drew apart, there was only the slightest smudge of blood on the bed covering. Jans looked at it in anguish. "Did I hurt you very much?"

"You didn't hurt me at all. It was lovely." We bathed together and dressed again. This time I thanked him for the clothes, and he said I was a very satisfying person to give presents to.

"Gerd taught me," I said.

"You and your brother, you were very close, weren't you?"

"Yes."

While we were eating lunch, he suddenly said, "Eroica, I realize it's hard for you to think about your brother—"

"No! It is not hard. I think about him all the time. He lives in me—only in me." I realized I should not say too much, but there were some things I could say to Jans now. I looked at him across the table. "One day I shall execute my brother's murderer and my mother's tormentor. I hope he does not get sick and die of something else first, because *I* want to kill him. Only I have the right."

Jans put his hand on my fist. "Eroica, you are too young to think like this. You are a beautiful young girl. There is nothing you will not be able to do. And you are already gifted with so much: beauty, passion, intelligence. An extraordinary life awaits you."

"Nothing will be mine until my brother's assassin is dead."

Jans smiled. "You know, for someone who was ready to commit suicide because she thought she was a murderess, aren't you somewhat too eager to kill someone else?"

"This is different. I just told you: it will be an execution."

"Why do you think your father caused your brother's death?"

"I know it."

"Except you have no overt physical evidence."

"When I have that, I shall kill him."

"Eroica, my parents were killed when I was six years old. My father was a professor of philology; my mother was a chemist. We lived in Warsaw. They were shot in front of me and in their last moments alive they would not even look at me for fear of endangering my life. I wanted to scream, but someone who knew my parents, a friend of my father's, held his hand over my mouth. My parents fell backward into a mass grave. To save me they had given me to a couple who were returning to Belgium. They adopted me. I saw the face of the man who shot my parents. Once I thought I would never forget him, but Eroica, I had to forget so that I would not suffocate with hatred. One day I said, 'It is over; look ahead. There is no way to bring them back. Accept that and start from there.' There were thousands of such deaths during the war. My story is different only because I survived."

I began to weep.

"Don't cry for my life," he said, coming over to my side of the table, "and don't destroy your own with revenge. Now, dry your tears and we shall go out. If you like, we can drive to Bonn and visit Beethoven's house. It's only twenty kilometers and I have to write an article on the 'Fascination of Bonn.' Who knows, you may have some sort of talent for this. Anyone who lies as well as you do would make an excellent correspondent."

I was glad to go out, although I worried about Lena. Jans said he was working on that and to stop thinking about it. So with my new white coat on over my lovely skirt and sweater, we drove along the Rhine toward Beethoven's birthplace. As we left Köln, Jans turned to me and said, "I remember now what I wanted to ask you. Why did your parents name you Eroica?"

I told him as much as I knew: my mother's hatred of

the name, my father's obsession with it, the fact that Gerd and I both liked the name, even my father's wild laughter while he was listening to the symphony the night before he left on his trip. To my surprise, Jans abruptly drove to the side of the road and stopped the car. "Do you know who the men were that were with your father that night?" I had briefly mentioned the scene in the foyer.

"No. I never saw them before."

"Do you think when we return tonight you could write down what your father said to them?" I told him that I could do that easily. He looked at me with great seriousness. "Eroica, when you heard your father talking, what did the name Barbarossa mean to you?"

"It didn't make any sense the way my father used it."

"Have you heard the name before?"

"I've heard it all my life. Barbarossa was Frederick the First. He became king of Germany in March 1152. He restored order among the warring German duchies simply by issuing a general order for peace. He added Italy to his kingdom and was made the Holy Roman Emperor in June of 1155, but he had a lot of trouble with the popes over who owned Sicily. Even so, he was fairly good at keeping order in Europe: he made an alliance with Henry the Second, of England, and he even managed to be on good terms with Louis the Seventh, the king of France. Hungary and Poland became part of his empire between 1166 and 1171.

"He had some serious troubles in Cologne once—a revolt."

"In Cologne?"

"Yes. Philip of Heinsberg was the archbishop of Cologne at the time, and the pope—that would be Urban the Third—instigated the trouble. But Urban fell over dead one day and the trouble was over. The king then joined the Third Crusade. He left Regensburg in May 1189 and marched into Asia Minor, where on June 10, 1190, while crossing the Calycadnus River near Seleucia, he drowned.

"He had five sons by his second wife, Beatrix. The eldest, Henry, became king of Italy and later Emperor Henry the Sixth. His grandson, Henry's child, was Frederick the Second. From all reports, he was a good ruler, fair and reasonable. He was said to be handsome, with flowing blond hair, blue eyes, and, of course, the red beard. His personal life was absolutely correct at all times. The English historian Carlyle praised him immensely as 'a terror to evil-doers.' Oh, I forgot something."

"Really?"

"Yes. He finally got Sicily by having his son Henry marry Constance, the daughter of Roger the Second, who was king of Sicily.

"No one knows where Frederick was finally buried, but there is a legend, which some people still believe, that holds that he is sitting in a cave in the Kyffhäuser mountain, in Thüringen, waiting until his country needs him again. Supposedly he will come to her rescue.

"Did you ever hear the word outside your history lessons?"

"What word?"

"Barbarossa."

"In a way I hear it all the time when anyone talks of my mother. She had the same family name as Frederick I. In fact, Gerd and I were told that he was an ancestor. Barbarossa was only a nickname, as in Alexander the Great, or Charles the Bald. He was Frederick the Redbeard."

"Is it true?"

"What?"

"That he was your ancestor?"

"I have no idea. There are some crests and shields at my mother's family home in Regensburg that are supposed to be proof. But what difference does it make? In those days anybody who could steal the most and have the biggest army declared himself a duke and started a dynastic rule."

"I'll bet they didn't tell you that in school."

"At my school? At my school they actually believed that we had royal ancestors. But Gerd said that was silly."

"Was he the one who told you that any clever thief could become a duke?"

"Yes, and he told me a funny thing about how people react to power."

"What was that?"

"He said that if a dragon moved into a city and ate ten people for breakfast one day, the remaining people would say, 'Oh, how dreadful,' but they would do nothing about it. After a while it would become a tradition and people would not think it was dreadful at all. In fact, they would eventually bring the ten people to the dragon at breakfast time and then back away, bowing and saying, '*Bon appétit,* Duke Dragon.' "

Jans laughed. "Your brother had good insight. But tell me, did you ever hear the name Barbarossa used in any other way?"

"I don't think so."

Jans smiled. "You know, I looked for your school, but it didn't take me too long before I realized that you must have made that up, too."

He started the car again and we drove on. "There is such a Catholic school, but I was never there." I told him the name of the school I went to before my father hired Pemsel.

"And your brother?"

"Before he started at the university he went to a private school not far from mine. My school was quite small, only about fifty girls."

"Do you miss it?"

"Not anymore. I never want to go to school again, except for ballet, but my father said I had to give up dancing because I have to be trained for a responsible position. I don't want a responsible position."

"What do you want to do with your life?"

"Nothing."

"Now, wait, don't answer so fast. Do you dream of becoming a dancer, or an actress?"

"No."

"Perhaps you are one of those girls who want to be doctors, astronomers, anthropologists."

"No."

"Eroica, everybody has plans, even those people who say they only live from one day to the next."

"I have no plans." I had never thought of that before, but it was true. "My dreams died with Gerd. That's another reason I am going to kill my father."

"Please, Eroica, do not say that again." He did not look at me as he spoke, but his voice has an unconcealed command in it.

We drove on in silence through Wesseling, where the Rhine is already very wide. By the time it reaches Cologne there are no more mountains or hills at its banks; it flows like a dark vein to an even darker North Sea. Wesseling itself is one of those towns where the leaves on the trees are sometimes pewter gray from the lignite mines, and like all mining towns it is inconsolably dreary. On the river I could see one of Father's double barges with its standard curling and snapping in the wind. My mind drifted as I watched it.

"Why do you say that?" Jans suddenly asked.

"What?"

"You said, 'Leave Germany.' "

"Did I?"

"Yes."

It was hard for me to realize that I had spoken out loud. "Gerd told me to leave Germany."

"When?"

"As soon as possible."

"No, I mean, when did he tell you that?"

"The night before he killed himself."

"Did he say why?"

"No." I told Jans about the fight and what Gerd had said about letting Mother die and leaving Father to his monuments.

"What monuments?"

"I don't know."

We were entering the capital. Jans lit a cigarette, holding the wheel steady with his elbows. "You know, of course, that it would be difficult for you to leave Germany; I mean, leave the country permanently."

"Why? When I am older and if I want to leave, I'll leave."

He shook his head. "You really are impossible. Don't you understand what's expected of you?"

"I would like it better if you would stop sounding like my father." He started to say something, but apparently changed his mind and looked away, smoking furiously. "I'm sorry I said that. You are very kind and not at all like my father."

"You were quite right. I was sounding off like a schoolmaster. Let's talk about something else." He touched the side of my face with a gentle hand. "What do you suppose I can put into that piece on Bonn?"

"You could always write about its past."

"Except that its past isn't here anymore, and tourists usually want the past pointed out to them in the form of castles and cathedrals and citadels."

"And crockery."

"That's very good. You're hired as my assistant."

"How much will I get paid?"

"Ah, the true German at last. I was beginning to wonder. Let's see what you are worth."

So we spent part of the afternoon looking for the "Fascination of Bonn," a once-drowsy university town that suddenly had fame awkwardly thrust upon it. As the capital of Western Germany it had acquired the nickname of the "federal village," with the railway station as its "only useful building." This slap at the German Parliament left no sting, since it was believed that the politicians had made the joke on themselves. "A sign of health," Jans said.

After we visited Beethoven's house, Jans asked, "Well, are you fascinated?"

"Only if he were buried here."

"That won't do. As an assistant you are supposed to come up with some fascinating ideas. We have to sell this hopeless village to tourists, and the only thing it has going for it is that Beethoven was born here."

"Then why don't you tell them something about Beethoven."

"Everything has already been written about him."

"Then why not write something that hasn't been written about him?"

Jans raised his eyebrows. "Such as?"

"His duel."

"His duel?"

"He left Bonn when he was twenty-two years old because of a matter of honor in which he had to fight a duel with a famous person who later died of his wounds. So he escaped to Vienna, where he had to stay for the rest of his life because he couldn't come back to Bonn, which he longed for until the day he died. All of his music came from a yearning for his homeland. He was a Rhinelander to the end. He lies buried in a strange, alien place, but his ghost wanders along his beloved Rhine, where anyone today can also wander and commune privately with the spirit of the greatest of all composers."

Jans looked at me with astonishment, then broke into sputtering laughter. "Eroica, the trivia has to touch the truth somewhere."

"Who can prove that he isn't haunting this place?"

"I can accept that. It's even rather good, but what about the duel?"

"Wouldn't most people believe it if they saw it in print? Gerd said people believe anything that's printed—true or not."

"Well, I have to admit that's fairly hard to argue with." He paused. "Eroica, didn't you say your brother read a lot?"

"Yes."

"What did he read?"

I told him about Gerd's books in my room and the set of classics in the reading alcove. "Gerd read all of them. He started me on them—long ago. I love the Greek plays best."

"Didn't he read newspapers or magazines?"

"No. Mother wouldn't have them in the house."

"What about television?"

"We don't have it."

"Do you know that your father manufactures them?"

"Yes, but my mother didn't like for us to have it."

"Didn't your brother ever object to this—this shielding?"

"Shielding? I don't know what you mean."

"Well, didn't you ever wonder why your mother didn't want you and your brother to see television?"

"She didn't like it, and she was always sick. Gerd said we should always do what she wanted. We didn't want her to get worse."

Jans looked at me for a few moments, then started the car without saying anything.

"What did you mean by 'shielding'?" I asked.

"I used the wrong word. I was only wondering why your mother didn't like television. It's not important. Let's drive about for a while and then we'll find a good place for dinner."

I gave him the smile I was beginning to sense he wanted. "I love it when you smile at me," he said, confirming my thoughts.

How easy it was to know what men liked. How quickly their faces said things about themselves. Even Father's, whose eyes said, "I hate everything," and Gerd's, which had said for so many years, "I love you."

We spent some time wandering in and out of shops. Jans bought me a white visored cap. There was a small yellow anchor embroidered onto the front of it. When he put it on my hair at a rakish angle, he said, "There, now you look like a Greek sailor." At a small antique junk shop I picked an imperial-harp shell off a table covered with odds and ends. It was a rare shell and enormously sought after by collectors.

"Do you want it?" asked Jans.

"It might be very expensive."

He laughed. "In this place?" He talked to the proprietress, gave her some money, and she gave me the shell without a word. Outside, I asked Jans what he had paid for it. "Almost nothing, a few marks."

I was amazed. "But it's a rare shell, and a beautiful specimen, no chips or breaks."

"But I gave her what she asked for it. Do you want me to go back and pay her some more?" He was grinning.

"I don't know."

"Eroica, I'm joking."

During dinner Jans told me more about his work. He wrote a regular travel column for an international magazine, and he free-lanced special articles for newspapers and organizational journals. "The money is good and now that the tourists are returning to Germany someone has to tell them what to take pictures of."

That night we made love again, and afterward, lying in the dimly lit room, he asked me cautiously where I had learned so much. "What do you mean?"

"Oh, the touching, the knowing about what is exciting to me—to any man. Earlier I almost stopped; something inside my head kept saying that you were not experienced. Then you reached out your hand, and, of course, I was lost."

"Maybe girls are born knowing that."

"Nonsense. Nobody is born knowing anything."

"Don't other girls know that?"

"Damn few that I've met." He turned his face to mine. "You don't have to talk about it if it embarrasses you."

I looked him straight in the eyes and said, "I had a close friend explain it to me."

"A man?"

"Yes."

He got up and wandered around the room looking for a cigarette.

"Do you always smoke when you don't like something?"

"I didn't say there was anything I didn't like. You mustn't misunderstand me; it was only idle curiosity." He puffed some smoke and sat on the edge of the bed, beside me. "What would you like to do tomorrow?"

"I must somehow get to Lena."

"I have a plan for that. Who answers the phones?"

"Father's are answered by a machine. The servants pick up the house phones. Gerd and I were not supposed to answer the phones, but sometimes he would. Usually he said wonderfully funny things that got people all mixed up. He would pretend that the person calling had reached a ship on the sea and go into long explanations about how the ship was sinking and they should send help at once." Without thinking, I had begun to cry. Jans quickly put his arms around me.

"My poor girl, don't grieve anymore."

I suddenly felt inconsolably sad. "I love him. I love him." I felt Jans hold me closer.

"Were you good friends?"

"Yes, he was my only friend." Jans stroked my hair with his gentle hands and rocked me back and forth as we sat on the bed.

"Of course," he said faintly, "of course."

8

When Jans called my home the next morning, it was Lena who answered. "Please listen," Jans said. "I was a friend of Gerd von Heyditch at the university. Miss von Heyditch is safe; she remembered her brother's mentioning me and she has asked me for help. It is important that you get this message straight: under no conditions are you to tell Mrs. Oper or Professor Pemsel that Miss von Heyditch has called you. If you do, she will not return at all." He stopped talking for quite a long time, his expression slowly changing to amusement.

"What is it? What?" I asked.

Jans silenced me. "I see. And no messages, you say?" Silence again. Then, "No, no, she is well, but remember, your silence must be absolute." He put down the receiver.

"What happened?" I began to pace.

"Professor Pemsel has decamped. Vera, it seems, lost her footing and fell down the wine-cellar stairs. She has to have three front teeth replaced and her nose mended. But she swears she doesn't know what happened. 'Where oh where is the dear child?' she keeps crying. 'Why did she run away?' " He was laughing.

"Do you think Lena will tell them of the phone call?"

"I'm sure she is telling them right now." His expression became serious. "Do you know if your brother had any friends at the university?"

I shook my head. "He was only there a few days."

"Then they will probably guess my statement is a lie. Pemsel, by the way, cannot even be reached at his former quarters. In any case, do you think Vera will have an explanation of why you ran away?"

"I don't know. I never ran away before."

"On what kind of terms are you with the two men?"

"I rarely talk to Karl, and Wilhelm and I can't stand each other. He calls me 'dummy.' " I told Jans of the incident concerning the car keys and my father's anger that his evening was spoiled.

"Where does your father go so consistently on Saturday evenings?"

I didn't know, but I did mention Vera's statement about the other men all drinking a great deal. "Not my father, though. He almost never drinks any more than a glass of wine at dinner."

"How do you know?"

"Gerd and I used to talk about that. We had both seen Wilhelm and Karl drunk plenty of times, but not Father. And I can't remember ever smelling whiskey on him."

"Do you know what your father meant by his statement on the phone—about not taking a taxi to the meeting?"

"No."

"Did he never take cabs?"

"He took them frequently, but not on Saturday nights."

"How long has he been going on those Saturday night excursions?"

I thought about this. "As far back as I can remember."

"Did your mother ever go with him?"

"No, she didn't like to go out. Anyway, Gerd thought Father went to a men's club of some kind."

"Was he sure of that?"

"I don't think so."

Jans was smoking one cigarette after another. I asked

him what was the matter. He put his freshly lit cigarette out, and said, "If Vera or Wilhelm panics, your picture will be on the front page of every newspaper in Europe."

"Why?"

"Because girls like you do not have the privilege of disappearing. You have no idea how many laws I broke when I brought you here."

"You mean you could get into trouble?"

He pulled me close to him on the couch. "My dear, lovely Eroica. I *am* in trouble. The only reason I am not in prison, or perhaps already shot, is that no one knows you are missing."

"Who would shoot you?" I was deeply shocked.

"Your father would not hesitate for a minute."

"But there are laws . . . and the police."

"Not for the very rich. I would simply disappear. I can easily imagine my bones spending eternity in one of your father's prefabricated building blocks."

"No!" He did not know what feelings of horror he struck in me. "Jans, there are all kinds of secret places along the Dalmation Coast. We could go hide there. No one would ever find us, and there are little islands where no one lives. Gerd and I used to talk about finding an island of our own and living on it forever."

"How extraordinary you are to think of something so lovely, but you must know that the world is not big enough for us to hide from your father. No, Eroica, you already live on one of the best-guarded islands in the world."

"I don't understand that."

He looked at me with unhappy eyes. "You are guarded by wealth and power: those are essentially the same things. More important, you are guarded by class, by hundreds of years of ancestors who took it for granted that the world was their private hunting lodge. Remember your brother's Duke Dragon?"

"But I don't want to be like that."

"You *are* like that. You have no choice. Those to the manner born do not live in barns." He lit a cigarette.

"Everyone must hate us."

"Almost everyone does."

My head began to hurt. I had not had a headache for several days. Jans must have seen something happen in my eyes because he suddenly put down his cigarette and cupped his hands on both sides of my face. "What is it, Eroica?"

"I have a headache."

"I'll get you something for it. I'm sorry we talked about this. I had not intended to do so. We only have a few days together, and it was certainly not my intention to hurt you. What I told you a moment ago has nothing to do with us. You must know how deeply I feel for you."

I mumbled something about his not having hurt me. "I get the headaches all the time."

"Migraines?"

"So there really are different kinds of headaches?"

"If one can believe the medical people, yes."

I told him about Pemsel's pronouncement about the superior German will, but he only smiled and brought me a small pill to take. "It will probably not do any good in the long run, but it will numb it for a little while. There seems to be no known cure for migraines. Would you like to lie down? I have to go do some work anyway."

I did not want to lie down; I wanted to go with him. "If we only have a few days, I would like to be with you."

He thought this over, walking back and forth in front of the window, occasionally glancing at me and rubbing his fine chin as though the beard were still there. "All right. I have to write a bunch of elegant half-truths for a travel brochure on a Rhine trip. It will take about two days by boat, but first I have to go to my office and pick up my mail. During that time I insist that you will your headache on to someone else. How about the professor?" He kissed me and stroked my hair, which I no longer wore in braids. "No, you wouldn't do that, would you? You might shoot him, but I suspect there is a streak of kindness in you that won't allow you to will these headaches on him."

After he left, I wandered around the apartment looking at his things. He wasn't much of a collector. There were no paintings on the walls and no knickknacks. He had a large lead-crystal ashtray on the table in front of the couch. I had put the imperial-harp seashell beside it the day before. Perhaps I would leave the shell when I had to go home since I had nothing else to give him. The more I thought about going home, the more my head hurt.

To distract myself, I began pulling books from a low shelf near the couch. I casually leafed through a half dozen volumes and experienced a curious delight in discovering Kafka and Joseph K. among them. There was one large flat book lying on its side beneath the upright ones and as I removed these latter ones, the cover of the book below was revealed to me by inches. It was black all over except for one small spot near the center which appeared to be painted red. I removed one more book. In that open space, the fringe of red enlarged into a bright scarlet oval. In its center was the black swastika which was carved on Father's medal.

At the time, I was kneeling on the floor in front of the bookcase, but I never remembered afterward having taken the book to the table in front of the couch or sitting down or even lifting the cover. The book was filled with photographs and very little writing. But then, very little writing beyond that title was needed. On a clean white page at the beginning were the words GERMANY'S CRIMES AGAINST MANKIND. Mesmerized with horror, I turned page after page. They seemed never to end: the piled-up corpses, the rows of dead children, the heaps of naked bones from which pale eyes stared at me. There were pages and pages of hanged men, still on the scaffolds, their heads tilted to one side as though they might be watching something quite interesting near the ground. Naked people stood in long lines while men in uniforms with swastikas on them gazed at them, their hands resting on their hips.

I read the few words: the names of the hundred and thirty-eight concentration camps, the approximate number of human beings who died in each, a description of the gas chambers and the incinerators. The name of the gas, Zyklon B, which was used to kill the people seemed to enter my mind in a nimble way and gambol about like a little tune. There was a graph done by a wartime economist showing how much more efficient and less expensive than bullets gas was in killing people. I had only recently learned how to make an economic graph and my mind followed this one with an abstract interest: yes, gas was much cheaper, basically. Less labor was needed for its administration, and it was one hundred percent effective; whereas shooting was not always fatal and took up much more space for its execution. The economist was quite correct. I was interested also in the little ridged wheel which was stamped over some of the blocklike buildings. On the last page was a picture of the award given to the man who had perfected the gas chambers and who had seen to their mass production and installation.

The picture was of Father's medal.

I was holding a flower—the crystal star—and Gerd was smiling. It was a thousand years ago and I remembered lying on that upland meadow where all the yellow butterflies danced over us and he said I had eyelashes like miniature fans. . . .

Suddenly a door opened. "You lied to me again," a voice shouted. "You're not seventeen years old! My God, Eroica. No wonder you are so ignorant."

That was not Gerd. He would not shout like that. Put the book away now and let's run down the hill past the house with the green shutters, with the red geraniums in the window box. I began to run, laughing because Gerd was behind me pretending he couldn't catch up with me. But he did, and he knocked me down and glass fell all over the hill. I could hear it fall for a long time and remembered wondering how glass could float.

When I woke up, I was wrapped in a white blanket, and the metamorphosis to a cocoon was almost complete. Arms held the covering around me, and a face was looking at me through a frosted magnifying glass. "If you promise not to try that again, I will let you loose." I nodded and the cocoon covering loosened, slipped away. "You must know, Eroica, that I was never going to show that to you. I collected the photographs for years; a gruesome game I played with myself so that I could one day end the rage and the madness and live something that resembled life. I tried to tell you that before."

Jans was sitting beside me, holding my wrists in an extraordinarily tight grip. There was glass all over the floor: the window was broken. His raincoat was wrapped around me. "I'll let you go if you promise, but you must promise."

"Promise?" I could only whisper. Why could I only whisper? "What do you want me to promise?" He looked fearfully toward the window.

"It's nine floors, Eroica; I'd have to go, too. I could not live with a death I had caused. I am sure you must know by now that I am a Jew."

Part II

9

My illness lasted longer than a year and it mystified everyone. To this day, I cannot remember the first few months of it, except for some bizarre images with words attached to them that floated above my face from time to time and then vanished again. Once, for example, Father stood beside my bed and looked down at me without speaking. Standing next to him, a man with white hair kept saying, "It's shock. She's had some kind of unacceptable, unthinkable experience. She's retreated into madness rather than face whatever it was that caused the shock. It's a form of suicide. This way she does not have to fend off the daily horror of living with whatever caused this. I believe her sanity will return in time and with it her speech."

My father stared down into my face like a beam of hot unbearable light. I felt as though I were nailed to the floor. "See to it that she survives. Get whomever you need."

"There are some very good people in Switzerland."

"Don't tell me about them; get them."

Sleeping was best, at least the warm going to sleep when they came running, when through the huge sounds inside my head I could hear their footsteps, when they came running and stuck the needle into my arm and I would drift out of the window, right through the bars that sometimes cast simple black and white patterns of lines on the opposite wall. I often drifted in and out of the pattern. I could see myself get up and float behind the stripes of the dark part of it where I would make myself long and thin so that I could not see myself from the bed where I was lying with my hands tied to something and something else wrapped across my midsection just below my breasts. Then I would come out into the light part of the pattern and lean against the dark part and smile at myself. Then the pattern would move and I would try to hold it to the wall but it would dissolve in my arms and the huge noise would begin inside my head and then, then the footsteps would come running and the needle would go into my arm and faces would float above me, faces without noses or mouths, pale-eyed faces that never blinked, and I would try not to blink too and in that trying, sleep would make it all disappear.

The awakening was the worst—the long, slow, exhausting struggle to reach the surface of things around me. I seemed to be walking on the floor of the sea, with the water as thick as syrup pushing against me from all sides. Sometimes I lost my footing and was carried along by sudden lurches of currents which I tried to hold back with my flailing and useless arms until something took them firmly and held them down while I tried to push with my shoulders and chest the thing that was buffeting and twisting me about. Then I would be in the white room where white figures moved soundlessly around me and over me, touching me with boneless hands that I tried to shrink away from but that always reached me, their fingers crawling on my skin like the worms inside my throat.

For a long time I didn't understand about the worms in my throat, any more than I understood why my hands were cemented into white stones that hung from the ends of my arms and that I screamed about but that no one paid any attention to even when they changed the stones, wrapping them around my half-clawed fingers in long strips until they were huge and heavy again, lying on the bed where I could see them and wonder about them without moving them, at least not until the strength came back and the person sitting in the chair was gone for a while and I could bring the stones to my mouth and rip at them with my teeth before the person—the hated person in white—came back and tore the stones away from my face, talking furiously and calling to someone between her harsh exasperated commands. "No. No. Your hands will never heal this way. Now, stop. Stop!" Then she would call a name and someone else in white would come in wheeling a high metal table and they would take off the shredded stones and make new ones.

It was better to awaken in the dark because the hateful whiteness wasn't everywhere crushing me with its terrible emptiness. But the dark was only soft until the other eyes, large and dead, which never blinked either, came from somewhere inside me and filled the room from which the darkness fled, eyes which stared and stared while I begged and pleaded with them to talk to me. When I screamed at them to blink, at least to do that, people came running again, bringing all the whiteness with them, and the roar in my head was constant until just after the needle went into my arm.

One day I awakened suddenly to a sound that was old and familiar and gentle. For a long time I lay still and tried to place this sound in which I found such comfort. I was alone in the room and my hands were not bandaged, nor were my arms tied down. There were still bars around my bed, and when I raised up to see if the window bars were also still there, I saw at once what made the sound: it was raining.

I leaned toward the open window and for the first time in what I believed to be years I smelled green leaves and the fragrant wet earth. The scent had actually overcome the strong odor of medicine and disinfectant. For a few minutes everything seemed quite clear to me: I was sick, my throat hurt, and I had injured my hands somehow. But then, as I tried to remember why my hands had been bandaged, I began to weep without being able to stop, and with that everything changed. When the nurse came in and found me crying, she became excited and left quickly, returning with some doctors who stood around and watched me and nodded. I wanted everyone to go away, but they remained, whispering to each other and still nodding until my father came and they all whispered to him in the open doorway. I don't know how long Father was there, because when I didn't stop weeping, one of the doctors put the needle into my arm and all the whispering faded away.

When I awakened again, the old struggle to come up from the bottom of the sea had returned, only I reached the surface much sooner. One day I awakened in a different room, which had a carpet on the floor and draperies on the windows; best of all, the walls were painted the soft green of willow trees. The nurses still moved around my bed, and from time to time the pain in my throat came back, and the needle was still a part of my sick life, but I began to think about things and watch people as they came and went and talked to each other. "If you ask me, they can give up on this one." Behind me, another voice, which was braiding my hair, said, "Don't advertise that opinion, or you won't last long around here." At times the voices sounded like rumblings inside my head that got all mixed up with the pain that was already there and everything became blurred and uncertain.

Sometimes a voice would coax me into doing the funniest things. "One more bite, dear child, one more bite for old Lena. One more little swallow, please; now, just one more. That's my good girl." Lena was trying to get me to eat baby food. Everything was all mashed into some sort of pulp. I could never taste any of the food in my mouth, but when I swallowed it, there always seemed to be pain.

Sometimes, even when I wasn't eating anything, my

throat hurt horribly: little worms were swarming inside the flesh, eating holes into it. Then Lena would come with her little bowls of mushy food and her whining, coaxing voice. "Now, that was good, wasn't it? Lena wouldn't fix anything for you that wasn't good. Now, after we're through we'll just go to the bathroom and get the water ready. 'Nice and hot,' those Swiss gentlemen said, as hot as we can get it without its being uncomfortable. That's my dear child; that's good; now, into the water and just float. No, no, you'll have to keep your head above the water. That's a dear child. Here, I'll hold you."

There seemed to be several distinct and totally different phases of time during this long illness; years later I was still trying to sort out which events belonged to which phase and I decided from what I later discovered that Lena and the baby food business was all in the second phase and that I was home by then, not in my own room but in one of the large guest rooms toward the back of the house which had a smaller sun room off it into which Lena had moved to take care of me.

Although there were three different phases, for a long time after I was well I was still confused about incidents that did not seem to belong in any of them. There was for example a harrowing ride in Jans' car in which all kinds of vehicles, huge Mercedes trucks and multicolored cars—their gun-sight hood ornaments all aimed at us—were trying to crush us against stone walls. Another time we were in his car and I opened the door, but he grabbed my arm fiercely and the car danced all over the street in a marvelous swinging and gliding way that made me laugh.

Why the illness changed from one phase to another was something I did not understand. Again and again I searched for the catalyst. Yet no matter how hard I tried, the reasons for these migrations always eluded me. Apparently I did not spend the first eleven months of my illness at home; I was in some kind of clinic, forcibly tied to a bed and watched constantly so that I would not pull out my own eyes. Whenever I was awake I screamed. From what I was later told some doctor decided that I would destroy my larynx if the continual screaming were permitted; so the deep sedative treatments were begun.

Vaguely, I remembered leaving the clinic, but I do not know why my father or the doctors sent me home. The only thing that seemed to have changed was that I began to dream of Gerd again.

The first dream came about a month before I left the clinic. Just before it began I had the odd sensation that I was holding my brother's nautilus shell, and stranger still was the unusual smell of cigarette smoke; but perhaps that was in the dream, too.

In my dream Gerd and I were back in the Julian Alps, staying at a massive walled estate belonging to some business friend of Father's, although there was a lovely old ivory-colored hotel on the opposite end of the lake. When we had actually stayed there before, Gerd and I had got up very early one morning and gone out rowing. We were both enormously excited about our getaway and Gerd rowed with what we both thought was great speed, since there was a fast boat of killer pirates not far behind us who wanted to hang us up by our thumbs and make us tell where the treasure was buried.

Finally exhausted, Gerd had rested on his oars, and for a time we had watched the mirror image of a small island on which an ancient church as white as a dawn moon grew out of a cluster of low trees. Subdued by the magical beauty of the setting, he had said softly, "Someday we'll come here to live, perhaps at the hotel, and we'll skate across the lake in the wintertime and row over in the summer." His manner began to change. "I think it would be a good idea to go and see if we're going to like the hotel. What do you say?" His eyes had a sudden marvelous sly look in them that I knew meant adventure.

"Oh, yes, yes." I never disagreed with my brother. I was about nine then.

We tied up to the hotel's pier and walked through the gardens and across a wide terrace where huge windows faced the water. I wanted to peer in one of the windows, but Gerd said that was not the correct thing to do. He walked right up to a door that was apparently a service entrance and knocked. A man in a black suit finally opened it and looked at us with considerable surprise, but before he could speak, Gerd said that we were staying at the duke's estate, and that the chef was out of eggs. The man did not seem to know what to do with this story. "You're from the duke's, you say?"

"Yes, yes," said Gerd in his best impatient voice. "We've been sent over to make a request."

"A request?"

"It will be returned to you tomorrow in perfect order and with no damage whatsoever."

"This is most extraordinary. The duke never contacts, or sees . . . that is, no one's been inside over there. We see the cars drive up, but . . . Are you sure you're from there? Perhaps we should phone or send someone."

"What? And wake everyone after they've all been up half the night? My dear man, I wouldn't do that if I were you. They wouldn't like it at all." By that time several people in various hotel uniforms had collected around us. "No. No. Do that and everyone will be extremely upset and difficult to get on with. The request is not great, but it would be deeply appreciated. The best thing is simply to use common sense and let everyone go on with his business." The man finally shrugged his shoulders and asked Gerd what he wanted. "An egg." Gerd never smiled at all as he said this. The others all looked at one another.

"One egg?" a chef, from the looks of his headgear, had asked.

"One egg."

The man walked to a huge basket, brought back an

egg and handed it to Gerd without any change of expression at all. Gerd handed the egg to me. "Thank you very much, gentlemen. This will not be forgotten." We turned and walked out into the small alley which took us back across the terrace. "Don't look back," Gerd whispered to me in French. We casually got into our boat, which had the duke's crest on it, and Gerd began to row in a steady, methodical way. I pretended to look toward the town beyond the hotel, but out of the side of my eye I could see all the people from the hotel kitchen standing on the terrace, watching us as we rowed away with their egg. Gerd never looked at them at all.

"Gerd, what are we going to do with this egg?"

"We are going to return it to them tomorrow."

"Why?"

"You wouldn't borrow something and not return it, would you, Eroica?"

"No, but why did we borrow it in the first place?"

"Would we stay in a hotel that would not lend his neighbor an egg?"

He was smiling his own secret smile as he rowed and I knew he was thinking of something that amused him in a curious way. "Consider this, Eroica: how many people do you suppose there are in the world who get the opportunity to lend an egg to a duke?" On the following morning, in the same fashion, we returned to the hotel and solemnly gave back the egg, plus an additional one we had sneaked out of the pantry during the night. The hotel kitchen had twice the crowd in it that it had the morning before. As I gave the two eggs to the chef, Gerd bowed slightly, and said, "The duke thanks you for your generosity and your trust." Wordlessly, the chef and everyone else bowed also. Again I took a surreptitious peek back at the hotel staff as they all stood on the terrace and watched us row away.

Somehow Father had found out about our little sojourns and he lectured us both, but particularly Gerd. "You will not get involved with the local people. You will not leave the grounds without my permission. You will not use any of the boats unless you clear it with the boatman. And you will not lead your sister astray by any more of these ridiculous shenanigans of yours, however harmless you think they may be." He spoke softly, but we knew he was livid.

Our host, a tall handsome man with gray hair and a military bearing and a great number of glassy-eyed deer heads attached to the walls in his huge house, did not seem to mind as much, although he kept saying, "An egg! I'll be damned. An egg!" Mother was rather amused about the whole thing; at least she had a soft, wistful smile on her face when she asked Gerd if we had worn our sweaters. Gerd assured her we had.

In my dream in the clinic we were again on the boat, but we never reached the hotel. We got out into the middle of the lake, but no matter how hard Gerd rowed, the boat would not move any further. I started to cry, but Gerd held my hands in his and said, "It's all right now. You'll see, everything will be all right."

More and more I dreamed of Gerd, the two of us together reliving some small amusing incident, at least partially reliving it, since the experiences never ended the way they did originally. Machinery broke down or we got lost in the forest or some terrible people barred our way and would not let us reach our intended goal or return to our destination. There was always some frightening interruption within the chronology of the dream.

The dream about the Spanish caves was the most horrifying of all. I was alone and I could hear Gerd calling me to follow him, but I could not see him and his voice echoed down a hundred corridors. Then a voice said, "Thank God we were able to find you; she's been weeping for hours." Then Gerd came and sat down beside me and lifted me up at the shoulders and put his arms around me and rocked me back and forth. "It's all right. It's all right, Eroica. I'm here."

"Oh, Gerd. We were in that terrible cave and I was lost and couldn't find you. I called and called."

"I'm here now. You're not in the cave anymore. It's all right. No more caves."

In the doorway there was a tall figure whose voice was familiar, but not from my past. "She still thinks you're her brother."

"Is that good?"

"Well, it's a link. Better that than nothing."

What an odd conversation, I thought. I'm here, Gerd; talk to me. Tell everyone else to go away. Gerd didn't say anything; he only made little shushing sounds through his lips and in a little while I could feel sleep lift me off the bed and carry me away a great distance.

Toward the end of my stay at the clinic, a man came daily to talk to me. I really did not want to talk to him, because he was one of those jolly types who was always smiling about nothing and saying idiotic things like, "How are we today?" (How could I know how he was?) "Does our little miss feel like a conversation, even if it's only a tiny one?" I never spoke to him at all, although he chatted away about all sorts of nonsense, asking me absurd questions about someone's frightening me. He showed me pictures of spilled ink on some pieces of paper and asked me what I thought they looked like. I thought they looked like spilled ink, but I never said so; if he couldn't see that, I certainly couldn't help him. One day he brought a bunch of pictures of parts of the human body, and more or less showed them to me; at least he kept letting them drop and then picking them up again, making sure I would see them. It was all very silly, so I just turned away from him while he scribbled something in a notebook he always carried.

I wished they would give me something to read. The only thing in the room besides the bed, two chairs and bedside table was Gerd's chambered nautilus. I kept that beside me on the pillow. It was a very good specimen and I didn't want anyone crushing or stealing it. Sometimes as I held it I was surprised that it was there.

Then one day my father was sitting beside the bed when I woke up, although I'm not sure I was really sleeping, because I had felt people walk in and out of the room all day, not just the usual nurses but people in ordinary clothes. "She's not responding here as we hoped. Home might be much more conducive to a recovery. I feel that it is worth an effort, but there are risks, of course." The man who spoke was the same white-haired man I had seen the day before, when he was talking to my father about shock—or perhaps it was a little longer than the day before. Time ended as fast as it began and I could not be sure about anything. My father only nodded and a little while later Lena was standing beside my bed.

She was crying and saying "poor dear child" over and over again. I reached out and touched her hand and the room became very still.

My father looked at the white-haired man, who said, "That rather decides it, I think." The same afternoon, I moved back home again, although not into my own bedroom.

The next stage of my recovery lasted about four months. Lena almost never let me out of her sight, and slowly she began to fill in the past that I had not lived. "There are two new maids now and that's the way it should be, and a boy that helps in the kitchen. The cook isn't at all like Vera was; she'll not move a muscle to clean under the cupboards and the stove, and she won't wash walls." So, Vera was gone. That seemed strange to me, but I didn't ask any questions; it seemed like a good time to listen. "We never got on, you know. I always knew she was a wicked woman." Lena was talking while she was making my bed. I was sitting in a wicker chair, looking down at the back garden, where everything was in its final summer bloom. There was something odd about the autumn flowers and the trees with their bronze-green leaves, but for some time the mystery eluded me.

Lena brought some of Mother's plants into my new room and one day I helped her water them. She seemed quite excited about that and kept saying, "That's a dear girl, a dear, dear girl." She had tears in her eyes. That night Father came to my room and asked me how I was feeling. I didn't really want to talk to him, but he had a rather anxious look on his face and I thought perhaps a word or two wouldn't hurt. However, I ended up not saying anything to him, and he left after standing around a bit and looking out the window, his hands clutched behind him.

I remembered by then that Gerd was dead; perhaps I had even remembered it much earlier. It is even possible that I never forgot it at all. As the weeks passed, Lena brought the remaining seashells and rocks from my old bedroom and placed them on a shelf where I could see them from my bed, although I no longer spent whole days in bed. Lena would cover the wicker chair with an eiderdown, and after I bathed and dressed in the morning I would sit there and do needlework. Sometimes I knitted, not anything particular, such as a sock, but merely a strip of knitting, which I would undo again, always somewhat fascinated at how quickly the yarn rippled out of the pattern and lost its identity.

When the cold winds came from the north, I finally realized what it was that was wrong about the garden: before I became ill, it had been late in the year—almost November—and when I left the clinic, it was still September. Time began to bother me; it was all mixed up. In a mysterious way it had gone backward at the same time that it had gone forward. Time was a mystery anyway and now it was acting irrationally. At night I listened to the rain and tried to put time in its place again. When was the last time Gerd and I had listened to the rain together? My memory drifted through many houses, listened from distant rooms and finally came to rest very near me. Our house had a large third floor which my parents had only used for storage. It had always been locked, but once Gerd and I had broken in by climbing on to a steeply sloping roof and crawling through one of the narrow casement windows. Inside, the rooms were filled with all kinds of heavy crates bound with metal bands. Gerd had tried to open one, but his tools were too light. Anyway, it had begun to rain, and after hearing the first steady drops, Gerd pulled two deep plush chairs from one of the bedrooms and placed them in front of the window, where we sat and listened to the lovely sound. It always made me drowsy. "Are you going to sleep, Eroica?" Gerd smiled at me. I nodded. "Come sit in my lap."

Within minutes of putting my head against his pleasantly warm neck while he caressed my arm, I slept. That was on a Sunday. Five days later, he was dead.

I tried to remember the words he shouted at Father as he ran from the house that night, but I heard only his terrible weeping and the unspeakably cruel line "Let Mother die."

How did Gerd learn about Father? What happened between that pleasant Sunday afternoon and that terrifying Thursday, between the time that I slept in my brother's arms and four days later when he wept in mine?

In the darkness of my mind Father's gleaming medal led me to the book full of the dead millions. I wandered through the pages, searching a lost world full of heedless bones for a single human face that would deny it all by its merely being able to blink its eyes. But no face rose up to meet my eyes; nor did a voice to answer my call. I drifted down a corridor of echoing screams—all my own. My father's house was a cement block, hollowed inside, where as many as thirty-seven people could live for seventeen minutes, their fingernails clawing the cement walls, before the Zyklon B ate up their lungs. My father built his house before I was born, before he even knew my mother, who was only a frail sound that went mute after I was born not a male child and all the wrong colors. When I finally saw the bloodied walls against which the doomed must have cursed my name, they had already been dead for too many years, and I, who arrived late upon the scene, found no one who could forgive me.

When the vision of the book returned to me, the last phase of my illness began and with it a clear memory of Jans: what had become of him? Did I only imagine that he had held me in his arms at the clinic and comforted me, or was that a dream of my dead brother, whose life I had still held in my hands during my madness? I decided that my speech was about to return, but not quite yet. Madness made me wily, although I believed myself to be completely well. Meanwhile there was much to be found out, and, as in another time, Lena had to be my source.

I began simply by looking at her; I would turn to her and frown as though I wished for something. "What is it, dear child? What can Lena get for you? Can't you try to tell me what it is?" After a while I would turn away and stare out the window. It was deep winter, and the rain pools were iced over. For several days I kept up this pattern of staring and each time she tried to find out what I wanted. "Would you like me to bring the rest of your things from your old room?" My face registered no change. "Would you like to see your father?" I was positively paralyzed. "What, then? How can Lena help you if you can't speak? I know you hear me, dear girl, and I believe you understand, but I don't know how to help you. If only your poor mother were alive." I grasped Lena's arm and looked at her with alarm. She let out a little cry. "Oh, God, save us." She quickly recovered. "Come sit down and I'll get someone, one of those fine doctors." I wouldn't let go of her arm. She sighed deeply and looked at me with such compassion I almost gave up the game to comfort her. Slowly she led me to the bed, where we both sat for a moment in silence. "I suppose I will have to tell you, since there is no one else, and those doctors"— she shook her head—

"what do they know?" She took both of my hands in hers. "You must try to remember and you must be very brave." Then with tears streaming down her face she told me that my mother and brother were dead. She told me that a professor had been engaged to tutor me. She paused. "Do you remember that?" I frowned faintly as though I were scanning my mind for old Pemsel's disgusting face. After a few moments, she went on. "Well, I don't know how much more you'll be able to remember, but something terrible happened to you. I should not have gone to church that day. I knew it the moment I saw those two with their heads together; I knew they had something nasty in mind. But Vera insisted I go, so I went. They were evil people. Your father got the professor to confess it later, when he had him found. There is no sin as terrible as to molest a child." This time I really did frown in honest confusion: the professor confessed that he had raped me? But Lena was already talking again, and I didn't want to miss anything. "If it hadn't been for the young man who found you wandering in the cemetery two days later, we don't know what would have happened to you. He brought your here because you went to your mother's tomb. Even in complete amnesia from the dreadful shock of that horrible professor's crime, you found your dear mother's grave. Thank God for that young man."

My mind was racing in several different directions. I peered into Lena's face. "Gerd?" I knew, of course, that she did not mean Gerd.

"No, no, dear child, not Gerd. The young man was a total—" She gasped. "Why, you've spoken. Oh, you're back with us." She hugged me and laughed and cried and wanted to run out and tell someone that I had returned from the dead—which was not quite the case, but that took me a little longer to discover. I held on to her and she sat back on the bed beside me, her wet face shimmering with relief and joy.

After a few minutes I whispered, "Lena, how old am I?"

I knew the question shocked Lena, but she soon realized that having been "away from a normal life," as she referred to it with the other servants, I would have no idea of the exact amount of time that had passed. She started to say something, apparently thought better of it, and finally after almost a minute said quietly, "You are seventeen. You had a birthday only a few days ago." She added nothing to this but she didn't have to. I could add as well as she. It had to be near the end of February: I had lost more than sixteen months.

The discovery that almost a year and a half was missing from my life left me speechless. Then, too, I was deeply worried about Jans. Since Lena was thanking God for the young man who had found me wandering around the cemetery, I assumed that he was alive, and since Pemsel had confessed to my rape, I did not have to fear that Jans would be accused. But how did Jans get me home? For some time I remembered breaking his window and trying to leap out, and now, sitting beside Lena, I looked at a scar that ran from my right little finger across my palm. Lena saw the look of uncertainty on my face and said, "The young man tore his shirt into pieces and bandaged your hands as best he could until he could get you here. There are some things we may never know. We believe you were held hostage somewhere and were cut making your escape. You had another girl's clothes on, not a stitch of your own. There are two missing days which no one could account for. The young man wrapped you up in his raincoat and brought you here. I myself helped hold you while he phoned your father's doctors."

The terrifying ride in Jans' car while he was trying to hold on to me and drive at the same time suddenly roared into my memory.

"What happened to the young man?" I asked as casually as I could.

"He asks about you every day, my dear. Every morning, without fail, no matter where he is, he phones me. Such a good person. Even when your father sends him on some important business halfway across the country, he still has time to call."

"My father sends him on business?"

"Oh, yes. He works for Von Heyditch Industries."

10

My return from being "away," as Lena so delicately put it, was not announced with any great joyous reception. When Lena excitedly wanted to tell my father that I could talk again, I clung to her arm and said that I was afraid. It took me a little while to realize that I was not lying. Lena, true to her instincts, thought about this briefly and saw more than I did in my fears. "It wouldn't be good if he began to ask you all sorts of questions," she said. And when my father came home, she told him that I had spoken to her, but that she thought I was still somewhat uncertain in my mind.

Thus, my first reunion with Father outside my room was more remarkable for its silence than for its conversation. We met at what must have been the most neutral of places: our huge formal drawing room, with its two great Venetian chandeliers and antique furniture and heavy brocade draperies. It was probably the most unfriendly room in all Germany. My mother had hated it and Gerd had always referred to it as the museum, saying that it smelled of dead ancestors. I was wearing a white organza dress which Lena had ordered for me, and my heavy braids were wound around my head.

Father was not in the drawing room when I first came down, and I assumed he was in his study and would come out when it pleased him to do so. But after a few minutes I heard him descend the stairs and when he entered the room, he stopped some six feet from me and looked at me with the nearest thing to a kind expression I had ever seen on his face.

Also, he seemed to be relaxed; all the harsh lines were gone from his face. He looked younger. His high smooth forehead gleamed from a fresh tan.

"Well, Eroica, I am pleased that you are better." There did not seem to be a necessary answer to his statement; so I remained silent. "Sit down, over here in this chair." He motioned toward two chairs facing each other and sat down opposite me. Looking at my father was like looking into a mirror: there was my forehead; there were my black eyebrows, my high cheekbones, which Gerd had once laughingly said were clear evidence of Apache blood. I could no longer delude myself with the fantasy that I was a love child of my mother and some splendid Greek or Spanish lover whom she had met for exquisite liaisons on golden shores of far-calling seas.

"I have perhaps neglected you, Eroica, or at least chosen unwisely the people who were to see to your needs. But that is all behind us now, and we can begin with a clean ledger." That certainly had a familiar ring: from the clean slate to the clean ledger. I was still a mathematical projection, a thin line on a graph. "Do you feel strong enough to talk about this?" His tone was quite soft and concerned.

"Yes, Father." I was stunned at my own calm voice. Why didn't I scream at him? Neglected? Neglected because you never touched me in my whole life? Because you murdered six million—and two? Because while I was mad you probably arranged and succeeded in the deaths of more millions? No, Father, you have not neglected me; you have formed and shaped me more completely after yourself than any loving, gentle, generous parent ever could have. You have made me a willing killer. I can kill anyone, Father, because we of the iron will have not only the right but apparently also the duty to cleanse the world of its weaknesses and follies. My rage exhausted me and I felt my fragile energies drain as I sat opposite him and sensed his new vitality and exuberance.

"Good. You will get your full health back in the next few weeks and then perhaps a good school, possibly in Switzerland. The change of location will do you good. But for the present, just rest and get well."

I could not help but draw my eyes toward his mouth: how could he talk and drink and breathe after all he had done? If there were gods, their very outrage should have bellowed out of the heart of the universe and crushed him.

One of the maids, a woman about forty whom I only knew as Marta and who sometimes came to talk to Lena, brought in a tray with a sherry decanter and two glasses. Father poured and held one of the filled glasses out to me. As I took it, no more than the edge of his fingernail touched my hand. My soul shuddered. With monumental control I kept the glass still. He raised his glass slightly. "Good. To a new beginning." I watched him drink. The old grim face of the man in the gilt helmet was gone. Something good had happened for him and I was convinced that he was celebrating something more than just my being better. I knew from some half-remembered incident which occurred during my illness that he wanted something from me, but the whole thing was a paradox which I mulled over with no intelligent conclusion whatsoever: my father did not like me, yet he expected something from me, something for himself which was important to him and which only I could give him. Gray voices, harshly whispered, came out of a white wall: "Was she damaged physically?"

"No, no, of course not."

"Then she can produce?"

"Of course. We need only to bring her out of shock and she will be as good as new."

Bitter laughter. "Do not use that expression again."

"I meant no offense sir."

"What about the other one?"

"Ah, yes. Unfortunately, she died on the operating table. Complications, you see. These things are not predictable, no matter how simple the operation."

"Is there a disposal problem?"

"Not at all. Closest relatives killed in the war. We thought cremation was best, under the circumstances, and less costly."

Finishing his sherry, my father said, "That's a pretty dress you have on. Did you wear it for me?"

Never did I want a compliment less. "It is the only one I have."

"We shall have to correct that. When you are up to it, Lena and you will do some shopping. You are not a child anymore." He poured himself another glass of sherry. "Buy whatever you wish, keeping in mind, of course, that you are a von Heyditch."

How could I forget! "Yes, Father."

"Now that all is going well, perhaps we might entertain a bit. What do you think of that?"

Entertain for what, Father? I hated his buoyance, his eagerness to begin again, his good health, his tan, his joy. I wondered who was paying for it all.

"I think we shall have a small reception in about four weeks. It's time for you to meet some people. Do you think you will be well enough for that?"

"Yes, Father." Why could I not scream at him? No, Father; I will never be well enough for anything that has anything to do with you. I don't want any stupid receptions. I don't want to meet some people. I don't want to meet *any* people. I don't want. I don't, don't. No. No. No. I am saying no to you, Father. I am screaming no at you, millions and millions of times. I deny you, Father, I deny you.

My mind raged on in a sick uncontrollable way as my body, calm and still, continued to sit opposite my father and drink sherry as though we were two old friends. "You are a little more grown-up for your age than most girls," he said. "I see no reason why you couldn't wear some of your mother's trinkets." He laughed a little at his own joke: Mother's jewelry, which she had hated wearing, was worth upward of a million marks. "I think one of her necklaces would be quite right for you. It would enhance your fine, long neck. And perhaps a little ring."

Really, Father? Will a little ring cover up my scarred hands? But my thought ended there: without warning, my head began to ache. I closed my eyes and took a long breath to get ready for the deeper pain I knew was coming.

"What is the matter?" My father's smile ended as abruptly as it came.

"I have a headache."

"I see. Yes, Lena did tell me you were subject to occasional head pain. Well, you must go lie down for a while and get rid of it."

We stood up at the same time. I felt odd realizing that my father was a handsome man. With the old bitterness and tightness in his face gone, I could see that he had handsome, even features. Above the pain I wondered why a man who had committed such unspeakable crimes didn't have snakes and worms crawling out of his mouth when he spoke? Why wasn't he struck dumb and paralytic and turned to stone? My head warned me to leave. "Good night, Father." I started to pass him.

"Eroica, if you feel better after a short nap, perhaps you will join me for dinner." It was neither a suggestion nor a request.

I didn't dare look at him, although he was very near me. He smelled of a shaving lotion that I had smelled somewhere before but could not place. "Yes, Father." I hurried past him and up the great curve of the stairs.

In my room, I quickly took off the silly ruffled dress and lay down on the bed in hopes of dealing with my headache. I could not remember having had headaches during my illness in the clinic, but in the last few months since I had been home they had returned with a vengeance. My mind said, "Think." My head said,

"Hurt." I leaned over to the wall shelf and took the lovely bonnet shell down and put it to my ear.

The whole house had a new feeling about it; there seemed to be a great deal of activity. Sometimes I heard cars on the gravel in the evenings and later on voices and laughter. There were more servants in the house and everything was humming along smoothly. What had happened that my father should bring life back into this mausoleum? Where were *his* demons? Mine had taken up permanent residence inside my soul, which by itself was not so bad, but they insisted upon long unreasonable conversations:

"Ask about Jans."

"I'm not supposed to know about Jans."

"What is he doing for your father?"

"I don't know. I'm not supposed to know about him."

"Lena told you about him, so asking will not make anyone suspicious."

"Maybe it will, though; and then he might be in trouble."

"If he were not supposed to be here they would have killed him with the other Jews."

"They didn't know about him; he was only six years old."

"They killed others who were only six years old and younger. Remember the huge container of baby shoes?"

I wanted to weep.

"But he was adopted by some people, so they couldn't find him."

"But they might find him now."

"No."

"Yes. He is doing a dangerous thing: he is living inside the dragon's mouth."

"Please, I have a headache."

"What does that have to do with Jans' safety? Remember how exquisitely he touched you?"

"Please stop."

"Touch yourself and remember. Think of Jans. Yes, that's it. Now think of his penis, so like a flower, the

most beautiful flower in the world, a velvet flower, rising, tall in seconds before your eyes. Yes, that's it. Look at it. Put your other hand around it. That's it. Lovely. See everything. See him looking at you as he pulls off your last garment. His eyes are looking; his hands are looking. Concentrate. His fingers are moving; his wonderful beautiful fingers moving fast, now very slowly, now almost stopping, now the faintest fluttering, the lovely strumming. Yes. His *fingers. Yes. Now. Now. Now."*

I lay still for a long time, exhausted, but the voices came back after a while. *"Don't you want that again?"*

"Yes."

"Then find him. Ask."

"No. If I ask, something terrible will happen."

"Not if you do it right."

"I don't know how."

"Don't be stupid. You know how. You can get anything from Lena. She loves playing mother to you, and she chatters about everything. Jans phones every day. When he calls tomorrow, be nearby. Ask Lena what he's saying. She'll hand you the phone quick enough."

"But what will I say to him? Please, tell me."

I discovered myself feverishly whispering into the shell. How ridiculous I was being. I could not afford to go mad again. I had to stop all nonsense and think clearly, carefully.

"All right. All right. What do I have to do?"

"First you have to go along with Father's plans. Have dinner with him tonight, and listen to him. If you listen long enough and hard enough, sooner or later the world will tell you everything. Then tell Lena that you want to go shopping tomorrow. When Mother did *dress up, she wore simple, elegant clothes. You know what to buy. Remember, you're a von Heyditch; so be what he wants you to be—a von Heyditch.*

I picked my dress up off the floor and rang for Lena. She had gone to the kitchen for some reason and was breathing heavily when she walked in. "Lena, tell the cook that I shall be having dinner with my father." She turned to leave. "Wait. Do we have any rouge in the house?"

"Rouge? I think so. I think Marta uses it."

"Get me some, and hurry back." She stood for a moment, looking at me with uncertainty. "Please, Lena." She left and I sat in front of the mirror at the dressing table and looked at my face. I did have a long neck. Jans had kissed it with exciting tenderness years ago, before the glass had floated around me and I began to drift through a corridor of echoing screams. Do not think of that. Remember what Jans said: "You look splendid in white, but all colors are put to shame when compared to your own." Coal-black hair—very appropriate, considering my birthplace. Lena walked in with a little cloth bag which she put on the dresser in front of me.

"Marta says she is glad to lend it." Lena looked at me with curiosity. "Would you like her to help you?"

"No, I don't think so." I inspected the little pots and sticks of color and carefully read the instructions. Lena was still standing beside me. This was a private ritual. "Lena, will you please tell my father that I shall be down for dinner at the usual time, and will you see that there are fresh flowers in the dining room?" She hesitated, but when I turned and smiled at her, she left.

I took the forest-green wax pencil and drew a line along my lashes: the green of my eyes positively leaped out. I dipped a finger into the rouge and rubbed it over the outer cheekbones below my eyes. Something began to shine in my face: the whites of my eyes gleamed. My skin took on a soft coral tone, as though I had just come in from a cool outdoors. I left my mouth alone; it had the same shape as Gerd's and Mother's, full and clearly delineated, and I had always felt that Gerd's mouth was beautiful. When Lena returned, she gasped a little and said I looked like a famous actress. Dear Lena, she didn't know how clairvoyant she was.

"We have to redo my hair. I do not want to part it in

the middle anymore." Lena combed it out and pulled it straight back, starting to make a figure eight, but I stopped her. "No, take the upper half of it and pin it in a bunch of some kind high in the back, then make two braids with the lower part and bring them around the other section." On the third try she was successful.

"Lovely," she said, pleased, "even if I do say so myself."

I thanked her and told her that we would go shopping the next day for some dresses and that Father was planning some kind of reception in a few weeks. "Lena, I will need your help. I am really well now, but there are things which I cannot remember."

"My dear child, of course I will help you." She hugged me. I hoped she wasn't going to get maudlin and cry.

"But you must not tell Father that I cannot remember things. I am afraid he will think I am still sick."

"Now, now. He'll hear nothing from me; you needn't worry about that. You and I will work out everything between us. Anyway, it's just as well that you don't remember everything."

"But there are some things I should know so that I don't make any stupid mistakes and embarrass Father."

"What a good girl, thinking of your father. Now, is there something in particular that you want to know?"

It was clear that she was ready to fill in my past with enthusiasm, but I knew I had to move carefully if I did not wish to get Jans into trouble. Gerd had once said that he was convinced that Father had all his important employees investigated until he knew which hand each of them used to direct his penis into a urinal. For the time, I decided to hold my questions.

When I came down for dinner with my newly prepared face, Father did a very strange thing: he got up when I came into the room and pulled out my chair for me. I thanked him the way Mother used to thank Gerd when he had done this.

Father told me that I looked quite lovely and that he was extremely pleased with my recovery.

We finished the soup and Marta took the plates out of the room. "You will have to put on a little weight. I'm glad to see you eating well."

"I'm sure I will; I'm always hungry."

"That's a good sign of health." He gave me a sudden smile and my mind snagged on something: hunger is a sign of health. I saw mountains of starved corpses. Quick, think of something else. Your hands are shaking; do something with your hands! On the table there was a bouquet of mixed flowers: pink winter cyclamen, scented yellow-green daphnes and wood anemones in blue, lavender, and white which Mother had domesticated for her garden. I snapped off one of the white anemones and casually, as if my mind were not even remotely aware of my actions, tilted my head down and laced the flower between the braid and the heavy coil of my hair. As I raised my head, I saw Father staring at me with a look of wonder. "You know, Eroica, you could become quite a remarkable woman. Perhaps a school in Switzerland might not be the thing for you at all. I'll have to give it some thought."

Incredible the things men find fascinating, but still more amazing was what one could learn from the things that impressed them so profoundly. Here was Father, just discovering that I was no longer a little girl whom he did not like. As a woman I had to be reckoned with quite differently: this much I did understand that night.

"Whatever you think is best, Father." I gave him what I was later to develop, with the benefit of a mirror—my mysterious tranquil smile.

Marta brought in our entrée, and as we ate, Father talked about business in England and France, even America. I was astonished to discover how much he knew, and remembered that in the past, wherever we had visited, our various hosts had talked about Father's great genius as a businessman.

During dessert he finally ended the subject on schools with, "Well, it's not a decision we have to make immediately." (We?) "Meanwhile, there are two more things I want to discuss, Eroica. I've returned the old gate to the family crypt. If you wish to visit from time to time, there would be no objection; but you must not try to relive the past and dwell on the dead."

I knew that I must not stare at him overly long. "I'm sorry, Father; I've dropped my napkin." I ducked down to retrieve what had never been dropped. Not dwell on the dead—my many, many dead. Oh, Father, they sustain me, they hover about me, crying out to be allowed to rest in peace. I am Antigone, Father, only I have millions to bury, millions besides my brother. My head, which had never stopped hurting, was ready to explode, and it was perhaps this pain which kept me from screaming obscenities at this murderer who sat so coolly handsome across the table from me. I sat up straight, but the smile wouldn't work. Just as well; it was not the time for it anyway. "Thank you, Father. You said there were two things?"

"Yes." He hesitated and drained the last of his wine. "There is a man in my employ whom you should probably meet. He is a Belgian, but of good ancestry. He has become quite a superior public-relations man and has many interesting ideas on expanding markets. I shall invite him to our little reception. Sooner or later you would learn of him anyway. It is my conviction that he probably saved your life during the earliest part of your illness. You're not expected to make a fuss over him, but he is deserving of some credit. Essentially, he will not fit in with our other guests, but under the circumstances we can make an exception. You need only to acknowledge him; I'm sure he's too much the gentleman to bring up anything out of the past." He smiled at me warmly.

Back in my room, I leaned my face against the cold windowpane. I did not need any of the seashells to hear the roaring around me. It would soon be spring and

Gerd would be dead three years. I was convinced that my father was reveling in some monstrous victory while Gerd's lost life remained unavenged. And Jans was to be treated like a good servant who had done a little something extra for the masters on their private game preserve. I was not to remember the dead, and all unpleasantness was completely behind us. I saw my face in the dark windowpane and realized what a failure I was. In the eighteenth year of my life, when I finally knew the truth about the murder of the millions, about my brother's death, my mother's tormented life, I was doomed to sit across the dinner table, enjoying my cream caramel dessert, with a man I hated beyond all fathoming, the man who was responsible for the crimes.

With almost no clear awareness of what I was doing I walked into the bathroom and vomited into the hand basin.

11

In the four weeks before the reception I discovered some things about myself that were immensely distressing to me. The first was that I was really still sick, or at least that there were hours when I wanted to creep back into the safety of my illness and take refuge from the choices which I knew I, alone, had to make. No matter how much I wanted to talk to Jans on the phone when he called, I had to choose not to do so. I also had to express pleasure each time my father gloated over some unusually good piece of business news: profits from exports were higher than expected; also, even though that part of the economy had slowed a bit, the nation itself was consuming more, and that took up the slack. "This means, Eroica, that Germany will soon have the highest standard of living in Europe." Such comments about the economy did not disturb me too much, but his excitement about the rise of Germany "out of the ashes" made me want to drive a stake through his black heart.

The second major thing I discovered was that I had gained a certain authority. I received a deference from the servants that was so novel I didn't recognize it at first. I thought merely that they were being a little strange. The younger maid, Mary Anne, who had entered the household during my illness, served tea one afternoon when Marta was busy elsewhere. She dropped a silver creamer on a china saucer, shattering the little plate and sending bits of imperial cobalt flying to the carpet. The girl turned to me in terror, her hand over her mouth. I wanted to laugh, but that inner voice advised me not to. "It's not important, Mary Anne. There is a good chance we have a few more saucers in the house."

"Oh, thank you, miss," she whispered, and made a charming curtsy when she left the room with the mess on the tray. I was ready to forget the incident, but when she returned a short time later, her eyes were red with crying and one of her cheeks was beginning to swell. I asked her what was wrong, but she said it was nothing.

After she left I sat drinking the tea, absently thinking about the piano, which had not been played in such a long time. I thought I might have it tuned. When she did not come to take the tray, I rang for her, but it was the cook who appeared. I had seen her several times before and my only impression had been that she reminded me of Vera, although they did not look alike at all. The former cook's whereabouts were still unknown to me. This new one picked up the tray and asked if I wished anything else.

"Yes, please put the tray down." The woman was somewhat startled but she returned the tray to the tea table. "Where is Mary Anne?"

"I sent her to scrub the back terrace; it will teach her not to break things."

"Did you hit her?"

"It's what she needed." She started toward the tray again.

"One moment please, Mrs. Erlich. You will not hit Mary Anne again, and Karl will scrub the back terrace, since he has the special machine with excellent brushes for cleaning all the floors."

The woman gave me an ugly look. "Mr. von Heyditch has given me full reign over the help," she said in a slow, measured way.

"Mrs. Erlich, I can change that with a single word. Please take out the tray." She picked up the tea things and marched out of the room as though special drums were beating for her.

That night at dinner I told my father that I felt the cook was not handling things properly. He looked at me with humorous amazement. "And what is it about her that you disapprove of?" He was smiling indulgently.

"I do not like for her to hit the maids the way she does."

The effect of my words was more startling than I had imagined it would be. He swore under his breath, then he stared at me intensely. "Do you think, Eroica, that you could interview a new cook yourself?"

"I am quite sure I could, but I did not hire Mrs. Erlich, Father; it is not my place to fire her. I think also that Lena can cook for a few days until I find us someone else."

My father nodded slowly. "Well," he said after a time, "I think I see the signs of a true von Heyditch at last."

I was unable to tell him that that wasn't the best news I had ever heard in my life. "Thank you, Father," I said with as much elaborate graciousness as I could. When we left the table, he complimented me on my white knit dress. We both knew that the compliment held other meanings and that it extended much further than my choice of a correct and becoming dress.

I never saw Mrs. Erlich again. Two days later, I hired a pleasant plump woman with good references. She seemed glad to get the job, and when she asked me if there were any particular rules that she should be aware of, I told her that there would be no hitting of the other servants.

"Oh, the heavens have mercy on us! I should think not," she said in dismay.

On that one day I discovered something I had never consciously known before: I discovered power. That is, I discovered that I had power, and one of the first things I realized was that one should never use more than one needs at any given time. There is a very special grace earned by controlling one's desire to overuse the power one has. I found various language tricks enormously useful to me. For example, after getting the cook fired, I never again worded anything in the form of a demand. I soon discovered that the servants were charmed by my "requests." "Marta, do you think I might have tea a bit later today, since Father won't be in for dinner until nine."

"Oh, but certainly, miss, whatever you wish."

I thanked her and asked her if she would please ask Mary Anne to come see me. Mary Anne showed up in my room before I had my lines fully rehearsed, but then, I was getting quite good at producing the speeches spontaneously. "Mary Anne, do you think you would like to spend part of your time helping me with my clothes? Lena says you are an excellent seamstress. What do you think?"

"Whatever you want me to do." Ever since the earlier incident with the cook, Mary Anne had looked at me with adoration.

"Well, I thought perhaps your talents were rather wasted in the kitchen, and I do need someone to see after these things. If Father is going to start entertaining, I shall have to extend my wardrobe and keep it in order. There is a sewing room off my mother's old bedroom; I shall have it opened and modernized for us. What do you think?" I used this last little question to some excess, but in spite of, or perhaps because of, its overuse, it was always effective.

Mary Anne was positively entranced about the idea of taking care of my wardrobe, and she was equally happy to leave the kitchen.

Later in the day, I sought out Lena, who was in Mother's garden room watering the plants. "Lena, I feel that you ought not to do any of the heavy work anymore. We need a general housekeeper to run things and one day soon we'll get someone, but I need you quite differently. I'm going to move into the large room opposite my father's and I would like you to move into the one next to it. There are connecting doors and I don't see how I can do without your companionship. Would you mind very much?"

She hugged me and told me that I was a true lady. Well, that was a bit much, since all my actions were carefully calculated to bring my father to some kind of ruin, but I accepted the compliment by kissing her on the cheek. Then she really did cry, and it dawned on me that except for my mother and brother—and, of course, Jans—I had never kissed anyone. I left her blowing her nose loudly and proceeded to the next objective—the kitchen.

The cook was surprised to see me, particularly when I said that I was perishing for a cup of hot chocolate, but she prepared it for me at once and asked if my father and I had found the meals acceptable. I told her they were excellent, but that I was somewhat concerned about the amount of work entailed, and I asked her if she thought I should hire more help for her since I had moved Mary Anne upstairs, to new duties.

"Well, there's Marta and her boy, and that should be enough for the time being."

I thanked her and left knowing I had another ally. Finally, at tea, I spoke to Marta about her son. She explained bitterly that her husband had abandoned her and the boy and that she had no skills except housework, "which is natural to all women anyway, so all I could do was hope for a position with a family that would accept my son as well." Lena had hired her for a decent salary but the boy, who was only eleven, was not paid wages of any kind. I told Marta that in the future he would receive a salary, although not a very large one, since he only worked about two hours a day, after school. She stared at me incredulously. I knew I was being presumptuous in proffering my private opinions upon this matter, but I felt particularly strongly about it. "Even a child needs a little money of his own in a world where everything costs. How else could he ever buy his mother a present if he wished to do so?"

She left the room rather quickly and I knew then that I had captured all the house staff. There were still the men, but they had never been part of my plans. There was no way to get to Wilhelm, and anyway I did not wish to. On the day he took Lena and me shopping I was coolly polite to him, thanking him for waiting for us and for carrying our packages. He looked at me with an expression that fell somewhere between distrust and curiosity. He seemed to be having some trouble with his old view of me as a dummy. I was convinced that he knew the story about the supposed rape. Karl must have known it, too. Since I no longer eavesdropped on people, I had no way of knowing what these two men thought of me in my new role. I did remember, however, that they knew of Father's secret activities, but it was a long time before I discovered that they were just as fooled as I was.

The living arrangements had not altered very much. Karl and Wilhelm still lived in the apartment over the carriage house, Marta and her son shared a room, the cook had Vera's old quarters and Mary Anne had the small room off the linen room.

At dinner that evening I told my father of the changes I had made. "I hope, Father, that you will not mind if I move into the room opposite yours."

He seemed both surprised and pleased by my reorganization of the household. "By all means, take whatever room you wish." He had an extra glass of wine that night and was unusually animated and witty. "Next you'll be running my businesses," he laughed.

I added an appreciative smile to his little joke, but my mind sped forward: that depends upon what they are, Father. At the time, I believed I was within twenty-four hours of finding out that information, since the following evening was our little reception.

The whole affair was catered, right down to the imported flowers which arrived early in the afternoon, huge bouquets of anthuriams from the Caribbean and massive sprays of yellow-green cymbidium orchids from Africa. There were also roses and peonies grown in hothouses in the city's nurseries. The people from the catering place had come to look the floor plan over the day before, and they made all kinds of pompous decisions, ordering everyone around with aggressive, impatient voices. I stayed out of their way, yet I watched with considerable attention: if I was to learn how to give a reception someday, I might as well learn from experts.

Gerd and I had been to large dinner parties and receptions over the years, but usually we were pushed off with other young people into side rooms where we looked glumly at the glum strangers around us. Sometimes we did not even speak the same languages. There was always a servant in charge, but Gerd and I usually got away through some prearranged ruse. Invariably we ended up in a storeroom or attic with a bottle of filched champagne with which we elaborately toasted our future plans. "Here's to the day," he said one night in a dusty castle tower on Lake Como, "when you and I begin our trip around the world."

That particular trip to Italy had nearly ended in tragedy: Mother almost died. She became ill quite suddenly and in a matter of minutes was taken off to a hospital while Father stormed back and forth in a huge hall on the floor below, the one on which Gerd and I were sequestered.

"How dare anyone discuss something like that with my wife. She is completely outside of all of it. She knows nothing and she is to go on knowing nothing. She is in extremely fragile health."

Then we heard a woman's voice, shaky and frightened. "Forgive me, sir, I presumed—"

But Father interrupted. "You presumed too much, madam." A door slammed and a woman's weeping reached us. "You stupid bitch, if she dies, we're dead, too." This last voice belonged to our host.

Later we discovered that Mother had taken an overdose of sleeping medicine, and it was that same summer, after we returned home, that she moved into a different bedroom in the house and Father remained alone in the elaborate master complex with its ornate sitting room and huge baths. I knew that Gerd worried about Mother and tried to find out what had made her so unhappy, but as far as I know, he never did.

Father's upcoming reception had the servants all excited and the uniforms had a little more starch in them than usual. Marta and Mary Anne were both to serve the trays of canapés with the help of two additional women from the caterer's. The cook was to see that the food was hot and well arranged on the trays before it left the pantry. Four waiters were to serve champagne or fill requests for other drinks.

Dressed in what Mary Anne called one of my serious dresses, I went downstairs to make sure Jans' name was on the guest list. It would be interesting to see if I could bluff the caterer, a rotund little man who made everyone nervous with his officious manner.

In the drawing room I ignored the caterer's presence and pointlessly moved a piece of Kaiser porcelain from one table to another. I knew the man was watching me. "Who are you?" he asked ungraciously. I did not answer him. Marta, who was just then coming from the foyer, must have heard the question, too.

"Marta, would you please bring me a cup of tea?"

She smiled and ignored the funny little man, as I had done. "Of course, Miss."

I moved about the room, rearranging things that did not need rearranging at all. When I came near the man, I was looking at one of Father's paintings, a fine old Flemish landscape. "I think that should be reframed. Much too ornate. Well, too late for now." I turned to the man abruptly. "Here, let me see your copy of the list; there has been a change."

He held on to it fiercely. "Just one moment! Who are you?"

He was at least four inches shorter than I, and he

drew himself up like Napoleon when I reached for the list. "I am Eroica von Heyditch; now, please give me the list." My voice was calm and low; I had finally learned how to imitate Father. He let go of the sheets of paper as though they were on fire. The list read like an embassy meeting, with the nationality of each person printed after his name. At the very end I read JANS DEBLIN, BELGIUM. "It's been corrected." I handed the papers back to the man, who took them hesitantly. Marta was just entering with a tray. "Would you leave it in the conservatory, please, Marta. I'll have it there."

An hour before the reception, Lena coiled my hair up onto the back of my head. I had slept earlier for two hours and had awakened thinking of my first meeting with Jans after a year and a half. His working for my father still mystified and frightened me. Lena, who understood my apprehensive mood but not the real reason for it, cooed gently. "Now, now, you'll be all right. Just walk tall and remember that you are a beautiful young woman from a noble family."

When she left, I looked at the black silk dress I was to wear for the evening. Though simple, it was daringly cut by the designer Father had sent to the house a week before. I was surprised at my father's interest, particularly when the designer told me, "Mr. von Heyditch does not wish your dress to be repeated at the reception. It must be one of a kind."

A few minutes before it was time for me to face seventy-four strangers, my father knocked on my bedroom door. I was not surprised to see him, since I knew there had to be some final instruction from him; there always was. But he did not give me any directive. He stopped just inside the door and stared at me, his eyes glistening brilliantly. For one horrible moment I felt naked, but the feeling passed and I managed to say, "Do you like the dress, Father?"

He did not answer. Instead he put his hand into the pocket of his evening coat and brought out a loose sparkling mass. Then he moved behind me and placed the diamond necklace around my neck. I watched this scene in the mirror in front of which we stood. The necklace was a new one, not one of Mother's. Father put his hands on my bare shoulders near my neck. The dress had a two-inch strip on each side that draped over the outer part of my shoulders and continued on into a deep-cut arc which revealed much of my back. I would have expected his hands to be like ice, but in fact they were quite warm. Before I could even think of shuddering, he removed his hands, and for a horrible moment our eyes met in the mirror. It was one of those mysterious looks that is charged with meanings—none of which I understood. Yet I knew something wild and grotesque had taken place. He gave a little laugh and walked out of the room with the springlike step of a young man.

I stumbled to the window and sat in my old wicker chair. My hands shook uncontrollably. "Stop! Stop! Stop!" I was whispering to my own body. "Get control! Get control!" A sharp knife twisted in my head. "No! No, I won't have a headache now! I have to think. Please, please, not now." I heard my own whining and stopped. "Get out of the chair. Stand up straight. You know what is expected of you. Stop being ridiculous. Find out what is happening. Move!" I did. I took a last look into the mirror to prepare my serene face. Father's necklace gleamed magnificently against my bare skin; the final stone, which seemed to hold a chain of diamonds together, was a huge oval surrounded by a circle of oddly staggered stones and hung pendantlike between my breasts. For a fraction of a second I thought I had seen the design before, but I failed to follow up the sensation of familiarity.

As I descended the broad stairway, the first guests were just entering. Cards were presented. A liveried man I had never seen took the people's wraps and announced names.

When Father first spoke of the reception, it was clearly understood between us that I was not expected to play hostess in any sense of the word. Yet in the last week or ten days before our "little evening" (Father's phrase) he had begun to make rather different statements in regard to my function. One night as he watched me across the dinner table he mentioned casually that I might be able to take on some responsibilities earlier than he had expected, since I had matured so suddenly. "You are a von Heyditch, Eroica, and it shows. I do not expect you to shoulder anything very heavy now, but I see that you make good judgments here with the running of the house, and this shows me promise. In time there may be some important occasions for which you will be much needed. Well, we shall see how it goes the first time."

For all that my father said, I still did not know my role, but it was obvious that he would be watching me to see what I could become. As I entered the foyer, I wondered briefly what potential he was looking for. Then I was surrounded by guests and too busy to think.

Father took my arm almost immediately. "Smile, Eroica." I did. He led me to a group of diplomat types and in a voice glazed with pride said, "Gentlemen, my daughter, Eroica."

Each of the men kissed my hand. It was all quite extraordinary. Father led me from one group to the next with always the same effect. The men were "charmed," the women polite. I made all the proper responses and continued smiling.

I had lived through dreamlike events before, in which reality was so diffuse that everything appeared to be happening in slow motion, in a somnolescent way, in which people conversed more in gestures than in words, floated rather than walked. Although the huge floral arrangements had softened the drawing room and the black-suited musicians in one far corner were humanizing it with their background music, the room still had the aura of the museum chamber in which a gathering of bowing and nodding automatons had been set in motion by some master mechanic. Gerd had once mentioned that even a victim at a public execution would be expected to act with decorum and propriety if that particular public consisted of upper-level society.

Through this meeting of people I thought constantly of Jans and how I would greet him before all these curious eyes. For a moment my thoughts must have shown on my face, for my father said, "What is it?"

Recover yourself. Say something! "Father, do I look all right?"

"Of course. You look splendid. Why do you ask such a thing?"

"Everyone stares at me."

He laughed with pleasure. "And well they should."

Then, suddenly, there was Jans, all dressed in evening clothes, and I barely heard my father's introduction as the blood rushed to my head. I used all the presence I had to keep from shaking.

He took my hand and kissed it exactly as the others had done. "A treasure, sir," he said to my father.

"Yes, everything considered." My father was watching me. I was unable to speak to the mask on Jans' face or to the cool voice which I hardly recognized. I felt physical pain in my chest. He released my hand at once; there had been no pressure as he held it, no subtlety to his touch as he kissed it. "Deblin, I don't think there is a memory of anything."

"There is no reason there should be, sir."

"No, of course not."

Jans turned to me. "I hope you are in good health, mademoiselle."

Through the pain I heard my voice. "Yes, thank you. I am."

Father and I moved on as Jans nodded and drifted away without any sign at all to me. "He's a good man, an excellent interpreter and he understands the kinds of markets we are looking for." Father introduced me to a few more people and then told me to "circulate and be pleasant to the guests, but remember always who you are."

I nodded. "Yes, Father."

A tray of elegant hors d'oeuvres was offered to me: foie gras and black caviar mountained on tiny islands of bread, pieces of lobster spiked by miniature lances. I took one, although I had no hunger, at least not for food. I moved about the room, nodding to the people to whom my father had introduced me. Again a tray of food appeared. Marta was looking at me with concern in her eyes. "The garden room, miss, quickly," she said softly. "Your father has his back turned."

"What?" But she was gone, offering the tray to a cluster of reaching hands. I drifted out of the room, across the foyer to my mother's conservatory. The room was dark; the draperies were pulled against the garden spotlights which lit the house from the outside. I pulled the door closed behind me and waited. When I felt his hands on my arms I was already shaking and crying. His mouth touched my face, my neck, my shoulders.

"Forgive me, Eroica."

"No, no, please don't say that."

"I almost killed you."

"No. No."

"I thought you would never get well again. Forgive me."

I covered his mouth with mine. "I love you. I have forgotten nothing. I love you." I felt his tears on my face and I wanted to cry out, Oh, Mother, Mother, if you can hear me, help us.

After a few minutes, he lowered his arms. "Eroica, you wear a diamond talisman; do not be alarmed at the way people look at you."

"What?"

"The diamond pendant you are wearing. It is his metal in miniature, in symbolic form." I gasped, and tried to reach for it. "That's not important now, but you should know it. His reasons for using this symbol now are still a mystery to me. I only know that the design keeps reappearing and that it is frightening to some and not to others. Now, listen to me. Meet me Sunday at the cemetery."

"The crypt?"

"No, it might be watched. The far end, where I lost you once."

"Among the Old Ones?"

"Yes. Is there a particular spot?"

"There is a monument of four obelisks made of black stone with laurel wreaths."

"Good. What time?"

"Dawn?"

In the darkness, he hesitated, but only for a moment. "Yes."

The reception was on a Thursday and finally broke up when the musicians, after playing background music for most of the two hours, suddenly began the national anthem. Trays of beautifully wrapped gifts were brought into the room and distributed. For the ladies there were sterling-silver pins, tiny replicas of the flags of their countries; and for the gentlemen, money clips with their countries' ensigns engraved on them. In a matter of minutes the first limousines purred up to the marble terrace, where, with a flourish of furs, the guests departed.

Out of the whole evening, the thing that worried me the most was the behavior of the servants. I could only assume that Lena had not told my father that Jans had called daily about my well-being, and I had no idea why Marta had taken such an enormous risk when she directed me to the garden room. Had my kindness and the increase in their salaries so fully won their loyalty? I pondered other motives: soon I would be mistress of the house; were they preparing for that? My father, in his sixties, might die soon, and I would be in complete control. However, with his recent display of vigor and vitality he could easily live another thirty years, unless I dispatched him sooner.

It did not occur to me that the servants' motives might be unselfish. For the time, I elected not to ask any questions.

When all the guests had left and the servants were putting the house back in order, my father complimented me. "You carried yourself very well; but then, blood always shows. You are a credit to your name. Did you leave the room?" His voice had not changed as he asked the question.

"Yes, Father."

"Why did you do that?"

I thought swiftly. "The waiters were behaving stupidly: they spilled champagne. I had to talk to that man in charge."

"Good for you. I think I did notice a bit of sloppiness. Perhaps we'll call in someone different next time."

"Whatever you think best, Father."

"Yes, we'll do that." He smiled congenially. "How do you feel?"

"Very well, thank you."

"Did you enjoy yourself?"

"Yes. At first I was a little afraid of all those important people, but after a while I was quite at ease."

"Eroica, they are not important people. *We* are important people. Always remember that."

"Yes, Father."

"Now then, I think I ought to put your new jewel in the safe."

I glanced at it only briefly as I took it off and handed it to my father, who casually slipped it into his coat pocket. "Next time, you may wear it again. We'll invite a different bunch." Again he smiled pleasantly.

"I'm a little tired, Father. Would you mind very much if I went to bed now?"

"Good idea. Get your rest. Have Lena bring you up something nourishing before you sleep."

"Yes, Father. Good night." I turned and walked across the room.

"Eroica."

I faced him. "Yes, Father?"

"You passed a very important test tonight. I want you to know that you passed it very well indeed."

In my room, I leaned against the closed door, exhausted; my very bones seemed to have gone limp. How was I serving Father? I felt myself shrink inside as I thought of having worn his medal around my neck. Also, Father was happy, even elated, and worst of all, he was dynamically healthy. I had never seen him like this before, and the more I considered his high spirits, the more I was convinced that he was up to something horrible. And whatever that was, I was part of it.

I wanted to sink into my old chair, curl up under the eiderdown and go back to being sick, back into the comfortable obliviousness of things, where I was someone else's problem. But I knew I could not do that. Once, in a serious moment when Gerd and I were making dreams for the future, he had said, "We won't really just be able to do whatever happens to amuse us, Eroica; the hallmark of aristocracy is responsibility." If it were not for the realization that I would see Jans on Sunday, I would have sunk into deep depression.

However, thoughts of Jans revived my energies and I set about trying to solve the problems of awakening before dawn on Sunday and then getting out of the house without anyone's knowledge. How stupid of me to have moved into the room across the mezzanine from Father's. I was certainly in the dragon's path. There was a thirty-foot drop from my window to Mother's rock garden, and I couldn't see myself climbing down the ivy, especially if it was raining at the time.

After pacing around my room for a while, I solved the problem of awakening by deciding not to go to sleep at all on Saturday night. Getting out of the house was not going to be as easy, and my dream that night did not help the matter. In it I lost my way, and when I did finally reach the dais with the four obelisks, there was Father, standing in the center of them, waiting for me.

On Friday I decided on a plan: I would stay in Mother's conservatory after dinner and read for a while. No one would think this unusual, since I frequently read there during the day. I reasoned that if Father knew I was there on Friday night, he would think it quite ordinary for me to be there on Saturday after dinner as well. Once the house quieted down, I would simply turn out the light, leave for the cemetery and wait for Jans there.

But Father did not come home for dinner on Friday. Marta said his office had called with the message that I was not to expect him. For hours after dinner I lay awake in the darkness of my room, waiting for his footsteps. After a time I slept fitfully, awakening often to night sounds intensified by my anxiety. Owls cried in the park, and farther away barge horns answered each other in low moans. I did not know if Father had come home or not and the plan for getting out of the house on Sunday seemed less and less sage.

On Saturday rain fell steadily all morning, my head hurt, and no one had heard from my father. Then, just before lunch, he burst into the foyer in the fiercest rage I had ever seen. His face was white and rigid as stone, his eyes were slits, and his mouth was clamped as tight as though it were glued. He rushed directly to his study.

Marta was just setting the table when he slammed his door violently enough to bring a painting off the wall. She came to stand by the open sliding panels between the two rooms. "What has happened?" I asked.

She shook her head. "I don't know." She went to the drawing room and picked up the painting and put it into a closet in the foyer.

I called Lena, who came in with a heavy shawl over her shoulders. "Lena, do you know what's going on?" I told her of my father's grim arrival.

"Oh, just some buisness thing, I suspect. Men always

go into fits if things don't go just the way they want them to."

I looked at Marta, who glanced at me and shook her head very slightly. She returned to setting the table. Lena patted my hand and clucked her usual banalities. "Don't worry your pretty head; he'll be over it by dinnertime."

But he was not over it by dinnertime. All afternoon he remained in his study. When Marta knocked on his door to ask if he wanted anything, he looked at her with blazing eyes. "No, and do not interrupt me again!" By then all the servants were tiptoeing around the house for fear of disturbing him.

All afternoon I worried about Jans, my imagination conjuring up horrible suspicions: Father had found out about him! Even though I knew Jans had called that morning, I worried anyway: Father might be waiting to trap him. I struggled with these fears through the afternoon. It's not possible. How would he know? You're being hysterical. Remain calm.

But my father's terrifying face left me agitated and alarmed. I tried to read, to sleep; instead I wandered through the silent rooms, sat on the stairs a dozen times, only to jump up again and continue drifting about the house, my fears skulking around with me.

Later I considered having dinner in my room, but I was afraid some business associate might show up and this was not the time to be missing, since my father no longer made his Saturday night excursions. When I had come out of my illness, it was one of the first things I had noticed.

I ate alone in the music room but couldn't really taste anything. If Father wanted to talk to me later, I would have to be there. Briefly I saw Jans waiting at the cemetery and then calling my name and worrying about something having happened to me. Lena came in and gently chided me for not having eaten much of my dinner. "Now, you mustn't let your father's business concerns interfere with your well-being. He wants you to be strong and healthy." She complained about her arthritis, told me to get a good night's sleep and retired.

Finally, around ten, my father came out of his study. His expression had changed into one of profound determination. "Could I get you something to eat, Father?"

He looked at me with an expression I could not read, except that he was not at all harsh when he spoke to me. "No." He paused, "Eroica, I'm going to be quite busy for a few days, a little more so than usual. You keep managing the house as you have been."

"Yes, Father."

"Why don't you go to bed and get some rest."

"Yes, Father." It was clear that he wanted me upstairs and away from whatever it was that had angered him earlier. He returned to his study without any further words. Once in my room, I kept the door slightly open, since it was obvious that he was waiting for someone. All the servants had retreated to their quarters.

Within thirty minutes the first car arrived. I stood in the half darkness of the mezzanine and watched Father let in several men. To my knowledge I had never seen any of them before. Two more cars drove up and again my father met the men at the door. The whole thing occurred without a single word's being spoken. The visitors looked like specters, with their black overcoats and their pale, drawn faces. They all went to Father's study and I listened for the door to close. It did.

I had no trouble keeping awake waiting for the men to leave. Twice I crept downstairs and listened with a racing heart for some sound from the study. I knew that this was an absurd expectation. The study had long ago been soundproofed.

At three the clock struck the hours, exploding the deep stillness. I was seated at the top of the stairs, terrified. I could wait no longer, although it was long before dawn. Dressed in black, with my black boots in my hand, I returned to the main floor, leaving the house through my mother's plant room. The rain had stopped and clouds floated in front of a transparent crescent moon. I made my way with ease to the park and on to the cemetery, where the gate creaked when I opened it.

12

"Eroica." Jans was standing against the wall just inside the gate. I reached out for him and felt his hands touch mine. He put his arms around me and held me close for a long still moment. With my head close to his chest I could hear his heart beating. "I've been insane with worry," he finally said. "Thank God you're early. Look, we're going to freeze here, or get wet when it rains again. My car is only a short distance away. Come." He took my hand and we left the cemetery and walked to his car. He drove, with only his parking lights on, to the other side of the park and stopped under an overhanging tree. I was still unable to speak. "Are you cold?"

"Yes."

He reached into the back seat and brought forth a blanket, with which he covered both of us. Then he rubbed my hands until the numbness left. "Better?"

"Yes. Jans, something has happened."

"What?"

"I don't know." I described the events which had taken place during the day and the men who were at that very moment with my father. Jans remained still. "What does it mean?"

"The government is going to extend the period during which new proceedings can be instituted against war criminals. It was decided yesterday. The statute-of-limitations deadline was to have been May of this year." He explained statute of limitations to me.

"You mean, Father can be tried for his crimes?"

"We don't know of any crimes he has committed."

"Jans! The gas rooms."

"Building them was no crime, at least not in the eyes of the law."

"It was a crime!"

"To you, to me, even to millions of others, it was a moral crime. Legally? Well, the law frequently has little to do with morality. Some of the men who were in charge of the camps have been tried and convicted of murder. Others escaped long ago and lost themselves in Germany or were taken in by other countries. I frankly do not understand your father's behavior. The talk at the office is that he is incensed because forces outside Germany can still dictate the country's internal affairs. Of course Bonn is under external pressure, and this enrages him; but there must be something more. It's that touch of panic in his rage that interests me. I have to conclude that he feels he is liable to court action for something in his past, or that this new development hinders some plan he has for the future. I know of at least two murders he could be tried for, but these cannot be proved."

"What two?"

"Professor Pemsel and your cook, Vera Oper."

"Dead? They are dead?"

"Yes. Vera died on the operating table; they gave her enough anesthesia to last a lifetime—about twenty minutes' worth."

"Oh, no!"

"Eroica, don't add that to your feelings of guilt. It had very little to do with you. She betrayed his house, and that was something he could never stand for. As for Pemsel, your father had his root removed for him."

"What?"

"He had his genitals removed. Your father believed that Pemsel violated the house of von Heyditch. Your vicious little professor survived the operation, but not the rat poison he lunched on later—of his own accord, possibly—but I could be mistaken."

I started to cry. "But he didn't. He didn't." In the dark I felt sick and miserable.

"My dear Eroica. Who should know better than I? Now, listen to me, you have no responsibility in any of this."

"But it's so dreadful."

"Murder generally is."

"But I *am* responsible. I wanted them dead."

"At one time or another most people wish someone dead, and there are those who believe that such thoughts are the same as killing. I don't happen to believe that. But this is irrelevant: we don't have the time to dwell on such philosophical points." For a long time he held me tightly as I wept. When I was finally able to stop, he said, "Eroica, there are some things I must tell you and some things that I must ask. You are going to have to absorb a great deal in a very short time." He turned on a small car light and looked into my face. "I would like to be generous and ask if you will be able to take some shocks, but I cannot do that."

I nodded. "Yes, I understand."

He breathed deeply. "All right. Now, listen carefully. After I brought you back—that is, after your father came home—the firm contacted me and your father offered me a job. You must understand why I took it."

"I know why you took it," I said. "To find out what my father is up to."

"Eroica, I don't know how it will end. If I'm lucky, I may find something from his past."

"Worse than the things you know he has already done?"

"Something provable. Something that will bring him to justice. As for what he is up to now . . . well, I'm going to need more than luck to discover that. For years there have been rumors about him, suspicions that he was trying to revive Nazism, or something like it. No one has ever been able to prove anything. He is into almost every kind of business imaginable. Of course, his factories still produce farm equipment, generators, prefabricated building materials, heavy tools, all of those sorts of things. But he has branched out from these, diversified into hundreds of other products: foods, furniture, hospital equipment, chemicals, medicines, textiles, television sets—everything from road-building machinery to preprocessed potatoes. And services, too: schools, hospitals, recreation centers, theaters, films. His salesmen look for customers wherever goods and services are needed. His products are excellent. When he finds a market, he sends in his experts to advise the local people on how to make the most expedient use of his goods. There are fine bridges in South America built with von Heyditch steel. There are new roads in the Near East put down by von Heyditch bulldozers and trucks. There is new housing in Mexico, Egypt, Spain, Chile, India, Iran, Turkey, all built with von Heyditch construction machinery. His electrical plants light the capitals of a dozen countries. His hydraulic structures and dams control dozens of rivers. Germans do not do the work, but VHI engineers supervise and direct these projects. This way, employment for the native people of those countries is created by Von Heyditch Industries.

"Every major power watches him with envy and anger. It is laughable, the number of spies hired by your father's firms. The truth is that he recruits them and then feeds them exactly the information that he wants them to have."

"He sees that they get lies?"

"Oh, no, he sees to it that they get the truth."

"What are they looking for?"

"Concealed war matériel, arms. . . . Who knows?"

"Does he produce those also?"

"There is not a single gun produced by Von Heyditch Industries, not even in his toy factories."

"Then how is he doing whatever you think he is?"

"Eroica, I have rejected those rumors about Nazism.

I don't know what he is doing, but I suspect that the destruction of Israel is involved."

"How did you get your suspicions?"

"Recently it was discovered that West Germany had secretly supplied arms to Israel. Egypt's President Nasser had a fit, of course, and he was quick to invite East Germany's Communist leader to tea. All this is common knowledge. Your father in no way participated in the arms deal, but privately he did not mind at all that Israel was being helped to arm itself. At the moment, the West German foreign policy involving Israel is up in the air. If Bonn establishes some agreement with the Israelis, the Arab states will break their diplomatic peace with West Germany entirely. All of this is about to happen, and your father—at least as of a few days ago—was still in high humor over it."

"But how can any of this make you think he is planning that country's destruction? Did he say something?"

In the faint light Jans' face took on a new half-smiling expression. "No. He didn't say anything, but somebody else did."

"Who?"

"My job with your father, Eroica, puts me at an interesting advantage. I am in direct touch with his customers around the world. Consequently, I am frequently the first to hear things. When several cement plants in Argentina stamped your father's ridged wheel on every part, I was among the first to know."

"The ridged wheel?" I never thought much about my father's trademarks; he had several, and none was particularly interesting.

"An oval ridged wheel, very pretty when made of diamonds. This insignia flies from all the von Heyditch ships which cut across the seas to bring materials for power plants, bridges, skyscrapers, entire factories, to the hungry countries that are supposed to be realizing themselves. Often these same countries use this flag as well, only inconspicuously over industrial sites. It is a relatively small flag, a lengthened triangle of red with a black ridged wheel in its center." He fell silent for a moment. "No. Your father did not say anything; he only laughed at the diplomats. But there was a man here at the time, from a South American nation, who was not amused. He said, 'So what if Israel and the Arabs have a little war? It will make no difference to anyone, in the long run. One day, when the Big Man gets tired of his game, he will crush Israel like a bug.' "

Jans seemed to be in pain; he was breathing haltingly. I put my arms around him. "What else? What else did he say?"

"Nothing. I tried to play it easy. I told him that the ridged wheel had no flags in Israel, that Von Heyditch Industries was concerned with human needs, not human destruction, and least of all with politics."

"What did he say?"

"He didn't say anything; he only laughed and continued to examine a table-model grain mill which was just perfect for his country's wheat."

"But what about everything else, all those Saturday night meetings?"

"A front; more of a ruse, actually."

"A front? What does that mean?"

"For years he has pretended to meet secretly with a group of ex-Nazis. Well, not ex, actually: losing the war did not change their views. These were Nazis who were never tried since there was never anything anyone could try them for. They were simply members of the party. But your father uses them as a means to distract a whole network of spies from discovering his real purposes. The group has not grown in ten years—I mean that no new members have been added to it—which should certainly tell those fool spies something; but apparently they don't consider that important. The British and the Americans probably know every word that is said at these little soirées. And everyone takes it seriously—the British, the Americans, even the not-so-ex Nazis. Everyone but your father. He has made sure that all his dark little organizations are known to interested governments, including his own. He had duped his old friends into believing that the party as they knew it would rise again. His trade arrangements are no secret; one can read about them in a half dozen international journals." Jans leaned forward and looked at the sky through the windshield. "And yet, there *is* a real purpose that remains hidden. And with every week that passes I feel more certain that it includes the death of Israel. I have no facts to support this, but his unconcern about Israel bothers me, his lack of interest. He has no trade with Israel. He does not make guns for the Arab nations. He refuses to deal with Russia, which must please the Americans." Jans lit a cigarette.

"*Is* there going to be a war in Israel?"

"Yes. I don't know when, but it's coming."

"All those Arabs against two million people who have already suffered so horribly. They will all be killed."

"No, I don't think so. The Israelies have surprised the Arabs before." He was silent while opening the window a little to let the smoke out.

"Why has my father been in such good spirits, at least until yesterday?"

"He's had some good reasons: the Americans have been at war for some time now."

"With whom?"

"North Vietnam, supposedly."

My mind raced back to Pemsel's maps: Vietnam, part of the Indochinese Peninsula. "But why? How could they be? Pemsel said it was only another dreary little Asiatic agricultural country that grew barely enough rice to feed itself."

"Eroica, if I understood American foreign policy, I could explain it to you." He shook his head. "No one calls it a war, except, I suspect, the people being shot at. The euphemism for it is 'police action,' but throughout February and this month, too, there have been reports of battles and bombings. Pictures are showing up of dead soldiers, bombed villages, and always, of course, the eternal refugees, plodding from nowhere to nowhere and getting in the way of the armies while doing it. No, I don't understand any of it. I'm not sure the Americans do either. They seemed to have inherited the war from the French, and they don't know how to give it back. Some journalist wag the other day called it de Gaulle's revenge. The allies treated de Gaulle rather shabbily during World War Two, and he has never forgiven them."

"Why should all this put my father into such high spirits?"

"Your father seems to have learned something from the Second World War: if a country uses up its resources for destruction, it will decrease its capacity to grow internally. There does not seem to be any way that 'America's little war,' as it's called in the press, can be profitable. Von Heyditch Industries will find new markets for human necessities while empty American shell casing and burned-out tanks rust after the monsoonal rains."

Jans put out his cigarette. We could begin to see streaks of a slate-colored sky. Despite my exhaustion, something hung on and nagged. "Jans, my father does not go to those Saturday-night meetings anymore."

"I know. All that ended last year. There was speculation that some internal dissension was destroying the group. But, of course, it all had to be von Heyditch's doing. No one else was of any consequence; he was the sole power. The members do not speak of it, but there was grumbling—secondhand—that your father lost interest. Since the organization was only a front, that explanation makes no sense.

"Other than that," he said wearily, "business among nations went on as usual—little skirmishes here and there, agreements, disagreements, decisions, indecisions, accusations, denials, warnings, counterwarnings. There were earthquakes in Japan and Alaska and under the Atlantic. Membership in the United Nations rose to one hundred and fifteen, over half of whom did not pay their bills to the organization. The squalor amid excessive prosperity continued without change, although there was a good deal of lamentation over how unfair it all was. China exploded a nuclear bomb. The population of the world was estimated at approximately three-point-three billion. And the pope suggested that all nations transcend all the obstacles that stand in the way of the effective brotherhood of all men."

He gave a short little laugh. I took his hand and kissed it. He smiled at me and touched my face lovingly. "I'm sorry, Eroica, it's hard not to become cynical. Tell me, how did I earn your love?"

"I don't know. I don't know how love happens, except I think about you all the time, and I worry about you."

"Stop worrying."

"I can't."

"Then let me reassure you. I know what I am doing. He's not going to kill me now."

"How can you be sure? He could find out about you—where you are from, your family."

"He knows all about my family. He had me thoroughly researched." I must have looked at him with a terrible expression because he laughed and kissed me. "He knows all about my father, who was a doctor born in Belgium, and my grandfather, who was also a doctor born in Belgium. I am sure that he has seen the hospital records of a Jans Bernhard Deblin, born in Belgium in 1936 to a Louisa Deblin, a German-born lady of considerable musical talents which unfortunately her son did not inherit. The boy was an only child of loving and indulgent parents whom he disappointed when he gave up his studies in medicine to pursue an uncertain career in linguistics."

"What happened to him after that?"

"Oh, he wandered about, spending a year in one country, then another, and so on, until he had collected a few languages which got him a dreary job as a tour director from which he went to a still drearier job writing travel columns for a magazine."

"How did he get out of that dreary business?"

"He kidnapped a young lady one day, and while he wasn't looking, she seduced him."

"Did she?"

He sighed deeply. "Yes, he was never the same after that. She was all black hair and green eyes and skin as lovely and fresh as a spring day. So, after he returned her to her father, the kindly old gentleman in gratitude offered him a job convincing foreigners that they should buy the handicrafts he produced in his little shops." Jans' face was close to mine; pain came into his eyes. "I didn't only take his offer in the hope of finding out what he was up to; I had to be near you, and that was as near as I could get."

I wanted to say I was sorry about all that lost time, but what good would saying that do? I tried to remember something from all those lost months. "Did you ever come to the clinic?"

"Twice. Both times at your father's request. You thought I was your brother."

I shook my head. "No, one of the times I realized it was you. Afterward, Lena told me you phoned every day, but she did not tell my father."

"Yes, I know. You once told me she was a friend. It was a risk, but I had to take it. She was sympathetic, and a friend."

"In a way she is, but please know that she hates Jews."

"Some of my closest acquaintances hate Jews. I enjoy the irony. They deride and mock the Jew, saying that he is without character, but they think I'm a sterling fellow."

"How can you stand them?"

"We've stood them for centuries."

It was impossible for me to understand how he could be so generous. "What did you do with the black book?"

He hesitated a second too long, which was why I did not believe him. "I burned it," he said.

"You should not have burned it."

"All those pictures are available in other books. It was time for me to burn it anyway."

We were silent for a few minutes. The sky was changing into dull, dark silver. He was looking at me intently. I had to ask something that had really been bothering me. "Are you still angry at me about my age?"

He shook his head and took my hands in his, kissing my fingers. "No, Eroica. That anger only lasted a little while. It dawned on me quite soon that your age had very little to do with the rest of your development. It was the inconsistencies that were confusing at first. You and your brother had been sealed off from the recent past. This was one of your father's mistakes, although in one respect a happy one: you were not raised with his hatred. I still don't understand why he didn't try to indoctrinate you from the time you were infants. Pemsel's attempts came years too late.

"Then, of course, there was your sexuality. I realized very quickly that your age had nothing to do with that. Your remarkable desire was already full-grown and ageless. You are marvelously sensual."

He began to kiss me and put his hand on my breast. I loved it and wanted to touch him back. His skin felt wonderfully warm and he smelled of some kind of delicious spice that I could not place. Always when I was near him I had the overpowering desire to taste him. I kissed his throat where his shirt was open and felt myself breathless and spinning. He raised my chin and smiled at me, his eyes shining. "Is that the way you've been thinking about me?"

"Yes." I was a little annoyed with myself for thinking of that just then when we had so many other things to think about, but I couldn't help it: I wished he would touch me. I kept thinking I had to stay in control, but I didn't really want to. He put his lips on mine, but it was not a kiss, exactly; he touched my tongue with his, moving very slowly. If he didn't do something else I knew I was going to explode. I took his hand and put it under my skirt, inside my panties. His fingers moved the way his tongue did—slowly, with a touch so exquisite it was almost painful. I wanted desperately to touch him, but he had buttons and belts and all such ridiculous obstacles which he finally helped me with. His penis was already tall and wonderful to hold. I don't remember exactly when he gushed because I was off the world and drifting amid the stars.

When I touched earth again, he had one arm tightly around my shoulders and with his other hand he was holding a handkerchief over the end of his penis, just above my hand. He looked mysterious in the predawn light, with his deep eyes close to mine, absorbing me. I wanted to tell him that we should drive away, at that moment, drive out of the city. By nighttime we could be in Regensburg. We could stay at Mother's estate: Uncle Teddy would help us and Father would never find us. The more I thought about it, the more reasonable it seemed. "Jans, let's go to Regensburg." I adjusted my skirt.

"That's the first place your father would look."

"But he could do nothing about it."

"He could do everything about it—bring you back, have me imprisoned, where I would get sick, according to all the records, and sent to a hospital for a cure. Believe me, Eroica, the cure would be fatal."

"No!"

"Oh, yes. We are presently quite powerless."

"But we must see each other; we must be together. Maybe Uncle Teddy could help us in some way. It is such a wonderful place. The air is fresh and there is a beautiful forest, with velvet moss on the ground and birds singing in the trees. There is no smell of factories, only wood smoke in the autumn, and we could stay in one of the big bedrooms that looks over the lake. We could stay in bed and watch the fire in the hearth, and have dinner sent up, and make love anytime we wanted to." Even as I spoke I knew we could do none of this until my father was dead. I must have sounded a little hysterical, because Jans was trying to comfort me, kissing me gently into silence.

"Eroica, my dear. That is all impossible. Your uncle is not your guardian and your father is one of the most powerful men in Europe. No one says no to him."

"I can say no to him. I can shoot him. That is a way to say no. There are guns in the house."

"Do you think you can shoot him and then go to Regensburg and live happily ever after? If you shot him, you would spend your life in a mental institution; you've already spent a year in one."

"Then I shall threaten him."

"Really?" He smiled. "With what?"

"I shall threaten to shoot myself if he does not let me go."

Jans was straightening up his clothes as I said this, but he stopped and grasped me by the shoulders. "You will not say that again. You will not even think it." He seemed quite angry and he shook me. "Do you understand? You will not think that again!"

"Why not? He wants me around now. I don't know why, but he does. He wants to have parties now, and he wants me to take charge of running the house. He was very pleased at my performance at his little reception. If I shoot myself, he will be alone."

Jans was still holding my shoulders with a firm grip. "I love you, Eroica. All that long time when you were ill, every day was suffering for me. At times I thought I was going mad. I would actually come here and walk in the cemetery because it gave me a kind of solace feeling that your lost mind might be here, that you had retreated into a time when your brother was alive. That's how far my own sanity went. If you die, I shall be alone, too, Eroica. If you love someone, you do not want the person you love to suffer."

I was exhausted and did not know how to answer

him. I knew he was trying to take an option away from me, but I could not fight his argument, because I did not want him to be alone. Actually, I did not want to shoot myself either. As Jans spoke, I began to see something I had not really been aware of before, even though I had just finished saying it myself: Father did not want to be alone. As angry as he had been the day before, he had come to me and with care and gentleness told me that he would be a bit busier than usual. Everything he said implied that we would go back to our routine of dinners and talking together. He loved for me to wear pretty clothes. He was delighted when his silly guests said I had grace and dignity. He had given up the idea of sending me away to school; he wanted me to be mistress of his house. Whatever horrors he had planned, he wanted me to stand beside him, to be part of some victory, which I did not understand.

Jans was looking at me with anxious eyes. "Eroica?"

"What?"

"What are you thinking about?"

"I was thinking about Father. I think Father could suffer, too; he could even suffer very badly."

"You'll have to explain that to me."

"I can't, because I don't know how I'm going to work it."

"Work what? Please make sense."

"I don't know yet what I am going to do; I only know that Father has my life all planned out in some way. All I have to do is find out what his plans are so I can ruin them for him. I don't think we are completely powerless."

"We are if you intend to shoot someone."

"He must have shot plenty of people, and everything seems to have worked out for him." I felt the old wretched anger return, black and murderous.

Jans was quiet for a time and then he said a terrible thing to me. He said it very fast and with a mean voice. "So, you want to be like him?"

I raised my fists without even thinking and started to

hit him. "You don't care that my brother died. He's nothing to you."

Jans grabbed my wrists and held them tightly while I struggled and cried. He didn't say anything at all, just let me carry on in this exhausting and sick way until I was too tired to move. Then he let go of my wrists and put his arms around me and held me close to him until I was all cried out. "Your brother means very much to me, Eroica, for reasons which are too complex for me to explain to you just now. Do not think I have forgotten him. I only know him through you, but if it is possible to love a man I never met, your brother is that man. It may surprise you to know that he lives in me, too. But we have to think out what we are going to do. We cannot rush about, doing things that will destroy us both. I intend very much to live, and I insist that you live, too. We are all victims of the same murderer: you, me, Gerd, your mother, my parents. I did not mean to imply that we will leave things as they are. First, though, we must discover your father's true plans."

I thought of Gerd's statement about responsibility: words were so easy; living them was impossible. Jans was looking at me with that same anxious look again. "Father hired Pemsel to train me for a responsible position. What did he mean by that?" I watched his face. For a moment he looked as if he were going to laugh, but he only made an exasperated sound.

"Eroica, do you really not know?" I shook my head. "You are his only heir. He is not merely preparing you to run the house; he is training you to run an empire. He wants you to take on enormous responsibilities someday."

"When do I get to do what I want to do?"

"Maybe never." He spoke gently.

"I can't believe that."

"I know you can't." He stopped for a moment, turning away and looking toward the windshield at the brightening sky. "Eroica, one day I visit a museum and I see a pretty girl whom I think I would like to meet. I ask her to allow me to call on her, to talk to her, to dance with her. 'There is hope for Germany after all,' I said to myself, 'because there are still pretty girls to hold in one's arms.' But my pretty girl is searching for the killer of a murdered brother, a torturer of a doomed mother. I am with her for only an hour before I lose her in a cemetery. When I find her again she wants to hang herself because two old perverts have abused her. I spend two extraordinary days with her. I sit beside the bed for hours while she sleeps, while I keep saying to myself, 'Don't get involved, you idiot; she is dangerous, dangerous.' My heart does not listen; it is busy loving; it cannot do anything but love, and in no time at all it convinces my head. I know then that the calm, obscure life I had planned for myself is no longer possible.

"Then, quite unwittingly, I hurt my pretty girl. I didn't just step on her toe or bump into her. No, nothing small or simple. I hurt her mortally. For a year she lay wrapped in self-protective bindings and screams and pain. It was too late for me to go back to being indifferent about my life. I had believed that there was no payment in laboring the past: I could not help the dead." He turned to me. "My God, Eroica, I truly let myself believe that it was all over. I began to curse the past for passing. Suddenly I wanted everyone to remember everything, but shouting it from the rooftops did not seem to be the most effective way of refreshing the world's memory or notifying it that I wanted to do something after all.

"Your father was impressed with my facility for languages. Essentially, I am his translator. For a year and a half I have been analyzing everything he says to foreign buyers. I spend whole days at a time with him. Sometimes he asks my views on market matters. Most of the time he trusts me. It is impossible for me to know how many tests he put me through. Every time I was contacted by someone from within the firm or someone from outside it I told him about it."

"Contacted? How do you mean, contacted?"

"People who offered me money for information."

"What kind of information?"

"All kinds: your father's personal life, tensions within the firm, who was moving up, who was moving out, who was visiting from what countries. I stopped being surprised at anything, and I assumed that anyone who asked me such questions was one of your father's spies. I reported everything to your father. As his interpreter, it is assumed by everyone that I know everything that goes on. Yet his master plan has eluded me. I must assume that he worked out his scheme long before I arrived and that his own employees in these foreign countries see to its completion. Yet I am constantly bribed. I told your father that we should keep thorough records of these incidents, that these people would obviously try to get to someone else. One day he even gave me a compliment of sorts, at least in his view of things."

"A compliment on your loyalty?"

"Yes, I suppose. He said, 'I understand your mother was German.' I told him that she was. That was one of the few times I ever saw him smile.

"He was impressed for other reasons; I work fourteen, fifteen, sixteen hours a day."

"As he does."

"Yes. Also, I have no close friends, neither men nor women. Many acquaintances, but no friends. He commented on it once. I told him that until I got ahead in life, I had no time for frivolities. He merely nodded."

"Did you know you were using one of his favorite expressions?"

"Frivolities?"

"Yes."

"I heard him use it only once, but not in that form. He made some such comment on Germany's youth, because they liked American music and American film stars."

"Why does he hate Americans?"

" 'Hate' may be the wrong word. He has contempt for them because they had the power, the force, to subjugate the world, and they didn't take it. There was a time when they could have vanquished Russia, and they didn't do it. Your father deeply believed in Germany's controlling the world. When he witnessed another country's ability to do the same thing and then throwing away its chance . . . well, what would he feel but contempt?"

He stopped talking and looked at me as he smoothed my hair off my face. His hand rested against my cheek. He again turned and looked at the sky. "It grows light. How did you get out?" I told him. "Will you have difficulty getting back in without being seen?"

"No. If you drive me to where the park turns, I am only a few minutes from the house. I have more than one way to get back in." Actually I was not sure that this was still true.

"I almost forgot something, Eroica: you have another friend. I managed to get Marta her job for her. She was a waitress in one of the plant cafés and very miserable with her position. She could not afford to have her son live with her. Some relatives in Frankfurt were taking care of the child. Now they are together, as they should be. She is an intelligent woman. You can count on her."

"What she did at the reception worried me."

He smiled. "I know. Trusting people occasionally is one of the risks we are going to have to take in the future." He paused. "Do you feel discouraged?"

"Yes."

"Don't be. We shall see each other."

"It seems impossible."

"I will not let it become impossible. I shall get word to you. My dear, beloved girl, you must make me a promise."

"What promise?"

"You must promise not to shoot anyone."

"I promise not to shoot anyone—today."

He looked at me darkly, with angry eyes. "That's not good enough."

"Jans, if we find that he is doing something horrible, and it is not illegal, we will have to kill him. If he harms you, I will shoot him. He has taken everything away from me that I loved: my brother, my mother, my dreams. There is nothing left that I love, except you. Do you think that if he harms you I will not kill him?"

"You must stop thinking about killing; it's just not natural."

"Maybe it is for me. Maybe I was born to it."

"No one is born to it."

"Then how do you explain everything that happened in the war?"

"I can't. People will be trying to explain that for years."

"Maybe Germans are natural killers, born that way."

"Nonsense. No one is born that way. People are taught everything."

"A man and woman stand beside a pit already filled with dead people and someone shoots them. Why? How can someone be taught to do that? For over three years I have wanted to kill my father. Jans, I was never taught to kill anything or anyone, nor even to want to, but I did want to. I do want to."

His expression turned to despair and he looked away to start the car. There were dark clouds on the horizon and they made me feel wretched and angry. I did not know what I had expected from this meeting with Jans, but all I got was more problems. He was too close to my father; any action on his part would be noticed at once. We could hardly keep meeting in the cemetery and making a kind of haphazard love in his car. I had to contrive some way to see him, some way that looked natural and ordinary. At the same time I had to make my father believe that I was willing and eager to become part of all his plans. I knew that the second of these was more urgent and this made me bitter and resentful: again Father was taking something away from me.

Jans drove slowly toward a spot where the park made

a right angle. There were trees and rhododendron shrubs growing there, and it was easy for me to return through the lime grove and then on to the greenhouse. He drove silently, without looking at me again. It hurt my chest to see his tight closed face. When he stopped the car, he spoke without looking at me. "Are you going to deprive me of any peace at all?"

I knew that I had to keep my options open; a hasty promise could take away choices that I believed I must never lose. "All right," I said, opening the door, "I promise not to shoot anyone tomorrow either." I slammed the door and he started off at once, very fast. I walked to the edge of the shrubbery, watching the car as long as I could. From the pain in my chest I was convinced my heart had broken and that only some fragments were left. Suddenly the car stopped and backed up, very fast. Jans got out and we ran to each other and embraced so hard I felt dizzy.

"You maniac," he said. "You wonderful, incredible maniac. Will you give me the day after tomorrow, too?"

"Yes," I said. We kissed each other, and then he looked into my eyes for a long moment. But he did not say anything; he only shook his head and got back into the car and drove away, but not as fast as before.

When I reached the back entrance to the greenhouse, I could see that all was still. Since it was Sunday, the servants would get up an hour later than usual.

The greenhouse was humid and the heat made me slightly ill, but I felt that I had better wait inside and watch a few minutes before I crept through the rose garden to the house. I walked down one of the aisles between the various bedding plants, wondering if there would be any begonias. Mother had loved them. In the summertime she filled glass bowls with the pink velvet blossoms she favored most and set them on the dining-room table.

Suddenly I stumbled over something on the path. At first I thought it was a sack, but when I regained my balance and took a second look, I realized it was a man.

He was dressed like one of Father's guests except that a black homburg covered his face. He looked exactly like a man taking a nap on a park bench. Why would a man take a nap in our greenhouse? Even as my mind rambled, I believe I knew the truth.

I dropped to my knees. Nothing in the world could have stopped me from looking at the man's face, although it took me three faltering motions of my hands before I could raise the hat. His eyes were open and he was smiling at me, at least it looked that way with his mouth pulled back slightly, showing a row of large lower teeth. To my knowledge I had never seen him before. All at once my hands began to shake uncontrollably. "Put the hat back. Put the hat back." I was talking aloud, urging myself into action. The third time I said it, it was a command, and I carefully placed the hat back over his face. "Now, get up and go to the conservatory. The door will be open." I did as I was told, leaving the greenhouse by the side door and walking without any particular concern to the small side terrace near Mother's plant room. I was right: the door was open. I went to the wicker couch and lay down among the pillows, pulling the knitted afghan over me.

"Don't go to sleep," I said.

"But I'm so tired," I whispered back.

"Never mind that. Don't go to sleep. Go upstairs to your room."

My quarrel was interrupted by a distant noise. I looked out from under the blanket. A car was moving along the narrow road. It stopped and three men got out and went into the greenhouse. I heard a second car, and I started to move toward the dining room. Suddenly I heard Father's voice and stopped, paralyzed. He must have been standing in the foyer.

"Bring the contracts to my office. I'll be there in twenty minutes. And call Deblin; we have that bunch from India here today. They're coming in at ten." There was no answer to these orders. Perhaps Father's employees only saluted him. The front door closed, and a few seconds later I heard Father's study door close also. I tore off my boots and slipped through the dining room to the foyer and up the stairs. The upper floor was in semidarkness and I stopped there in the huge, cool mezzanine, my heart racing. I heard footsteps below and dropped to my knees. Father was back in the foyer. He stopped in front of the clock, looked at it and then at his own watch. Apparently, there were no adjustments to be made. It seemed that everything was on time, on schedule, on . . . on . . . on. . . . Kneeling behind the richly carved dark balustrade, clutching my boots against my chest, I heard myself mumbling incoherently as Father left the house.

13

If I were asked what single incident most affected my thinking after my return from the clinic, I would have to say it was the way Father casually checked his watch in the foyer after he had someone dispose of the fashionably dressed dead man in our greenhouse. I was convinced that Father had murdered him. If Gerd's death had turned me murderous and Jans' black book made my dedication to killing impersonal, the homburged house guest did something quite different to me: he gave me a direction. My vague plans to kill Father were exactly that: vague. But my greenhouse acquaintance showed me a specific way to reach Father, who was, after all, first and last, a businessman.

This direction did not go into effect immediately. For two days I was ill, lying in bed, refusing food and at times unable to stop shuddering. The vision of Father going on with business as usual just after he had murdered someone revolted me horribly. A year and a half before, when I thought that I had killed Vera, I wanted to hang myself. All Father did after his crime was check his watch against the foyer clock and jauntily walk out of the house to his waiting limousine.

As I lay in bed for the next two days, my mind went through weird convolutions. The worst part of it was that I could not sleep; I was unable to let go of my shocked senses, and as exhausted as I was, my mind continued to work itself into pointless idiotic problems: the square footage of my room, the compounded images of infinity represented in one mirrored closet door reflecting another, the number of repeated wallpaper patterns which resembled small hanging cages with abstract birds resting inside them. For a time it rained and the angle at which the water struck the leaded rectangular panes brought up a new collection of trivial questions.

As the hours passed, I became increasingly frantic over my inability to sleep, and I remembered my mother's desperate pleas for just one full night's rest. Memories of my mother had been returning to me with increasing frequency and clarity since my illness. Once, when we had been in Switzerland, she had stayed in her room all day. After tea, Gerd was playing the piano when he suddenly stopped in the middle of a Chopin étude and started for the stairs. I followed him to Mother's room. He knocked hesitantly, and when there was no answer, he opened the door: Mother was not there. Gerd sat down on the disheveled bed, frowning. I asked him if we should ask our hosts to find out if she had gone somewhere. He shook his head slowly. A light snow had begun to fall and Gerd got up to open the draperies all the way. I hard him gasp and I ran to the window: Mother was standing out in the snow with her head thrown back and her arms held up toward the sky. She was wearing only a nightdress and her hair, covered with snowflakes, hung to her waist. Gerd tore open the door to the balcony and ran down the narrow wooden stairs. Together we half carried, half pulled Mother back up to the bedroom. She was moaning.

"Eroica, find some dry clothes for her." I pulled open dresser drawers and picked out a flannel nightgown. She did not help us at all. "Quick, get some towels," Gerd said. I ran into the bathroom, and when I returned with all the towels that were there, Gerd had pulled off the wet gown and covered her with the new one. "Dry her hair." I knelt on the bed behind her and dried the long wheat-colored hair. Then Gerd lifted her fully onto the bed. She did not speak to us, but her eyes were open. We covered her with blankets and an eider-down and Gerd added logs to the fire until it was roaring. For an hour we sat next to her.

"Gerd, doesn't she know she could catch cold?"

He looked at me unhappily. "She knows, Eroica, she knows," he whispered.

When Mother finally spoke, all she said was, "Gerd, are you taking care of your sister?"

"Yes, Mother," he answered. She nodded faintly and closed her eyes.

For a time we stood by the window, looking out at the falling snow. "Is she in pain, Gerd?"

He hesitated before he answered. "Perhaps not just this moment," he said.

All afternoon, images of the past returned to haunt me. Questions that I knew had always been waiting to be asked came into the foreground of my mind. "Gerd, why didn't you stay alive to take care of me? Even when you found out what Father was, why did you leave me alone with him? If you knew that Mother was trying to die, how could you leave me?" As always, I expected a voice to speak out of the heart of the universe. But all was silent.

By early evening I was hallucinating. The big-eyed dead man was sitting beside my bed talking. *"What are you going to do about me?"* The room began to fill up with people. At the foot of the bed stood a couple who both looked like Jans: the man had the same light hair and handsome features; the woman, too, had the same coloring and gentle eyes. They both had fresh blood on their necks and chests. Near them a little boy was struggling to scream, but someone was holding a hand over his mouth. My mother was crying, begging to be allowed to sleep, but I could not see her. Gerd was talking, too: *"Are you going to deprive me of any peace at all?"* At the door a man slipped a gun into his pocket. He straightened his tie, adjusted his hat, checked his watch. I tried to scream at him, but I only heard the voices of the others. The caged birds in the wallpaper began to beat their wings. I tried to scream again but heard nothing. A woman came toward me out of the shadows. She lifted my head up off the pillow and put a cup to my mouth.

"Drink this." I drank, clutching her hand which held the container. "I told your father that you had got chilled and had a slight fever. He suggested you stay in bed until you feel better."

I did not know what she gave me to drink, but in a few minutes all the people except the woman with the cup had left the room. She sat on the bed near my pillow and continued to hold up my head. "Drink all of it." I did. The liquid was warm and tasted a little like sweetened milk. Slowly she lowered my head to the pillow and took away the cup. I looked up at her; by then I recognized her voice.

"What's wrong with me, Marta?"

"You're suffering from exhaustion, but you'll sleep now. First go wash your face and empty your bladder."

I got up and at once began to fall. Marta caught me and led me to the bathroom, helping me to the toilet. After that, when I looked into the mirror, I could not believe my face: there were smears of mud all over it. Marta ran some warm water and washed it off. "Where are the clothes you wore last night?"

"I don't remember." Apparently I was well enough to lie.

"He called a little while ago and wanted to know if you were safe. Now, where are the clothes?"

"On the floor in a corner of one of the closets."

"I'll take care of them later." She led me back to the bed and helped me into it; then she sat in the chair the dead man had sat in. No, that was silly; the dead man could not have sat in the chair. The last thing I remembered before I fell asleep was Marta's watching me with a deeply penetrating concern.

On the morning of the second day I awoke with a

bitter taste in my mouth. It was still raining and I felt weak, but at least there was no crowd in my room. I contemplated getting up. I wondered where Father was. More interesting . . . where was the dead man?

There was a tray beside my bed. I considered the food on it. The cup of chocolate was cold. There was an egg, some rolls, and my favorite stewed fruit: figs in heavy syrup. Several snowdrop flowers stood in a thin crystal vase. How clear the petals were: three white outer ones and three smaller inner ones edged with green. Winter-blooming and lovely, they defied all the hardship that an indifferent sky could heap upon them. On bleak and stormy days one could see them lean with the wind.

I got out of bed and tried to ignore my feeling of dizziness—not very successfully, however, since I had to grab on to things to keep from falling. I decided to try my father's routine on waking: a cold shower. I stepped into the tub and instantly thought it was a pretty stupid way to begin the day. It was a wonder Father didn't die of pneumonia. I wrapped myself in a towel and fought the impulse to crawl back into bed. Instead I sat down and ate the figs. I was considering the cold chocolate when Lena peeked into the room. "Oh, you're up. And how do you feel?" She came in full of good cheer and bad news. "Everyone will be so glad you're better. We don't want you getting sick again. You gave us quite a little fright, but Marta said it was only a chill and would pass. I think it was a delayed reaction from the reception. Cook thinks so, too. But I can see that you're fine now and could take on another reception and sail right through it, which you may be doing quite soon. My, how exciting things are getting."

"What?"

"Wilhelm says your father is planning just that."

"What?"

Lena was making up the bed. "Oh, yes. Of course, I only got it secondhand, but that's what he says. He always likes to be first with any news."

"What, Lena? What is Father planning?"

"Well, I'm not sure it's a reception, but it's some kind of celebration. I don't think Wilhelm knows for certain, either, what it's going to be. But to hear him talk, one would think the master had asked his advice."

I was fascinated by the speed of her mouth and sat down at my desk to watch. "Is Father home?"

"Oh, my, no; he's had lunch and gone back to his office." She crossed the room with the tray and I lifted the flower vase off it and placed it on my desk. Lena smiled at me. "Marta picked the flowers for you. I thought it was very sweet of her."

"Yes, it was. Did Father say he would be home at the usual time for dinner?"

"Yes. He was quite concerned about you and told Marta to call the doctor if you weren't better today. So you see, dear child, he loves his little daughter after all. I think your long illness brought you and your father much closer together. After all, he has no one else. And it seems his business problems were only temporary. He is in excellent humor again and full of plans."

I wondered how the death of the man in the greenhouse had solved Father's problems.

While I was getting dressed, I saw my boots, mudless and polished. I looked for the other things I had worn on Sunday. They were laundered and exactly where they should be. It was time to become acquainted with Marta.

I found her in the pantry, polishing silver. She got up as I came in. "Would you like something to eat?"

I said that I would and she left at once for the kitchen. I wondered what Gerd would have thought of Marta, with her direct but rather melancholy eyes. She was quite handsome now without the bitterness in her face. Her mouth was no longer severe in its expression and she walked less stiffly than when I had first seen her. She had changed her hair, too; before, she had worn it pulled back into a tight knot on the back of her head, but now she waved it and secured it with a clasp at the nape of her neck.

When she came back into the room, she seemed surprised to see me seated at her work table. "Would you like your lunch in the music room?" Her voice, too, had a new soft quality to it; one night I heard her reading to her child and they had both laughed at something. It seemed quite incongruous that a child should laugh in our house, and I had listened to it with a feeling of regret and perhaps even envy.

"No. I would like it here. Of course, I do not wish to disturb your work."

She smiled faintly. "Here?"

"Yes. Is that all right?"

"Anything you want is all right." She put the tray down and got a lace mat from one of the drawers, arranging my lunch on it. She started to take away the polish and the silver.

"You can leave it. I would like to talk to you."

She gave me one of those quick puzzled looks people give you when they wonder what you're up to. "Of course," she said. "I'll just clear this away first." After she removed her work, she came back and stood looking at me expectantly. I felt awkward asking her if she wouldn't like to sit down. She sat opposite me and waited silently.

There didn't seem to be any point in small talk: we both knew it was raining and she obviously understood the state of my health better than I did. "I want to thank you for whatever you gave me that made me sleep. And for taking care of my boots and clothes." She nodded. "And for telling my father I had a cold or a chill or whatever you said."

She smiled. "A chill. It doesn't really mean anything, but almost everyone assumes it does, and one can recover from it at will."

I instantly wished I were as smart as she was. "My father thinks that we ought to have a housekeeper. We had one once, but she left. I don't remember why my mother never hired a new one. I was hoping that perhaps you would take on the responsibility." She sat back in the chair, her direct gaze never leaving my eyes. "We shall have to hire another maid for the kitchen—or two, if you think it's necessary."

"One should be sufficient. We can get temporary help if there's to be more entertaining."

"That sounds reasonable. We should make some changes in the living arrangements, too. The things in the large storage area off your room can be moved into the carriage house. There is space for five cars and not all of the area is being used. That way you will have two rooms. The new maid you hire will have to live out."

"They frequently prefer to, these days anyway."

I was hoping that I would not run out of things to talk about, but, of course, I did. But she was smarter than I and knew when to pick up the disappearing thread of the discussion before it slipped away altogether. "Will you notify the others yourself?" she asked.

That had to take a yes answer. "I'll do that today."

"And would you like me to take the incoming calls?" Her serious, almost formal tone had not changed at all.

"Yes, that would be right, wouldn't it?"

"I think so."

Her expression altered slightly from its calm one to a certain questioning gaze. "Will your father agree to these changes?"

I answered without any consideration. "Yes, Mrs. Henneg, he will." At my calling her by her formal name, a curious contract was abruptly sealed. She smiled at me and in the intelligence of her solemn eyes I found a bond. It was a high moment for me: I had never looked into the person of another woman before. I had touched something which was both strange and familiar, comforting and filling.

There seemed to be nothing more to say; that is, I

could think of nothing more. But she added something. "There is an opinion that you should learn to drive a car."

Her statement caught me off guard; I had turned to my forgotten lunch. "My father—did he say so?"

"No." She got up and for the merest moment she hesitated, watching me closely until she saw that I understood.

After lunch I spent the remainder of the day gently notifying everyone of the changes in our household. When I finally got around to Wilhelm, with whom I felt gentleness was a wasted effort, he listened with a sullen expression while he polished the inside of the car, spitting occasionally out of the open door onto the cement floor. "Something else: please clear out the storage area next to Mrs. Henneg's room. After that, there are some pieces of furniture from upstairs that I want moved into her room." He glanced at me with obvious vexation.

"Are these your father's orders?"

"I'm sure you know the answer to that." This had to be one of the great ploys in dealing with men like Wilhelm and Karl. "And Wilhelm, perhaps tomorrow you can teach me how to drive." The cigarette which he had just lit almost fell out of his mouth. As I retreated to my room, I decided that I had come a long way since I threw the keys to the Mercedes into the storm drain. I did not know how far until Father and I sat across the table from each other at dinner that night and he asked after my health.

"Eroica, you're looking very well. One of the women said something about a chill, but it must have been a very small one."

I smiled back at him. Not so small, Father. It wore a black overcoat and had a grin hanging on its dead face. Whatever did you do with it?

"I'm in excellent health, Father. I may even decide never to be sick again."

"That's what I like to hear." He ate vigorously.

I decided to take advantage of his high spirits. "Father, I want to learn how to drive."

He looked up from his plate. "A splendid idea." He was positively glowing. The idea wasn't all that splendid.

He continued eating. I watched his finely sculptured hands, with their long fingers and clearly mooned nails. In that moment, as I was preparing some precise words for my father, I was actually thinking of something quite different: across the table from me sat a killer who had my hands.

"And, Father"—I spoke carefully—"I want to learn about business; I mean, the firm. I want to work with you in whatever way I can."

His reaction almost knocked me out of my chair. An expression of dynamic energy came into his face; he seemed to radiate force and heat. I held his gaze, knowing that I must not break under that fierce concentration. I saw flames, heard screams; saw people suffocating in agony; my brother's dead face; my mother's hollow, unseeing eyes; Jans, crushed in concrete. I held on. Years passed, telescoped into rage and violence. Around me the world was spinning. The sun shone directly into my eyes as my body was disintegrating, dissolving, swept away, ashes, dust, nothing. I held on.

Then only the candles were burning, three quite ordinary candles, their flames straight and golden in that enormous room where my father had passed through my soul without touching it. He was smiling, then laughing, a rich, low laughter, his eyes drawn away from mine, and directed toward his wine glass. "Eroica, take up your glass." I moved, amazed to discover that I still had a hand which could react to a command.

"To us," he said, hissing the words electrically.

I drank, watching the fierce pleasure in his eyes. The bitter burning in my throat was no fault of the wine.

He launched into his plans at once, his face animated. "Eroica, since the night of the reception a special idea has been forming itself in my mind, and now you make a suggestion that complements my idea perfectly. There is no reason at all that a daughter of mine should not in time carry on with my work. You are of my blood, which runs deep and pure and strong. The accident of birth that made you a woman is of no consequence if that woman thinks as a man does. And this, I have felt for some time now, is your true nature. It is strength that counts and the will to use that strength where it will be most effective. The most efficient use of all of our faculties is in one area alone: to gain, to preserve and to exercise power. Nothing is second to power, Eroica. All nations hunger for it; if they do not, they decay, or they are swept under by nations that have it. Those who have gained it by superior will and determination have the right to use it. More than that: they have the duty to use it." He stopped, his wild eyes gloating.

I could not stop staring at him. He emanated power, walked in its blazing reality like some demon who knew the ultimate truth of Man's black heart.

All I had was my little act; my pretense at excitement and overwhelming admiration. There was one truth I was unable to deny: he fascinated me.

Father was still speaking. "But now—that aside for the moment—my plan." His face was calmer, his eyes showing a glint of enigmatic humor. "Sometime this year, Eroica. we are going to celebrate your birthday."

"My birthday?"

"Yes. We have somewhat neglected such celebrations the last few years, and I believe the time has come for you to have a party." I was confused; my birthday was in the spring. I did not have to remind him of this, since he was giving me an acceptable explanation of this chronological discrepancy. "There is no reason one can't celebrate one's birthday whenever one wishes." That seemed reasonable, and I was rather touched that he wanted to give me a party, although I did not want one.

"We'll celebrate it in the fall, and it will be a very special occasion." He smiled at me again and drained his glass. "On the ninth of November, you will become twenty-one."

14

My father rarely gave reasons for the things he did; it probably never dawned on a man in his position to have to answer to anyone. And the world in which he was known apparently concurred with this view. Thus when Father did give me a reason for anything it was generally because some whim moved him to it at the time. Perhaps it was the expression on my face or the fact that I had appeared to close ranks with him that caused him to comment further on the subject of my twenty-first birthday. "For our purposes it is better that the world believe you are of age."

As Father said this, it occurred to me that if Gerd were alive, he would have been of age. This sudden awareness remained in my mind like blunted yet persistent pain as my father continued to speak of the future, liberally using such words as "we" and "us" and "our." It became obvious to me that Father trusted me, and I believed that it was only a matter of time before he would reveal all his plans to me.

In my simple view of things my method of destroying Father was clear: once I discovered what he was up to, I would tell Jans, who would disclose the whole horrible scheme to the police, and Father would be tried and executed for the criminal that he was. The world could breathe a big sigh of relief, Israel would not be crushed, and Jans would be a hero.

There would be no question this time as to what was criminal and what was merely immoral. Perfecting gas chambers may not have been illegal, but certainly a murdered man in a greenhouse was not something the law could overlook.

Jans was right: it would be ridiculous for me to kill Father myself when the authorities would do it for me. The thing to do was to acquaint Jans with the greenhouse murder as soon as I could. But, for the moment, listening carefully to Father as he talked on about my coming of age was of the greatest importance. I concurred easily with this new idea after the first shock settled. Why shouldn't I be twenty-one, or thirty-one, or a hundred and one? "Is that old enough, Father?"

"For our purposes, yes." He looked wonderfully satisfied, his handsome face mellow with its warm smile.

Perhaps if I had been a hundred and one, I might have asked him what, exactly, "our purposes" were. But I believed that I should move with caution; a man who trusted no one couldn't be rushed. "The first thing we must do, Eroica, is prepare you for your entrance on the stage, as the saying goes."

"Yes, Father." Poor poetic Father didn't know how prepared I was.

"Now then, in the next few months it will be made known that there will be no change in von Heyditch policy, regardless of any untimely event. The policies of the leadership will go on as usual."

"Untimely event?"

"Eroica, I anticipate a long life, perhaps another twenty, thirty years. However, sooner or later there will be those who will begin to consider my age. Also, I am not without enemies. There are those who think there is no heir in this house, and this view must be erased entirely." He paused and gave me the most loving look I had ever had from him. "You have become a comfort to me, Eroica."

I gave him a shy smile.

"You have some fine qualities. Few women have the

ability to make good decisions at the right time. Wilhelm tells me you have reorganized the household. After reviewing your decisions, I quite agree with your arrangements. May I assume, though, that they are now stabilized?" His attitude was pure indulgence.

"Yes, Father. I trust Mrs. Henneg completely. She is capable of more than scraping plates."

"She impressed me the same way, but never trust anyone completely. Always keep a private reservation."

"I shall remember that, Father." Behind the immediate coloring of his eyes I saw something that looked like ancient stone, impervious, indecipherable.

He paused a moment, then said, "Wilhelm told me that you had spoken to him about learning to drive. But he objects to being your teacher. I am inclined to agree with him."

"As a chauffeur, wouldn't he be an expert?"

"I think someone else would be better, Eroica. Perhaps a woman." I wondered if Father was concerned about another attack upon my virtue. "What about Mrs. Henneg?" asked Father. "Does she drive?" It seemed like a straightforward question; yet, why Mrs. Henneg?

"I don't know," I said.

"You get on with her, don't you?"

"Yes."

"Well, let's find out." He pressed the buzzer on the floor with his foot, without even glancing down. I heard it, a faint motor sound in the kitchen. Almost at once, Marta came into the dining room carrying an empty tray. She did not look at me at all as she picked up our plates, her face intent on her work. Father watched her for a few moments and then asked her if she knew how to drive.

"Yes, sir."

"Good. You are licensed?"

"Yes, sir."

"Then, when time permits, you will teach my daughter. The park roads will be an ideal place to begin."

"Yes, sir."

"You will not move into traffic until I tell you to. I shall have a car brought around for you tomorrow; then you may start whenever the conditions are best."

With our dishes on her tray, and waiting to leave, Marta again said, "Yes, sir."

Dinner finally ended with Father's making a number of somewhat vague plans and uttering a few pleasantries. "In a little while I shall arrange a visit for you to my offices. Then, a little later, I'll have a guide for you. You will be able to visit the various concerns in the local area and become acquainted with our products. The most important thing is for you to be seen. Everyone must know who you are. Perhaps you should consider a new wardrobe for this undertaking."

"Yes, Father."

"Good. Then make your own plans about that. You seem to have a knack for it, so I'll not concern myself. But remember who you are." He had to say it! Gerd once said that this particular statement of his, about remembering who we were, was computerized into Father's brain and that he was no longer even aware that he said it. "You must know, Eroica, that you are very attractive and that you carry yourself well. This pleases me."

"Thank you, Father."

I thought that was the end of it, but as we got up from the table, he added two more comments. "After your birthday, we shall have to think in terms of a mate for you; a family like ours must never be allowed to end." I was too stunned to say "Yes, Father," but perhaps he was not listening to me anyway, since he went on. "We must have grandsons." He left me standing at the far side of the dining room, momentarily paralyzed. At least one thing was clear: the plural referred to his royal self.

In my room, I sat in the dark and listened to the roar in my head. A mate! He wanted to breed me. The old need to murder returned. In the sick darkness I visualized his death. I saw the yellow teeth of my old rat community in the wine cellar take pieces out of him. Slowly, dear friends, only a nibble at a time. I listened for his screams: he was in a big cage, and each day I let in a few hungry rats. One of them nipped off the end of his nose, and I began to laugh. Why, Father, you've lost your handsome profile. You really look very funny without a nose. I laughed and laughed until the door opened and Lena stood silhouetted in the light from her room.

"What is it?" She came in and turned on the lamp beside my chair. I wanted to shrink away from her, but the ordeal with Father had exhausted me and I felt numbed and sick. I was becoming aware that my composed pretense in his presence was a deadly strain on my nerves. In the region between my loathing of him and my pretended love for him, I balanced my narrow life: in one moment, shuddering with fear; in the next, trembling with self-hatred.

"Are you all right?" Lena's face was full of concern.

I took a deep breath. "Of course. I just remembered a joke." I smiled and patted her hand. "But not a very nice one. I'm sorry I awakened you."

"Dear child, I was not asleep at all." She still had a worried expression in her eyes.

"Lena, could I ask something of you? I know it's late, but I would be very grateful to you."

"Why, anything at all, dear girl." Her face began to settle down.

"Would you brush my hair? You are so good at it and it makes me wonderfully sleepy."

As I saw my face in the mirror, with Lena sitting on a chair behind me, brushing my hair and chatting constantly, I tried to think of nothing. But Father's last words kept echoing out of the walls. I refused to believe that my marrying and having children was my only involvement in his plans. I was convinced that ultimately he would reveal all his secret criminal machinations to me. It could not be otherwise. If he was, in fact, making sure that his policies would continue if—my mind snagged on the word—*when* he died, he would have to tell them to someone, and I was his only heir.

I knew that these ideas did not necessarily follow logically. More and more I thought of that night when the departing men in the foyer had applauded my father's strange speech on some future victory which the world would commend. Obviously there were others who already knew of Father's plans, and as far as I knew, these men with their briefcases were scattered around the world—waiting.

Yet, they took their orders from Father, and if he were not alive to give orders, who would give them? Gerd had once said that Father trusted no one. The more I considered our new relationship, the more I believed that Father had come to trust me. I did not have to be of age to marry; I could have married with his consent at any time.

"Am I pulling too hard?" Lena had stopped brushing.

"No, it feels lovely. Why do you ask?"

"You were shaking your head. I thought perhaps I was too rough."

"No, not at all. Do you mind doing it some more?"

"Listen to her: do I mind. For my dear girl I'll do anything. And one day I'll be taking care of your babies and brushing their hair."

That was definitely the wrong subject. "Were you ever married, Lena?"

"Oh, yes—a good, gentle man." She was blinking rapidly.

"You don't have to talk about it if you don't want to. I don't want to pry."

"You're not prying, child. It's all history now. He died in the war, in North Africa. His commanding officer sent me a lovely letter. I was grateful for that."

"You loved him?"

"My, yes. He wasn't what people called handsome; but then, I wasn't pretty, so we were suited."

"You had no children?"

"No, the war came so soon after we were married. I was in service with a family who gave me little time off. I should have quit, but we hoped to buy a small farm when the war was over. Then, everything was wasted; he was dead. No children. No farm." She was weeping. "You were the only child I was ever allowed to care for." Her shoulders shook, "When you touched my hand at the hospital and the master said I was to take care of you, you can't know what it meant to me."

I took the brush out of her hand and put my arms around her, not knowing what to say. After a time she was back in good spirits, wiping away her tears and telling me that I had given her something that she once thought she would never have. I wanted to tell her that I had used the key which she had left in a sweater pocket for me long ago, but I didn't. I was still my father's child: I was keeping a reservation.

After Lena returned to her own room, I listened to the cold spring wind that swept through the Ruhr and up the Rhine like an enraged Valkyrie. For a time I paced the floor, unable to calm the violent rancor that seethed inside me like a suppressed scream. How dare Father even think that he could pick my future husband for me. I imagined his choice: a cold, loveless brute commissioned to fulfill a contract.

A question from the clinic came back to me. "Can she produce?" Why hadn't I considered that question before? Father always spoke in the language of business; he wanted business to go on as usual. Anyone else would have asked, "Can she bear a child?" Vera's words about my mother's miscarriages suddenly returned to me, and for the first time in my life I saw my father as a sexual person; that is, for the first time I contemplated the fact that Father had genitals, that he could cover a woman, enter her, experience a brief spasm and fall away sated. Could I really give that the same name as Jans' and my tender lovemaking? No! I envisioned Father in the act: he was swinish, cruel and quick, entering my mother's bedroom, where I saw her shivering and terrified, and taking her without a word, his huge penis plunging into her, ripping her, tearing her. Transient madness danced in my rage. No, Father, you'll not force me into that. Convulsively I struck at the brutal plunderer my father had sent to my bed. My gripping fist slashed away, the knife gleaming, then bloody. He screamed and I looked toward his face: Father!

It was almost an hour later before I had the strength to go downstairs. A solitary lamp burned in the drawing room. Father must still be in his study. Beyond the kitchen were the servants' quarters, and to my relief a thin light came from under Marta's door in the little hallway. She did not seem particularly surprised to see me, but she quickly closed the door to the other room, where her child slept, and motioned me to sit.

I felt my own awkwardness deeply as I stood before her, not knowing how to begin. This was not a cute act in front of Lena; I was about to break a major rule: I was going to trust someone completely.

She sat in the desk chair, smiling gently, and waited for me to speak.

"I have to see him," I said. She nodded. "Perhaps you could drive me somewhere during the lesson."

"No. We will probably be watched constantly while I teach you to drive." I must have appeared stunned at this idea, because she smiled and said, "Didn't you think of that?"

"No."

"The car may even have a listening device in it. Your father does not intend for anything to happen to you again."

"Then it's impossible. Everything is impossible."

"No, just difficult. The best thing to do is the obvious. Do whatever you had planned for this week."

"I have to shop for some clothes, some suits. Father has plans for me to visit his office. Usually when I go shopping, Wilhelm drives us into the city."

"Does he follow you around?"

"Yes."

"Does he come into the shops?"

"No, he waits for us outside."

"Are there any particular shops you prefer?"

"Not any more. I used to go to certain ones that Father had on a list, but now I go where I want. If I see something I like in a window, I go there."

"How do you pay for what you buy?"

"I have them call a number that Father gave me."

"Do you ever pay anyone directly?"

"Yes, for little things."

"Would you like to go shopping tomorrow? Lena's arthritis is very bad when it rains. I'll go with you instead."

"Oh! And I asked her to brush my hair. I didn't think."

"I'm sure she understands. If it is raining while you are in the shops, where does Wilhelm go?"

"He goes to a restaurant. Usually he drinks beer. But he never goes very far away and he always tells us where he is going to be."

"Does he carry a gun?"

This was another thing I had not thought about. "I don't know."

"He probably does," she said casually. "Well, we'll both go shopping tomorrow. We need new linens for the house. Things have not been kept up very well."

"I guess no one's really been in charge since Vera."

Marta nodded slowly, turning to the papers on the desk. "I've been making lists of things that have to be brought up to date. Our shopping may take quite a long time tomorrow." She went on, detailing various problems having to do with household matters. I wondered what Jans was doing just at that moment. It seemed as though months had passed since I saw him drive away from the park. Marta had stopped talking and was looking at me with a somewhat amused expression on her face. "I can see that the house linen interests you deeply."

"I'm sorry, I should have been listening."

After a little silence she said, "You are a young girl. You have a right to dream. I cannot make you any promises, but there is a very good chance that you will see him tomorrow." She stood up. "Why don't you go dream about that."

I made my way back through the darkened rooms. The lamp was still lit outside Father's study. At the top of the stairs I listened to the house. I heard sighs and moans, whispering and weeping; voices, muffled and muted, called, beseeched, pleaded. My father's house. My mad father's madhouse! I stood with my back to the balustrade and looked into the gloom of the two long halls that stretched away from the mezzanine. In that uncertain darkness, with the voices of the dead reaching for me, a sudden wave of terrible fear washed over me: if Father trusted no one, then he did not trust Jans. Possibly, that very moment, Jans was being watched, followed, denounced. I rushed to my room and lay trembling on the bed. Outside the wind beat against the shutters like demons demanding entrance.

For a long time I shivered at the fearful possibilities, and when at last I slept, it was not Jans I dreamed of. I was with Mother and Gerd in a compartment on a train. In my sleep I dreamed I had awakened to find Mother sitting next to me, dying. I screamed to Gerd to stop her, but he did nothing, only stared out of the window. When I pulled at his shoulder, he turned toward me, and I saw that it was not Gerd's face at all.

The next morning we left Wilhelm outside the couturiere's. He grumbled when we could not tell him how long we'd be, but he finally agreed to wait in a small Brauhaus across the street.

"Very well, then, we shall send someone for you when we are ready." When he was gone, Marta turned to me. "You have an hour and a half to buy what you need. Then we shall have lunch at the American hotel. Wilhelm can eat wherever he wants, and I shall tell him that we are sorry to inconvenience him but that we must shop for some household goods this afternoon. Things have worked out better than expected; your father is not going home for lunch." I nodded to all this. It was very pleasant to be with Marta.

I bought five suits. Marta gave her opinion when I asked her for it. Once, she complimented me. "You have excellent taste." I said that it was easy to have good taste when the cost did not count. But she demurred. "Some of the wealthiest women in the world look frumpish because they have no taste. Their money does not help."

When Wilhelm dropped us at the hotel, Marta turned to me, looking troubled. "Do you have any extra money with you so he can have a nice lunch somewhere?"

I took out enough for twenty lunches. "Will this be enough, Wilhelm?" I asked hesitantly.

His eyes glinted. "Yeah, that's probably enough." He took the money and shoved it into his pocket.

Marta was watching without apparent interest and told him just to pick us up in two hours. When he drove off, a sly leer on his face, she said, "The dirty cheat. You gave him half a week's wages."

We walked into the lobby, past the desk, to the elevators, and pressed the button for the seventh floor. When we got off the elevator, she turned to me. "I'm leaving you here now. I shall be in the coffee shop when you are ready to leave. Pay no attention to anyone. Act like a hotel guest. Remember that you have only two hours and Wilhelm will be on time. The room number is seven-fifty-seven." She got on a down elevator and I was left alone in the hall.

In front of seven-fifty-seven, I put out my hand to knock, but the door opened before I touched it. Jans held his arms out to me and I fell into them with such relief to see him well that all my appalling fears vanished. He held me tightly against his chest, kissing my face and hair in a lovely tender way that made me forget everything.

"Eroica, I had some lunch sent up." We both looked

toward the table where silver covered dishes were elegantly arranged beside plates and wine glasses. I looked at the bed. Americans certainly liked big beds.

"Could we make love first?"

"I like your priorities," he said laughing. I decided to think that over later. We began to take our clothes off, and he looked so beautiful I couldn't stop myself from touching him. He brought his arms around me to unhook my brassiere, and with his warm, wonderfully scented shoulder touching my mouth I really wanted more than anything else to taste him. I was still standing up, but my legs didn't seem to know about it and I had the odd sensation that all the feeling in my arms and legs had converged to that one place between my legs which was waiting for the touch of his fingers. Vaguely I remember his taking off my underpants and bringing me down on the bed very slowly, but he didn't touch me, at least not when I expected him to. He touched me with his tongue instead, and it seemed only a little time before I became a part of the immense universe and, upon returning, discovered to my dismay that I was crying. He didn't pay any attention to that, but was fully on the bed by then and kneeling between my legs, bringing his penis down to where his tongue had been, using it in the same caressing way, and in a minute I went right out into space again.

I think I came back before he did, because his penis was inside of me and he was clutching my shoulders and making a long low sound in his throat, which he stopped by biting my neck, but not so it hurt. It was lovely listening to him and feeling him sort of settle down as though he had been flying and was just then landing. I thought of some water birds I had seen somewhere coming over a lake very fast with eloquent wings, which seemed to dip suddenly and then to settle on the water with a kind of shiver before they quieted altogether.

In the stillness that followed he brushed his mouth back and forth against the side of my neck. I had my arms around him and it felt lovely to stroke his back, particularly the center, which dipped between his shoulders and ran to his waist, where it rose again to make the sensuous line of his buttocks.

Jans moved, rising above me and slipping away to lie at my side. He glanced at his wristwatch, but I placed my hand over it. "Eroica, we have to think of the time."

"I don't want to think of the time. I want to stay here forever."

He raised himself up on his elbows. "I know," he said. "I know what you want. But we have other demands upon us." He was right, of course, but I still didn't like it.

He sat on the edge of the bed and became serious. "Now, listen to me, Eroica. We have used up almost a third of our time. We must get dressed."

"I don't want to get dressed."

He picked up all my clothes and placed them beside me on the bed; then he began to get dressed. There didn't seem to be any choice in the matter, although I grumbled about it, but he only seemed to be amused at my protests. When we were both dressed, he asked me if anything further had happened on Sunday. We were seated at the table, picking at the lunch. The vichyssoise was not bad.

"After I left you at the park, I found a dead man in our greenhouse."

Jans started to rise out of the chair but sat back down, a look of horror on his face. "A dead man?"

"Yes."

"What did he look like?"

"Dead."

"Eroica, please!"

"He looked like one of Father's friends."

"Then, you had seen him before?"

"No."

"Then how do you know he was one of your father's friends?"

"All my father's friends look alike. They wear the

same kind of clothes and hats and they all walk the same way."

"They walk the same way?"

"Like someone put too much starch in their shirts, or they had a board of some kind holding them up straight. It's hard to describe."

"You're doing very well. What happened to the dead man?"

"Some men came and took him away."

"No. I mean, was he shot, or stabbed, or hit with something?"

"I don't know." Thinking back to that morning, I realized I had not spent any time looking for bullet holes or knife wounds in him. I remembered then that I had not seen any blood, and I told Jans this.

Jans got up and went to his raincoat, from which he took a folded newspaper that was stuck in the pocket. "Is this the man?"

There he was, staring off the newspaper with an even bigger smile squashed all over his face. "Yes. Only he was wearing a homburg over his fat face when I met him."

"He was cremated yesterday. A special service is being held for him today. That's where your father is now. The man is named Friedrich Hauser; he was found dead in his bed early Sunday afternoon by his housekeeper. It says here that he died of a heart attack sometime Sunday night."

"I wonder if he was wearing his hat."

"I suspect he was wearing pajamas."

"Why did my father kill him?"

"What makes you think your father killed him?"

"Doesn't he kill everyone—sooner or later?"

Jans started to say something, but stopped. He poured some white wine into our glasses. "You must not lose heart, Eroica."

Lose heart! I was living with a madman who just took another three years away from my life and who wanted to breed me with some huge monster, and I was not supposed to lose heart. But Jans had such an anxious look on his face I couldn't bear to say these things to him. I nodded and decided that if it were possible to "keep heart," or whatever was the opposite of losing it, I would certainly try to do that. "If the man wasn't murdered, why didn't my father just call a doctor or an ambulance? Why did they put him on the floor of the greenhouse?"

"I don't know, Eroica. But there is something I can tell you: articles have been appearing in the foreign press suggesting that there will be several new indictments brought against a number of suspected war criminals. No names have been mentioned by the media, but in the capital there was quiet talk of some of these men. Friedrich Hauser was one of them. It's possible that Hauser's trial might have brought out evidence against your father."

He paused a moment, frowning, "It's strange that no one seems to know where your father was during the last days of the war. He disappeared for a time and then reappeared in a hospital, suffering from shock and a head injury. Most of his records, his vital business records, were missing. People close to him vanished by the time the postwar trials at Nürnberg were under way. It was believed that your father might be tried for having used slave labor, but at the time there were bigger fish on trial before him.

"The trials dragged; the public lost interest. And, after all, industrialists created jobs. Then, an incredible blunder by the Russians: the Berlin blockade. After that it was inevitable that alliances would shift. The Allies needed a strong Germany to keep Russia in her place, so they had to help put their old enemy back on her feet. Result: European Recovery Program. By the middle of 1949, Germany had its own Allied-sanctioned government in fascinating Bonn"—he smiled—"and the Russians, never trusted by the other Allies and never trusting anybody, become the enemy.

"Your father had been running his business from various places. He had foreign investments. No one knows their total extent, but he was obviously not short of money. What he did not have was the right to rebuild his factories on any great scale. The Allies had intended to turn Germany into a big peaceful farm, with happy farmers singing in the fields. It was absurd. It was impossible. Perhaps Siegfried's sword couldn't be reforged, but the anvil was definitely needed.

"Neighboring nations also needed the Germans back in business: foreign ports counted on German shipping; foreign merchants needed this huge hungry customer; the whole continent of which Germany is the heart, at least geographically, needed her coal, her steel, her insatiable vitality, her extraordinary efficiency, and always her genius for research, for making a good product and making it quickly. I sometimes think the Germans invented the work ethic.

"Then, in 1950, war broke out in Korea. The Americans took a new view of trying industrialists, and your father, although never entirely forgotten in another context, was needed to rebuild his factories. They left him alone to do just that. Your father's blueprints for peacetime machinery, his models for nonmilitary tools, were in various neutral countries where he controlled small unimportant-appearing plants. These untroubled neutrals were above it all; they took their cut and kept silent. Your father's other great asset—his skilled workers, who were scattered across a ruined and chaotic nation—hitchhiked home. It was business as usual, twenty-four hours a day. Only two things had changed: the government, and the products. To von Heyditch these were not even changes. He was a businessman: his concern was the marketplace for his goods, whatever they were. And he had one—the world." Jans took a deep breath. "That's where we are today."

"But why did he need to play games? Why the pretense of a secret organization?"

"That, my dear Eroica, is the other side of the moon."

"And the dead man?"

"An urn of ashes today, and being mourned by some old friends." He paused and lit a cigarette. "It is possible that Hauser could have placed your father at a given spot at the end of the war. It was months before anyone knew who the injured derelict was in the hospital; he had been brought in wearing beggar's clothes. Your mother was at Regensburg with her newborn son. She was unable to tell the authorities anything about her husband's whereabouts."

"How do you know all this?"

"There are interested organizations which have files on Nazi-party members. If your father knew of my recent contacts with them, I would be dead."

"Would my father's whereabouts at the end of the war convict him of anything?"

"Answer unknown. But an interesting question. On May seventh in 1945 General Jodl signed the unconditional surrender at American headquarters at Rheims. Hitler had committed suicide on April thirtieth. SS men vanished into the ruins of a devastated Germany. Anonymity was the order of the day."

"Near that time—I don't know exactly when—my father was in Bergen."

"Bergen?" Jans stood up. "Bergen? What was he doing there?" He had a deep frown on his face.

"I don't know; I wasn't born yet."

"Then how did you know where he was?" I gave him a brief account of the rat business, telling him also what Vera had said about Father's having to help bury dead prisoners. Jans looked at me and rubbed his forehead furiously. "The British freed Belsen on April fourteenth of 1945. Cologne had fallen to the Allies in the early part of March, about the same time that the Americans crossed the Rhine at Remagen. At that time Cologne was in ruins and your father among the missing.

"There must have been quite a few fires on the home front not caused by Allied bombing. The lack of records—who ordered what to be done to whom—later became a major block in winning convictions."

"What about the victims, people who were still alive?"

"The trials of the industrialists did not start immediately, Eroica, although plans for them date back to 1942. Germany was starving and freezing to death in that first winter after the surrender, and she had plenty of company. Somebody once said that the currency then in central Europe was American candy bars. Neither the Nazis nor their ex-prisoners had enough to eat. The victims wanted out of the horror as quickly as possible and were more interested in emigrating than in giving evidence. There was a scarcity of everything except suffering and death, and the bad smell of both. Victims vanished from the cities where they had been held, some shuffled into displaced-person camps and from there out of Germany. Only recently are some of them being found, and some of these are now willing to testify."

"Then my father was never tried for anything?"

"No. His semisecret cabal was like a private men's club, and he was one of the first who refused to produce anything but peacetime goods, even after the restrictions were removed. When others were ultimately allowed to return to the production of munitions, Von Heyditch Industries declined. Your father was once reported to have said, 'The trains must run on time so men can get to work.' He produced rails, locomotive parts, barges, roadbed equipment—anything to get the country moving again. It was a sound position to take, and he knew it. No one could fault him for it. His private life since the war has been unimpeachable.

"There were many who were not tried. They reclaimed their property when the times permitted it, and they are respected citizens today. They will live out their lives without a backward glance at all that unpleasantness. They will show pictures of their grandchildren to people much like themselves and they will die peacefully in their beds and memorials will be held for them. The snow will return each year to fall on their graves in exactly the same way that it does on the graves of the murdered dead."

He lit a cigarette. "Are you sure the name of the place was Bergen?" He turned to look at me. "Eroica, what is it?"

"My father is also waiting for grandchildren. He wants me to marry after my twenty-first birthday."

"That's quite a wait for your father."

"He's planning on living a long time." I must have begun to shiver, because Jans was staring at me very hard.

"There's something else, isn't there? Eroica, what do you want to tell me?"

I shook my head. "Nothing."

He leaned toward me slightly. "Is he planning on sending you away—to school, perhaps?"

"No. I'm going to visit his offices and some of the plants. He wants me to be noticed. He is looking for a mate for me."

"Now?"

"I think so."

"Well, he *has* a reputation for planning well in advance, but this seems somewhat premature."

"No, it's my birthday that is going to be premature."

"I don't understand that."

"I don't understand it completely either, but he wants me to become twenty-one years old in November."

"Which November?"

"The coming one, this year."

"That black-hearted bastard!"

"He assured me that he would find the right man. He wants grandsons, a lot of them." Jans was staring at me with wild rage, and I realized that with that statement I had jeopardized his life. How would he act around Father now! I stood up and walked around the table to him. "Jans, I am never going to marry anyone my father picks for me, so you don't have to worry about that." I took his hands and held them in mine. "Anyway, he doesn't realize it, but making me twenty-one releases me from his custody. Then I can choose for myself. Once he has changed all the records and has his big celebration, we can leave for Mother's estate. We'll be safe. He won't be able to do anything about it . . . about us." Jans was looking at me with sadness. "Please say you'll come with me to Regensburg," I said. He was shaking his head slowly. "Oh, Jans, you'll act differently around him and give yourself away."

"Eroica, I've lasted this long. I'm very careful."

"I'm so afraid for you. Can't we just leave Germany?"

"No, Eroica, we are bound to it now. Do you think we have choices the way other people do who don't happen to like the climate?" He hesitated. "Eroica, I cannot leave Germany, or even Cologne, and least of all VHI." His expression was dark and desperate. "I'm committed now. I have to know what he is up to."

"Maybe he isn't up to anything."

"You know better than that."

"Don't you see how afraid for you I am?"

"Don't worry about me. Realize that you are in danger yourself."

I thought about that briefly. "No. I never feel endangered around Father—only powerless."

He held my hands tightly. "Look, I have been working on a theory that is still in the preposterous stage, but daily it gathers possibilities. It needs more research, and this takes time."

"What is it? Is it something that will get him into trouble if the police find out about it? Tell me."

"Eroica, I can't discuss it yet."

"It's not something illegal, is it?"

He hesitated. "I don't know."

"You do know. You don't trust me." I began to feel a black resentment toward him.

"Of course I don't trust you," he said angrily. "How can I trust you when you threaten to go around shooting someone? You're very dangerous." He stopped, but his anger was still there. "Whose idea was it that you visit the plants?"

"Mine."

"I should have known. What did you expect to find? Secret documents and a network of sinister-looking people doing evil things? Eroica, your father's factories are run by cool-headed executives who admire him, staffed by skilled and industrious workers who love him. Yes, Eroica—who *love* him. He pays well, gives fringe benefits, and has a fine pension program; in return he gets hard work and absolute loyalty.

"Why do you think he accepts your idea for visiting the plants?" He didn't wait for an answer. "He wants you to be seen by his staff, his workers, his competitors, his enemies—in fact, everyone. He wants it known that there is an heir who will follow him, someone who will continue his aims when he is no longer there. What do you think the ridged-wheel diamond was for?

"And there is another thing: your father's expectations are also the workers' expectations. They too want to see you get married and bear sons. That is your position in life."

"You sound like you agree with him."

"Eroica, how could I agree with him? I just don't want you asking odd questions of the guides your father is going to supply you with at the plants. I want you to do exactly as he expects."

"Jans, just how long do you expect me to *act* my life?" I had moved away from him because I didn't want to do anything stupid, like hit him again.

"Right now, Eroica, our lives are only as good as we can pretend them."

"I can't pretend mine anymore."

"Yes, you can. You were going to do just that until November, weren't you?"

I knew that he was right, but it was difficult to control my rage. "Then I am only some kind of container for everybody's use."

"Stop that." Jans came to me quickly. "You won't be able to help yourself if you give in to that. When I first met you, Eroica, the thing about you that I found most fascinating was that you did not give in to self-pity. You wept when you told me of your brother's death, but not with grief. You were enraged. I knew then that you would not rest until you knew the reason for his death. Are you going to stop now?"

"I already know."

"I don't think you do. Your brother did not kill himself for a simple reason."

"He killed himself because of what Father did in the war."

"No."

I was stunned, and looked up at him quickly to see his expression. He had spoken softly, but his eyes had a desperate look in them. "Eroica, he survived that," he said in a near whisper.

"No. I don't believe you. Gerd couldn't bear what Father had done. He found out the truth about the war and Father's part in all the killings. He found out about the medal and Father tried to explain it, but Gerd couldn't bear it. He couldn't. That's why he's dead. He didn't survive it." I went on in this way, outraged that Jans couldn't see the obvious. But he only kept shaking his head slowly, trying to calm me down by putting his hands on my shoulders, but I shook them off. "What reason, then?"

He lowered his head, hiding his eyes. "I cannot tell you that." Again his voice was just above a whisper.

"You must." I grasped his hand and felt him shiver. "You must. You must!" I was screaming at him.

He faced me then, pain and fear in his eyes, but his face set, his mouth tight. "No. You will have to trust me."

"I cannot trust you if you won't tell me that." I released his hand. "I'll hate you if you won't tell me that."

"Please, Eroica, don't make it worse for me. I can't tell you yet, and this is very hard for me. You would—" He started to say something more, but stopped abruptly.

"I would what? What?"

Again he shook his head and motioned toward me with encircling arms. "I'm sorry. You'll have to trust me."

I backed away from him. "I don't trust you if you keep that from me. You have no right to keep that from me." I was crying. "You're my enemy."

He looked stricken. "Eroica, it's because of you that I can't tell you. Please accept that."

"I don't accept it. I don't understand it."

"Believe me. . . ."

"I don't believe anything you say. I'll never believe anything you say again." I took my coat and ran out of the room. Going down the elevator, the last image of his tragic face, his open arms reaching toward me, haunted me unbearably.

15

Marta said nothing about my distressed state when I joined her in the coffee shop, and for the next two hours I silently followed her around while she shopped for the household. Wilhelm, cheerful and picking his teeth with a penknife, collected us in the late afternoon.

In the weeks that followed I lived two different lives. Throughout the daytime hours I pretended to be calm to the point of listless indifference and managed the expected responses to the comments of others with studied care. I learned to drive without ever entering traffic; I listened to reports on household matters, which I forgot instantly; and I indulged Lena's need to play mother as she chatted about my future as one of Germany's heiresses.

In the late afternoons I read to escape the restlessness which was the surface side of the anxiety I experienced at night. My reading took me through Gerd's copy of Shakespeare's plays, and always my brother's underlined passages seemed to apply to my life in some unacceptable way: "Our fears do make us traitors" . . . "A dog's obeyed in office" . . . "There is no darkness but ignorance" . . . and a hundred similar ones all hitting the mark somewhere and making me feel uneasy or useless and always depressed.

To escape Gerd's silent voice, I abandoned the books when they became unbearable and took refuge in the park, only to discover that the slightest memory fragment of my brother's life sent me running desperately back to the house. Dawn and sunset had been the times of day we loved most; yet, after Gerd's death, the moments of sundown made me shiver with a nameless malaise that threw me into a frenzy of lamp-lighting.

But it was dinner with Father that marked the real transition between my two lives. In a limbo of controlled hatred I sat opposite him and returned his pleasantries in kind, the burden of concealing the malice in my murderous heart taking its toll in hideous nightmares and distorted memories of Gerd. One night I dreamed *I* had killed my brother.

In the long nights of that spring when I should have been trying to reinforce myself with energy for the daily masquerade with Father, I paced my room for hours, my mind relentlessly searching for the last week of my brother's life. Jans' guarded statement about Gerd's suicide continued to haunt and enrage me, not because Jans refused to tell me what he thought but because I had the tormenting suspicion that he was right. Gerd had discovered Father's gas chambers, but he had survived that knowledge. Between the time he learned of that and the time of his terrible quarrel with Father, Gerd had discovered something else, and it was this new horror that caused him to give up his life.

Night upon night, as my insomnia returned, I hunted the dark places in my memory for words and images that would solve this agonizing mystery. One night I crawled painfully back through the months of madness, through my mother's long dying, through totally black periods marked only with screams and moans into the sudden unexpected sunshine of a Sunday in the park and Gerd's face bright from the midday spring sun and an unconcealable excitement. "Eroica, tomorrow I start my serious formal studies. Let's celebrate."

"If we can get into the wine cellar, we can get a bottle of champagne."

"A very good idea." We were standing at the outer

edge of the garden when a mass of fast-moving clouds suddenly blotted out the sun, and Gerd, looking up at the house, held his gaze for a long moment, saying pensively, "But first, I think it's time we explored the top floor."

I followed his line of vision, and as I looked at the house and saw its great height, its steep angular roofs, its rows of bolted balconied windows, I shivered inwardly.

On Monday, Mother was sick and did not come down to dinner. Father was silent. Later, in his room, Gerd spoke eagerly of his university classes. "In some ways I'm way ahead. I'll take extra examinations to place in a higher level. I intend to be at Oxford before I'm twenty."

Tuesday: Father was in a foul mood and no one spoke a word. Mother drank a few sips of wine but didn't touch her dinner. Gerd looked from one to the other with strange, anxious eyes.

Wednesday: Mother was sick again. What did Father talk about at dinner? Gerd had been listening to him, staring at him with a piercing gaze, then looking away but drawing his eyes back again at Father as though he had no control over them. After dinner I went to his room. He was lying in bed in the dark. "Do you want to be alone, Gerd?" He turned on the bedside lamp and shook his head. I lay down beside him, but he did not talk. Sometime during the night, while I slept, he carried me back to my room.

Thursday: I did not see Mother all day. Father came out of his study just before dinner, but he left the table halfway through the meal without saying anything. I could tell that he was in a mean mood by the way he meticulously placed his knife and fork.

No one would tell me why Gerd was late getting home from the university. Vera did not even acknowledge my questions. I waited for him in my room, troubled by an increasing dread that I did not understand. When I finally heard him, he was shouting—suddenly, and without any warning that he was even in the house, as though he had come from behind a closed door in mid-sentence, his fury out of control and skirting madness.

I ran out of my room and from the second landing on the stairs saw him run into a tree. His words to me as I knelt beside him on the ground, with Father's long shadow from the terrace cast over us, were forever committed to my memory: "Leave Germany. Let Mother die."

But what had he screamed at Father? With hypnotic effort I concentrated on those wild words which later events had obliterated from my memory. For hours I lay in the darkness searching for those few minutes that had so totally been swept away.

Finally I went behind the minutes, back to the dinner table, where Father set down his knife with that excessive and studied calm that always told us that things weren't going his way. He had said nothing about Gerd's absence.

I sat up, realizing Father had said nothing because he knew where Gerd was. Wilhelm's word came back then. "The Old Man should have trained the kid better. The kid got it all wrong."

Questions shrieked at me from the darkness: when did Gerd come home? was he in the house during dinner? what had gone wrong for Father?

I got up and turned on the light. It was after three. I opened the door to the hall and stood outside in the darkened mezzanine and listened. My head roared. "Will you be a hero again, Father?" The words echoed out of a deep unknown place.

I sank to my knees. Oh, Gerd, what else? What else. Help me to remember. But it was over for that night, and I lay awake until dawn, obsessed with the conviction that Gerd knew Father's plans.

After a particularly bad day when I had used up all my wavering strength to carry on the daily charade that had become my life, I fled to the park, only to rush back to the garden when a jackdaw streaked out of a tree, terrifying me with its cry. It was as I stood gasping with exhaustion in the shadow of the towering house that I again remembered the long distant Sunday when Gerd and I, in a fever of excitement, with thunder rolling from the sky, climbed out of a window, scaled a steep roof and broke into the top floor.

The following dawn, I climbed out of the same window, scaled the same sloping roof (barefoot), pried loose the same leaded pane and entered the room where Gerd and I had listened to the rain together for the last time.

The furniture was still there just as I remembered it, and the wooden crates with the metal bands were scattered about in much the same way, but there was one thing different about them: they were open. That is, they were agape, like steamer trunks. I saw at once that the metal bands had never sealed them in the way Gerd and I had thought they had. The crates were actually carefully designed, interior-hinged cabinets large enough for me to walk into. They were all empty. I searched the rooms, with no clear idea of what I expected to find or even of what I was looking for. In the sitting room, which was reached by a heavy staircase, long sealed at the bottom, there was only a huge armoire. It too was empty.

An hour after daybreak, seated dejectedly in the chair where once I slept in my brother's arms, I watched the sun filter through the windows: my footprints were all over the dusty floor. But there were other footprints, older than mine, where dust had settled into dust; and these marked a path to the armoire in the sitting room.

The piece of furniture was set into a niche that might have been a recessed window, only it wasn't. I opened it again. Gerd and I had believed so deeply in hidden chambers and secret corridors that they were almost a mania with us. We never found any, either at the Köln house or at Regensburg, nor did we ultimately expect to; and so completely did I cease to believe in them that when the left side panel of the armoire turned out to be a door and whined at my touch, I almost went into shock. Beyond it was a narrow flight of stairs which I knew at once led to the master-bedroom complex.

I left everything as it was, sweeping away my footprints with a furniture cover and returning to my room, experiencing a certain satisfaction at having discovered Father's stairway. Yet I was no closer to the reason for Gerd's suicide. That he had executed himself in expiation of Father's crimes became increasingly unacceptable to me as the day passed. Also, amid the other enigmas remained Gerd's cruel words "Let Mother die." Among my collection of sorrows this statement was the most incomprehensible of all. Her life seemed always to have been a helpless ghost that haunted ours and one to which Gerd ministered a gentle or continuing care until that terrible night. No matter how carefully I averted my thoughts from these oppressive griefs or tried to slink past them, they were always there, with that same unacceptability one has of children's begging in the streets at night.

Marta, who was never fooled by my pretense, let me know that Jans called each day. Then, one morning three weeks after my meeting with him at the hotel, Marta asked me if I would like to go somewhere after lunch.

I looked up immediately. "Yes."

"Wilhelm is driving your father to the capital this afternoon. He won't be home for lunch. Wouldn't you like to get out a bit, perhaps visit a museum?" I nodded. "Good, I'll have the cook get your lunch. Dress warmly; there is going to be cold weather." She paused a moment; then she commented, in the most casual voice imaginable, "I understand there is an exhibit of old manuscripts at the museum library. You're always reading; you might like that." She left my room.

I washed, then tore around the room, deciphering Marta's message while I dressed. The museum. Jans and I had met at the museum library. I stopped short. When we parted the last time, I had quarreled with him, made him feel wretched. He took all the risks while I slept late and went driving in the park. I raged at myself as I considered my face in the mirror. Bring him something . . . important.

I reviewed the "key" situation. Lena still cleaned Father's study. At that moment she was in the kitchen having lunch.

On the table beside her bed I picked up her ring of keys and slipped downstairs to the study, but once inside I was in complete confusion. What could I bring Jans that would be of use to him or to the organizations he spoke of? I had only a few minutes, and no idea where to look. I opened one file cabinet after another. None of the folders meant anything to me. Then I found something incredible: a cabinet marked DEAD FILES. I took one folder at random from each of the five drawers and put them under my sweater. I left the study, carefully checking first to make sure everything looked normal, and then locked the door. Upstairs I took the folders and hid them in the zippered fur lining of my coat.

Lena came in to tell me lunch was ready. "Marta says you're going out. It will be good for you." She stopped, turned white and gasped, her mouth remaining open. On the bed was the ring of keys.

"Lena, I . . . wanted to see Gerd's room."

She released her breath. "Of course you did. But you mustn't say anything, ever!"

"No, no. I won't say anything." I handed her the keys. Perhaps it was only my imagination that she trembled a little.

A muted gray coat with a muffler and a knit cap made me look like any schoolgirl. No Dior suit for this outing.

In the museum Marta bought a brochure describing the rare manuscripts, and we began to examine the works in their glass-topped tables. I wanted desperately to look around the exhibit room for Jans, but Marta pretended to be interested only in the exhibit, so I did the same with wild impatience.

When I saw him, his face was reflected against some dark scrolls at which I was looking, and in that moment of recognition I was stunned at his tormented expression. He was standing next to me, leaning over the case, looking down, but he straightened up and said casually, "Shall we go." I nodded. Marta was at the next display case, her back to us.

We left the museum and walked to a rented car, but he did not start it immediately; he watched the rearview mirror for a few moments before we drove away. Then he headed downriver to a small park where children were at play; there he turned the car so that we faced the Rhine. During this drive he was silent and it hurt my heart to see the dispirited look on his face. I wanted to tell him I was sorry for hurting him, but he spoke first.

"Marta tells me you are not sleeping well."

"That's not important." More than anything I wanted to help him, to give him something that would make him trust me. I uncinched the belt of my coat and took out the gray folders. "I stole these from Father's study. They were in a cabinet marked 'Dead Files.' I was hoping it meant people he had killed, but I suppose if it did, he would probably not have called it that. I only had a few minutes. I didn't know what to take."

Jans opened the first folder and glanced through it. Then, quickly, he opened all the others and scanned those, too. For the first time since we met, he looked less drawn and weary. He looked at me with a faintly amused expression.

"Tell me, Eroica, did you ever vacation in Liechtenstein?"

"Yes, several times a year. We have a house there."

"And do you like it?"

"No. It's one of those mountain houses—a chalet, only much larger—built up against a hillside. It has silly, ornate shutters and animal heads hanging from all the walls."

"No, I mean did you like the charming little principality?"

"I have no feelings about it one way or the other. Mother didn't like the place. She always went to bed right away and just stayed there until we left."

"Does your father have business to tend to there?"

"Yes, he has an office there. Why are you talking as though you were an adult asking a small child how she is doing in kindergarten?"

He smiled, leaning back and holding the five folders against his chest.

"Well? What are they?" I asked.

"Dead files."

"What does that mean?"

"In business, it usually means a file which is closed to further use."

"Is that what those are?"

"Yes, as far as your Father is concerned. I frankly don't understand why he saved them." He put the files between us on the seat and took my hands, pulling off the mittens. "If you had ever got past kindergarten, you might have known what dead files were and you would never have brought me these. You might have picked something quite useless."

"They are important? What are they?"

"They are documents transferring property to a holding company your father owned in Liechtenstein before the war."

"A holding company?"

"Yes. Do you know what that is?"

"It's a corporation which owns other corporations."

"A Pemselian definition?"

"Yes."

"Nothing wrong with it; somewhat generalized. Specifically, holding companies have numerous functions. The one involved here held property in trust for its owners; that is, the property did not belong to the holding company; it was only supposed to be kept by it for a given period of time. After that, it would have been returned to the owners."

"How is that important?"

"The property was never returned to the owners."

"Then the business isn't finished," I said.

Jans breathed in sharply and looked away toward the playground. "It's finished," he said slowly. "The owners are dead."

"My father killed them?"

He looked back at me. "There are a few notes and letters in the files. Eroica, their origin is Bergen."

"Bergen?" There it was again: the name that always conjured up rats.

"Yes. The concentration camp there was Belsen, as you now know. There were some unique differences about that camp. Witnesses, now vanished or dead, were reported to have said that many of the Jews imprisoned there were convinced they would survive because they believed they were being held for exchange purposes." He let go of my hand and lit a cigarette.

"Exchange?"

"Yes. Someone convinced them that they would be exchanged for German prisoners. They believed someone with influence would intercede with the government in their behalf because they had certain reliable arrangements. The witnesses claimed that it must have been true because within a year they were all gone."

"They were exchanged?"

"No, they were all murdered."

"How do you know?"

"When you told me about your father's having been in Bergen at the end of the war, we—that is, the organization with which I am in contact—rechecked the surviving Belsen records. Wilhelm and Karl were prison guards there, but we could find nothing else that tied your father to that camp—no records, no witnesses. It was very disappointing. And Karl and Wilhelm had no records of atrocities. Quite the contrary; according to investigations made after the war was over, they were apparently more kindly disposed toward the prisoners than any of the other guards.

"There was one curious incident: when the British arrived in 1945, they found three camp administrators shot to death. They were all seated at their desks, with their guns in their holsters. It was obvious that whoever killed them was known to them and trusted by them. Someone had also made a bonfire of some of the records, but that was common to most of the camps."

"But why would the people with the property trust my father?"

"They were businessmen who had probably dealt with him before—in a time when the laws meant something. Also, the property in these files was situated in foreign countries and therefore safer, considering the times; and your father's concerns, even then, were multinational.

"In an effort to rid Germany of all Jews the government in the late thirties began a program in which all property belonging to Jews was supposed to have gone to the nation. Initially the Jews were given some opportunity to liquidate their businesses: one can imagine the losses in panic sales. Supposedly the 'Aryanization'—that's what the process was called—of Jewish property was to be voluntary. These men who did business with VHI assumed that their troubles were quite temporary. They probably had sound contracts retaining ultimate title to their possessions. By April of 1938, every Jew had to report all of his domestic and foreign holdings. Obviously some kept a few things back. By July, the government issued an order that all Jewish businesses were to be terminated by the end of the year—finished, closed out, or in non-Jewish hands. But as it turned out, they were terminated a little sooner. In early November a Polish-Jewish student whose parents had lived in Germany but who were being deported to Poland assassinated the third secretary of the German embassy in Paris. Result: instant martyrdom for the embassy man and carefully planned spontaneous demonstrations against the Jews: murder, arson, looting, and the arrest of twenty thousand Jewish men. The breaking of the plate glass of the shop windows and the synagogues and the homes of Jews all over Germany gave the pogrom its name: 'Crystalnight,' or 'Night of Glass.' From November ninth on, it was open season on Jews."

"November ninth?" I turned away from Jans and looked at the great river. For thousands of centuries it had slithered out of glaciers, thundered down mountains, roared its way between gorges, drinking up other rivers along the way, pulling them into itself until it was wide and full and fat, like a great primitive creature that slid on its belly and put its forked tongue into the sea. I shook my head; it was stupid to think that way. Gerd had seen the river as a wondrous mystery to be studied and admired and loved.

Jans put his hand on my cap and slowly pulled it off. "Does that date mean anything to you?"

A white pleasure ship was floating by. It had bright red-and-blue-striped umbrellas on one of its decks, and people seated under them seemed to be eating and talking. "That is the day I will be twenty-one, and he picked that day because of that other tie in November, back in 1938. Didn't he?"

Jans' hand tightened on my shoulder. "Look at me. Eroica, turn this way." He placed the folders on the back seat, then pulled me close to him.

"My father had Wilhelm and Karl make sure all the people who trusted him got killed, didn't he?" I began to shudder. "Didn't he?"

"Don't suffer, Eroica. It's got nothing to do with you."

"I'm his daughter. He always said that blood is the same."

"Was Gerd like him?" Jans was looking at me angrily.

"No!" I screamed.

"Neither are you."

"Gerd was better than I. He and my mother were alike. I'm like Father."

"No!"

"How do you know? I want to kill him." I began to cry. "All those people trusted him and he stole everything from them and killed them."

"Don't, Eroica. We have some real evidence now. He stole from his own government as well. The documents are all dated before November 1938. The Night of Glass was a piece of luck for him. He was supposed to have transferred all this property over to the German government at that time, but considering the madness, it was not difficult for him merely to keep it. And it was impossible for any of these people to bring a charge against him. The Jews had no rights. Their last hope was their foreign businesses. In these cases"—he motioned toward the files—"two manufacturing plants in Argentina, one in Sweden, one in France and a silver mine in Mexico could have bought tickets out of Germany if a man of influence had pulled a few strings. Instead—"

"Instead he had them arrested and killed as quickly as possible, and he goes right on living as though nothing ever happened."

"Not quite: his son is dead," said Jans softly.

I should have looked at that statement longer, or perhaps at the way he said it, but I didn't. Anyway, he started to talk about something else very quickly.

"I told you last time that I was working on something which seemed preposterous, but it doesn't seem that way anymore. Your father deals with many economically backward countries. These are good markets and safe investments because Bonn manages the financing for at least ten years and guarantees up to eighty percent of it. Germany needs foreign markets, and the government's backing of an industrialist is a great incentive for a company. For a long time I have known that only over these nations does the ridged wheel fly. In other countries there are different trademarks of his, but in the backward ones the red and black flag is the only trade emblem he uses, no matter what the merchandise is.

"For months I have noticed some peculiar behavior with representatives from these countries—a subtle anxiety, not at all the good cheer one finds in other visitors. Then, last week, I congratulated a new customer on his country's recent admission to the UN. The man blazed into anger and stalked out of the room. Your father laughed.

"I think VHI has control of the UN votes in the ridged-wheel nations."

"But how could that happen?"

"Economic blackmail is the new means of holding a knife to a nation's throat."

"Is that his plan—to control the UN?"

"No, he is too cynical about the UN to take it seriously. He calls it the Jockey Club—little men riding horses that go nowhere—but it amuses him to know that he can manipulate the odds. I think he is using it as a testing device. I don't know what kind of real race it's tied up to."

"But don't the people in those countries own their railroads and bridges once they are built? They can stop dealing with him then, can't they?"

"Of course, your father couldn't very well take his bridges and go home, but he has a multitude of other enterprises over which VHI has control."

"But he would lose money if he closed factories or things like that. He is always talking about new markets."

Jans seemed to be watching some barges headed downriver. "A new, young nation is a strange creature, Eroica; it is about ninety-five-percent pride, and when pride is involved, blackmail becomes politically and morally acceptable under the name of expediency. A closed factory is a loss of national pride; the unemployment resulting from the closing causes unrest: If the foreign industrialist seems to have unlimited wealth elsewhere, the new nation does not consider *his* loss, only its own."

"Couldn't they just take it away from him?"

"Not if they want help from other industrialists. Foreign aid, loans, everything, abruptly ends when there is trouble of that kind. No one will take a chance with a nation like that. Also, Eroica, I don't think you realize how big VHI is now. It has enormous prestige all over the world. Industrialists in other nations watch him closely: if VHI invests, it must be good."

"Then why can't someone figure out what he's up to?"

"He hasn't done anything to give himself away. I don't think that the nations whose political vote he controls know what he has planned."

"If that's true, then Father wouldn't let just anyone know about it, would he?"

"No, why do you ask?"

"One night I heard Pemsel and the others talk about a 'noble purpose.' Could they have known?"

"No. Many of your father's employees believe that VHI is helping other countries arm themselves, that his scientists and engineers are helping underdeveloped nations manufacture munitions. This is not true."

"What about the men who had the 'rendezvous with the future,' who had their armor in their briefcases?"

"Eroica, I don't even know who they are. God knows I think about them often enough. I'm sure they know the plan, and they are loose upon the world." He fell silent.

"I wish I could remember more about that night. I should have counted how many men there were. I always had the impression that there were at least nine or ten, maybe even eleven. They surrounded Father completely."

"There was no reason for you to count them."

"Gerd would have counted them. It might make a difference knowing that."

"I doubt it. You mustn't start worrying over things like that. Save your energies. Marta is worried about you. I hope the formal announcement didn't bother you. Many things can happen between now and November, especially now that we have something to go on. Then, too, people rarely remember anything like that for long."

"What formal announcement?" I knew at once from his expression that my coming birthday was already public record. "Where was it made?"

Jans brushed his hand across his mouth and chin; he was biting his lower lip. "You didn't know?" I shook my head. "It was written up in the firm's newspaper and the general press had an item about it. I thought perhaps that you were having trouble with your father about it, because of what Marta said about your not sleeping well."

"That has nothing to do with November. I have been trying to remember things that happened three years ago, all the things my brother said in those days before he died."

Jans smoothed down my hair, his hand resting on my cheek. "Don't go over it, Eroica."

"I have to. He said things that made no sense then, but now everything has so many meanings. Jans, please tell me what else was in the newspaper."

"Your father announced that you would be of age, that there would be a birthday celebration, and that a further statement would be made at that time."

"That monster."

"Eroica, take heart. At least we have something with these files. But you know, of course, that these present a terrible problem."

"What problem? You said it was real evidence."

"Eroica, don't you understand that you have endangered yourself?"

"With Father? No, he will never suspect me."

"He's certainly going to suspect someone. The moment he hears of an investigation regarding Bergen-

Belsen, he will recheck everything. What will you say if he questions you?"

"Why should he question me?"

"Because he trusts no one." Jans sounded exasperated.

I knew that Father trusted no one, at least not until recently. "He trusts me," I said. Of course, I was still not completely sure this was true. It had never really been tested. It was like the old saying about liars: the horror of being a liar did not rest in no one's ultimately believing *anything* the liar said; it rested on the fact that the liar could never believe what others said. "I will act innocent, or sick, or outraged, or whatever seems right at the time."

Jans looked at me anxiously. "Listen, I no longer live where I used to." He took a key from his coat pocket. "If you ever believe you are in danger, take a taxi and go to the address I'm going to give you." He took out a pen. "No, I don't think I'll write it down. You'll have to memorize it." He told it to me and made me repeat it until I knew it well.

As he started the car, I remembered something that had been bothering me. "Jans, why hasn't Father taken me to his offices, as he planned?" He looked away angrily. "Please, Jans, I can't continue to act from ignorance. If you know anything, tell me."

"I think he is waiting for some special guests."

"Who?"

"Some oil people."

I laughed. "Don't worry, Jans, he's not going to give me away to the Arabs."

"I'm glad you're sure of that."

"I'm sure of that." We drove in silence for a few minutes. "Jans, how soon will it be before we know about the files?"

"I don't know. I'm not even sure what will happen. I'm hoping for a serious legal action against him."

"You mean, this evidence isn't strong enough to arrest him?"

"Eroica, your father is one of the most powerful men in Europe. People like that are not arrested casually, and he has the best legal minds in the world at his disposal. Don't hope for too much right away."

"Are you saying that even if the authorities know what he has done, he might not have to pay for it?"

Jans answered this slowly. "No, I'm not saying that at all, but I want you to realize that an indictment is not proof of guilt. All these things take time and a great deal of investigation. Our best hope is that this will at least stop him from carrying out his plans for the future."

"But he must be tried for the past, too."

"Yes, I know." He breathed in deeply. "You must be patient and not get discouraged." He hesitated. "And you must not try to do anything . . . yourself. In the end the law will get him. Also, you must remember that your father's death might not stop the men who know his plan. It might even cause them to act . . . to do whatever he wanted done." After this, he glanced at me nervously several times as he drove.

I did not want to argue with him, so I changed the subject. "There was something else I meant to tell you. The night before Gerd died, I thought he had come home late from the university, but I don't think so anymore. I believe he was on the third floor that afternoon and found something about Father in some crates that are there. That terrible row he had with Father only made sense to me after I saw your black book." I told him about the sealed-up third story and the stairway between the two sitting rooms.

Jans listened attentively, then said, "Your house was built in the last century, when it was not uncommon to construct a private easeway of that kind. The times demanded a moral behavior that the body couldn't always live with. The Germans were not excluded from the Victorian repressions of the time, and hypocrisy was as much the mark of that age as it is of this one—only the emphasis is different. In your father's case the stairs were probably a means of getting to his secret files, though I still don't understand why he saved these particular ones."

Back at the museum we did not say anything to each other; nor did we touch. There was a shadow in his face, a dark and desperate concern in his eyes that took no words to convey.

The two weeks after that meeting went by quietly. My father was jovial, the household ran smoothly, and the garden was rich with color. It was full spring and all things seemed to be making their demand for life.

Then, in the course of forty-eight hours, everything came apart: the government announced an investigation into Father's wartime activities; Father turned the full force of his rage upon his own house with astonishing ferocity; and Jans was missing.

Part III

16

The automobiles raced up our drive and fanned out in front of the house like a flock of predatory birds. There was no order in their parking; they even drove upon the grassed area in the center of the circular drive.

I first heard them at eleven in the morning as I was coming downstairs to go for a walk. Marta was just on her way to open the door when I reached the second landing. "There are about a million people out there," I called to her.

She stopped walking and looked up at me. "Go to your room and wait there."

"Who are they?"

She shook her head and waited for me to go back upstairs, but I only went as far as the mezzanine, where I could hear Marta's angry voice clearly.

"He is not at home, and we do not know when he will return," she said when they asked to see von Heyditch. But they forced their way in and from behind the balustrade I could see them swarming through the downstairs rooms with cameras and note pads. I heard Lena, pulling back the drapes in the garden room, suddenly stop singing. Then, "Heavens, what is happening!"

Doors opened and closed loudly. A voice from the foyer called, "Let's talk to the girl." I ran back to my room and locked the door. When the wild beating of my heart calmed a little, I looked out of the window and saw men wandering around in the garden; they were taking pictures of the house. I pulled back from the window quickly as I saw a man swing his camera upward.

A little while later, Marta came to my room. Her voice was quite calm, but her eyes were full of fear. "Your father has been indicted. I do not know the charges against him. Those people were reporters." She sat down on my desk chair.

"What will happen?" I asked.

"The reporters are not going to leave us alone for long. Some of them are probably parked just outside the gate." She laughed a little nervously. "The cook threatened one with a pot of boiling water if he did not leave her kitchen. At the moment we are bolted in." I thought that was peculiar wording: weren't they bolted out? But I did not comment on it. "The phones have been ringing constantly, so you must not be alarmed if we do not hear from Jans today. He will probably not be able to get through." She got up and paced back and forth. "Hector will be coming home on the bus, and they will probably stop him."

I liked her son's name. She told me one day during our driving lessons that she had once intended to go to the university and study ancient cultures, but that naming her child "Hector" was as close as she managed to get. "They wouldn't harm him, would they?" I asked.

"They will frighten him."

"Then I shall go get him."

She turned her astonished eyes toward me. "Impossible."

"Why? No one knows my face, and I have ways of getting in and out that they would never think of." A plan of my own was beginning to form.

"You can't. I forbid it."

While Marta, on the edge of tears, pleaded with me to be sensible, I raced into my clothes, tucking my hair under my cap and carefully hiding the key Jans gave me in the fingers of one of my gloves. "Don't worry. I know what I am doing."

Her eyes were dark with fear. "I can't let you do this."

"One of us has to get Hector, and I'm the only one who can." She told me which school he attended and I told her not to worry if I was a little longer than might be expected: I was going to take the long way around.

She put her hands over her face and shivered. "What if—"

"We don't have time for 'what-ifs.' The best time to act is when everything is in an uproar." She followed me to the plant room, where she suddenly embraced me.

I left, making my way to the greenhouse and from there to the orchard and on to the park. I walked easily, with my gloved hands in my pockets, my cap pulled down and my coat collar turned up. Fortunately, there was a funeral going on at the cemetery. I stood around a bit in the subdued and mourning crowd, and then, dabbing my eyes, I went back to the street and hired one of the taxis. The driver started to say that he was waiting for a particular group, but I told him that the service wouldn't be over for a while and that he could drive me home and get back in time for his other mourners. I gave him Jans' address and he drove there without further question.

Jans' new quarters were in a fashionable district, apparently only recently completed. The landscaping had that unsettled look of a garden full-grown in one place and then simply transplanted in another. There wasn't a weed in sight. Jans' apartment was on the second floor and I met no one as I let myself inside with the key he had given me.

As I stood in the living room, I felt a quickening of my heart. This was where he lived, ate and slept. I went to his bedroom closet and put my face against his clothes and longed for him. But I pushed those thoughts aside quickly, remembering why I had come. I returned to the living room and began to search for his black book.

Jans did extraordinary things in open, ordinary ways. If he had acted true to past form, then the book had to be with the other books, in open view. But it was not with the other books; I found it halfway down a neat stack of Von Heyditch Industries annual public-relations reports. Father put out some very high-grade brochures printed on thick paper and covered with colored photographs of his products.

I embraced the book. So, Father was at last going to be tried for his crimes. Well, that was the world's business. I had a trial of my own in mind. Putting the book in the lining of my coat, I realized I had to leave Jans a clue as to who had taken it. I looked around the room and saw his photograph and records. After a hurried search, I found Beethoven's Third Symphony and placed it where the book had been.

Everything went smoothly. I left the apartment and had no trouble getting a taxi to the school where I got the boy out by telling the headmaster that I was a maid in the house where his mother worked and that she had become quite ill with flu and that the boy was probably infected. They let him go at once.

"Your mother wants you to come home so she can check your throat." He looked at me a little oddly, but he had no particular reason to distrust me, and getting away from the school was one of those hopeless little hopes that always hang around a child's daydreams. I knew the feeling, and he knew a good chance when he saw one. He smiled and we walked away from the headmaster as casually as we could.

Two blocks from the school, I hired a third taxi and told Hector that we were going to sneak home and surprise everyone and that he was to do exactly as I told him.

The cab dropped us at the bend in the park and we walked carefully toward the orchard. We were in the greenhouse when I suddenly realized I hadn't seen Wilhelm or Karl all morning.

As soon as Marta saw us she embraced Hector as though he had been lost for months and rushed him off to the kitchen. I went upstairs to change and, unable to think of a better place, left the book in the lining of my coat.

When I returned downstairs, Marta was standing outside the music room, her whole body tensed and listening. "What is it?" I asked.

She looked at me anxiously. "I don't know. This feeling of being locked in leaves me fearful. And I can't understand why your father hasn't sent someone to reassure us. What happened to the men? I heard Wilhelm bring the car back, but I haven't seen him."

I told Marta that there was not much else we could do but wait and went out to see if the cars were both there. They were, with the keys in them. Standing there, I remembered Marta's startling question. "Does he carry a gun?"

When I opened the glove compartment and took out the pistol, I experienced an acute sense of distance from my action, as though a part of me were standing away from myself, watching me examine the gun. Unconsciously I spoke aloud to my brother. "I have failed you. Even when you were still alive, I failed you. I should not have left you alone. But this time, I shall not fail you."

I got out of the car, making sure I left no sign behind me, and climbed the stairs to the men's quarters certain they would not be there. The five rooms were in order, and from what I could tell, the men had simply got dressed and left. Their overcoats were gone, but the closets still held the bulk of their clothing. In a wooden cabinet I found three handsome boxes in which handguns had rested; the raised molds looked like deep patterns in the snow. I took one of the small pamphlets which told how to care for the gun.

I searched the rooms for a letter or note from Father,

since it occurred to me that Father would certainly have sent someone to the house if he knew that the men were not here, but there was nothing.

When I got back to the house, I could hear Marta on the phone: "We do not know when he will be in. Please call his office. Do not call here again."

I quickly went to my room, placed the gun under my pillow and went back downstairs. The phone was ringing. Marta picked it up angrily, apparently certain that it was another reporter. She listened a moment but did not speak, then thrust the receiver toward me, whispering, "Your father."

I took the phone, trying to keep my hand from trembling and my voice calm. "Father?" He wanted to know what was happening. I told him about the reporters' entering the house. He cursed briefly and told me to call Wilhelm to the phone at once.

"He's not here, Father." He asked about Karl. "He's not here either." I could almost hear Father thinking. Finally he asked which car was gone, and I told him both were in the carriage house with the keys in them. There was a long silence, and then he asked to speak to Marta. She took the phone from my hand with a look of deep anxiety.

"No, they said nothing about leaving. . . . About ten, the cook saw Karl going up to their rooms. . . . No, sir, no one saw them after that." She went into some detail about the reporters, finishing up with the statement that we were safely bolted in. She looked toward me suddenly. "She's very well. No, she was the least frightened of all of us. . . . Yes, of course, sir, we wouldn't think of it." She said "yes" once more and hung up.

"What wouldn't we think of?"

"Leaving the house. Also, we are not to answer the door or the telephones again. He is sending some guards who will remain outside and to whom we are not to speak."

I could not read Marta's thoughts, but I could feel

her terror. Within an hour, a car arrived, and we counted a half dozen armed men who took up positions around the house. The phones continued to ring until finally I unhooked them, knowing with a sinking feeling that one caller might have been Jans.

For the rest of the day we all went through our routine in silence. Looking at the guards from an upstairs balcony I wondered if they were acting as our protectors or if they simply formed a barrier against our escape.

Just before ten o'clock Father came home. Marta and I were in the music room talking when we heard the door wrench against the chain. She went at once to open it and my first view of him was so totally astonishing that for a second I did not recognize him. His black overcoat was open and flapping, his tie was loosened, and his inevitable black fedora was missing, though Father always left the house with his hat on and entered it with his hat on. I remembered the night I had put the rats in his study and he had fired the gun wildly into the walls. That was a madness filled with terror and loathing. This face, however distraught, held a deadly implacable rage.

Details of this scene left their imprints in my memory for hours: Marta swaying a little, even though she still held on to the door; the black shadows of the guards slanting obliquely from the frail light of the foyer; my father's fists, white-knuckled and clenched tightly enough to crush bone. Father said something to the men, then pulled the door away from Marta, who staggered backward, and shut it. "Get me all the keys to the carriage house."

Marta walked hurriedly past me toward the kitchen. Father remained in the middle of the foyer. If he saw me, he made no outward note of it.

Marta returned quickly and handed him the keys. He took them, saying only, "Make sure Lena is here when I return. I won't be long."

Marta looked at me. "What does he want with

Lena?" I shrugged, but a deep fear began to take hold of me: Lena, the keeper of the keys! Frightful possibilities sped through my mind: Father suspected me! He had not spoken to me at all. Usually he was eager for us to talk, and even said a few nights before that it was a joy to come home and find me waiting for him. I shivered as Marta and I went to the window and watched Father go to the rooms above the carriage house, where one after another the lights went on. When we saw Father descend to the tool room, Marta left to get Lena, and a few minutes later I heard him at the door. He was talking to one of the guards as he came in.

"You will find their pictures and other descriptions in the files. They are armed: three pistols. Put everyone on it. Contact the airlines, the trains, our people at the frontiers. Have someone work the city; you'll find a list in the files of their friends, their favorite bars, their whores. Avoid any extravagances unless absolutely necessary: I prefer them able to talk." A minute later a car roared away into the darkness. Father came back to the music room just as Lena, a sweater over her flannel nightgown, was descending the stairs with Marta. She was in a state of repressed panic. Father motioned both women to chairs and sat down at the far side of the table. I remained watching, but he continued to ignore me.

"I want to know who has been in my study in the last few weeks." Lena's round white face seemed to turn gray, but perhaps it was only the shadow made by her loosened hair. "To my knowledge, Lena, you are the only one who has a key to the study. Do you have it on you?"

"Oh, yes, sir." She reached into her sweater pocket and brought out a bunch of keys.

"Put them on the table." My father's eyes never left her face. "Did you for any reason ever give the key to the study to any of the men? Now, think carefully. Do not be in a hurry to answer."

Lena's brown-spotted hand shook as she lowered it to

the table. If Father saw fear as proof of guilt, Lena was condemned. "No, sir, I never gave the keys to the men. Never." She stopped and gave a little gasp. "Oh, that's not true." My father leaned forward slightly. "A long time ago . . . you remember, sir, I had to open the door for them so they could get the rats out."

Father sat back stiffly in his chair. "Were you with them in the room while they looked for the rodents?" His voice was less steady, and as I looked at him, I noticed a curious thing: he appeared to have lost weight; his neck seemed longer.

Lena was trying to remember what had happened three years earlier. "It was the day after you saw the rats that the men went in to kill them."

"Were you with them?" Father's voice was calmer.

"No, Wilhelm told me to get out, that I was interfering with the work."

"How long were he and Karl in the study?"

"I'm not sure. They were in and out all day."

"Did you give them the key, or did you leave the door open?"

"They took my key."

"So they had it all day?"

"Yes."

"Do you remember whether or not either of the men left in the car that day?"

"No, I don't remember that, sir."

"One or the other could have left for a brief time without your knowing it, couldn't he?"

"Yes. I suppose. When I iron, I can't hear anything that goes on up front. And if I'm cleaning a bath or something where there is water running, I don't always know."

"When did Wilhelm return the key?"

"Oh, I got it back that night, sir. It was my responsibility, you see. You told me never to give it up and I . . ." She stopped talking and my heart stopped beating.

"What were you going to say?" asked my father.

Lena did not look at me. I waited in horror for her to

remember that she had once given me the key and that she had seen it in my possession again two weeks ago, but she said, "It was only something Wilhelm said that I just remembered."

"And what was that?"

"Well, he had had trouble with the car keys that time he lost both sets to the limousine."

"What does that have to do with the study key?"

"Well, Wilhelm said that there should be more than one key." I saw Father's nostrils pull in sharply. He continued to face Lena, but his eyes had a dark inward look, searching, examining.

I understood his confusion only too well: Wilhelm and Karl had run because they were once Father's hired killers and an investigation of Father's wartime activities would certainly bring their own crimes to the surface, but they would not steal the files, since it was these very documents which would cause such an investigation.

Father turned his attention to Marta. "Have you ever used Lena's keys?"

"No, sir."

"When was the last time you were in the study?"

"I have never been in the study. Mrs. Schweiger informed me when I was hired that she alone had access to the study and to the master bedrooms, and I have observed that privacy to the letter."

Father gazed at her a moment longer without saying anything, then turned back to Lena. "Now, I want you to consider this carefully, Lena. Has either of the men made any comments at mealtimes—for that matter, at any time—which sounded angry or complaining?"

Lena blinked several times. "Well, they always grumble, sir."

"What about?"

"Oh, they complain about the meals and the price of cigarettes and the government and the weather. . . ."

"Yes, yes, I know those complaints. What else?"

I watched Father's angry eyes. He was hunting for a

reason why Wilhelm and Karl should steal the files. A bitter statement from either of the men about the recent disbanding of Father's phony cabal would have convicted them on the spot. I began to put together possible answers that I knew had to be in Father's mind: Wilhelm and Karl had been paid by members of the disgruntled Nazi organization to steal the files. In return, they were promised a fortune and protection in another country. Believe it, Father, believe it! You took away all their dreams of ever having power again. You betrayed them, so now they have betrayed you. They stole your secrets and are out there somewhere trying to destroy you.

Father had a hideous glazed look in his eyes that made me sick with fear. If he ever stopped suspecting the men, those dreadful eyes would turn upon me. I struggled to remain calm and watched the whole proceeding with a facade of curiosity and interest. When Lena could not seem to remember anything more, the session came to an unsatisfactory end and Father dismissed the two women for the night.

"Erocia," he began softly, "I want you to hear the reason for this commotion from my own lips. A charge has been made against the firm involving some property. The whole thing is an absurd and malicious lie, but, as always happens in these cases, many of my enemies wish to blacken our good name. We who work the hardest and achieve our ends are always envied by malcontents and failures who hate us." He spoke in a thick, tight voice, his face rigid and white. Then, slowly, his expression became more gentle. "Your mother allowed herself to become disheartened by just such people, and that is what killed her. You must be strong, Eroica. If you hear things that trouble you, you must ask me about them. Listen to no one else. I will keep you informed of anything you should know. In the meantime, do not worry yourself over anything. My legal staff has everything under control. In a few days it will all be over." He smiled a little. "Now then, why don't you bring me a glass of sherry, and then get some rest. I don't want you thinking about any of this, and more than ever it is important that you remain well and strong."

"Yes, Father." I was amazed that I could carry out his request so calmly. I went to the cabinet in the dining room. So, his legal staff had everything under control. My fear began to turn into a terrible rage. "An indictment is not proof of guilt," Jans had said. "He has the best legal minds in the world at his disposal. These things take time." Time? For three years Gerd's death had gone unavenged; it seemed more like ten. And here was Father, knowing of his own horrible crimes, already dismissing the indictment against him, only twelve hours after it was brought out. Everything was under control—his control. Even time. In a few days it would be all over and he would be able to relax again in the security of his vast power. I poured the rich amber liquid into a crystal glass. Night of Glass. Night of Glass. On that joyous occasion our daughter will carry on . . . carry on . . . in the case of some untimely . . . untimely . . . untimely event . . . event . . . event. . . .

I shook my head and walked carefully back to the music room. The clock was just chiming eleven. The day seemed so long that I could not remember its beginning. Father smiled as I handed him the sherry, and raised his glass to me. I smiled back. "Sleep well, Father."

On the second landing I looked out and saw Gerd weeping beneath the tree. At my feet lay my mother, gasping sobs without tears. I dragged myself up to my room and quickly clutched the gun. I could kill him now, while he was gloating over his control of things. But what if Jans were right about the men who knew Father's plan? The bastards, the bastards! I wanted to shoot them all.

I argued against Jans' warning: if I shot Father now, before he found Wilhelm and Karl and questioned them, then Jans was forever safe. If I did not shoot Father now, and if he believed Wilhelm and Karl, who would say they only ran because of the indictment, it would be but a matter of time before he began to turn his suspicions on me. He would question Lena again, and if he asked her a different set of questions, she would soon give me away with her panic. She would ultimately tell him that Jans phoned every day. Horrors climbed on horrors.

I took out the pamphlet on the care of the gun and, upon slipping out the weapon's magazine, discovered that it was loaded, something I had forgotten to consider before. I studied the diagram, checking for the bullet in the chamber, which the instructions cautioned about. Apparently it took some skill to shoot accurately, even at close range, the major problem being steady control of the wrist so that the gun won't swing through a wide arc. I practiced holding the gun still, aiming at myself in the mirror on the closet door. By gripping my shooting wrist with my free hand, I could keep the gun fairly steady. But, of course, I could only pass the real test for that when I fired it.

I put the gun on safety and tiptoed barefoot to the second landing on the stairs, where I had to stop to get my breathing under control and my heart to slow down. Jans' voice was loud in my mind. "In the end the law will get him. . . . Your father's death might cause those men to act . . . to *do* whatever he wanted done." In the foyer, I was still shaking my head to all Jans' arguments, but, as it turned out, he had won for the moment: Father was gone.

That night I slept with surprising peacefulness, dreaming fond and fragile dreams of Mother and Gerd and I on a boat anchored in a still, pale sea both strange and familiar.

But when I woke up, it was with an odd sense of shock, as though someone had called my name. For a second I even believed I had answered, that I had actually spoken some words aloud. I got up, took the gun from under my pillow and hid it in the lining of my coat, and then dressed quickly. Coming down the stairs, I discovered that it was six in the morning, and it was during the chiming of the clock that I heard Father's angry voice. "Do not tell me that it could not have been avoided. I told you I wanted them alive. . . . Idiot! They would not have fired on you if you had not been chasing them. We could have picked them up later. What good are they to me now?" I thought he had hung up, but after a moment he said, "That goes without saying. What you don't seem to understand is that I wanted them alive, for the present. I need some answers. I want to talk to the man who got to the bodies first. . . . Never mind the police. Our people will be there inside the hour; they will take care of the police. It can't come out. This is exactly the kind of incident those fools in the government will leap on. I warn you, the Jews are behind this indictment and they will stop at nothing." The sound of the phone crashing on its base followed this last statement.

Father's use of the word "Jews" and his sudden thrusting down of the phone so stunned and horrified me that I raced back upstairs to the mezzanine, where I waited in the shadows, straining my ears for Father's next move. So, someone had been extravagant, after all.

A moment later, Father came out of his study looking fiercely agitated and extremely pale. He still wore the same clothes he had worn the night before. Twice he started for the stairs, but stopped abruptly and turned back toward the drawing room. Then he paced back and forth in the foyer, finally reaching into his pocket and pulling out a cylinder of some kind. He opened it and, with a jerking motion of his right hand, let three or four pills fall into his open left palm, which he then thrust to his mouth. He threw his head back like a man gulping air. In the next moment he was bounding up the stairs, pulling off his tie.

I ran to my room and waited; twenty minutes later, he left the house without a word to anyone.

Marta looked at me quizzically when I came into the kitchen. "What's happening?" she asked.

"Wilhelm and Karl are dead."

She gave a loud gasp but quickly clapped her hand over her mouth, her eyes filled with alarm. "How do you know?" she whispered.

I told her about Father's telephone conversation. "It's obvious that the two were being chased and someone shot them. Father is wild; he wanted to talk to them first. He wanted to know why they ran away."

Marta slowly poured coffee into a cup, her face cast down as though she were involved in some enormously complex action. When she looked up at me, her eyes were deeply troubled. "Then he will turn back upon us."

"Why should he?" I was amazed at what she had said.

"I don't know. Frustration, perhaps. Or . . . he suspects someone else of having caused his present troubles."

I wondered how much she knew. "Why should he suspect us?"

"He suspects someone in this house," she whispered. "Obviously someone took something from his study. For what other reason would he have questioned Lena about the keys the way he did? And Lena is paralyzed with fright. No, he will not let it go with the death of the men, and people as powerful as he can do anything, find out anything."

Marta was right: Father's spies might find out how the documents got to the organization with which Jans worked; or he might question Lena again, and one word from her about Jans and Father's suspicions would take a violent shift.

Marta was watching me apprehensively. "If he questions Lena again in her present state of mind, she would confess to things that are not even true," she said slowly. "And he will want to clear everything up for certain. He does not do things halfway. He will look at everyone."

She paused, and then whispered, "She will tell him about Mr. Deblin's calls."

With these words it became increasingly obvious to me how much Marta knew. I shifted the subject. "Father did not go to bed at all last night, and this morning he swallowed a bunch of pills."

"He's on amphetamines."

"What's that?"

"It's a drug that stimulates the nervous system; it lifts one's mood, artificially makes one feel better. He must be taking quite a large dose, since he worked all night."

"How do you know that?"

"I heard him. After that harassment from the press yesterday I slept badly, and I got up several times to check some noise. Your father's study door was open. He was burning things most of the night."

I felt wretchedly depressed as I realized that Father had burned the remaining evidence. It was time to make new plans. "Marta, there is something I want you to do. In the next day or so—I shall let you know when—you must take Hector, Mary Anne and Lena by train to Regensburg, to my mother's estate, and tell my uncle that I sent you. I shall write out the details and give you money. Dismiss the cook and whoever else comes in by the day." Marta was looking at me with disbelief. "Tell my uncle that I've sent you on ahead and that I'll be following in a few days."

"No. I can't leave you here."

"Of course you can. He's not going to do anything to me."

"Do you think you can withstand his questioning?"

"Easily. He trusts me completely."

"He trusts no one completely."

"Even if that's true, he won't harm me. I'm his immortality. Without me he has no heir."

Marta shook her head rapidly. "No, I can't leave you alone with that man."

"Yes you can, and you must go when I tell you. The guards will be gone soon; if not, go through the park, through the back. Hector already knows the way. Beyond the park, you can get a cab easily. Take nothing with you, but dress warmly. My uncle will take care of you. I'll get word to you soon." She again shook her head. "Don't start to protest. He killed the cook we used to have here. He can have anyone killed. He killed my old professor. He killed one of his own friends only a few weeks ago. He would have killed Wilhelm and Karl had he caught them, but they managed to get themselves shot a little before he wanted them dead." I took her hand. "You are my friend. You know if he knew about Jans, he would kill him at once, and you as Jans' accomplice. What do you think would happen to Hector then?" I did not wait for her to answer. "Now do you know why you must go?" She nodded. "Good. I shall answer the phones from now on." I left the room, leaving Marta at the table, her hands covering her face.

All morning I waited for Jans' call, but only the newspapers called. I told them I was the housekeeper and in the process of closing the house and that all von Heyditch matters would be handled through the head office of VHI.

Jans did not call in the afternoon either, nor did Father come home for lunch. I tried to read, but terrifying questions kept entering my mind as the day passed into evening: what if Father already suspected Jans? what if Father really suspected me? what if the gun doesn't go off?

Marta kept reassuring me that Jans was only being prudent and careful. "It's possible that the phones are tapped by now," she said. Again I was astonished that I had not thought of that myself.

Father come home at seven, somewhat early for him, and went directly to his study. Marta gave me an anguished glance when he came in without saying a word to anyone. As usual I was in the music room, waiting. Father looked drained and unwell, yet he walked rapidly.

Just before dinner I went up to see Lena, who had

been sick all day and refused to eat. Not wishing to awaken her in case she was asleep, I came into the room quietly. But she was not asleep; she was listening to her radio, and the subject at that moment was my father. The indictments against him did not involve the murder of any Jews: they were concerned with the "appropriation" of government-owned property in the year 1938 and with VHI's possible involvement in the death of three prison officials in the year 1945. The government was going to need some time to prepare its case against Rolf von Heyditch, since many records were missing and there seemed to be no living witnesses.

I stood quietly in the dark and listened. There was another news item coincidentally related to VHI. Two employees of the company—their names were given—were killed when their car, apparently out of control, failed to make a turn on a narrow mountain road in Switzerland. The men were believed to be on holiday at the time.

When I turned on the light, Lena was sitting up in bed, trembling, her agonized face staring at the radio in horror. I tried to talk to her. "It's all right, Lena. Everything will be all right." But she did not seem to hear me. Marta came in a moment later, her face too contorted with fear. "What is it?" I asked.

"He wants to see Lena in his study." She stared at the numbed and helpless Lena. "Now."

"That's impossible. Tell him she is too sick to get out of bed." But Marta did not move. "I'll tell him. Do what you can for her. I can't get her to answer me."

When I knocked on Father's study door, he seemed remotely surprised to see me. His expression softened quickly, although he looked exhausted and his eyes were excessively bright. "Father, Lena is very ill. Could this wait until tomorrow?"

"If she is that ill, Eroica, she must be hospitalized. Tell Marta to get her ready."

"I can take care of her here, Father." I was willing to try anything to keep her out of one of Father's hospitals. "It's only fair," I said smiling. "After all, she did take care of me."

"Nonsense. Have Marta get her ready. I'll have an ambulance here shortly."

I knew that to protest further was to endanger everyone. I returned to the foyer, my mind racing ahead. They had to leave tonight. At the hospital, Lena would be given a sedative tonight, and tomorrow Father would question her and the whole truth would be out. Marta had to get away and get in touch with Jans and warn him.

Upstairs, Marta was still trying, unsuccessfully, to calm Lena. I motioned her into my room. "Father has called an ambulance. He will not be able to talk to her tonight, not in the state she is in, but the morning will be a different matter. You must leave tonight. Before you get on the train tonight, phone Jans and warn him. Tell him to call me from a public telephone at exactly eleven tomorrow morning. Tell him not to speak at all and to hang up as soon as I answer. I must know if he is all right. Marta, everything depends upon his call. Do you understand? If he does not call, I will assume that my father has caught him. Please tell him that. If, for any reason you cannot reach him, you must call me. One of you must call me." I thought a moment. "Marta, you will easily reach Regensburg by morning. After you are settled, phone me. Make it around noon and be casual—only a few words, so that I know you are all safe."

She nodded. "What about you?"

"Don't worry about me. I have plans of my own." Marta's dark eyes glistened. "If you don't go, your deaths will lie in my soul. Lena's will soon be there. Please do not interfere with what I have to do." She took my hand and gripped it in both of hers.

"Come with us," she pleaded. "You must not remain alone with that man." She was weeping.

I retrieved my hand. "Nonsense." I realized that I sounded just like Father.

When we tried to dress Lena, she began to moan; and when the stretcher carriers and a doctor arrived, she wailed plaintively until the doctor gave her an injection of some kind and she relaxed almost at once. I took a last look at her as they carried her out: her eyes were open and I believe she was looking straight at me. I could feel the tears fill my eyes and run down my cheeks. I wanted desperately to tell her that I was sorry that I could not save her life. Briefly I remembered Vera's words. "Do not get involved unless you wish to inherit the dragon's wrath." Lena, poor, dear Lena of the good heart; what could she know of protecting herself from dragons? I knew she was going to die in that hospital even if she never told Father anything. She was familiar with the dragon's lair and therefore might someday be called as a witness to describe what she had seen in it over the years. Father left nothing to chance.

When the ambulance was gone and all was quiet, Father and I sat down to dinner. Although he looked fatigued, Father's good spirits seemed to be returning and he began talking almost at once. "Eroica, you will be happy to hear that the charges against us have come to nothing." He smiled. "The firm may have to pay a little fine over a misunderstanding that happened a long time ago, but that is nothing. My lawyers have just informed me that the other charges are groundless and will be dropped."

"Then you are not in any trouble?"

"No, of course not."

"But it seemed so . . . serious, with all the newspaper people coming to the house."

"They always make a lot of fuss about nothing. And you must realize that people like us will always have enemies. Even now, there is a mystery as to how all this got started, but be assured I shall not rest until I find out who these enemies are. My staff is working on it now, and we have some good friends in the capital who will bring in some answers quite soon." He are heartily and refilled his wineglass twice.

I kept my face turned down; if Father had seen in my eyes the terror with which his words filled me, he would have known at once who his greatest enemy was. I finally mastered enough composure to keep up another hour's conversation with him, since I knew that Marta would warn Jans that very night and he would be able to get away. He could take a plane to the other side of the world and disappear in a strange country. But even as I reassured myself, I remembered Jans' telling me, "The world is not big enough for us to hide from your father." And Father had caught Wilhelm and Karl in another country before twenty hours had gone by.

I watched him eat. Father had to die before he found out anything about Jans. I didn't want any last orders left with Father's gang of killers. Jans had to be made safe forever.

In a few hours Father and I would be alone in the house. Perhaps I always knew that one day I would be walking toward him with a gun in my hand and I would shoot him and shoot him and shoot him until I vanished into the very gun itself and became the last, the finally articulate, bullet, in which all my hatred and fear of him crashed into his heart exploding, exploding—outward, outward, outward—until he was a million bits, then vapor, then nothing, and Gerd and I were free forever.

In retrospect, it was always a mystery to me that on the first day of Father's troubles I had the premonition that in the end, when his troubles dissolved and he was cheerful again, I would be the one who would be walking toward him, holding the gun and saying what no one else had been able to say: "Die! Die! Die!"

"You're not eating your dinner, Eroica."

I managed a smile. "It's just that it's such a relief to know that everything is finally all right."

"I am pleased that you were concerned about me. In a few days I shall have my weight back, and then, with a little rest, all will be back to normal."

I asked about Wilhelm and Karl. He became somber.

"Still a puzzle, I'm afraid; but I'm sure it will resolve itself in a day or two." A few minutes later we said good night to each other and I went to my room and he to his study.

I locked the door that connected Lena's room and mine; I could not bear to think about her. After taking the gun out of my coat, I lay a long time in the dark, waiting for Father to come upstairs. Once I thought I heard him, but it must have been a shutter, or perhaps it was Marta and the others, leaving. Seeing Lena being carted off to the hospital was the final incident that convinced her that there were no options left. Around midnight I crept downstairs to her room: they were all gone.

The lamp still burned outside Father's study. Since he had not slept the night before, I felt that he would go to bed soon. I would wait for him upstairs. Several times I thought I heard footsteps, and each time I crept to the mezzanine and listened. All was still in the house. I was exhausted from waiting. Lena's wide-open eyes looked at me from the dark. "Dear child, my dear child. I will die because of you." The last time I returned to my room I discovered I was weeping. I lay on the bed and thought of Gerd and Mother. Jans was safe. I heard owls calling in the orchard. And then I did the most stupid of all things: I fell asleep.

Sounds I did not recognize awakened me. At first I thought they were human voices, a steady chant of human voices. I rushed to pull open the draperies; a heavy rain fell straight down from a gray-white sky. It was after seven. My mind was all muddled. Father! The gun! The gun was under my pillow. I returned it to my coat pocket and cautiously left my room. I listened at Father's bedroom door. Silence.

Downstairs all was the same as the night before, except that Father was gone. I drifted from room to room: everything was neat and in order. It was not uncommon for Father to leave the house at five without disturbing anyone and have his breakfast in his office;

therefore, he would not notice that the servants were gone. All this mundane reasoning ran through my mind in the hopeless wish to escape the facts: Father would go to the clinic sometime during the day and Lena would tell him that I had been in his study. Or some "friend" in the government would call him and tell him that it was his own interpreter who had given the files to the investigating organization.

I prepared some tea and took it to Mother's plant room, where I watched the rain and waited for Jans' call. At least he was safe no matter what Father found out today. If Lena told him I had had the key to the study, he would talk to me first to find out what I had done with the documents. There was a good chance that Lena would never mention Jans' calls. Since she had not been answering the phones for some weeks now, there was no reason for her to bring up Jans at all. An imaginary conversation came into my mind. "So you gave her the key so she could go to her brother's room. . . ." "Oh, no sir, I didn't give it to her, but I thought it was all right because the dear child was so depressed and lonely. . . ." "That's enough." I saw my father motion to someone nearby; then there was a hypodermic needle and then Lena was sleeping, her eyes open, and someone was asking if there was a disposal problem.

With the teacup in my hand I wandered around the huge empty house trying to shake these dark images out of my mind. The hours lagged. Twice I checked the phone to see that it was working. In the music room I searched for old chords on the piano; they sounded loud and hollow in the stillness. I tried to read, but the words faded off the page as my mind concentrated on the creeping minutes.

Eleven finally came as I sat in front of the phone, watching it. The clock Westminster-chimed pleasantly and then tolled the hours, which I counted with increasing dread. At ten minutes after eleven I was already desperate. At half past the hour I was on the edge of panic: Jans would call if he could; Marta would call if she had been unable to reach him.

At noon, with dangerous unconcern for Jans' safety or mine, I called Von Heyditch Industries and asked to speak to Jans Deblin. I was told to hold. After a few minutes a man came on the line and said that Jans Deblin had left on holiday that very morning and was not expected back for some time. The person on the other end wanted to know if the matter was urgent and if anyone else could be of help. I hung up without answering.

17

On holiday. How pleasant that sounded. He had worked hard, many hours, did not give himself over to frivolity, and now he was on holiday. No one deserved it more. Karl and Wilhelm had gone on holiday.

I wondered how Father had killed him.

The vision of the block of concrete kept vaulting into my mind and I hurled it out with all the force of will I had. Think of something else. Anything. Mother's tulips were blooming and the heavy rain was beating them all to pieces. Go pick them. Put a big glass bowl of them on the dining-room table. What had happened to Marta and the others? If she could have, Marta would have called earlier, to tell me that she was not able to reach Jans or that she and the others were safe in Regensburg. She must be dead, too, and Mary Anne and the boy, Hector. I thought of the heaps of dead children in Jans' black book. Think of something else. Anything, anything, anything.

With monumental calm I went to my room, where I bathed and put on fresh clothes—one of the white knit dresses Father liked so much. I brushed my hair loose and let it hang to my waist. Father liked that, too. I took out my coat, with Jans' black book and the gun in it, and left it on top of my bed.

It was still early afternoon, and Father might not be home until very late. That did not matter. I could wait now because there was nothing left to wait for. For a long time I sat on one of the steps near the bottom of the great arched staircase and leaned my face against the balustrade. On just such an afternoon I had come home from school and sat on this very step, wondering where my brother was. As on that day, the house was silent and cold. On that day, too, I had listened to the river horns as they called to each other like people lost in caves.

All my fear had left me, perhaps because there was nothing left to fear. Jans was dead. A single resolve stopped me from following him: before I killed Father, I would force him to look at his crimes. I wanted him to know that I knew everything, that I loathed him unspeakably, and that it was I who had betrayed his house.

Just as the clock struck three he walked in the door. He still looked extremely tired and stood just inside the foyer in a detached and bemused way that was not like him at all. I walked toward him. "Father?" He took off his hat and smiled at me, but he did not say anything. "How very nice to have you home early." I took his hat and helped him off with his coat. He merely watched me as I put the garments into the dressing room off the foyer. "You look tired, Father. May I pour you a sherry?"

He smiled again. "Yes. Why not? I'm going upstairs; why don't you bring it up to me and we can sit and talk." At another time I might have had qualms over the extra softness of his voice, but that time was long past. There was no longer any need to wonder what Father was thinking.

In the dining room I put the sherry bottle and two glasses on a tray. So, we were going to talk. How pleasant. Just Father and I making plans for a future that could only exist in hell. When I reached his sitting room, the door was open. I placed the tray on a table and lit the fire in the hearth. Then I went to my room and returned with Jans' black book and my coat, which

I placed on the seat of an elegant wing chair. After pouring our sherry I waited for Father to come from his bedroom.

When he came in, he looked quite well; he had put a wine-colored smoking jacket on and a white scarf around his neck with the ends neatly tucked inside the collar of the coat. His hair was brushed back with some kind of pomade. After he sat in a large chair near the fire, I handed him his sherry and sat on a sofa opposite him. As he had been given to doing lately, he raised his glass to me and nodded, but said nothing. I returned the gesture. We drank. After a few moments of silence, as he watched me, I asked after Lena.

"I am sorry to have to tell you this, Eroica—I have been trying to think of some gentle way to tell you—but the truth is she died during the night. I know you were fond of her."

"Yes, Father, I was." I had already known what to expect, so Lena's death was hardly a surprise. "What did she die of, Father?"

"A heart attack," he answered without hesitation. He added, a moment later, "But life goes on for the living, and we must make plans for the future. It is particularly important that we have this discussion now, since I made arrangements today that will affect you deeply, and soon." His eyes looked at me fondly, with contentment and quite obvious pride. "After this recent difficulty, Eroica, I thought it best that there exist a clear statement of inheritance. My legal staff has seen to this. Now, if something should happen to me, there will be a smooth transition of ownership." He spoke almost pensively. "As my only heir, you will carry on our traditions and policies as though my hand were guiding you. It was to your brother that I would have passed the torch . . ."

In that moment I understood why Gerd had killed himself and what Jans had meant when he said, "Your brother survived your Father's past." What he had refused to tell me was that Gerd had not survived Father's future. Suddenly Jans' enigmatic statement—"It is because of you that I cannot tell you"—made all the sense in the world. If Gerd killed himself to deprive Father of an heir, then I—by living—was betraying my brother. The last von Heyditch had to die to purify the world.

". . . but when you marry," Father went on, "there will be a special dispensation made regarding the name. Your sons must carry the name." His expression changed, his eyes glittering with triumph, their gaze burning into mine hypnotically. "For a thousand years will this name be reckoned with." Father's eyes were gazing through me down the centuries.

In one wild instant my hatred of him reached its own triumph. "Is that what you told Gerd, Father, that the world had to suffer us for another thousand years?"

He looked blank for a moment; then his thick eyebrows lowered into a deep frown. "What?"

"Is that when he screamed at you that he'd rather be dead than carry on this accursed name?" I stood up. "What else did you tell him, Father? That he could be the most powerful man in the world as long as he killed everyone who got in his way?" Father remained seated, staring at me with angry disbelief. I picked up the coat and draped it over the back of the sofa so that the pocket with the gun in it was easily within my reach; then I thrust Jans' black book into his hands.

He looked up at me, his frown replaced with a look of cautious interest with which I was quite familiar. I sat down again beside my coat, watching him as he opened the book.

He turned the pages rapidly, stopping momentarily at two or three spots to examine something more closely. I don't know exactly what I expected. Perhaps I wanted to hear him shriek and howl at me, but he did nothing of the sort. He laughed. Halfway through the book he began to chuckle as though he were looking at a book filled with mildly amusing jokes. When he finally came to the end, he closed the cover and said, "Not a new one in the whole bunch. . . . Eroica, is this how you have been wasting your time?" He sipped his sherry.

I was unable to speak, or even to move, which may have been a good thing, because I might have tried to shoot him then and surely would have botched it somehow. He had reopened the book, and he tore out the title page, which he squeezed into a ball and threw it into the fire. I found my voice and discovered that it was calm and controlled. "That's your medal on the last page, Father."

"Of course it's my medal. I earned it." He looked a little sterner.

That look was easier for me to deal with. "Then it's all true, and you deny none of it."

"What's all true?"

"That all those millions were murdered, and you are responsible."

"Come now, Eroica, you can't believe that one man can have the credit for all this." He waved vaguely at the book, which he had placed on the table beside him. "All Europe deserves the credit. Do you really believe that if people everywhere didn't want this, they would have let it happen? Consider this, Eroica, out of nine million Jews in Europe, approximately six million were killed. Do you think I could do that all by myself?" He laughed again. "Do you think Germany could do that all by herself? Be realistic. Germany only did what the world wanted done, and believe me, the world was a great help. It sat back and relaxed and was content to have someone else do the work and go through the expense."

"There were people who didn't want it . . . who knew it was wrong, horrible, horrible. Mother knew it was horrible." I had a hard time making a clear argument.

"Your mother, Eroica, was horrified at her Church. Forty-five percent of Germany is Catholic. That's almost half the people—if I need to point that out to you. Do you know how much your mother's Church protested the policy the government was taking regarding the Jews? It's laughable. All that humanitarian blubbering, you see, didn't really extend to the Jews. What happens in the world, Eroica, happens because the world lets it happen. Do you think the head of the Church said no to the solution of the Jewish problem? Do you think the British and American heads of state didn't know what was happening? They knew more than most ordinary Germans on the street. They said later that there was nothing they could have done anyway. That's absurd. Long before the war, the Jews could have left Germany, but no one wanted them, Eroica. The English government sneaked Jews in undercover. Why undercover? Because their people did not want them any more than our people did. But there was a great deal of wringing of hands at the plight of the poor Jews.

"I must thank you for the gift of this book, but it's quite mediocre. Now, if you really want to see some interesting pictures, you should see *my* collection. I have many reels of film, also. Quite interesting. In the cabinet over there you will find a projector, and if you look closely at the wall behind you, you'll discover it to be a screen, a full-size film screen. You need a little more education. By the way, how did you get these?" He motioned toward the book.

"I stole them."

"You went through a lot of trouble. I have some originals, Eroica, some extremely interesting pictures from Ravensbrück, Dachau, Buchenwald. They were originally intended to go into medical archives, but I managed to get them for a very small price; and one should always keep a good record of certain achievements.

"Come now, if you would like to see a really good collection, you must see mine. You only need open the doors there and press the button. It's all set for immediate viewing. Go on; turn it on." I did not move. "Come now, I know you are stronger than your brother was, and there is a certain eroticism to these that might interest you."

"Were these films and pictures in the crates on the third floor?"

"So, you've been up there, have you? Yes, I kept them there for a time, among other things. Your mother was not capable of understanding these things; unfortunately, she did discover them. But you're made of much sterner stuff."

"I would like to know something, Father."

"What?"

"Did you shoot those three prison officials at Bergen?"

"Of course not. Do you think I go around shooting people?"

"But you were in Bergen?"

"Yes, some business. But a crazed soldier hit me on the head as I was getting into my car. I was trying to get to Regensburg, to your mother. The soldier took my car and I ended up in a hospital ward—an excellent place to get temporarily lost, by the way. Things were quite untidy outside."

"What about the dead man in the greenhouse?"

"What dead man?"

"A Mr. Hauser."

"He died of heart failure."

"In our greenhouse?"

"No, in our drawing room."

"Why was he in the greenhouse?"

"He was easier to pick up from there; there was no point in alarming the servants, and I did not wish him to be found dead in our drawing room. It would have been unseemly. We returned him to his own bed, since it's what he would have wanted, and he did convenience everyone by giving out just when he did. Frightened men are dangerous men, Eroica; remember that. And he was in a bit of trouble that threatened to spill over on his friends. He was getting old, and who knows what he might have said under pressure. How did you run into him?" Father sounded genuinely curious, although there was a hard edge to his voice by then but still no real anger.

I ignored the question. "Did you force Gerd to look at your films?"

"I didn't have to, Eroica. I think he was quite fascinated by them, couldn't tear his eyes away." He laughed.

I reached into my coat pocket and brought out the pistol, aiming it at him. Then Father really laughed. "My, my, what a cannon!"

Although I had prepared for this moment, planning to remain calm and steady, my hands shook badly and my voice trembled. "This cannon, Father, is going to blow you to bits."

"Well, Eroica, you again prove me right. Any other woman would have used poison, but a daughter of mine uses an automatic pistol. Yes, you definitely have more character than your brother had. But then, you are more like me."

I released the safety. "Don't think I don't know how to use it, Father."

"I'm sure you do. You wouldn't be my daughter if you didn't. How like me you are. Of course you want me dead. It will all be yours, then. You will be the House of von Heyditch. Have sons, Eroica; make sure there is someone to carry on after you, too, are gone. The House must go on." He looked at me with a slight frown. "Did you think it out by yourself?" He shook his head admiringly. "Of course you did. You must have seen the possibilities at once when I made you of age. Well, it's a good sign. None of this idiotic sentimentality. You knew what was yours and you knew how to take it.

"Place the gun in my hand afterward and say that I spoke of ill health. Everyone will believe you. Call my lawyers at once. Tell them you heard the shot—only one, so don't make any mistakes—and that you came running. Don't touch anything else. Take your sherry glass and your things out. Perhaps I should leave a note."

He put his head back and laughed. "Like me. Who would have thought it—a woman being like me? Gerd could never have done it. You should have been my son. He was like a girl, incapable of taking over and carrying on my work. But you . . . you are just like me. He was a great disappointment to me, too cowardly to accept his responsibilities. But you . . . you have the true German will. . . ."

"Stop saying that; I'm not like you! You're a . . . killer."

"Eroica, look at you. You're doing exactly what I would do. There's nothing wrong with killing if it's done for the right reasons. Do you know what I offered your brother? I gave him a chance to control all Europe. Think of it. And he hanged himself. I assure you, if someone had offered *me* that at seventeen, I would have been shouting for joy, and so will you." He smiled a vulgar cynical smile. "There is one more thing, Eroica: be careful whom you marry. Centuries of good pure blood run in your veins, and this must always be the first consideration in marriage."

I aimed the gun at his sneering face, gripping my wrist with my free hand. He wouldn't even close his eyes or stop smiling. My hands shook. I tried to think of Gerd hanging from the study ceiling, Mother's emaciated face, Jans crushed in concrete, but nothing came to me except Father's straight, unflinching stare into the gun barrel. I lowered the gun slowly.

"Now then, Eroica, if that foolishness is over, I think it's time that we straighten out a few things." He refilled his glass. "Who put you up to this nonsense, where did you get this book, and whose gun is that?"

"The gun?" I looked down at the weapon. "Why, it's my gun, Father. Yes, it's meant for me. I've been mistaken all along. You, Father, are the one who has to stay alone for . . . how long did you say? Another twenty, thirty years? Yes, Father. You, all alone for the next thirty years. You and your pictures, your records of certain achievements, all alone, with no sons and no grandsons." I raised the barrel to my temple.

Horror ran across his face for the first time and he began to shake his head rapidly. "No," he whispered loudly.

"Yes," I answered.

"Eroica, there is no need for you to do this."

"Yes, there is, Father, a very great need. You see, I can't live in the same world with you. Just as Gerd and Mother couldn't."

"You can't do this." He was still whispering.

"Yes, I can. Really. Quite easily."

"No, you're my daughter. You're the last. Please, Eroica, I beg you. . . ." He began to moan.

"Why, Father, you're whining. Don't whine, Father, it's un-German." He started to rise. "One move and I shall be dead," I hissed at him. He fell back into his chair, a deep groan in his throat. Then, suddenly, he was weeping. "No!" I screamed. "Don't you dare cry. You don't get to cry. That's only for sentimental, blubbering humanitarians who wring their hands over people being murdered by the millions. That's what ties all those people together, Father—the dead and the living—their tears. But not us, Father; we can have no tears. Mother knew that. She had only dry gasps to weep. We are the desert, Father. We are the dead sand in the desert where nothing grows." I was weeping as I pushed my hair away from my forehead and positioned the gun farther back on my temple. Father shrieked and sank down in his chair, one hand reaching spread-fingered toward me. He opened his mouth but did not speak. He opened it wider and wider; then his whole face began to quiver and he made gagging sounds in his throat. At the same time his whole body gave a curious lurching motion; his legs shot out straight in front of him and his head twisted back so that his chest rose upward, where it heaved violently for a few seconds before it fell in, and his head jerked forward, twitching obscenely before it hung loose and motionless. His legs stuck out stiffly in front of him and his body lay half off the chair.

I still held the gun to my head, but my hand shook uncontrollably as I lowered it and stared at my father's gaping mouth. With only one of his eyes open, he had a ludicrous wink on his face. "Father?" I touched his shoulder, but he did not move. "Father." I began to scream at him. "Don't you dare die. I'm not finished. It was I who violated your house. I stole your records. Do you hear me, Father?" I grabbed the lapel of his coat. "Hear it! It was I!" I began to tug at the lapel.

"He can't hear you, Eroica." Jans strode into the room swiftly, taking the gun from my hand and placing it on the mantel. I was crying wildly, but Jans was busy with Father, loosening his scarf and listening to his chest. He stood up and took a folded afghan and covered him. Then he returned to me and grasped my shoulders. "Stop it, Eroica."

"You're alive," I gasped.

"Yes, and so is he." Jans looked toward Father and then picked up the phone.

Two hours later, Father was still alive but in deep paralysis. The three doctors who hovered over him met with Jans and me in the music room.

"Did he complain of head pains?" asked one.

Jans lit a cigarette and inhaled deeply. "No, not at all. We were reviewing some matters—a particular project of his of which he was quite fond—confidential, of course"—all three doctors nodded soberly—"when suddenly he seemed to enter into some kind of convulsion. I loosened his clothing and covered him at once. He did not respond to my voice."

The oldest of the doctors turned to me. "We might as well tell you, the situation does not look promising. Your father has had what is commonly known as a stroke. A full clinical picture of its severity is developing. We do not wish to give you any false hopes; his condition is serious, grave. He may linger for hours, days, weeks. Time will tell. He may regain consciousness, possibly even some movement and speech. Again, it is a matter of time. We advise that he be moved to a clinic in a day or so, when we know more."

"That's not possible," I said. "When my father was ill before, he refused to go to a clinic. He told me many times that if he becomes ill, he is to be kept here."

The doctors looked at each other with anxious expressions. "My dear young lady," began one of them, "this is most irregular."

"Not at all," I said calmly. "My mother died in this house. She, too, refused to go to a clinic, and my father agreed with her. He often said that if something untimely should happen to him, I should stay with him, here."

"But he must have full-time care . . . around the clock."

"That can be arranged here," I said.

Again the doctors glanced at each other with misgivings. Jans looked at me cautiously, but remained silent. One of the doctors looked at his watch. "Perhaps we should decide later, when we know—"

"You may decide whatever you wish, but it is my father's will that he remain here, and his will always prevails. I speak in his behalf." I stood up. "I shall go to him now."

Jans and the doctors rose quickly, and I had the odd sensation that I had just entered an enormous room where a great audience was watching me. I turned toward Jans. "Mr. Deblin, during my father's recent difficulties with the government, he instructed me to contact you in case anything happened to him. Did he speak to you of this?"

Jans nodded slowly. "Yes, mademoiselle, he did."

I paused a moment, deeply aware of the attentive and waiting doctors. "There will, of course, be no change of policy and tradition at VHI," I said quietly. "In the meantime, I think you and these gentlemen must prepare a statement for the press." I faced the listening doctors. "Can we conceal the severity of his condition?"

The silence in the room was charged with surprise.

"For a time," said one of them slowly, taking a deep breath.

"Please do your best."

They nodded somberly as I left them.

In Father's room I told the nurse to wait outside. She seemed offended but left without saying anything. Father looked much as I last saw him, except that he was in bed and his mouth hung open only slightly. He still had the monstrous wink on his face, and with the open eye turned upward he seemed to be snickering at a hugely indecent joke.

"Father?" I did not expect an answer, yet seeing him lie in bed with that grotesque grin on his face frightened me at first. He could regain consciousness at any time, and even if he couldn't speak immediately, he might yet reveal his feelings through some expression in his eyes. Also, the doctors might be wrong. Father might sit up at any moment and point his accusing finger at me: I had betrayed the House; I had tried to kill him; I had paralyzed him.

As I stood at the foot of the bed, looking at him, some stark memories of him began to return to me. "You have become a comfort to me, Eroica, and a pride." He had trusted me completely! My heart seemed to wither with this realization, and I wanted to sink into nothingness. Gerd had done it right; he hadn't lied and betrayed. He had known what he had to do and he had done it quietly, using no one. I had caused Lena to die.

Jans came into the room and stood beside me. "You must not despair," he said, looking hard at my face.

"Everything went wrong. I did it all wrong." I seemed unable to word my sorrows clearly.

"Eroica, listen to me. They suggested I prepare you for his death. They do not think he will last the week."

During that long first night, while the doctors moved all kinds of medical apparatus into Father's room, Jans and I finally had time to talk privately. He had already told me that Marta had reached him by phone and that he had moved into the house an hour after he put Marta and the others up at a hotel for a few days, telling them not to go to Regensburg until he contacted them.

"Why didn't you let me know you were alive?"

"You know very well why. If you had killed him, you would have killed us, and I couldn't help you make that decision."

"But I thought you were dead."

"That had nothing to do with it. It was essential to you that you couldn't kill him. It was essential to me. However, I didn't doubt for a minute that you intended to kill yourself. My biggest problem was getting to you before you managed to pull it off. I stood behind that door with my heart in my hand while you and your father reached the final hour."

"But if Father had not had the stroke and you would have come into the room to stop me, you would have endangered yourself."

"I had a story prepared. Marta was supposed to have called me because you were acting wildly and she feared that you might try something desperate. It wasn't a very good story, but it was at least plausible, and your carrying a gun around gave it a good deal of weight. I might also add that the story would have been true. What do you think I thought when you sent everyone away?"

"Marta was supposed to warn you that you were in danger."

"Eroica, you were the one who was in danger. I knew immediately that once he told you that there was no chance of his being tried, you would have your own private trial for him, whether I was in danger or not."

He was right, of course, and as I heard the anger in his voice, I knew that he was thinking of Father's unknown plans for the future. I had destroyed any chance of his discovering those plans. "Jans, did you hear everything Father said?" He nodded. "What did he mean when he said that he had offered Gerd the chance to control all Europe?"

Jans looked down at Father. "Those words have been pounding in my head like a drumbeat."

"I ruined everything. He might have told me about that if I hadn't been so stupid."

"Don't worry about the mistakes. We must look at what we have. You did a very good job with those doctors; they are convinced that there is an absolute replica of von Heyditch waiting to take over, and they will spread that word quickly. No one will disbelieve them: first, because they are doctors; and second, because your father has only recently clarified your position with VHI. You *are* VHI."

I backed away from the bed. "No, I can't."

"Yes you can."

"I don't know anything."

"But you have extraordinary instincts. That line about contacting me . . . really, Eroica, it positively stunned me. You have an intelligence you don't know anything about. In a few words you put me beside you in a way that no one will question. By the time those doctors tell the story the second time, they'll be saying they *heard* your father telling you to contact me in case something happened to him, and my having been his translator strengthens it all immeasurably. We'll find out what he's up to."

His confidence made me feel better, but as I looked down at Father's sly face, an ominous foreboding shivered through me; my instincts weren't telling me anything encouraging.

Father did not die that week, as the doctors had predicted. Nor the next. Spring melted into summer and still he hung on. At first the nurses took care of him completely and I only sat beside his bed a few hours each day, but as the time passed, I took over more and more of their duties, leaving them only the intravenous feeding to perform. One after another the women quit, complaining to the doctors that I refused to let them do their work. Without knowing why, I knew that he was my responsibility, that there was no one else in the whole world who should be asked or expected to do this. Each day I washed his deteriorating body: by the middle of the summer he looked like the starved skeletons in Jans' black book. His hair was falling out rapidly, his once-muscular legs and arms were only sticks, and his genitals were shrunken and gray. Jans wanted to help me, but by then I refused to let anyone help, saying only that it was my duty and no one else's. Jans nodded unhappily and looked away. The doctors, who came daily, always bringing new specialists with them, remarked on my great devotion and love for my father. Jans said their stories of my care and dedication brought tears to people's eyes.

As the weeks passed and it became increasingly evident to us that Jans could find nothing in all the records of VHI—to which he now had full access—of some pending doom for Israel, my hatred of my father began to return with febrile intensity. After watching Jans, resolute but exhausted, spend weeks rereading foreign contracts for a clue to VHI's power over the ridged-wheel nations, I found myself talking in loud whispers to Father. "Please, please, Father . . . stay alive. Tell me what you want done." Then I would curse myself for pleading to him. But a day later Jans' discouraged face would send me into a new frenzy of whispered begging of the living dead man, who no longer even resembled my father, to stay alive.

One day, as I was changing the bedsheets and cleaning the feces from his bony hips, I suddenly heard myself no longer whispering. "You bastard, either live or die. But one way or another, tell us." Bitterly I thought of his mock death: he couldn't control his bowels, yet he clutched a large part of the world in his monstrous power.

Late one night, as I was adjusting the reading lamp I read by as I sat beside his bed, I thought I saw a gleam of intelligence in his eye, a sudden glint of light coming from within him and directed straight at me. I shrank back and cried out, which brought Jans running from Father's sitting room, which he used for an office when he was not at Father's offices.

"He looked at me," I screamed. "I swear he looked at me. He can see and hear everything. He's just pretending." I was still screaming when I tore a pillow away from under Father's feet, which were covered with damp bedsores, and brought it down over his face. Jans wrenched it out of my hands and pushed me away from the bed.

After that, Jans rarely left me alone. When he had to be away at the VHI offices, he made sure Marta was with me. My headaches returned and with them the insomnia and a frightening inability to stop weeping for hours at a time. When I did sleep, my dreams were peopled with the dead and always with Father's mocking face.

Fifteen weeks after I had aimed my gun at the spot between Father's eyes, he died. It was about noon. He had been breathing quietly as I watched his skull-face, and then my mind wandered off vacantly, as if leading me down a barren road; when I returned, my father was dead. About three minutes had passed while I was elsewhere.

Exhausted and in deep pain, I sat back in the chair and watched his motionless profile. Even when he was emaciated, the bones of his face stood out in bleak triumph beneath the dead and shriveled flesh. I walked out into the mezzanine and stood quietly in the gloom, listening to the silence in the house. Fog pressed against the glass of the great oval windows on the stair landings. I felt a profound sense of loss that I could not understand. A moment later, coming out of the sitting room and finding me standing in the hall, Jans looked into my face and with a sharp intake of breath quickly walked past me to Father's room.

We were alone now, and all our desperate hopes that Father might have revealed his secret to us before he died went with him to the grave. Our first fear was that Father's death might be a signal of some kind to set his plan in motion. We listened to news broadcasts like addicts; yet we did not know what we were listening for. Jans increased his search among the records with a fury that left him gaunt and restless.

While we were proceeding with the dreary charade of having Father's bones prepared for burial, a whole secretarial staff spent days answering the letters and telegrams of condolence. To me these messages of deep sorrow were ridiculous lies and nonsense, but still Jans and I read them all, looking for a clue, a pattern, a developing picture of a code, that would break the secret.

"We have to assume," said Jans one night as we sat across the music-room table from each other, rereading all the cables from the ridged-wheel nations, "that whoever is in this believes that you know all about it. We have to assume further that someone is expecting to hear from you."

I gasped, but he quickly put his hand on mine. "Don't panic. That may be our best break. It gives us time. If we get any anxious messages in the next few days or weeks, we may be able to put something together. In the meantime, we can only . . ."—he flinched at the word as he watched my face—"wait."

Father's sealed coffin lay in the great banquet hall on the second floor of VHI's central office complex for three days while employees and guests paid their tributes to him. All the flags on his factories and mines and ships flew at half mast. His will had specified that there be no religious service for him; thus, my first public appearance was at the family crypt, where his coffin was to be placed beside Mother's. Jans had insisted that I attend this ritual. "You are the bereaved daughter. We do not know who is watching!"

Heavily veiled and with Jans beside me, I stood next to Father's flag-draped casket and silently wept with rage. Strangers pressed my gloved hand and burst into tears while news cameras recorded the occasion in remarkable numbers. I noticed that people looked at Jans with interest and curiosity as he shielded me from aggressive newsmen. I did not answer a single question.

It took me a little time to realize that Jans' depression was as deep as mine, but he seemed better able to live with his. Only a few times did he reveal his profound despair, and the reasons were always the same: he had followed some promising clue only to have it mean nothing after hours of work. In these times of disappointment he would hold his head in his hands, his elbows on the desk, and visibly tremble for a few moments before taking a deep breath, the expression of grim determination returning to his face, and starting again.

I had convinced Uncle Teddy to stay with me for a few days, but our reunion had the aura of an amateur play in which people forgot their lines or repeated them at the wrong times. He was not well, and when his limousine finally drove away, I was glad to see him go. He had never worked a day in his life, unless pasting stamps into a book could be classified as work. He was not comfortable in Cologne. He said that Rhinelanders lived much too primitively for his tastes. When I thought of Mother's estate, I rather knew what he meant: the great manor house where Gerd was born was full of peace and quiet. It belonged in another world, in a time long past. Its elegant towers lifted their loveliness in the midst of a shadowy forest where deer drank, without fear, at the grassy banks of mountain streams. It was part of the green world full of a strange, unreachable innocence.

Uncle Teddy did leave me a copy of his will, and all it did was add more wealth to everything that Father left me.

As far as the world knew, I was almost twenty-one.

Father's ability to have records changed was extraordinarily thorough. Uncle Teddy seemed indifferent to my age; he wanted to get back to civilization. Father's efficient, cool-headed executives continued to run things, even though Jans watched from the inside and they knew that he was my voice.

Our search for Father's plans ultimately centered on the employees. We had to find the men whom Father had sent out on a mission years ago, on the very day that Jans and I had first met. Jans was convinced that the men at the VHI office in Cologne knew nothing about any plot, even the few old dour ones from the war days, whom he forced into retirement within a month after Father's death. These he replaced with younger men who were eager to get on in the world.

"It is my conviction that those men, with their rendezvous in the future, are still where he sent them that night," he said as he gazed at the lists of VHI employees in foreign countries. "In the last year I have been present at every one of your father's major business meetings involving VHI interests in foreign countries. Not once did he bring together a group of his own men from all or even a few of the different countries. He met with the men from Argentina or Tunisia or Iran separately, but never together, not even when the enterprises were the same. I have read the biannual progress and quality reports of every plant and factory from every one of the ridged-wheel nations; there is nothing unusual about any of them. Here are the names of all VHI employees in these firms and there is not a politician among them—in the strict sense of the word. They are technicians, advisors, engineers; and their ages range from the middle twenties to the late sixties." He paused.

I shook my head. "I'm sorry, I can't tell you their ages. It was dark on the stairs and from above I couldn't see their faces. I had the impression that they were Father's age, but Father always looked so much younger than he was, so the men could have been ten or fifteen years younger than Father, maybe more. To me

Father was perpetually forty. Gerd once said jokingly that Father willed himself to stop aging at forty, because he wanted to live forever."

Jans smiled abstractedly. "We'll start at that age, and by assuming that none of the men was younger than forty, we can cut the list in half."

"What if those men aren't even on the list?"

Jans frowned and looked down at the papers in front of him. "No, your father doesn't think that way, and we have to think the way he does."

"Jans, you're doing it again, you're talking about him as though he were still alive."

"He is alive as long as his plan is alive."

"And we have to think as he did?"

"Yes."

I shuddered. "Jans, I want to think in any way except the way my father did."

"Eroica, we don't have to become him; we only have to know how he thinks."

"Well, then think the worst, because that's what he did. He used everybody. Others did all the rotten things for him. Remember his statement to me: 'Do you think I go around shooting people?' " We were in Father's study at the time, sitting at a library table with the VHI employee lists spread out in front of us. Jans looked up from the lists slowly.

"Yes, he'll have someone else do it for him, and the men we are looking for will follow the same pattern—someone else will do it for them—and VHI won't even seem to be in on it anywhere." He stood up. "It's not something having to do with economics at all. It's not going to be a matter of closing down factories and throwing people out of work or humiliating a backward country with the threat of economic failure." He stood staring at Father's desk. "The cabal had the appearance of being a phony organization. His control over the ridged-wheel nations has the appearance of economic blackmail. . . ." He ran his hands through his hair.

"There's nowhere to go from there. We have to go back over the way we came."

And that's what we did. For weeks we went back over the records, checking out every employee working abroad, his age, his wartime whereabouts, his position with VHI. No patterns developed. There were a few SS men with relatively unimportant supervisory jobs in various foreign-based factories. Jans left them alone. "We can get rid of them later. We can't do anything now that looks as though VHI is changing its policies."

In the late fall we went to Liechtenstein, where we again spent days going over records. There was no visible evidence of the old war crimes. The holding company's files contained documents of the transfers of hundreds of small foreign firms into the VHI concern, but they were all dated in the nineteen fifties and they were all legally transacted and so marked.

The chalet was as I remembered it: quaintly uncomfortable, full of kitsch furniture and clocks with cuckoos whose necks I wanted to wring. Jans stopped all their mechanisms, which insulted the couple who were employed to care for the house. There was one room which had a large window facing the river. Here Gerd and I had contemplated the swift headwaters of the Rhine. "It's all only in process, Eroica; the mountains, the rivers, everything is in a constant state of change. That's the most intense reality of life—its constant change." I saw his bright smile and sunlit hair as he spoke and found myself in deep mourning. Jans sensed my moods before I could give them names, and he quickly made some staff changes, ordered the chalet sold, and took us home.

In the capital he worked at becoming chummy with the representatives from some of the ridged-wheel nations. They were polite and suspicious. "Every time I'm near one of their people I can sense their secret hostility in my heart. I'd like to walk up to one and point-blank ask him how the Old Dragon plans to use his country."

I did finally visit Father's office, at the top of his twenty-story office building, and was surprised at how sparsely he had furnished it. Yet, in another sense the whole world was in it. One wall, built in a concave arc formation over thirty feet long, had a map of the world on it. Jans explained all the little lights as he sat behind Father's desk and pressed various buttons on a control panel on the desk. I sat beside him and watched as he talked. "Textiles." He pressed a button and little white lights went on all over the world. "Chemicals." Blue lights went on. Halfway through the control-table demonstration, I suddenly hit at the buttons with my fists.

"Father's toy! The world is Father's toy." I began to curse his neon wall and Jans quickly put his arms around me to quiet me down. We drove home in silence.

As the days passed, we lived in the shadow of the wheel. Jans again reviewed contracts, delving into areas where a country's economy might be jeopardized by some action on VHI's part. He followed up every rumor, hint, and suggestion made by a foreign guest that something had gone abnormally awry in his country. It all came to nothing. His greatest fear now was that time was running out. We waited for signs, portents, errors. We waited for anything and everything.

October came and I began to rage at our failure. The worse horror I felt was the absolute conviction that the continuation of VHI policies in all business areas also included Father's private policy in his intended destruction of the Jewish state. In a violent moment I threw Father's medal into the fire; whatever was left of it was later plowed under in the lime orchard. As for the pendant, I studied it for hours, swore at it, and then one day ran out to the tool room and placed it on the anvil. Jans, running behind me, stopped the hammer just in time. "Now, listen to me: you're going to drive yourself mad worrying like this. We have to remain sane. Destroying this may be a mistake; someday we may need it."

"What do you suggest? Shall I wear it to one of those idiotic embassy parties we are always being invited to?" We stared at each other as the idea began to touch us in a lurid and fascinating way. For hours we talked it over: should we accept the next invitation, and should I wear the pendant? It was dangerous; we decided against it, and Jans returned the diamond to the safe.

My nightmares increased alarmingly, until I woke up screaming every night. Marta finally convinced Jans that we should leave Cologne for a few days and during that time forget everything. We both knew that forgetting was not possible, but Jans had a real concern for my sanity.

We left for Regensburg on a beautiful autumn morning, spending the first few days at Mother's estate. We were alone, except for the servants, because Uncle Teddy was off "taking the waters" at some spa in Switzerland, which Gerd had once called the hot-water bag of the world. Teddy had a long history of taking the waters, and for once his health addiction was convenient as well as amusing. No one expected anything of us. We made love and then rested. We awakened and made love again. I took Jans through the elaborate gardens and on to the forest, where I experienced one of those strange moments one believes one has lived before in exactly the same way. Jans was lying on his back with silvered sunlight slipping past the leaves and flickering on his hair and skin. "We weren't even living anymore. Do you know that?" he said. Lying beside him, I only nodded, and he turned to me, his eyes tender and loving.

One day during that visit I called Jans "Gerd." Perhaps we both knew that a time would come when I had to let go of my brother. We were making love, and as I kissed the satin heart of Jans' penis, I said my brother's name. I began to weep and tried to tell him I was sorry, but Jans only held me very tightly, as though he were trying to keep me from physically falling apart. "Eroica, your dead brother is not someone I can be jealous of. In fact, I am grateful to him. God alone knows what would have happened to you if he had not taught you so much." Jans knew better than I that I would have to come to terms with my dead lover and accept the living one.

One of the many things that Jans and I talked about on that trip was Father's collection of films. "Did you see them?" I asked him.

"Yes. That first day, when you thought you were alone in the house, I searched the top floor and your father's living quarters. I found the projectors and his gruesome collection. I viewed them all."

"What are we going to do with them?"

"They are yours to do with as you wish. I can tell you one thing: Gerd did not enjoy them. I believe they were the final horror that convinced him that he had to end the House of von Heyditch. How resolute his conviction must have been that it could so turn him from all other considerations—your mother's life . . . his love for you. He believed that his way was the only way. This is usually the tragedy of the idealist. The villains always know when to compromise."

"Do you think I should see them?"

"Good God, no! You would have screaming nightmares for the rest of your life."

When we returned home a few days later, I had Jans give Father's films and photographs to the nation as a bequest. Then we, with our somewhat renurtured spirits, plunged back into the search for the phantoms who seemed to become more and more elusive as time passed. Jans hit on the idea of feeding into computers every bit of information that he had about VHI employees abroad. The machines told us everything about them except which dozen or so were in a position to coerce some nations into murder.

We were wretchedly disappointed. "It's like one of those Chinese puzzles," said Jans late one night as he was returning some files to his briefcase. "I open a door expecting to find what I'm looking for, but there is only another door, and inside of that one there is another, and so on. I have a feeling that one day I really will get to the very last minute, infinitesimal chamber, and I shall open it, and everything will blow up in my face."

Toward the end of October, Jans brought home a curious cable: it came from a VHI man in Bolivia who wanted to know if the celebration would be held on schedule.

"What celebration?" I asked Jans. The cable was addressed to me.

He shook his head slowly, but said, "Your birthday?"

We had done nothing about my pending birthday party; in fact, we had forgotten about it, just as Jans said people would. There were no invitations out or even ordered and no further announcements had been made. There was a good deal of gossip about Jans' and my relationship; and the media people had us married in a dozen different places in secret ceremonies attended by people we did not even know. We ignored the speculations and titillating rumors.

Jans had long since become recognized as the power behind the huge firm and was both envied and admired. There were those who said that he worked hard enough to be the Old Man's son himself, and everyone believed that Father had spoken his last words to his trusted interpreter.

Thirty-six hours after the first cable arrived, a second wire with a similar message came from a VHI employee in Libya. Jans immediately fed all the information that he had about the two men into a computer: both were engineers in their late forties; both had been with VHI during the war, doing essential work which exempted them from military duty; both had families who lived with them abroad. But they did not arrive at their foreign posts at the same time, neither had belonged to the Nazi party, and they were not in the same line of work. The Bolivia man worked as an operational advisor at a hydroelectric plant in Bogota. The man in Libya was involved in research design at a transmission station near Tripoli. Jans matched up dozens of other facts about them, none of them telling us anything unusual.

In Father's office we waited for the third wire, Jans pacing back and forth in front of the map—between South America and North Africa—repeating "Celebration, celebration" every few minutes in such a frenzy of despair that watching him was almost unbearable for me. "Jans, let's wire them that there won't be a celebration."

He stopped walking and stared at me, his face pale and haggard. "What will that tell them?"

"I don't know, but we have to answer them." I was seated in Father's leather chair, swiveling slightly. I pressed the TEXTILE button on his control panel and Jans glanced briefly at the map as the white lights went on. I pressed another button and looked toward the map. There were no lights. I pressed it again. "The lights didn't go on."

For a moment Jans didn't say anything; he was looking at the map rather abstractedly. "It's been three days since we received the first cable . . . What did you say?"

"The lights didn't go on."

He bounded toward me and brought his hand forcefully down upon mine on the controls. "Which button?" he said, his face wild with energy. He raised his hand off mine slowly as we both looked down on the panel.

"Electrical-power plants," I said.

Jans laughed. "Oh my God. A hydroelectric plant, a transmission station! Of course they're in the same line of work, and they are both within reach of the capitals of those countries, and so are nine others in nine other capitals where the lights are also going to go out all at once like the candles of a birthday cake. Oh, happy birthday, Eroica." He swayed drunkenly, then steadied himself against the control panel. "And I used to think he didn't have a sense of humor. How like him to give expert engineers phony titles that downgraded their real purpose and ability—an advisor, a researcher!" Jans stared at me, shaking his head rapidly. "Don't you see—you could have killed him and he'd still be laughing in hell, and he knew it."

"Jans, please tell me. What is he up to?"

"It's lights, Eroica, lights that won't go on. Lights that will not go on in homes or hospitals, not in stores or streets, not in factories, not in offices, not in train stations, not in trains." He was breathing wildly. "Huge cities without lights. Rows and rows of tall buildings like dead things in the dark. Elevators, furnaces, pumps—none of them working. No trains, no radios. A silent, cold, lightless world. Oh, my God." Fiercely, he pounded the button that produced no light and laughed again. "He must have pressed it so often in anticipation he wore it out. You once said the world was his toy. His toy!" Then suddenly he became quite calm, closing his eyes and breathing deeply. "Actually, it's probably only a short." He had a wonderful smile on his face. "Come, we have things to do." He was talking rapidly.

"What? What is it? What do we have to do?"

"First we shall send cables. One should always answer one's cables. No, first we'll get the names of all those confident men who aren't expecting cables because they know a command when they hear one, not like our two nervous nincompoops. 'There will, of course, be no change of policy and tradition at VHI.' How does it feel, my dear Eroica, to have sent out an order to start a war?"

"Jans, I don't know what you're talking about. Please stop running." We were walking very fast to his private office. He stopped suddenly.

"Eroica, there were eleven men around your father

that night four years ago when he played your symphony, and I know exactly where they are and what they are up to and when they think they are going to do it." All the wild humor was gone from him and he looked at me with glistening eyes. "Eroica, the order went out four years ago, and in seven days, on the ninth, on your birthday, no, on your nonbirthday, the lights will go out; no, not just the lights, everything, everything powered by electricity will go out in eleven capitals of the world and will stay out unless we—you—send eleven cables notifying eleven men that the celebration has been postponed."

It was almost midnight as we stood in that empty corridor with the black carpets and the blood-red velvet wallpaper on the plush top floor of Father's office building, staring at each other in explosive amazement. "Those men are the dragon's teeth, Eroica."

"Jans, why would my father do that? He already had their votes whenever he wanted them."

"That's just it: he didn't want their votes. He wanted people to think that, just as he wanted people to think that he didn't believe in guns."

"But he doesn't . . . didn't."

"He wants a war, Eroica, but not one that involves his own country. He wants someone else to fight it. He wants an all-out war that will destroy his enemies without himself ever getting involved.

"A shutdown of power plants in those capital cities of the world is his blackmail, his leverage, to force those countries to aid Israel's enemies. The war is coming and your father plans to assure its success for the enemy. With economic embargos, military aid, and God knows what else he can force out of those countries, he intends finally to destroy the symbol of his thwarted will. For a long time I knew there was something different about your father's hatred of Israel. It's never really been just a country full of Jews to him. It's a symbol of all the opposing forces that worked against Germany. The

Third Reich attempted to destroy the Jew. The creation of Israel is an attempt to preserve him. Don't you see the way he thinks? To him, Israel is a living symbol of everything that opposed his iron will. Your brother said no by dying.

"In all the time I worked for your father I never heard him laugh the way other men did at jokes about the Jews. He didn't laugh, because he had a vengeful respect for the Jews. He hated them for what they had done to him: they had survived his careful plans of totally eliminating them. He built the instruments to destroy them and they wouldn't stay destroyed. One day he was reading a report on the Near East and he suddenly ripped it to bits. 'That miserable piece of desert is flourishing,' he said. Do you see, Eroica—they overcame him. He said 'die' and they wouldn't die.

"That's why he saved everything—to convince himself of his achievements. He needed evidence of his success. In those dark hours when he knew his old enemy could turn the desert into a garden, he went to his films, his old documents that said he had won. . . . What did he call them?"

"Records of certain achievements."

"A bit ambiguous on the 'certain,' but either meaning was applicable for him."

"Jans, you're talking about him in the past."

He looked at me with strange, calm eyes. "Your father is dead, Eroica."

We didn't send cables to the eleven men telling them that the celebration had been postponed. In a few hours Jans contacted the governments in each of the eleven countries and had the men quietly arrested and deported to Germany, where Jans retired them without explanation. In the following weeks new men whom Jans chose with great care took their places.

After that I felt enormously free and buoyant, but Jans' sudden distant expression at times left me uneasy.

I was disturbed at the way he still worried over every VHI employee in a foreign country. When I questioned him about his concern, he said, "We can't ever assume that your father would have been satisfied after a war in the Near East had destroyed one of his enemies. His thinking didn't stop there. He wanted the world at odds with itself. He wanted the two great powers to go after each other on the soils of the little nations. He loved the war in Southeast Asia. It actually made him happy. His old enemies were eating each other up and all those Pemselian inferior peoples were being destroyed in the bargain."

"But, Jans, you can't worry about everyone in the world."

He chuckled. "Well, I don't think I'm doing that."

I was happy to see his spirits pick up, although I continued to sense a dark pessimism in him that he tried in a hundred ways to hide. I remembered the day long ago when he had shaved off his beard and told me that he was "twenty-seven, going on thirty-eight hundred," and I had not understood, because I knew nothing of Jews. But now, watching him trying to conceal his melancholy hours from me, I began to ponder the centuries of sorrows that stood like homeless ghosts behind him.

For generations my own ancestors had been born on soil that was theirs without question. They had taken the certainty of an eternal homeland as much for granted as they did the stars. On their burial places monuments in stone smugly clarified for the world their place in time.

In an unmarked mass grave over which wild grasses lived and died with the seasons lay the bones of Jans' parents.

"It's that other thirty-eight hundred years, isn't it?" I said to him one night some months after we were married at a quiet civil ceremony at Regensburg.

He seemed to be watching the rain, but I knew he was staring inwardly.

He looked up, startled. "What is?"

"Whatever it is that keeps you from feeling the way I do."

"And how do you feel?"

"Wonderful, because you're safe, because we're safe."

"I'll work on it," he said without smiling.

In a curious way, being safe meant not having any more cruel and terrifying mysteries in one's life. It meant knowing what was happening around you. It seemed to me that from the hours I had tried to open my dead brother's hand to the moment I had pressed the lightless control button on Father's desk, my life had been a series of monstrous enigmas, agonizing and calamitous. I wanted peace and I believed in its possibility totally because I felt that now we could decide what would happen in our lives.

"Don't you see what I mean, Jans? Before, when we were still hunting for the men my father had sent out, someone else controlled everything. We didn't even know what we were looking for or what was going to happen. Someone else was in control. That was the form and shape of our enemy: that terrible feeling that someone else was actually directing everything we did. Even the statement we gave the press when Father was ill was exactly the statement he wanted me to give and it was actually a message for those dreadful men at the power plants. But now the things we say come from us, not him; and the things we do are for our lives, not his."

Jans didn't argue with me over my view that only we had control of our lives; he smiled and made some funny comment about the optimism of youth, but I knew that behind that gentle acquiescence he kept a quiet and watchful reservation.

A year later our first child was born. For a short time we stayed in the old house in Cologne, but after a few months we bought an estate farther into the countryside, away from the cemetery where I had clung so tenaciously to the dead. By then, even Jans began to believe in the possibility of serenity in our lives, although the rest of the world seemed to be having a nervous breakdown. We were removed from it all not only by an actual effort on our part—avoiding the parties and receptions and other superficial gatherings—but also by the joy that was ours in our love for each other and in our child. The way Jans held his son and looked into the small sleeping face was lovely to watch, and when we were alone and we touched in our moments of tender love or lay side by side afterward and shared our secret thoughts, we believed there was no world but the one we made.

It was almost a month after the baby was born that we finally got around to looking at the last of the hundreds of gifts we had received for our son. Jans and I were opening them in one of the large bedrooms in our new home, where the April breeze fluttered the curtains at the windows. My secretary had made a list of the cards and letters that came with the gifts. On each package she had taped the name of the sender. Marta had offered to have them all opened and all Jans and I would have had to do was look at them, but there is something lovely about opening these gifts and I did not want us to lose this. It was easy enough to write down the gifts next to the sender's name, and it made it all more personal to us and memorable. There were a few that had no cards. Presumably the cards got lost or mixed up with someone else's gift. We were never sure. It was one of these unidentified ones that I was opening while Jans held up another native costume. "Guess."

I looked at the little shirt made of bright-colored cotton. "Nigeria?"

"Close. Next door: Dahomey."

Inside the unmarked box I had opened there was another box, and inside of that one still another. Slowly a feeling of dread came over me as I remembered Jans' statement, which he had made over a year before, about the Chinese puzzle. Frantically I tore open the fourth box, but I could go no further; there was yet another one. Jans, seeing the look on my face, rushed toward me and tore the box from my hand. "It's all right. It's all right," he said.

"Open it." I heard my own harsh voice come through my chattering teeth. I knew what it was even before Jans opened the last tiny velvet box and found the ring, the ridged-wheel ring, made of cobalt-blue sapphire that matched the design of my pendant in the safe.

I could not scream in the presence of the laughter—my father's wild sardonic laughter—to which my shocked and unwilling memory was listening. Jans took the ring from its box and we both stared at it in silence. It was a blue flame in his hand. "It looks like gas—burning," I whispered.

Jans quickly put his arms around me. "Don't talk." After a moment he said, "Someone has given himself away in this stupid gesture." He began to caress my face with his hand. "You must not think morbid thoughts. You have to remain calm. Do you understand?" I nodded, knowing that he was thinking of our child, whom I was nursing. "Now then, point out to me every scrap of paper and packing material that came from this package."

Jans took all the paper and boxes in which the ring had been packaged and had the laboratory people at VHI find out everything they could about it. From the beginning, Jans' reassurances did not work on me. The boxes carried no manufacturer's mark; the paper was produced by Von Heyditch Industries and we exported it to over thirty nations and sold it in Germany as well; the ring's box could have been purchased anywhere in Europe, or anywhere on the Western Hemisphere. None of the servants remembered when the package came; it could have been delivered first to one of the VHI plants and sent to the house by messenger along with dozens of other packages. It had not been mailed; there was not a word or a letter or a symbol on any part of the packaging. Jans had every receiving and mailing department check its records for the arrival of an unaddressed package. No one marked its arrival and no one remembered it. Since there were other unaddressed packages that were hand-delivered for the "VHI baby," no one thought about any of them. It could have come from anywhere in the world, carried by courier and casually dropped into the bin of a delivery truck without anyone's ever being aware of anything.

Then there was the ring. Jans hired a select group of men who sought out every major gem merchant, jewelry cutter, mounter, and private collector in Europe, looking for anyone who could identify the artisans who had anything to do with the sapphire ring, whose picture the men carried around with them. The detectives used any handy lie they could to conceal their real purposes: how much would it cost to have it copied? It was stolen: had someone been trying to sell it? It was believed to be reset: had anyone seen the central stone, the design, the platinum mounting? Everything ended in failure.

As the days passed, I saw Jans' disappointment increase. However, the more it became obvious that the ring would be an unsolved mystery in our lives, the more I felt a developing awareness about the sender of the ring. After a time I decided that it did not matter whether I was right or not in my suspicions about the ring; I could no longer bear to watch Jans' dispirited face or listen to the crushing silence as he stared away at a great distance. I wondered at the apparent listening tilt of his head. What sounds did he hear? Gunfire, faint and muted? What memory was he looking back toward? Two bodies in slow motion, turning slightly, falling backward, falling, graceful in death, their heads turning, a dead glance over the shoulder at the dead below them who were waiting for them, waiting for their falling?

It was during one of these long still times that I decided to tell him. "Jans, I know who sent the ring."

He came out of his silence like an explosion, rising in a single wild motion out of his favorite chair, where he had been looking into the fire and chain-smoking cigarettes, probably without even knowing that he was smoking at all. "What?"

"My father sent it." I was standing in front of him, beside the hearth in our bedroom. For a moment I thought he was going to shake me. Not that I would have blamed him: it was a bizarre notion that my father could send anything back from hell—even by special courier. "It's really not at all difficult to understand, but, of course, you have to have known Father. I think he had the ring made up a long time ago. It doesn't matter where or when. He had it packaged and put away somewhere—in a bank vault perhaps. At the announcement of the birth of a son to VHI it was to be delivered, and it is more than probable that whoever delivered it, or whoever set its delivery in motion, had no idea of the contents of the package. Perhaps it was only a rather routine order left with some lawyer, some banker, some old friend of Father's. It doesn't matter with whom."

Jans was frowning deeply and looking at me with an amazed expression.

"Well, what do you think? Can you believe that?" I asked.

"Can you?"

"Of course. Father's last, most crucial plan was to have grandsons who would carry on his work, who would become leaders in the world—his kind of leaders. And doesn't it all have Father's touch to it? His mark is on it, that element of terror, that feeling we have that someone else is in control."

I desperately wanted him to accept my theory, to believe it completely; but there were those extra years, and they looked at me down though the centuries through Jans' eyes.

"Do you think," he said quietly, "that those harmless-looking eleven men preparing a meeting with a dark future were the last of their kind? I don't mean engineers at power plants, Eroica, I mean just ordinary men talking to their children." He took my hand and held it silently for a long time. "You're going to have to come to terms with those thirty-eight hundred years."

In the daytime, when one is occupied with all the things that hourly living demands, the ghosts of the past are stilled; but in the night their voices come out of one's memory and they whisper and whisper until one is forced to listen. Their faces, too, come out of the dark, slivers of gray transparent light hovering all around with sightless eyes. It was in that dreadful darkness that I sometimes awakened, alone and fearful, to hear my father's words. "What happens in the world, Eroica, happens because the world lets it happen." It was then, when that whispering came to me in the living, moving night, that I saw through the darkness, through the fog, the faces of the dead in Jans' black book, that I heard the running footsteps, actually heard them clear and sharp on the street, and behind them the command to halt, and still the running footsteps and then the gunfire and the scream and the silence all in the same few seconds. It was then that I saw Pemsel's mad face and heard Father's grotesque laughter and saw the ridged wheel repeated millions of times in great, high clusters, huge gears meshing together, moving, crushing everything before them, pushing loosely connected mountains of bones that tumbled over and over each other and left them not in pits but piled high in front of me, where I, only a cipher in a world gone mad, stood paralyzed and mute in front of them. In those moments of lucid madness I could hear my father with absolute clarity. "Is there a disposal problem?"

And then another voice, unidentifiable: "No sir. No one wants them. We thought cremation was best, under the circumstances."

I was always stunned, in those moments when I knew I was mad, when I could barely breathe in the enormous presence of my own listening and waiting, to discover that Jans was also awake. Had I moaned, screamed? He would quickly move toward me, sheltering me with his arms, and it was during this touching, this tender quiet love when words were lost to us, when we entered each other's souls, that we prevailed over the long nights of our fierce aloneness and vanquished all the terrors of the world.